THE GATHERING OF SOULS

GERRY O'CARROLL

AND JEFF GULVIN

LIB
ERT
IES

A special thanks to Robert Kirby, who never lost the faith

Dublin
Sunday 31st August, 9.45 pm

Eva could see how pale she looked reflected in the darkened glass. It was a year to the day since her son had set off for Tommy O'Driscoll's house only for a car to come flying around the corner, the driver drunk or high on drugs or just full of malice.

Downstairs, the phone was ringing. She hoped it wasn't her husband. After seeing him this afternoon at the cemetery, she couldn't talk to him now. She should talk to him; she knew she should; his loss was as great as hers. She blamed him, and he knew it – though it didn't make any sense. But he was a policeman. They had scrapings of paint and traces of metal from the car. They had tyre marks. And yet he, the man who'd made his name at Dublin crime scenes, couldn't locate the hit-and-run driver who had killed their only son. Somehow it had created a vacuum between them. Too much to think about, too many emotions; no space, no peace to try and work it out. She realised she had the telephone receiver in her hand. 'Hello?' she said. 'Hello?'

'Eva, it's Paddy. Are you OK?'

Patrick Maguire, her mentor, the man who allowed her to talk while he sat across the kitchen table and listened.

'Paddy,' she said softly. 'I'm fine. How are you?'

'I'm sorry to call so late, but I've been worried about you. There were so many people at the cemetery today; I was concerned it would overwhelm you.'

'It did a bit, to be honest,' she admitted. 'I didn't get a moment alone with Danny.'

'That's what I thought.'

'There were so many people, they'd all come to mark the day, and I . . . I didn't want to say anything.'

'You're his mother. Everyone knows you. You're entitled to some private time with him.'

'I know, but I had Jess and Laura to think about. Did you see the flowers, Paddy? Everyone brought so many beautiful flowers.'

'I know; they were fantastic. Look, Eva, I'm sorry you didn't get any time with him.'

'It's all right,' she said, 'there'll be other days. God knows there will be lots of other days.'

Tears threatened suddenly, and she could feel the lump in her throat. 'Oh Pad,' she whispered, 'I don't know what I'm doing. I feel so empty, so confused. I hardly know what to do with myself.'

'Listen,' he said, 'it's the first anniversary, and it was always going to be the hardest. Just go with it: feel what you feel and make no apologies either to yourself or to anyone else. Nobody can feel what you do; nobody else was his mother.'

His voice was so gentle. She could see his face, his smile; the tenderness in his eyes. She wondered for a moment then, as she'd wondered a few times, what life might've been like if she'd not been so taken with Moss all those years ago.

'Did you speak to him?' Patrick asked, as if guessing her thoughts.

'Not properly. I just can't seem to. It's been a year, and whoever did this is out there living their life, and here I am with my twelve-year-old in the ground. I blame my husband – at least for not finding out who did it. I know it's irrational, and I know I shouldn't, and I know it's hurting people. But I can't seem to get beyond it. He catches criminals but he can't catch this one. Doesn't he understand? This is the only one that matters.' Sobs tightened her throat, and she struggled to hold them back. 'I know it's not his fault, and I know he's hurting just as much as I am, but somehow I can't grieve with him; I have to grieve on my own.'

'You'll come through it,' Patrick told her gently. 'Like everything else it will take time, but you *will* come through it.'

'I don't know. I don't know. Really, I'm not sure I will.'

'You will, Eva. I promise. You just have to give it time.'

'It's been six months,' she reminded him. 'Moss moved out just before the trial, and the . . . the truth is I'm not sure any more. I'm not sure there's any coming back from where we are now.'

Walking through to the living room, she caught another glimpse of her reflection in the window. 'I hate myself for what it's doing to the girls,' she said. 'I mean, on top of Danny's death and everything. But I just can't help it.' The tears threatened to swamp her now. 'Paddy,' she said, haltingly, 'I'm thinking of moving back to Kerry.'

For a moment he was silent. 'Really?'

'My mam is there, and my sisters, and with what happened up here, I can't deal with Dublin any more.'

'What about Moss?'

'I don't know; perhaps we'll get a divorce.'

There, she'd said it: at last she'd voiced what she had been thinking for so long. But she couldn't talk any more tonight; saying goodbye to Patrick, she hung up and stood before the window. She looked like a fragile piece of sculpture. All she could think about was her son: she had two daughters who needed her now more than ever, but all she could see was Danny.

She couldn't leave him. She couldn't leave him on his own, not without a few words, not today of all days: they had had no time earlier, and there was so much she wanted to say.

*

Across the street he stood in shadow, as earlier he'd stood among gravestones. Above the city, the clouds had parted, and moonlight spilled onto the dirty pavement. Puddles lapped kerbstones as they'd marked paths in the cemetery. He had watched the way she'd dealt with everyone; she had been unfailingly polite and gracious, yet he knew how desperate she was. He had watched the way she was around her husband, together and yet separate, the distance between them tangible.

He watched her now silhouetted in the living room window.

*

Eva hated herself for leaving the girls, but she couldn't let this day pass without having a moment alone with her son. Listening for sounds from upstairs, she grabbed her car keys and stepped outside. The rain had gone, but the air was damp and the avenue lay in darkness. The three-storey Georgian houses stood shoulder to shoulder, grey stone and greyer slate; street lights illuminating steps and railings, the parked cars half-hidden behind the massive chestnut trees. She glanced up at her daughters' bedroom windows: she wouldn't be long, half an hour at the most. Nothing could happen in half an hour; she would be back and feeling better, and they'd never even know she'd been gone. Yet crossing the road to her car, she knew that this was wrong. This was very wrong; it wasn't rational. She almost went back. But Danny beckoned; her son called her, as he had never called her before.

*

He watched as she paused there on the step. He watched as she got in her car. He watched as the engine fired and the lights came on and she glanced furtively at the upstairs windows. Then she pulled out and, gunning the engine, drove quickly to the T-junction. Without indicating, she swung onto the main road. Stepping from the trees, he stole a lingering look at the house: the upstairs in perfect darkness; lights from the hall below.

Sunday 31st August
9.45 pm

A light burned in the Bureau of Criminal Investigation. South of the river on the fifth floor at Harcourt Square, thirty-nine-year-old Inspector Moss Quinn sat hunched over his desk. At six foot, give or take an inch, he was leanly built, with hair flecked grey at the temples. He wore an Armani suit; his tie was undone and gold links hung at the cuffs of his shirt.

Sunday night, and there was no other detective in the suite. Sitting there in the half-dark, he could see Eva as she'd been in the cemetery: how gaunt and hopeless she'd looked; the hollow expression in her eyes. He reminded himself that he had come in to collate the files: five women – five single mothers who had disappeared, leaving their children behind. Their cases went back six years, to Janice Long and Karen Brady, and tomorrow he and Detective Murphy were making the temporary transfer to a new unit in Naas. Since the collapse of Maggs's trial, there had been questions raised in the Dáil; questions about him; his career had been publicly scrutinised for the first time. He didn't like it; he didn't like it at all. But now, perhaps, he had a chance to redeem himself. In the words of the justice minister, the souls of these five wretched women must finally be laid to rest.

There was another file on Quinn's desk – a case Murphy had asked about on Friday. He'd been reminded of it again that morning, when he'd noticed the necklace his wife was wearing. He turned the pages, a fist pressed to his jowls. The night of the music festival, Mary Harrington had died of thirst and Conor Maggs had confessed.

Quinn sat back, arms folded. He could hear the words; he didn't have to read them. The murder trial; the defendant taking the stand in the Four Courts; the barrister giving him the pages, telling him to read them aloud.

Conor Maggs's confession
The Four Courts, Dublin
Monday 15th April
2 pm

For a moment Maggs just sat there. He peered at Quinn; he stared hard at Doyle. Then he spoke, his tongue snaking his lips and his hand shaking slightly as it held the page.

I spoke to her outside the corner shop. She came teetering up from Jett O'Carroll's pub on a pair of high heels that looked as though they were going to turn her ankle. A little later I saw her again: she was trying to light a cigarette standing in the shadows cast by the solicitor's building.

'Hey,' I said, 'it's you again. We keep bumping into each other.'

She looked up with a squint, the lighted match wavering.

'Up the road, remember? You bumped into me and had to sit down on the window.'

'Did I?' she muttered.

'You'd had a run-in with your girlfriend'.

'Yeah, well there you go. What the fuck, eh? Who cares?' She looked as

though she was about to fall over; taking her hand, I steadied her. She was peering at me, blinking slowly, but she didn't pull away. Moving closer, I could smell the scent she was wearing: I could see the glint of perspiration where it gathered at the base of her throat.

'What's your name?' I asked her.

'Mary.'

'I'm Conor.' I smiled now, still holding her hand. Turning her palm upwards, I studied the lines in the skin. 'You know you have a very long love line. Has anyone ever told you? It's really strong, look.' I paused then, and added: 'Your life line is a little short, mind.'

She pulled her hand away but made no move to leave. She just stood there sucking on her cigarette.

I glanced across the square towards the big marquee, where a band was playing. 'I've had enough of the music,' I said. 'Been here all night. What about you? Do you fancy going somewhere?'

Mary shrugged.

'If you've had a fight with your friend, why don't I bring you somewhere?'

'Where?'

'I don't know, the beach maybe. What do you think? We could go to Ballybunion and take a look at the sea.'

She thought about that for a moment. 'Have you got a car?'

What a question! Jesus, I had a Ford Granada: a classic, just like the one Jack Regan had driven in the old TV series 'The Sweeney'. Immaculate in silver, with a black vinyl roof and perfect upholstery, it was parked round the corner in a side road. Settling her in the passenger seat, I fired up the engine.

Halfway to the coast, she cracked her window a fraction, took the pack of cigarettes from her bag and lit one.

Like a wave, the anger washed over me. I hate smoking; I mean, I really hate it. She hadn't asked; no one smoked in my car. I stared ahead, knuckles white on the steering wheel. She didn't say anything. She just sat there, dragging on her fag like she was suckling. I saw ash break and spill onto the seat.

It was as if someone had struck me: I could feel a tremor, my jaw was tight.

Slowing the car, I looked for somewhere to turn.

'I thought you were bringing me to the beach,' she said.

'It's too far, there's not enough time. I'll just pull off and we can look at the moon or something.'

'The moon,' she said, flicking at the end of the cigarette. 'What d'you want to look at the moon for?'

The ash fell on the carpet. I turned up a track that ran between farmers' fields. A hundred yards off the road, it widened at a five-bar gate. Pulling over, I switched off the engine. Neither of us spoke now: my window down, I rested an elbow on the sill.

'Come on,' I said finally, 'let's get some air. You've had a few to drink, and the last thing I need is you chucking up in my car.'

Getting out, I walked round the front and opened her door. Then, taking her hand, I helped her out. She lolled against me, the heels of her shoes catching in the stones on the track. I led her to the gate and she rested against it, still sucking on her cigarette. Without thinking, she blew smoke in my face.

I looked away in disgust; I looked at the ground, and then up. The moon was bright, the sky streaked with cloud. I stepped across her where she leant with her back to the gate; my hands at her waist and one leg either side of her. I kissed her. She tasted of cigarettes; it reminded me of my mother.

Hooking her hands around my neck, she tried to kiss me. I backed away: all I could taste, all I could smell, was cigarettes.

'Are you all right?' she asked. 'What's the matter with you?'

I didn't reply. I was looking across the fields to the lights of a house in the distance.

'What's up?' she was slurring. 'What did you say your name was? Colin, was it? Shit, I don't remember.' She was giggling now. 'What's the matter, Colin, is your girlfriend back there or something?'

I didn't reply; I just stared at her.

'Let's go back,' she said. 'What the hell, we never got to the beach, did we, and I never fancied you anyway.'

'We can't go back,' I said.

'What do you mean, we can't go back? Of course we can. Take me back, Colin. Come on, let's go back and listen to some music.'

'It's Conor, all right. My name is Conor, not Colin.'

Something sparked in her eyes. She had her palms pressed to my chest now, and I could feel the anxiety rising in her suddenly. I pointed above her head.

'Look at the moon, would you? Can you not see how beautiful it is?' She didn't look up. She looked at me: uncertainty, the beginnings of fear, maybe.

'I want to go back,' she said. 'My friends will be waiting. They'll be wondering where I am.'

'No they won't, you told me you'd had a fight.'

I had her pinned now, and she pushed at me. She tried to force me away with her elbows in my chest.

But I wouldn't move. Spinning her round, I slammed her into the gate. She cried out. Covering her mouth, I dragged her down to the ground. She was terrified: eyes wide, lips parted, there was blood against her teeth. She was trying to scream, to cry out. I lay across her but somehow she managed to push me off and wriggle free. Grabbing her leg, I dragged her back and smashed her across the face.

She cried now. She tried to scream but I stuffed the heel of my hand in her mouth. I had her: she was prostrate beneath me. But I no longer wanted her. There was no desire in me. I did hate her, though: I hated her for the way she looked; I hated her for the way she'd led me on. I hated her for lighting a cigarette and dropping ash in my car.

*

Sitting at his desk, Quinn let go the breath he'd not realised was caught in his chest. He could still see Maggs in the witness box: dark hair and dark eyes, hunched up in his seat like a child. He had scrutinised every mannerism, every expression, every movement. He recalled thinking that no matter what he was trying to get across to the jury, there was a part of him that was enjoying the whole experience. He was the centre of attention, and he read so eloquently, and with such passion, that every eye was turned his way, including that of Eva, who was sitting in the public gallery wearing the necklace he'd given her.

*

I savoured every moment. With the belt around her neck, I could control how slowly she suffocated. It was incredible, empowering: to extinguish another person's life. It was overwhelming. I tightened the belt; I tightened it till my knuckles whitened, before releasing it again. A gasp, and her body went into convulsion; twitching like a chicken with its head ripped off. That really intrigued me: when the oxygen was gone, she didn't merely go limp: she went into a kind of fit. I realised I was at peace, a sense of quiet exultation working through my veins; this was the culmination of experience; it was action and reaction, authority without responsibility.

Lying back, I stared at the sky. The Milky Way was plainly visible; dusted stars, gathered like souls, cut a swathe through the firmament. I'm no writer, but lying there, I thought I could compose a poem. The stillness, the moon above, and the salty air drifting in from the sea.

Getting to my feet, I fetched a roll of tape from the boot of the car. She lay where I'd left her. For a moment, I thought she was dead. Bu she couldn't be dead: not yet, at least. Bending close, I could feel her breath on my cheek. Relieved now, I tore off a strip of tape and fixed it over her mouth. I didn't want any noise when she came to, but I didn't want her to die either. Leaving her nostrils exposed, I bound her ankles, then her wrists, then left her lying in the shadows while I took a moment to think.

I knew this part of the country pretty well, and it didn't take long to decide where I would take her. It began to rain; lifting her into the boot, I stood with the moon hidden and my eyes closed, letting the water roll off my face.

The engine running, I flicked on the headlights, then backed around and headed for the main road. I made for Ballylongford and O'Connor country; the ruins of Lislaughtin Abbey. Across the field was the old keep at Carrigafoyle: a stronghold the O'Connors had claimed was impregnable. In 1580, however, William Pelham had pounded it into ruins using small cannons and naval guns commandeered from English ships anchored in the bay.

Beyond the keep was one of the many broken-down cottages that littered this part of the River Shannon. Long and low it was, like a crofter's place, a relic from the past; no one ever went there. I parked in front of a gate close to the house where Jimmy Hanrahan lived with his father. I'd seen Jimmy at the festival, though his father hadn't been there. His dad hardly ever went out. His wife had thrown herself into the estuary after Jimmy had been charged with battering an old woman half to death. Ever since then, the poor old fool had seen dead people in his kitchen.

She was still unconscious as I lifted her, slippery where I'd wrapped her in a plastic tarp. Shoving open the gate, I made my way across boggy grass that sloped to rough banks and darkened water beyond. Coming to suddenly, she wriggled like a worm; I slapped her. She was heavy; the rain made the plastic oil slick, and it was all could do to hold her. I walked in a half-crouch a hundred yards along the shore.

By the time I made it to the cottage, I was breathing hard. Soaking wet, I could see the shell of the keep, and beyond it the remains of Lislaughtin Abbey.

The cottage had no roof, the wooden cross-beams breaking the sky overhead. Fatigued now, my legs felt like jelly. Inside, it took a moment for my eyes to grow accustomed to the dark. She was trying to cry out, muffled sounds coming from behind the tape. There was no one to hear her.

There were three rooms, one of which had been tacked on as an afterthought – a toilet or a scullery, perhaps. I considered the floors, carpet sticking to old boards, slivers of rotten linoleum. Many of the boards were decayed, the nails that held them, rusty. When I lifted them and felt in the darkness underneath, it was clear that there was a space a couple of feet deep. This was perfect: a body could putrefy here, and no one would ever know. I broke boards where I had to, laid them to one side. After a while, the openinng was big enough. Then I looked her in the eye. What I saw was terror, pure and absolute. That terror thrilled me.

I laid her in the hole and pressed her down so that she was wedged tight and couldn't move; no one would hear her cry. Leaving enough room for her to breathe, I covered the aperture with a few boards and the stinking remains of carpet.

A few hours later, I did drive to Ballybunion, only this time an extremely drunk young woman called Molly Parkinson was in the passenger seat with her eyes closed and her cheek pressed to the window. She was a hairdresser from Dublin: she'd cut my hair, and a few weeks ago we'd started going out. I'd rented a caravan on the headland overlooking the twin beaches where, in the old days, male and female bathers used to be segregated.

Molly was really out of it, and I had to carry her inside. There was a double bed at the back that was separated from the main living area by a partition. She was muttering about wanting another drink, but she didn't object when I told her she'd had enough, and she moved only listlessly as I took her clothes off.

The blood pumping suddenly, I took her the moment she was naked. Afterwards, I sat on the step under the awning with rain rattling the canvas roof. I had half a bottle of wine and I nursed it; the caravan door was open and Molly was already in bed. I'd seen her drunk before and knew she'd have the mother of all hangovers in the morning. Earlier, she'd passed out completely. It was the perfect alibi: when she woke up, she would remember nothing about tonight at all. I could tell her she'd danced naked through the streets and she'd believe me. All I had to do was say we'd been together, and she'd be so embarrassed she'd back me up completely.

Sunday 31st August
10.05 pm

Danny was buried in Glasnevin Cemetery close to the Botanic Gardens. Eva had to drive through the residential area west of Dalcassian Downs and cross the little bridge that was all but covered with trees.

The pool of light from her headlights spilled briefly over the railway lines before exposing the first of the headstones. Leaving the car, she walked now, banks of stones on both left and right, until she came to the path that led to the south-eastern corner of the cemetery. There the railway line bisected the trees before the canal, but it was as close as they could get to the water; Danny had loved the canal.

Again she faltered, there in the darkness with the sound of a tram on the Luas line, cars on Finglas Road. She had an aching feeling that she should never have left the two girls in the house by themselves. She wondered what their father would say if he knew what she was doing; she wondered if he would understand.

She should not have left them. But they were asleep, and there was no fire in the grate and no one could get in. Then she realised that she hadn't even brought a phone, let alone a purse or a bag: her mobile phone was in her handbag, and that was on the table in the hall.

She hesitated, then half-turned, looking across the rows of sleepers to the shadow of her car beyond.

*

Hidden in the trees, he heard her. When she paused, he could imagine what she was thinking: the children at home on their own. They were alone because their father no longer lived with them. If he had still been part of the family, none of what she was doing here would matter. Her presence set the pulse working at his temple. He knew how her son called to her and that, having come this far, she would not rush home.

*

Looking down on the flowers that covered the white pebbles that lay on top of the grave, Eva imagined his face. She could picture him in his room; with a rugby ball; she could see him getting ready for school.

She dropped to her knees, the ground sodden from all the rain. There were so many flowers; a year now, and so many people wanting to pay their respects.

*

Still he watched, though he was no longer in the trees. He was standing behind her, silently.

She looked so small and pitiful, her shoulders drooping as if the weight of the last year was too much for her to bear. When he spoke, his voice was a whisper. 'Eva,' he said.

The sound came from directly behind her. It was so sudden, so unexpected, that Eva cried out. Before she could move, she felt a hand grip her shoulder; another covered her mouth. She was forced face down on the grave. She lay on her belly. Then he was on top of her; her mouth in the flowers, the sharp stones pressing into her cheek. He rolled her onto her back and she lifted her hands. 'Please,' she cried. 'Please don't. Please, what are you doing?'

'No sound.' His voice was a hiss, a guttural rasp; something told her she had heard it before. 'No words now, or I'll kill you.' He was covering her mouth, his shapeless head close to hers. 'I'll stamp you to death, do you hear me? I'll stamp you to death right here on the stones of your son's grave.'

All she could see was shadow. There was no whitened patch where his face should be, whoever he was. He was all in black, his features covered by a mask.

She lay there with his fist jammed between her teeth, so that the only sound she could utter was a pathetic kind of gurgle. She couldn't move; her pulse was so thick that she felt the blood would stop flowing. Then her muscles seemed to come to life and she scrabbled to get up. In a flash, he forced her down again. She kicked out, and he cracked her across the mouth. He was on top of her, peering through the narrow slits of a ski mask; he could see the fear in her eyes. He kissed her.

He couldn't help it: a moment of lust. He kissed her through the mask; he could taste blood where he had split her lip. His eyes rolled and, grabbing a handful of her hair, he wiped the blood from his mask. Then he saw the glint of gold at her throat.

The necklace, the pendant: the sacred heart of Christ bloodied by a crown of thorns. Gently now, he stroked the heel of his thumb back and forth across it. Then he tore the heart from the chain.

Stuffing it into a pocket, he took a roll of tape and, tearing off a strip, he twisted Eva's head to one side and stuck it over her mouth.

He bound her wrists and ankles. Cloud blanketed the stars. Rain began to fall. For a moment, he looked into her face. She was helpless now; walking off a few paces, he took the pendant out again. The cemetery was silent and empty; only the ghosts of those who couldn't sleep were taking any notice.

Eva was shaking, quivering with fear, cold with disgust. She was disgusted with herself for allowing this to happen, for leaving Laura and Jessie alone. She stared at the headstone, at her son's name; her son beneath the soil. Tears clogged her throat; she could barely breathe. Snot from her nose ran over the tape covering her mouth. She heard the scrape of leather on stone, then he was above her again.

Tears like fragments of glass. She could no longer see the headstone, or the grass, or the broken flowers where he'd pressed himself against her.

Sunday 31st August
10.05 pm

Moss Quinn, still sitting at his desk, turned the pages of Mary's file.

Once more he was back in the courtroom. And he could see Conor Maggs, his head bowed now as he finished reading. Very slowly, very deliberately, he laid the signed confession on the edge of the witness box. He shot a glance to where his barrister, Senior Counsel Phelan, was standing.

'Thank you, Conor,' Phelan said.

For a few moments, Phelan considered the notes on the lectern. Turning to the members of the jury, he looked each of them in the eye and then peered beyond the counsel for the prosecution, to where the three Gards who had brought the case were sitting. Briefly, Quinn felt the weight of Phelan's gaze, before it settled on Doyle. The sergeant, originally from Kerry, was a big, heavy-set man; at fifty years of age, his face was seamed like old leather, his eyes a cobalt blue. The close-cut grey hair bristled across his scalp.

'Poetic,' the barrister stated. 'One could describe it almost as whimsical. A tale to rival any told in this city of Sean O'Casey.' He gesticulated flamboyantly. 'A modern-day Juno; a veritable Ulysses.'

His features darkened considerably. 'However one wants to describe it, it is a work of fiction.'

For a few moments there was no sound in the courtroom: nobody moved; nobody coughed; nobody seemed to breathe.

'Your honour,' Phelan said to the judge, 'the so-called confession was written by a police officer with a flair for the language; the signature extracted by force. The defendant was hit so hard and so often that he wrote down word for word exactly what he was told.' Again he paused, his lips forming a single line. 'And then he was forced to sign it.'

A ripple of unease spread through the public gallery. The judge reached for his gavel. Glancing at Quinn, Doyle blanched slightly. He hooked one finger into the collar of his shirt, where it was suddenly constricting.

Phelan took a series of photographs from his desk; he passed them, together with medical reports, to the bench. 'Here are the pictures taken at the hospital,' he explained, 'and here are some the defendant took twenty-four hours before he was arrested. You can see clearly that before the guards "spoke" to him, his body was unmarked.' He looked long and hard at Doyle; the big man could not return his stare. Doyle's gaze fell on Quinn and Frank Maguire, and neither of them looked back. 'Conor knew the Guards were coming. For years they'd been looking for an excuse, and he knew what would happen when they got it.'

The barrister allowed his words to settle before turning once more to the witness box.

'Now, Conor,' he said, 'in your own words this time, why don't you tell the court exactly how it happened?'

Shifting in his seat, Maggs risked a glance in the direction of Doyle, who was peering at him from under hooded brows. Maggs's eyes were hunted, the flesh around them wrinkled. Then his gaze shifted to the public gallery, and Quinn saw it fix on Eva. For a long moment he stared at her. Eyes closed now, he passed a hand across his face. He shook his head; his shoulders hunched to his jowls. When he spoke, he voice wavered.

'The metal door was ajar,' he began. 'It took me a while to notice, and when I did I stared hard. I didn't understand: why was the door ajar? The door was always either wide open or it was locked. It was never, ever ajar. And the silence; the silence was new, and disturbing. Sitting on the narrow bed, with its thin mattress and single pillow, next to the tiny sink and the seat-less toilet, the silence was suddenly terrifying. Midnight, and I'd woken to a crack of light breaking around the door jamb. They had nothing: I mean, no evidence, not a shred of anything to link me to the crime I was accused of. Yet they wanted it to be me; they needed it to be me – Doyle particularly, with all his hatred, but Quinn too.

'And then, as if to confirm my worst fears, I could hear the foot-fall of the big man. I knew who it was. Not Quinn: he wouldn't get his hands dirty. I began to tremble: this awful dream I could not wake up from was gradually becoming a nightmare. I knew what was about to happen; I knew how they were when they didn't get what they wanted. I knew how they'd bend the truth; create their own truth so that they got the result they wanted.

'I realised then that the block was empty: Jesus, mine was the only cell that had anyone in it. Nobody would hear; there would be no one to witness what was about to happen.

'I felt the weight all at once in my bladder. I wanted to pee. I would pee my pants at the very least; I would pee my pants, I knew it. This was personal; this had always been personal. And because it was so personal, it was terrifying. I was trembling, shaking; I could hear myself whimpering like a child.

'Then the door was pushed open and the half-light from the cor-ridor was partially blocked by shadow.'

Sitting there listening to it all, Quinn saw him cast a glance once more at the gallery. Only this time he was starring at Jane Finucane. On remand at Mountjoy, Maggs had written a letter to an evangelical church group in Harold's Cross. He'd told them how, after Doyle had finished with him, he'd been in and out of consciousness and then had suddenly woken up. He claimed that the cell was bathed in a white light and that Christ was standing before him. He showed him the marks in his hands; he showed him the hole in his side. He told him that he wasn't alone. They'd heard how Jane had read that letter and afterwards had gone to see him. They had been together ever since. Further along the same row, and hunched up like a rag, Quinn could see Molly Parkinson, the girl who'd originally given Maggs his alibi.

At the barrister's lectern, Phelan was speaking again. 'Your honour,' he said, 'the photographs show that my client was beaten so savagely the muscles were detached from his ribs.'

Quinn watched as the judge considered the pictures. He saw his eyes darken and the tip of his nose grow white. He could see Maggs watching the way the judge's gaze began to narrow under the powdered wig; the way he regarded Quinn and Frank Maguire, Patrick's brother, the senior investigating officer. Doyle sat impassively, his thick fingers spread in his lap, his cropped hair almost transparent under the courtroom lights. His eyes were as blue as Maggs's were black, and Maggs was staring at him.

'Coercion, your honour,' Phelan stated, 'Coercion, brutality, torture.'

*

Getting up from his desk, Quinn closed the file. Thanks to the medical reports and the photographs Maggs had taken in advance of his arrest and interrogation, the case collapsed. The judge tore into the police and the prosecution for bringing the case in the first place.

For Quinn, it was as vivid a memory now as Maggs on the witness stand.

*

Staring coldly at Doyle, the judge demanded an investigation.

The court emptied, but Quinn remained where he was. Frank Maguire remained where he was too, his face ashen, the nausea of the moment etched deeply into his skin. Only Doyle got up. He stood for a moment, working saliva into his mouth, then turned on his heel and stalked out.

Gathering up his papers, Phelan threw a glance at Quinn. 'Moss,' he muttered, 'what the hell was all that about?' He turned to Maguire. 'And you, Frank, what were you thinking, bringing such a ragtag of a case to court?' He grinned then. 'Still, I'll chalk it up as a victory nonetheless. Word of advice to the both of you: if I were you, I'd get the Doyler out to grass and do it quickly. Did you not know we're in Europe, lads? We have been for a while now.'

Outside, Quinn paused as Maggs made a statement to the press. He could smell the Liffey, that particular scent that was part city, part salt and part history, maybe. Jane Finucane was holding Maggs's hand, and across the road Doyle was leaning on the wall, gazing upriver.

'I've only a few words,' Maggs was saying. 'All this has taken its toll, and I want to move on – and quickly. My life has changed; nothing is as it was before. What I want to tell you is that no matter who you are, no matter that you're in the darkest moment of adversity, never forget that just around the corner there's a moment of triumph waiting. I had nothing to do with Mary's death, but the police had targeted me long ago. I ought to sue them; I ought to take them for every penny I can; my lawyer advises me to do just that. But that night in the cell, the Lord himself came to me, and his suffering was far worse than anything I'd been through. Christ didn't seek revenge; instead, he offered comfort to his enemies; he offered forgiveness.'

Maggs broke off and looked down the road, to where Doyle had turned and was watching him. 'I want to tell you that God is alive and well and is living among us, just as he always was. I know, because I've seen him with my own eyes. I will not bear a grudge, I will not seek retribution. I forgive Sergeant Doyle for what he did to me. I forgive An Garda Síochána – a misguided police force perhaps, but not one that's morally corrupt.'

He clutched Jane's hand. 'This woman believed in me. When I was at my lowest ebb, she came to me, and we're together now. We're leaving Ireland. We're going to London to start a new life. My story is one of salvation, and my only desire now is to be able to tell it. Thank you; that's all.'

As Maggs finished speaking, the scrum of reporters and cameramen flocked over to Doyle. He stood where he was with his arms folded, staring at Maggs, before briefly glancing at Quinn.

He said nothing, and ignored the questions. Quinn watched him walk away from the cameras and walk over O'Donovan Bridge. He'd left his car on the other side of the river; no doubt he was heading for Jocky O'Connell's on Richmond Street and a couple of quiet pints. Quinn saw Maggs and Jane Finucane get into a car. He saw Molly Parkinson with a bitter look on her face. He saw his wife cast a glance his way before ducking her head and hurrying to the corner, where a taxi was waiting.

*

Crossing the detectives' suite with his hands in his pockets, Quinn could see Eva again as she had been that day. His mouth was dry suddenly; he'd been pushed aside, and there was nothing he could do. At least Maggs had left the country for good: he and his new girlfriend had gone to London, as he'd said they would, to spread the Gospel – or whatever it was they planned to do. According to a couple of contacts Doyle had in the Met, they were living in Muswell Hill.

Doyle had been in the job for three decades. He had never married, and was living in digs with his landlady, Mrs Mulroney, as he'd been doing for twenty years. His life was the job, the pub, the dog track – the streets of this old city, which had seen so much from so many.

Pausing at the window, his thoughts drifted. The office looked out on Harcourt Street and, beyond it, St Stephen's Green. A stone's throw to the north-west was Dublin Castle, from where the British had ruled until 1922. For a moment, Quinn reflected: the old building was where the Archbishop of Cashel had been tortured in the days of Elizabeth I. His jailers had fashioned a metal boot for his leg, then filled it with oil and salt and 'cooked' it over an open fire.

Downstairs, Sergeant Dunne was on duty. Dunne, originally from the country, was a long-time crony of Doyle's. He was unkempt, with a large belly and a shiny, bald head. He looked up as Quinn opened the security door.

'Did you find what you were looking for?' Dunne asked. 'Coming in of a Sunday night . . . I'm not sure that could be classed as conscientious so much as masochistic, maybe.'

Quinn half-smiled. 'Are you still here, Davey? If you must know, I came looking for a packet of smokes I was hiding after telling myself it was time to knock it on the head.'

'Took me a year and a day to quit,' Dunne observed, 'but I got there in the end.'

'So there's hope for me yet, is there? Thank God for that. Night, Davey.'

'Goodnight, Moss. Take care of yourself.'

At the gate, Quinn felt in his pocket for the cigarettes, but he needed a drink, and with the hotel only across the street, there was little point in lighting up. He had to wait for a couple of taxis to trundle past, then an old man and a handful of tourists. Dublin was like a magnet for tourists these days, and Quinn could spot the 'blow-ins' a mile off. 'Too long in one city,' he told himself. 'Your whole life in the one place . . . it's not good for you, Moss.'

Sitting at the bar he ordered a Guinness, and while it was settling the barman gave him a small glass of Jameson. Quinn nursed it, his mobile phone on the bar and Murphy's number at the top of the list. His palm itched. The Guinness settled and he watched as Billy topped it off.

'No Doyle tonight, then?' Billy asked him.

'It's Sunday: you've no music and the old buzzard will be on Talbot Street, most likely.'

Quinn sipped the Guinness, still conscious of Murphy's number. Billy wiped the polished bar, flipped the cloth over his shoulder and wiped it again.

'Is it right you and Doyle had a bit of a falling-out?' he asked. 'After that case was in all the papers, I heard that the two of you had words.'

Quinn sat back. 'That was six months ago, Billy. But yeah you're right, we did. Sometimes the Doyler has the subtlety of a flying house brick, and I reminded him of as much after a few pints when we were toe to toe on Abbey Street.'

'That's what I heard: the two of you going at it, with Daniel O'Connell watching.'

'It didn't come to blows, Billy. I'm not so stupid I'd mix it with the old mouldy-arse.'

He felt a strong urge to call Murphy. She was young and she was attractive and, like him, she was married. Since the Naas inquiry had been ordered, the two of them had been working closely together. They shared the same car, sometimes the same desk, and they had pored over those five missing-person files sitting side by side. He had never strayed from his wife, had never intended to. But then he'd never imagined he'd be living above the Garda Club either, a year after his son's death.

He stepped outside for a smoke and, leaning back against the railings, gazed across the road to the flat roof of Harcourt Square – like the head of an insect bristling with antennae. In the palm of his hand he held the mobile, Murphy's number still showing. Thinking about her now, the saliva was draining. It was only when she answered that he realised he'd even dialled the number.

'Hello Moss.' Her voice sounded soft and warm and inviting.

His sounded thick in his throat. 'Keira,' he said, 'what're you doing?'

*

When he got to the corner of Harrington Street, she climbed out of her car. He noticed her dark hair and olive skin; she considered him with a smile. Quinn realised that he was trembling. The anticipation of being alone with this woman, when he'd spent the last six months trying to save his marriage, was suddenly intoxicating.

All was quiet: nothing going on at the club tonight, no function, no Brazilian dancing or whatever the samba sound he heard so often was. Across the way, St Kevin's Church dominated, and as they stood there among fallen autumn leaves the rain began to fall.

'What did you tell your husband?' he asked her.

'I didn't tell him anything. He's not at home. He's in Wicklow playing golf with his brother: they've been away all weekend and won't be home till tomorrow. I was going to mention it on Friday, when we were packing the stuff for Naas, but . . . '

They entered the building by the side door. It was as if Quinn's senses were suddenly heightened: he could hear every rustle of her clothing; he could hear the beating of his heart. He could scent her womanhood like a hint of perfumed gossamer.

She walked in front of him wearing jeans and a tight-fitting top. He watched the way the denim hugged the contours of her thighs and he could feel his breath grow short. At the door she turned so he could fit the key in the lock, and her breasts brushed against him. He could see his wife, only she had pushed him away; he could see the son he wasn't allowed to grieve.

The flat was the last one the Garda retained. It was no more than a living room with a kitchenette and a bathroom. Through the open door to the other room, he could see the bed, which was still unmade.

Murphy perched on the settee, her gaze almost unnervingly on his. Her hair was drawn back, the gold loops of her earrings piercing the exact centre of each lobe. Quinn studied her openly now as he'd done covertly for more than a couple of months. There was something about this woman that touched the loneliness that had first engulfed him twelve months previously. He had a bottle of wine in the fridge. He poured two glasses, fetched an ashtray and produced the half-packet of cigarettes from his jacket pocket. Deliberately, he switched off his phone.

'You know, I was in the office earlier,' he said. 'I was kicking my heels, and we're moving tomorrow and . . . '

'Are we taking Mary Harrington's file with us?'

He pushed out his lips. 'You asked me that on Friday and I said no. I dug it out just now because today at the memorial, Eva was still wearing the necklace Maggs gave her. She put it on after Danny was killed and she's been wearing it pretty much ever since.' He lifted his shoulders. 'I don't know why: some comfort in what she used to believe, or something.'

'So have you changed your mind then?'

He thought about that for a moment. 'About Mary, no. They were single mothers, Murph: that's the common factor. We know Mary was pregnant, but only because of an autopsy.'

Murphy sat back, her wineglass cupped between both palms, and the faintest imprint of her lips around the rim. Neither of them spoke now; there was an awkwardness between them that he'd not been aware of before.

'Maybe I shouldn't have come,' she suggested.

Quinn studied her. 'You could've said no.'

'I know I could.'

'Why didn't you?'

She laughed then. 'Because I wanted to see you: I've been wanting to see you since the moment I was assigned.'

'Doyle suspects there's something going on between us; you know that, don't you. Jesus. I might be the DI, Murph, but he still behaves like I'm fresh out of Templemore.'

Suddenly the awkwardness was gone. Quinn didn't care anymore. Murphy didn't care. Setting down her glass, she got to her feet. Then, slowly, she bent to where he was sitting and, cupping his cheek, she kissed him. The touch of her lips – forbidden, unlooked-for but suddenly sublime. It was wrong, it was too complicated, and yet there was a simplicity to it as well that sent a shudder through him. Hand in hand now, they went through to the bedroom.

Naked, he lay against her.

This was more than sex, this was more than lust or desire or loneliness: this was the culmination of six weeks working together so closely that they knew the sound of each other's footsteps. This was more than frustration or relief, it was more than anger. For the last year, almost, he'd been helpless.

He had witnessed the look in his wife's eyes when their son was taken, and he'd had to watch as the light that burned for him had quietly faded. He'd seen her reaction when they set the date for Maggs's trial and she'd told him he was looking for a scapegoat. She'd told him it wasn't about Maggs at all; it wasn't even about the murder of Mary Harrington. It was about Moss Quinn, Dublin's finest: the copper who couldn't catch the man who killed his son.

Sunday 31st August
10.10 pm

Eva's hands were bound, her feet tied at the ankles; with the tape across her mouth, she was unable to speak. He peered into her eyes. She was quaking, quivering – muscle spasms caused by fear and confusion. The incomprehension of what was happening showed in her face. Did she know him?

Did she think she knew him? Did she recognise his voice?

Crouching beside her, he rested the flat of a forearm across his thigh and cocked his head to one side. His voice rattled like water over stone. 'Do you want one last word with him? Do you wish you'd had the chance to tell him you loved him? Do you wish you could've said goodbye, instead of coming upon him as you did, with his skull smashed and his brains all over the pavement?'

With tears in her eyes, she just stared at him. 'There was no one to take responsibility; no one to blame. No one except your husband.' He fell silent then for a moment. 'Of course, it means you're on your own now. It's what you asked for, but I wonder – is it what you wanted?' He peered at her through the ski mask. 'You don't know, do you? You're so confused. Of course you are. It is confusing.' He got to his feet and looked down, silhouetted against the trees. 'But it's too late. You understand that, don't you? Too late, Eva: too late to change it now.'

Eva couldn't move: all she could think about was Laura and Jess at home by themselves; desperately, she tried to free her hands. She tried to get up but her ankles were so tightly bound she could no longer feel her feet. She tried to scream but a swath of sticky tape covered her mouth. Tears streamed; her panic was absolute. There was nothing she could do. He hoisted her over his shoulder and, with her head hanging down and blood rushing to it, he carried her into the trees.

Sunday 31st August
10.17 pm

John Hanrahan knew his son wasn't home. He was lying in bed in his dilapidated house on the banks of the Shannon estuary, a flattened expanse of reed and water where fishermen liked to trawl. Jimmy hadn't been home all day: he'd been in late last night and was gone again this morning. It was late now, and old John knew the boy wouldn't be home.

He lay in the dark and listened. Every night he listened. But when his son was home, when Jimmy was there, it wasn't quite so bad. Jimmy never got up to go downstairs with him; Jimmy never witnessed anything. But just knowing he was in the house made the task a little easier.

When John was alone, however, and the wind howled, it was almost impossible to climb out of bed.

When he did finally get up, sometimes the fear was so intense that it stopped the blood from flowing. His legs would seize before he was halfway down the stairs. Then he couldn't go down at all and he'd have to wake Jimmy, and the lad would come out shouting the odds about the old man and his ravings. But he wasn't mad; whatever they said, John knew he wasn't mad.

He saw the dead in his kitchen; they'd be sitting at his table when the devil came to cut cards for their souls. They all said he was mad; Jimmy said he was mad. But old John knew how it was: this wasn't madness, it was penance for all he had never been to Lizzy. His poor wife, she'd taken her own life and was in purgatory now, and it was his task to plead for her. In all these years, he'd not seen her. He'd seen that girl, though. He'd told them he'd seen her when they dug her up across the way, but they didn't believe him. The coppers, they just gave him a pat on the back and said 'Thanks, John'. But that was all they did. He'd not seen her again, of course; he rarely saw anyone twice.

He heard them all the time, though. And he could hear them now, and the knowledge that they were down there sent a shiver down his spine. He had to get up. He dare not stay in bed, because if he didn't get up and Lizzy came and he missed her, the torment would go on and on.

He could hear them in the kitchen.

He could hear them all the clearer because his son wasn't home. Voices they were, low and hoarse, whispers almost; one by one, they called him.

Monday 1st September
3 am

Waking from the dream, Patrick Maguire could still see her face. He could hear her voice, almost smell her cigarette: he could picture the way a single line of smoke would eddy to a ceiling stained yellow by years of the same. Sitting upright, he could hear her again as if she were in some darkened corner of the room. But the voice was inside his head; the way she spoke to his brother and never to him. He could picture her refusing even to look at him.

There was stillness in the air after the rain: even with the windows open, the old city seemed rather quiet. It was a weighty silence, thick and heavy, yet alive in a stifling kind of way. It was exactly 3 am, and he hadn't woken from a dream so much as from a memory: it was the only one he had, and after all these years he was weary of it. His mother in the chair, with her lank, plaited hair, that stinking cigarette between fingers so waxen from nicotine they looked jaundiced. Her voice was ruined: no more than a cackle, like the old witch who buried her sons in the wood. Drink and smoke, and sitting there bitching about what having two boys had done to her. It was 'Frankie this' and 'Frankie that', and without them she would still have had a husband.

Patrick could see damp seeping through the walls; he could see lime scale, thick and brown, clogging the sink in the kitchen: he could see it foul like dried shit in the bowl of the toilet. He could picture her cold, almost soulless eyes, the way she ignored and humiliated him, behaved as if he wasn't there.

Angry suddenly, he grabbed his dressing gown and went through to the kitchen, pausing to stare at the photograph that for some reason he still kept on the mantelpiece. There she was with her eyes glazed, the wineglass hidden, but the ubiquitous cigarette between her fingers, with an inch of grey ash about to fall in her lap. And there they were, fatherless, yet dutiful as a mother's sons should be; him and Frankie, stoic as ever, either side of her chair.

Her mouth was narrow and pinched; orange-coloured lipstick smeared over horizontal lines that belonged to a woman more than twice her age. He considered her face, her hair; the way she occupied the chair. Looking closer still, he noticed the gold necklace glimmering at her throat.

Monday 1st September
6 am

Jessica Quinn woke to the silence, not sure what day it was – though she hoped it was Saturday.

The house felt cold; it felt odd. She had a strange feeling in her stomach and she couldn't imagine why. Getting out of bed, she grabbed her teddy bear and, hugging him close, crossed to her sister's room.

Laura was still asleep but, as if she could sense that someone was there, she opened her eyes.

'What is it?' she said. 'What is it, Jess? What's wrong?'

Jess hunched her shoulders. Laura rolled on her back then, sitting upright, she glanced at the large-faced clock beside the bed.

'What are you doing up so early?' Jess just stood there.

'I miss my dad,' she said.

'Phone him up, then. He said we could phone any time. He told you again yesterday.'

'Why did mam send him away?'

Laura clicked her tongue. 'She didn't send him away. It's not like that. You're too young, Jessie: you don't understand.'

'I'm ten.'

'You're not ten till December. You don't understand.'

Jess had tears in her eyes. 'We were all together, then Danny got knocked down, and since then mam is a different person. It's as if she blames our dad, Laura. How can she blame Dad?'

Laura sighed. 'I don't know, but policemen are supposed to be able to catch the people who do bad things, aren't they? Dad couldn't catch whoever killed Danny. I don't know, Jess. But you know what he said yesterday: he doesn't blame our mam for blaming him. She's not very well but she'll get better. She just needs time.'

'I know that, but we're on our own now; with dad not here, there's only mam to look after us.'

Sitting down on her sister's bed, Jessica tugged at the ear of her teddy.

'It's Monday,' she said. 'I thought it was Saturday it's so quiet, but it's school today, it's Monday.' Laura lay down again.

'Mam's not even up yet. You should go back to bed, Jess.'

Jess shook her head. 'I'm going downstairs.'

She shuffled out of the room and across the landing. One hand on the banister, she made her way downstairs, then went into the kitchen. A few moments later, Laura came down wearing pyjamas and dressing gown. She took the kettle from where Jess was trying to fill it, standing precariously on a three-legged stool.

'You'll burn yourself with the steam,' she said. 'Like you did before: remember?'

A couple of years previously, Jess had burned her wrist and they'd had to go to hospital. Laura put the kettle on and got a cup from the cupboard. Jess fetched a tea bag and, between them, they made their mother some tea.

A few minutes later, with Laura carrying the cup, they went back upstairs. Their mother's bedroom door was ajar, and Jess noticed that the landing light was still on. That wasn't normal. Their mother always closed her door, and she switched the landing light off when she came to bed. The bedroom was empty; their mother wasn't there. The bed was untouched, the duvet smooth and flat, and pulled up to the pillows.

'Where is she?' Jess asked.

Laura didn't know. She didn't reply.

'Where is she, Laura? She's not downstairs.' The hint of panic began to stretch Jessie's voice; anxiously, she worked a hand through her hair. Placing the cup on the bedside table, Laura stared at the bed as if she thought her mother would suddenly appear. Then she turned to her sister.

'Where is she?' Jessie repeated. 'Why isn't she here?'

Laura crossed to the window. 'Her car's not there, maybe she went to the shop. We used up most of the milk last night, didn't we? She must be at the shop, Jess. She'll be back in a minute. We'd better get dressed; we'd better get ready for school.'

Half an hour later, they were sitting at the kitchen table, the remnants of a packet of cornflakes in two bowls but not enough milk to pour over them. The only sound was the ticking of the wall clock.

'She didn't go to the shop, did she?' Jess said.

Laura didn't answer: she sat where she was, her expression fixed, holding her spoon as if she was about to eat.

'I'm going to phone Dad,' she said. Sliding off the chair, she went through to the hall. Their father's mobile number was plugged into the handset. Laura scrolled through the options, and dialled. She waited, then, frowning heavily, turned to her sister. 'There's no one there; his phone's switched off.'

'Try it again,' Jess told her.

Laura redialled but still no answer. 'What's Dad doing with his phone turned off?' she sounded suddenly panicky. 'His phone is never turned off.'

Jess clutched at her hand now. 'No Mam; no Dad. Where are they?'

'It's all right,' Laura said. 'Dad's just not switched his phone on yet today, that's all – or maybe the battery ran out.' She was thinking hard, trying to work out what to do. She walked the length of the hall and opened the front door. Last night's rain lay in puddles at the bottom of the steps. Hand in hand, the two girls looked up and down the road, but there was no sign of their mother.

Back inside, Laura took the address book from the telephone table and flicked through the pages.

'What're you doing?' Jess asked.

'I'm going to phone Uncle Joe.' Laura picked up the phone. 'Nanny and Granddad Quinn are away and Nanny Clare is in Kerry. I'm going to phone Uncle Joe, Jess: he'll know what to do.'

Monday 1st September
7 am

Yet more rain seemed to be blowing in from the west. Pulling into the drive, Jimmy Hanrahan shut off the engine and climbed from the short-wheelbase Land Rover into weeds that reached to his knees. Taking a moment to roll a smoke, he could hear his father's horse shifting around in the stable. He'd have to muck the horse out; the old feller didn't seem capable any more, and if Jimmy didn't do it, it wouldn't get done.

He sucked on the cigarette, just a few threads of tobacco; the way he'd learned to make them when he'd been banged up as a kid. He worked his shoulders, looking at the sky and listening through the kitchen window to his father muttering away like a mad thing. No doubt he'd been up in the night spreading the holy water the priest from Ballylongford had given him.

He took another drag and, letting the smoke drift, squatted on the old motorbike, which was a rust bucket these days. Resting one heel on the foot peg, he considered how low and bruised the clouds were as they gathered above what was left of Lislaughtin Abbey. From here, he could see the five-bar gate and the broken-down cottage where that American tourist had gone for a leak a couple of years back. The smell had attracted him; the maggots; millions of flies still in the larval stage.

Jimmy had watched from this very spot, smoking a roll-up just as he was now. Shades all over the place, an ambulance, a helicopter; search teams in white suits; Quinn and Doyle down from Dublin.

His father had dressed in his dark suit and wrapped a scarf round his neck before harnessing the horse between the shafts and offering his services as pall-bearer. Doyle had been kind enough, he supposed, humouring the old feller when he'd started coming out with his stories. Doyle was a Dublin man these days, though Jimmy knew him from here. He remembered how it had been when Maggs's mother was found dead with her insides burned to bejaysus. He remembered stories told about how when Doyle joined the Guards, his eldest brother had told him not to come knocking on his granny's door of a Saturday night. He grinned now wolfishly, licking at his teeth and wondering how a Kerryman from such a hardline family could end up with his nose in a trough of pigswill.

He thought about how Doyle used to watch out for Eva in the days before she took up with Quinn and every mother's son was trying to get inside her knickers. Jimmy had fancied a bit of that himself, and no matter what he tried to tell anyone, so had Conor Maggs. The sad fuck thought she fancied him just because she was the only girl in the county who'd give him the time of day. With the rumours her uncle spread, it was a surprise to no one but Maggs that people liked to avoid him. Maybe it was a streak of defiance in Eva – her way of telling Doyle she was old enough to look after herself – but all it did was to give the Maggot the impression there was something between them.

Eva had been one of those girls, though; the kind that just didn't know how beautiful they were. Either that or when she was really young, some priest had told her that 'lilies that fester smell far worse than weeds', and she'd never forgotten the comment.

The clouds descended and he yelled at the horse to shut its noise, then went inside to make the old nutter a bowl of porridge. He wondered why he bothered; better to let them toss him in a mental home and be done with it. But then Jimmy liked the money the Social dished out, and without the old man there would be none of that.

His father was in the living room moulded to his chair, with the cartoons playing on the TV.

'Jimmy?' he called. 'Jimmy? Is that you, lad? Where the devil have ya been?'

Jimmy didn't answer.

He closed the kitchen door. The place was so filthy he'd have to clean up or the social would stop the money. He shifted his shotgun and hunting rifle where they leant against the side of the fridge. The magnet fell off the door and two Polaroids came with it. Cursing softly Jimmy, picked them up: one of him with a stag he'd poached on the other side of the hill, the other with half a dozen rabbits he had hanging from a leather string.

The door opened and his father stood there. 'Jimmy, for the love of God, did you not hear me calling?'

'Of course I heard you.' Jimmy looked sour. ''Tis all I ever hear. Now go on back to 'Tom & Jerry' before I drag you down to Fletcher's bog and throw your carcass in.'

Monday 1st September
7 am

Sitting in his car across the river from the Dublin city moorings, Doyle considered John Finucane's boat. Sixty-two feet of ocean-going cabin cruiser, all white paint and smoked glass. Business was obviously good for the only property developer in Dublin who discouraged competition by tying industrial chains round the feet of his enemies and taking them out to sea.

They'd had word that the clogger was employing illegal immigrants on some of his northside building developments. It wasn't something that Doyle would normally bother with: at fifty, and a sergeant in the National Bureau of Criminal Investigation, he didn't concern himself with things like immigration. But this was Johnny Clogs, who had no trouble winning government contracts because there were a few in the government paid good money to see that's how it remained. Any angle was a good angle; one of these days, Doyle would nail the bastard.

Even now, with so much new competition, Johnny was still the northside's most notorious, no matter that he was Doyle's age. The fact that he was running Ukrainians would piss off Alexei

Bris-Mintov, and that was no bad thing. From Kiev to Dublin via Berlin, 'Minty' had been around for about five years now; he had already carved up much of the 'business' on the south of the river. The old boss down there, Lorne McGeady, had been so miffed that he'd tried to create some kind of tie-up with Johnny, but the clogger was having none of it; not so far, anyway. It wasn't like the old days, though, when the city had been ruled by hard men like the General. In those days, even amongst the villains there was order: there was honour and a certain amount of respect. But since the Celtic Tiger started to bear its teeth, everything had changed.

Across the water, he saw Finucane poke his bald pate out of the main salon, sniff the rain like a reluctant dog and duck back inside again. How he managed to keep his boat at the moorings for as long as he did was another indication of how good his friends were: it was supposed to be a public mooring. Further up the quay, a replica of the old sailing ship *The Jeanie Johnston* was moored, but apart from her, all you ever saw was Johnny's gin palace. Doyle glanced at *The Jeanie Johnston* again: a training ship, a graceful three-master; the original had been used to take emigrants to America back in the nineteenth century. Funny how things had changed, he thought: these days everyone was coming here.

He had yet to go home and change after last night. He'd been in O'Shea's for the music, before crossing the river to the little drinker he frequented behind Connolly Station. It was a private club where the bar was tended by Maureen, a wonderfully bosomy woman with whom he'd had a thing going for a while now.

He could still smell her on him. She was warm and sensuous; always with a laugh and a smile, and a hint of her mighty cleavage to add some spice to a seat at her bar. She and Doyle went way back: he'd known her when she lived in Tralee, and when she moved to Dublin he'd helped her find work. Over the years, their on-off relationship had survived her three marriages.

His phone rang where it lay on the seat beside him. A glance at the dashboard clock told him it was barely seven; he wondered who was phoning at this time. Probably Maureen, to tell him he'd left something at her place. It wasn't Maureen; it was Quinn's home number. 'Hello,' he said. 'This is Doyle.'

'Uncle Joe, is that you?'

Doyle narrowed his eyes: one of the girls. He could hear the unease in her voice.

'Uncle Joe?'

'Who's that now, Jessie or Laura?'

'It's Laura.'

'I thought it was. How are you, Laura?'

'Uncle Joe . . . ' Her voice faltered.

'What is it, love?'

'It's our mam, she's not here. I don't know where she is and I can't get hold of my dad.'

'Sit tight, I'll be right there.'

Scrolling through the numbers on his phone, he came to Quinn's and dialled. No answer; his phone was switched off. In all their years working together, Doyle had never known Quinn to have his phone switched off. He was a detective inspector in the Garda, for Christ's sake; what was he doing with his phone switched off? As Doyle spun the car around, his mind was working overtime: yesterday had been the first anniversary of Danny's death, and both Eva and Moss had been at the cemetery. But they hadn't been together; they'd not been together in a year.

Doyle had no wife and no children but he'd seen how those two girls were. He'd seen how much they were hurting, and he would like to have taken his niece by one hand and his partner by the other and metaphorically knocked their heads together; as if the boy's death was not enough, without everything else breaking down because of it.

He was concerned, though: he'd seen how Eva had been yesterday. He could see beyond the smiles, of course: she was his brother's girl. This wasn't like her. This wasn't like her at all.

Again he dialled Quinn's number, but again he got nothing. 'Moss,' he muttered softly, 'why haven't you got your phone on?'

Monday 1st September
7.30 am

Murphy was still in the shower. They'd made love most of the night, and Quinn was nursing a cup of coffee with the kind of glow in his belly he'd not felt in years. He wasn't sure what it meant. He wasn't sure he cared what it meant: after the trauma of yesterday and how distant Eva had been, he was happy just to feel something.

'Listen,' he called through to her, 'I'm going to the Square to get those files together for Naas. I'll see you when you get there, all right? It's probably better that we don't show up together.'

Murphy was working shampoo into her scalp. He watched it trickle down her shoulders, slip deliciously onto the fullness of her breasts: he watched it work in rivulets down her belly. 'Go ahead,' Murphy told him. 'I'll be discreet when I let myself out, so don't worry.'

Leaving her in the flat, Quinn trotted down the stairs and onto the autumnal street. The wind was blowing, and the rain was falling in a charcoal mist between the trees. They'd had so much rain through August that it felt as though half the country had been flooded for weeks. In his car, he flicked on the radio; a few minutes later, he was beyond the barrier at Harcourt Square and parking in the underground car park. Just behind him, Frank Maguire came down the ramp in his big silver Opel.

Quinn waited. He'd seen the man yesterday; like so many other people, Frank had crossed the river to pay his respects to Danny's memory. Patrick had been there, of course; thinking of Paddy, Quinn needed to talk to him: his best mate from their rugby days – and Frank Maguire's little brother. He was a social worker, a prison visitor; as a family friend, he'd offered to counsel Eva. He was a good listener; he was still counselling her almost a year later.

Quinn watched the superintendent get out of his car: at forty-six, he was a career copper – a man with ambitions at Garda HQ. He liked to socialise with the upper echelons but in reality Quinn knew the commissioner, Tom Calhoun, better than he did. It galled Maguire, of course: he was the senior officer and, given his golf-club and Masonic connections, it made little sense that Quinn was more 'in' with the top brass than he was. But Calhoun had been a veteran No. 8 when Quinn first made the Dublin second XV, and they'd played together for a couple of years before Calhoun hung up his rugby boots. Maguire had light-coloured hair cut short and brushed forward at an angle across his forehead. He was married to an investment banker who was always flying to London or New York.

Everything about him was proper: where he lived, where he played golf. To top it all, he wore hand-made suits. He was a daily communicant at St Kevin's Church, across the road from the Garda Club: given that that was where Quinn was squatting, at least temporarily, he'd have to be careful if he was planning on seeing Murphy.

'Morning, Moss,' Maguire said, shaking his hand. 'Did you manage to get through it yesterday?'

For a chill moment, Quinn thought of his son in his grave; the image was juxtaposed with that of another woman in his bed.

'I tried to phone you last night,' Maguire told him. 'My wife is away, and I thought I'd invite you over for a small one.'

'What time was this?'

'Around ten, I suppose.'

'I was here then still, I think,' Quinn told him. 'Don't ask me why, Frank, but I was at my desk looking over the files Murphy and I are taking to Naas.'

'Your phone was switched off,' Maguire said. 'I didn't think to call your desk.'

Quinn felt in his pocket and discovered that his phone was still switched off. He'd missed a few calls: two from his house in Glasnevin, another from Frank, and two more this morning from Doyle.

That had been at seven. What the hell did the Doyler want so early? At that moment, the phone rang again. Maguire was holding the lift but Quinn nodded for him to go on. 'Doyler,' he said when he answered. 'That's three times already and it's not yet eight o'clock.'

'Why the hell was your phone off?' Doyle demanded.

His tone sent the hairs rising on the nape of Quinn's neck. 'What is it now? What's up?'

'Laura tried to phone you, lad, but she couldn't get a reply. It's Eva, Moss: she's not here, and her bed doesn't look as though it's been slept in.'

Monday 1st September
7.50 am

Eva's car was not in its usual spot. As Quinn pulled up he was conscious of the knot tightening in the pit of his stomach. He could see his youngest daughter's face at the window: she was waiting for him, her nose to the glass, peering out anxiously. He climbed the steps and the front door flew open; Laura threw herself into his arms.

'Hey,' he said, 'it's all right. It's OK, Laura, everything's going to be fine.'

Doyle was at the far end of the hall with breakfast dishes in his hands. The two men exchanged a concerned glance. Laura was holding on to him tightly. 'Dad, she's not here. Mam's not here. We don't know where she is.'

'We phoned you, but your phone was off,' Jess was almost shouting as she came rushing out of the living room.

'I know, love. I'm sorry.' Quinn bent to pick her up and, with both of them clinging to him, glanced at Doyle again. 'I turned the bloody thing off and forgot to switch it on again. It's a good job you could get hold of your Uncle Joe, girls, wasn't it?'

In the lounge, he sat down on the sofa with a daughter on each knee. 'Mam wasn't in her room when you woke up?' he asked. 'Is that how it was?'

Jess nodded. 'It was awful quiet, Dad. I woke up first and went through to Laura's room. It was so quiet I thought it was Saturday or something.'

'Well it's not,' he said with a reassuring smile. 'It's Monday. I expect your mam had to nip out. She'll be back soon. Now I think the best thing you two can do is get your things together and I'll drive you to school.'

'School?' Laura looked almost shocked.

'Your mam will be fine, love. You need to be at school.'

The two girls went upstairs to get their shoes.

Doyle touched Quinn lightly on the arm. 'There's tea brewed, Moss, if you want a cup.'

Quinn shook his head. Hands on his hips, he was studying the picture of him and Danny fishing the Tolka. Eva had taken the photograph only a couple of weeks before the boy had been killed.

Guilt pricked him – a sickening sensation in his gut. It had been a year and a day, and there was no sign, no word – and him a detective inspector with as good a network of touts as any copper working.

'So what do you know?' Doyle asked him.

Quinn pushed out his lips. 'I'm just glad you were on the end of the phone.'

'I was with Maureen last night, so I didn't get back to Harold's Cross. This morning I drove to the quays thinking I might have words with your man about those Ukrainians he's got working for him. I was sitting there when Laura phoned.'

'I went to the office last night, Doyler. Like I told you, I forgot to switch my phone back on.'

'Getting the files together for this thing down in Naas, were you?'

'The justice minister's pet project,' Quinn replied, nodding.

Doyle shoved his hands in his pockets. 'So what about this, then? What about little Eva taking off somewhere and not telling anyone where she was going?'

'Have you been upstairs?' Quinn asked him.

Doyle nodded. 'The girls are right: it doesn't look as though the bed's been slept in.'

Quinn could see the unease etched in his face. 'Let's get the kids to school,' he said. 'I know what you're thinking but it'll be fine. Eva's not one to do anything stupid: you know she's not.'

For years, Quinn had been subordinate to the older man. He had been a young copper when Doyle was already a sergeant; then Quinn made detective and they'd been sergeants together for a while before Quinn was promoted to inspector. Doyle never had designs on anything beyond the rank of sergeant, and his methods had been gleaned from the 'Brano Five Team', who were called out to the trouble spots in the late sixties and early seventies. They were led by Jim 'Lugs' Brannigan, a legendary Dublin policeman who boxed for Ireland but didn't use the Queensberry Rules when dealing with the city's lowlifes. Lugs used to give the so-called hard men the choice of fighting him or appearing in court; most of them chose the latter. He was famous for taking on a gang in Dolphin's Barn one night, and he was the one they called when a drunk from Meath Street used a hachet as currency to get served in the pub.

Between them, Quinn and Doyle got the girls into the car, and Doyle drove the short distance to the school. Quinn kissed them and told them not to worry, then watched as they padded across the playground.

'Do you not want to let the headteacher know what's gone on, maybe?' Doyle suggested.

Quinn shook his head. 'I don't want to let anyone know, Doyler. Eva's not herself, we both know that. We'll just find out where she is and bring her home.' He looked at his watch. 'Fuck it,' he said.

'I'm supposed to be going to Naas.'

Taking his mobile phone out, he stepped away from Doyle and called Murphy. 'Listen, Murph,' he said, 'something's come up. Can you take the files to Naas and brief the team without me?'

'Of course. What's happened?'

'It's my wife,' he said, hoarsely. 'She went out and left the girls on their own. Keep a lid on it, will you? Me and Doyle will find her, then I'll get down to Naas.'

Doyle was standing with his hands in his pockets and his collar turned up under his ears. He had a distant expression on his face. He looked round as Quinn hung up the phone.

'So you know what I'm thinking,' Doyle said. He looked square-ly at Quinn. It's not like her; but then it's not like anyone, is it? You saw her yesterday, Mossie – how she was just about coping and no more. I'm going to say it because it has to be said: I can't help but wonder if she's not fetched herself off for the rope.'

Monday 1st September
8.30 am

Conor Maggs made a pot of coffee. He was in the tiny kitchen. Beyond the concrete balcony he could see the back of the hotel, where Polish chambermaids were shaking out the bed sheets. He could smell breakfast: eggs and bacon; black and white pudding; the semolina grits poor people used to eat in America.

He moved to the living room, where he sat down and opened his Bible – a modern version, not the King James one that his aunt had bought him for his First Communion. His aunt had been good to him; she'd given him and his brothers and sisters a home when they had nowhere else, even though she knew that her sister was a drunk who funded her habit by lying on her back. For a moment, Maggs thought about his mother. It wasn't her fault, but she'd been old with the drink. Old and ugly: too much drink and too many men; too many cigarettes.

*

She'd been up before he left for school that morning. This was very unusual: normally she was still all-but-comatose from the drink the

58

night before. This morning, though, it was almost as if she knew she'd done something very bad; although she couldn't have known quite how bad, she knew that he'd find out.

His aunt had already left for work. Conor came down from his little room with its narrow bed at the front of the pebble-dash council semi. He was washed and dressed in his uniform of white shirt and blue jumper, the tie only loosely knotted. His aunt always made sure his tie was neat before he left the house. His mother didn't care. She was overweight and her hair was a mess; and she was wearing the loose nylon dressing gown that was pretty much see-through.

When he sat down to a bowl of cereal, she had a smoke going, leaning with one hand on the worktop, her crimson nail varnish chipped like that of some cheap checkout girl who said little and snapped gum. The cigarette smoke was stifling, and with the windows shut, the fug sucked the air from the room.

His mother was resting with her back to the cooker. She didn't speak to him, just crossed one leg over the other, the white flesh of her thigh exposed between the folds of the dressing gown. He could see her breasts – she wasn't wearing a bra – and colour rose from his jowls. Avoiding her eye, he poured milk over the cereal and spooned on some sugar. The work surface was littered with empty bottles. Sherry, mostly, along with a few wine bottles from the supermarket: the German stuff, sweet and cheap; she didn't care what it tasted like just so long as she could tip it down her throat.

His aunt never got in from work before six-thirty. She worked long hours in a small factory and had to travel all the way to Tralee. His mother had the house to herself during the day; when he finished school, Conor would wander down to the river and sit there watching the otters and the little birds that nested among the reeds. Not wanting to walk in on anything, he did his homework down there or, when it was cold or raining, he'd go to the library.

The other kids would be hanging out and they'd either come

looking to give him a kicking or would just take the piss. They'd been doing that pretty much all the time since he and his mother had moved there five years ago. And it wasn't just the kids; everyone seemed to know what his mother was: the local families, the Guards, the clergy. He was judged because of it, though perhaps not by the priest: his aunt was devout and made sure he went to Mass at least twice a week. It was at Mass that Conor had seen Eva.

He thought about her as he sat there spooning mushy Weetabix into his mouth. She was the only person at school who had any time for him; since he was nine years old, she'd made his life bearable.

She wore his necklace, the one he'd persuaded his aunt to buy for her as a present for his First Communion. It had been a thank-you for her consideration and little kindnesses towards him.

His mother coughed and Conor glanced up at her now, aware of her looking at him guiltily. If he held her gaze for any length of time, she had to look away.

'Come home early today,' she said gently. 'I'll make you your tea.'

He was stunned: he could not recall the last time she'd made him any food – or even offered to, for that matter. It was his aunt who did the cooking; after his mother had got rid of her last 'client', she would sink into the bottle for the rest of the day.

'I've homework, mam,' he muttered. 'I'll just go to the library. I don't mind.'

'Suit yerself.' He could see the pain in her eyes as, with a shrug, she dragged on her cigarette, held the butt under the running tap and shuffled upstairs.

The walk to school took him a mile across town, out of the estate and up through the square, where he saw a group of kids hanging around the shops. Jimmy Hanrahan and his mates – half a dozen of them – roamed the playground at break-time looking for someone to pick on. They hadn't seen him yet; Conor ducked into the doorway of the Indian restaurant until they'd moved on. They were dawdling, though, and he'd have no choice but to dawdle behind them: he couldn't risk trying to pass them in the street. Jimmy would never allow that. Jimmy was the local hardchaw, a bully; picking on Conor Maggs was his favourite pastime. At fourteen, he was six months older than Conor, but he was nowhere near as bright: the only lesson he seemed to do OK in was literature – a flair he'd got from his mam, who was supposed to be something of a culchie. His old man, on the other hand, was a vicious drunk who spent the hours when he wasn't boozing, poaching illicit deer.

Conor waited until it was safe to leave the doorway. As he stepped out to cross the road, Eva's Uncle Joe swept past in his car and he had to step back again sharply. For a brief moment, their eyes met. The copper looked at him as he always did – with suspicion and malice. He'd been like that since Eva's father died.

When the car had passed, Conor crossed quickly. It wasn't often he saw Doyle down here: he was a Guard up in Dublin these days and only came down when he had a few days off. He knew what Conor's mother was – he'd always known – and he was a prime example of how judgemental people can be.

Doyle had been there the day Conor, Eva and their classmates made their First communion, and Conor knew he'd been against Eva accepting the gift. But her mother was as sweet a soul as her youngest, and told the old bastard not to be so prejudiced.

It was all because of his mother. Conor knew that: he'd never known anything else. He had no clue who his dad was; he could've been one of dozens. Fathers had never been spoken about in their house: there was only him and his mother. Here the Guards seemed to turn a blind eye to her 'business'. In Limerick, they'd been in a tiny flat before the council kicked them out. It seemed as though the door had been knocked all hours of the day. He used to hear the customers bouncing away on top of her, and he'd bury his head in the pillow to try and shut the noise out.

Jimmy was at the school gates: Jimmy who, ironically, had been in the same catechism class as him and Eva. Not that he took any notice: his old man had made him go for the sake of his mother's religion. A skinny kid, he was brutal and very strong; and he was leaning against the gate with a whole gaggle of other kids around him. One of them looked up as Conor came round the corner; he muttered something to Jimmy and then they all turned. Conor faltered; he could feel the blood rising in his cheeks. He studied the tarmac, acutely conscious that he would have to walk past them.

There were twenty of them maybe, not just from his year but from the years above and below.

Older kids, younger. One of them yelled out suddenly: 'Hey maggot, how's your ma? How's she feeling this morning?'

The others cackled away like mad things. Conor was trembling; he could feel heat in his bladder; there were tears behind his eyes. This was much worse than usual, but he had no choice, there was no other way to get into the school. He'd had to run this kind of gauntlet more times than he could remember. He did it most days, and he could do it today; it was just that there were more of them this morning.

'She's got a right pair on her, doesn't she?' another kid scoffed. 'They sag like spuds in a sack, mind, but they are fuckin' big.'

Conor stopped dead. He could hear the taunts, but across the playground, by the netball posts, he glimpsed Eva. With her auburn hair and freckles across her nose, she was a thing of beauty – the only thing of beauty in his life. And she always had a kind word for him. She could see the crowd; she would know what was going on.

'She's pig-ugly, lads, I can tell you.' It was Jimmy's voice. He was holding a Polaroid photograph, and the other kids were gathering round to take a look. 'I'm charging for this,' Jimmy cracked. 'I need to get me money back somehow. Big floppy tits, she has, and a really hairy box.'

Conor's mouth fell open.

'Do you want to take a look, maggot? Naw, bollocks do you, you don't need to, do you? You get to see the old witch every day.' He held up the picture, flapping it at Conor like a fan.

'She doesn't know I took it. She was shit-faced, the fat bitch.'

Conor flew at him. Forcing his way through the other kids like an animal, he leapt. Jimmy was too quick, though: he whipped the photo away and, in the same movement, whacked Conor on the side of the head. Off balance already, he went sprawling; then he was on his hands and knees, and the other kids, girls as well as boys, were kicking lumps out of him.

The next thing he knew, the crowd was scattering and he heard one of the teachers yelling across the playground. He was on his face, with blood in his mouth, and as he lifted his head, there was Jimmy waving the picture of his half-naked mother in front of his eyes. Then the photo was gone, and Jimmy was gone, and Conor had a teacher hauling him up by the elbow.

'Are you all right?' he asked, his tone terse, not kindly. 'You need to get yourself to class, lad, you're late enough as it is.'

Conor stumbled across the playground. He could still see Eva watching, and for a moment he thought she might come and speak to him. But she didn't. He wiped his lip with the back of his hand and it came away bloody.

'Go to the bathroom before you go to class,' the teacher told him. 'Clean yourself up: you're a mess, Maggs. And you're late. Get yourself cleaned up.'

*

Any man who had the price: old or young, it didn't seem to matter. The picture was a trophy, a memento of the day Jimmy Hanrahan lost his virginity. He'd thought it a great laugh. That picture did the rounds for months afterwards: more than twenty years later, it was as firmly imprinted on Maggs's mind as the night Doyle took his fists to him.

With steam rising from the coffee cup, he considered what he would talk about with the community group that night. He'd spoken to them a few times but not for some months. He wasn't sure what to prepare: something inspirational, maybe, or something more doctrinal, such as the Catholic belief that in the Mass Christ really was manifest as flesh and blood in the sacraments. It was the only bit of the Roman idolatry he still believed in; the rest had been usurped by evangelical fervour after his experience in the cell at Rathfarnham. That was another vivid memory – and one that brought him out in a mix of cold sweat and elation. One minute he had Doyle in his ear, telling him he knew what he'd done not just to the girl from Limerick but to his own mother. Then the Lord himself, in all his suffering, was looking down where Maggs lay; where Doyle had left him.

All at once, he knew what he would talk about. Martyrs: he would talk about those who had suffered for their faith. Like Peter, the Lord's favourite, who had been crucified upside down by the Romans because he didn't believe he was worthy to meet death in the same fashion as his master.

Monday 1st September
8.45 am

Back at the house in Glasnevin, Quinn and Doyle were ringing round every hospital in the city to see if anyone answering Eva's description had been brought in. Her handbag was on the hall table, together with her purse, her driving licence, her mobile phone; everything, in fact, other than her car keys. So far, they had found nothing, and right now Quinn was on his landline to the Mater Hospital, situated directly across the road from Mountjoy Prison. Doyle was in the kitchen on his mobile phone; he came through, then, his face taut with anxiety.

'Moss,' he said, 'I just spoke to the City Centre Morgue.'

Amiens Street, right next door to the garda station. Quinn's heart was thumping.

'They dragged a body from Spencer Dock,' Doyle told him. 'A woman in her thirties, and wearing a wedding band.'

Quinn stared at him. And for a moment he couldn't breathe: a woman in her thirties, a wedding band. How many times had he been called to a scene where a body had been found after someone had been reported missing?

It was always the person they were looking for.

He could feel the colour draining from his face, and the sweat breaking out on his scalp. He looked at Doyle and saw the same fear etched in his granite features. He could see Murphy naked beneath him; he could feel the softness of her breasts, the warmth of her in his bed. He couldn't deal with this; not after Danny, not after yesterday. He had to clamp his jaws together to stop himself from breaking down. He tried to steel himself; he tried to think.

Eyes closed, he asked: 'Was her car down there? Did they find her car?'

Doyle shook his head. 'I don't know. I didn't ask, Moss. I didn't ask about the car.'

They drove south with Doyle and followed Quinn towards the centre of town. Quinn was just about holding things together and for his part Doyle tried to concentrate on the crisis that was unfolding. But this was family, his brother's youngest, and all he could think about was the three-hour drive to Kerry. He could not imagine having to tell his sister-in-law that her youngest had taken her life because her son was gone and she hadn't been able to cope.

Only once had he had to tell that to a family. He'd arrested Jimmy Hanrahan when he was fifteen, after he and a couple of mates had broken into the spinster Bolton's house on the Ballybunion Road. They'd stolen jewellery which had been given to the old woman by her mother. When she wouldn't tell them where she kept her savings, Jimmy battered her over the head with her fire poker. She needed thirty-two stitches in her scalp.

It had been a bad business. Jimmy's old man had always been a toe-rag, and when his mother found out that her boy had gone the same way, she rowed out into the Shannon in a little boat and drowned herself.

Doyle had been the one to tell her husband; John Hanrahan swore that, from that day on, he would never touch another drop of drink. Guilt besieged him because, according to the faith his wife had kept, she would be in purgatory now, her soul neither God's nor the devil's. In a bid to contact her, he'd started to visit mediums; not long after that, the souls of the dead started visiting his kitchen. But it wasn't just the dead; according to old John, it was Beelzebub himself sitting there at the table.

In the car park, Quinn sat in his car. His palms were sweating; he reached for the glovebox and the half-smoked packet of cigarettes he'd brought from the flat this morning. All manner of memories were whizzing through his head: Eva the first time he'd seen her, beautiful, with ochre-coloured hair and eyes the green of polished emeralds. A rugby tour in Kerry, him and Paddy Maguire; they'd won the first match and they were in the bar with Doyle telling Quinn who Eva was, and that he needed to keep his mucky mitts to himself.

Crossing the car park, Doyle opened the door and laid a gentle hand on his shoulder. 'Are you set?' he asked.

Quinn had been to the morgue many times. He'd seen autopsies being performed; he'd seen more corpses than he could count. But never had he been here like this.

He could picture his wife only yesterday at Danny's grave, sur-rounded by people yet enveloped in her own silence. He realised then that she could have done it. In the state of mind she was in then, she could've gone to Spencer Dock and thrown herself into the water.

He had to pause for breath. 'Jesus, Doyler, I'm not sure I can do this.'

Doyle nodded. His own eyes were haunted, his features stiff with tension. 'Do you want to stay here?' he asked. 'Do you want me to do it?'

Quinn swallowed, then, looking sharply at the old Victorian walls, shook his head slowly. 'If it is her, I have to know. If I have to tell the kids, I have to have seen her myself.'

They made their way past reception, and again he had to catch his breath. As they were walking down the short corridor to the heavy swing doors, which were part-wood and part-plastic, his heart thumped; the knot in his gut was a physical pain now. Pushing open the door, he found a mortuary assistant in the office off to the left.

The odour of disinfectant assaulted his nostrils: he saw white tiled walls, and a tiled floor that had been scrubbed till it squeaked. The assistant, who was wearing a pair of rubber boots, looked up at them through a pane of security glass.

'DI Quinn.' Quinn's voice was little more than a whisper. 'We were told you had a possible suicide brought in.'

The young man pushed a strand of thin black hair away from his eyes. 'That's right,' he said. 'They dragged her out of Spencer Dock just this morning.' He closed the office door, then led the way through another door to where the cold rooms and sluices were.

'I'd say she was in her late thirties,' the assistant told them. 'She's got reddish-brown hair and bluish eyes. Dark skirt; white top; no shoes. She's wearing a wedding ring: nothing particular, just a gold band.'

'What kind of a gold band?'

'A narrow one, not unlike that, now you come to mention it,' he said, nodding towards the one Quinn was fingering.

Doyle crossed himself.

The assistant led the way through the next set of doors, where four stainless-steel tables were set side by side, a few feet apart. Each had a lip along the edge and steel slats running crosswise the full length of the table so that bodily fluids could drain into the belly pan below. The tang of disinfectant was overpowering.

This was where Dublin's dead were brought. Suicides, victims of road-traffic accidents and murders; they were cleaned up and patched up so that those with the task of identifying the body would be put through as little trauma as possible.

The door to the cold room stood open, and a polished pine

casket stood on one table. Beyond was the mortuary itself, the walls filled with refrigerated cabinets, each of which held five trays, one on top of the other. The assistant opened the fourth rack at the second level and slid the tray all the way out. The body was covered in opaque polythene sheeting.

Quinn looked down as he'd done countless times before; only now, he imagined Jess and Laura at school trying to concentrate on their lessons.

He was trembling.

Before he was ready, before he could think about what was to come, the assistant drew back the plastic sheet. She lay with her eyes closed, her skin like candle wax, and strands of auburn hair were matted around her face. She looked pained and weary in death. Quinn tried to part his lips, but his mouth was as dry as an old bone.

'Have you any idea who she is?' the assistant asked him.

'No,' he whispered. 'I don't.'

Monday 1st September
9 am

Outside, the two men leant against the brick wall as if they'd both just run a marathon. Quinn was still shaking; with a sharp exhalation of breath, Doyle crossed himself for the umpteenth time.

'Thank the Blessed Virgin,' he muttered. 'Jesus, Moss, that was a moment and no mistake.' Quinn stared at the grubby concrete, bits of paper, slivers of old gum.

They were quiet for a few moments, then Doyle cleared his throat. 'So now then,' he said. 'You're the one that made inspector: where the devil is she?'

Quinn lit a cigarette and as he smoked it, his mind settled. 'She's at the cemetery, Joe, that's where she is.'

'Ah,' Doyle said, nodding slowly. 'Of course she is. And you know what? If we'd taken a step back and thought about it for just a moment, we'd have figured that out a lot sooner.'

'We're coppers. We think hospital and mortuary; that's just the way it is.' Straightening up, Quinn dropped the cigarette and worked it under his heel. Then he took his phone out of his pocket and called Patrick Maguire.

'Paddy, it's Moss,' he said. 'Listen, have you spoken to Eva?'

'Not today,' Maguire told him. 'I saw you both yesterday, of course, and I called the house last night to make sure she was all right.'

'You phoned her?' Quinn held the phone a little tighter.

'I did, Moss. Just before ten, I think. I was worried about her; you know how she was yesterday.'

Covering the mouthpiece for a moment, Quinn turned to Doyle. 'Paddy phoned her a little before ten last night,' he said. Doyle checked his watch. 'How was she, Pat?' Quinn asked. 'When you spoke to her?'

'She sounded OK, I suppose; you know, given the day and everything. But I've been worried about her. I told you that: the last few times we've spoken, there was a sense of hopelessness I'd not seen before. I put it down to the run-up to the first anniversary and . . . '

'Her husband not being able to find her son's killer,' Quinn said, finishing the sentence for him.

'Irrational as it is, I suppose, yes.'

'It's not that irrational. I'm a Guard, Pat: a copper, me and the Doyler both. Her husband and her uncle: we managed to get the kid she'd befriended into the dock, but we couldn't do anything about her son's killer. She can't help it, she juxtaposes those two events.'

'You can't blame her, Moss,' Maguire said. 'She's not blaming you deliberately, and I don't even think it's as clear-cut as you say. Anyway, how is she this morning? I was going to phone but I'm up here at the 'Joy.'

Quinn looked sideways at Doyle, who was still leaning against the mortuary wall with his hands in his pockets. 'That's just it, Patrick,' Quinn said. 'She's missing.'

'Missing?'

'Yes, and from what you just told me, you were the last person to speak to her. We're at the city morgue now, and . . . '

'Jesus Christ, she's not . . . '

'No, but we thought she might be. They dragged a floater from Spencer Dock who answered her description. I'm thinking she's at the cemetery, Paddy. What do you reckon?'

Maguire mulled that over for a moment. 'Yeah,' he said, 'if she's not at home, that's as likely a place as any.'

'That's what I thought. OK, bud, thanks. I'll be talking to you.'

'Mossie?'

'Yes?'

'Make sure you give me a call – I mean when you find her. Tell her if she wants to get together, that's fine. Tell her anytime; I can change my appointments.'

*

In the prisoners' reception at Mountjoy, Patrick Maguire switched off his phone. The doors were unlocked and he went through to the inner vestibule; then the doors were locked again behind him. A second set of doors was unlocked and, nodding to the warder, he made his way to the interview room, where Karl Crame was waiting.

Crame sat with his arms resting on the table. Tattoos from wrist to shoulder: snakes; women; a tapestry of orange, red and blue. His hair was shaved to the skull, and at twenty-two his eyes were cold and grey.

'Patrick Pearse, there y'are, I was beginning to think you weren't coming.'

'Sorry, Karl.' Maguire sat down and placed his soft leather briefcase by his feet. 'I got held up.'

'Listen.' Crame reached across the table and gripped him by the wrist. 'I need to know you'll do what you can for me. The lads in here tell me you're the man, Paddy – that you actually mean what you say.'

'Of course I do,' Maguire said. 'Why else would I spend so much time with lowlife such as you?'

Crame didn't smile.

'It's a joke, Karl.' Maguire was Quinn's age, though a bit smaller and a little wirier, maybe.

'Chill out, will you, for Christ's sake? What I said was a joke.'

'A joke, right. Ha, ha.' Crame's eyes were tight. 'Listen, Patrick, I don't want to fuck about with any counselling bullshit. I don't need any of that. I have to talk to you about my girlfriend. I mean, the bitch is determined I'll never see my son.'

'Whoa, whoa, slow down, will you?' Maguire said, facing his palms downwards. 'What girlfriend? What son? You've lost me.'

Crame looked suddenly bitter. 'I've spoken to some of the lads in here, and they told me that if a lad's got shite going on, sometimes you can help.'

Again, Maguire studied him. There was something about his eyes, which were bleak and empty; it was an expression he was seeing more and more these days. The man reeked of violence: naked street violence.

'I didn't know you had a son, Karl,' Maguire said.

'Well I do, and that bitch from Jobstown . . . ' Crame broke off and looked hard at him. That's where I live: the Kilmahon estate. Do you know it?'

'Who doesn't? The Guards have just doubled their patrols down there.'

'Yeah, well, some of them bastards ought to try living there. Anyway, that's not the point. The point is I'm stuck in here. But it's not going to be forever, and that cow is trying to stop me from seeing my little boy.'

For the first time, Maguire could see some real emotion. He sat back now as Crame gesticulated. 'I might not be any good as a dad, Patrick, and I might not like his mammy very much, but I love that babby, and stuck in here, he's pretty much all I think about.'

'What're you in for, Karl? Dealing, was it?' There was no accusation, no judgement in Maguire's voice.

Crame nodded. 'I was a dealer, yeah, but small-time, you know what I mean. I had a little bit of turf down there in Kilmahon, but it was nothing much. They gave me seven years, and she's saying she's not bringing my boy in any more. By the time I get out, the lad won't know me.'

Maguire nodded. 'How old is he?'

'Jesus, he's only five, and she's threatening to take him away, move out of Dublin, leave Ireland altogether maybe.' His eyes were dull now, his hands balled into fists. 'I was working down at Poolbeg when the bastards laid me off. I had the dole but it wasn't enough, so I took up with the dealing. I pissed off a couple of players, though: you know, a couple of Dub bastards already in the game. Anyway, they set me up, and that's how I'm in here: it's not my fault. I was only trying to make a living, and I don't deserve to have that woman take my son away from me.'

Maguire sat back. This was the kind of inmate he saw all the time, someone who'd stumbled through a difficult beginning and an impossible childhood – and, almost inevitably, had ended up in Mountjoy Prison. With the influx of drugs, gangs were springing up both north and south of the river. And they weren't like the old gangs: they were getting younger and younger, and they were capable of the kind of violence that even the old-school boys from Ballyfermot might have baulked at.

'Listen, Karl,' he said, 'if you're telling me that when you get out, you're not just going to go back to how it was – and by that I mean get hold of your supplier and start over – then I might be able to help you.'

Crame looked a little more hopeful. 'That's what the lads said: they told me you were that kind of man. They say you used to be with the Brothers, Paddy. Is that right?'

Patrick hissed a short breath. 'I had a misspent youth, same as you, but that's not what we're talking about. I can't promise anything, but if I get the chance, I'll see what I can do.'

'Ah Jesus, thanks Patrick. I knew you'd help me out.'

'She's on her own, is she, your ex-missus?' Maguire took out a pen and paper to write down the details. 'I mean, I'm not going to show up and find some hairy-arsed ape waiting to pound on my head, am I?'

Monday 1st September
9.10 am

Leaving his partner, Quinn drove up to Doyle's Corner before head-
ing west on the North Circular Road. Crossing the Royal Canal at
Dalcassian Downs, he skirted the southern lip of the Botanic
Gardens and turned off for the lower section of the cemetery.

He found Eva's car parked just beyond the bridge. Pulling up
behind it, he sat for a moment, not quite sure what he was going to
say to her. If her bed hadn't been slept in, she'd either been sitting
up all night or she'd been here since after Paddy phoned her. Either
way, the implications were not good. He had to think carefully about
how he was going to handle the situation. Eva was not irresponsible
– it wasn't in her nature – but she was grieving still, and she'd left
Jess and Laura alone. Quinn was beginning to wonder if he might
have to think about getting someone a little more qualified than Pat
Maguire to talk to her.

Sitting there, he thought back to last night, and what he had
been doing at the Garda Club. He remembered how warm he had
felt in Keira's arms. He told himself that it didn't matter; he told
himself that for now, at least, he had to forget about it. He could
deal with his guilt later: what mattered right now was Eva's state of

mind. He still loved her – he had always loved her – and deep down somewhere under all the grief, he believed she still loved him.

That was enough; what had happened last night did not change anything. It had been a moment; ill-timed, no doubt, but he told himself that nothing was ruined, nothing was lost. Eva didn't ever have to know.

Nobody did.

He'd never intended for it to happen, and if he'd still been living at home, it never would have done. He only agreed to move out at all because things had got to the point where the atmosphere was so bad that it was affecting Laura and Jess.

So many things had happened: just a year since Danny's death, and a week after that Maggs had been charged with murder.

It was then that Eva had started wearing the Sacred Heart. Quinn hadn't allowed it to faze him. He knew why she was wearing it: it was nothing to do with Maggs – and all to do with Danny. It was God and heaven and everything like that: the kind of things people turn to when they are trying to make sense of a child's death.

It was true, though, that she didn't believe that Maggs had killed Mary Harrington. She'd said as much before the trial; she'd talked about the day they'd met, and how in her opinion Quinn had marked Maggs's card as early as back then.

It was as if, with her son gone, she had to revisit the past constantly. She talked about school the day Jimmy 'the Poker' had been flashing the Polaroid around. Maggs had been just thirteen then, and everyone had been laughing at him: not just the kids but some of the teachers as well, behind his back. Eva was the only one who had stood up for him.

She had stood up for him in her living room in Glasnevin more than twenty years later, when she had reminded her husband that they had had no physical evidence and that the confession had been forced from his lips. He stared at her car, reading and re-reading the licence plate as if he had to convince himself that the car really was hers.

What was he going to say to her? How would she be when he showed up and she came to her senses and realised that she'd left her daughters alone to be with her dead son.

'Gentle, Moss,' he muttered. 'Just make sure you're gentle, lad; that's all.'

Locking the car, he made his way towards the far corner of the cemetery, the thicket of trees, the railway line and the canal waters beyond.

He stopped in his tracks and stared. She wasn't there. There was no one at the grave; no one sitting on any of the benches. In fact, there was no one around at all. Quinn couldn't understand it. He looked for her; he almost called her name. Perhaps she was on the towpath somewhere. Then another grim thought occurred to him, and he revisited the ashen face of the drowned woman he had seen earlier.

He was a few yards from his son's headstone when his phone started ringing. 'Quinn,' he said, holding it to his ear.

For a moment, there was nothing but silence. Quinn was only half-concentrating. He was staring at yesterday's flowers and, beyond the grave, the railway line where trains thundered along, and, further on still, the dark waters of the Royal Canal.

'This is Detective Inspector Quinn,' he repeated.

'Tick-tock.' A strained, rasping voice: no kind of voice at all. 'Tick-tock, the mouse and the clock. Tick-tick-tock. The clock's gonna stop. '

The line went dead, and Quinn stood holding the phone.

*

He was rooted to the spot, the voice still sounding in his head. His wife's car was parked by the bridge, and yet she wasn't there. He could feel sweat forming on the palms of his hands; he could feel the knot of tension, which had been with him all day, tighten.

He moved closer to the grave: there was something odd about it, something out of place. He realised that some of the flowers looked flattened, trampled almost. The stems broken; petals strewn on the ground. He could make out footmarks in the grass. It had rained so much, and for so long, the ground was mush, and the marks were indelibly imprinted. There was something about them that disturbed him. They were too close to the stones; they were facing this way and that: he picked out some made by a woman's shoe and others made by a man's.

He heard the voice in his head again. Suddenly, cold sweat washed over him like a wave: all at once, he understood what had happened.

Hearing someone on the path behind him, he turned quickly and saw an elderly woman carrying a bunch of flowers. He waved to her, fumbling in his pocket for ID. 'I'm a policeman,' he called. 'Please, would you stand still?'

Looking slightly bemused, she stopped dead. Quinn reassured her with a smile. 'Look, I'm sorry,' he said, 'I know you've come to visit someone, but I need you to turn around and go back the way you came.'

He needed to call Doyle, but first he had to secure the scene. From the back of his car, he took a roll of blue and white tape; walking towards the bridge, he wound it across the gates. Once he was inside the gates, he tied the tape to the railings, then retraced his steps, trailing the tape, until he'd created a flexible handrail all the way to Danny's grave. He started again from the headstone, working his way back to the gate until he'd established a corridor. All the time he was working, he was trying to get his head round what had happened: a voice disguised; a clock ticking. He felt cold now like he'd never felt cold before.

Monday 1st September
9.21am

On the fifth floor at Harcourt Square, Doyle fetched a cup of coffee from the machine and carried it back to his desk. Murphy was yet to leave for Naas. She'd been sidetracked by a phone call from one of the outlying police stations: a priest had been found dead in his church, and the locals needed someone from the Bureau to attend. She'd put off briefing the new unit until midday and made an initial assessment before passing the notes to a colleague. She was stuffing the files into a briefcase when the door opened and a lad from the post room came in.

'Is Inspector Quinn about?' he asked her.

Murphy noticed that the lad was carrying a white envelope. 'Is that for him? I can take it.'

Then she noticed how he was holding it: he had the ends of the envelope against the flat of his palms, and was barely touching the surface. Quinn's name in letters cut from a newspaper.

Walking past with his coffee, Doyle stopped dead. He peered at the envelope, then at Murphy. Finally, placing his cup on her desk, he took a handkerchief from his trouser pocket and spread it flat on the desk. The other detectives had picked up on the silence and, one by one, they looked up.

'Put the envelope down on the hanky,' Doyle instructed.

The lad from the post room did as he was asked. Taking a letter opener from the inspectors' office, Doyle slit the top. Inside was a single Polaroid photograph: a picture of a dark-coloured stone on a patch of sand. Doyle squinted. Murphy raised an eyebrow, and the other detectives began to gather round.

'Sarge?' Murphy said.

Picking up the phone, Doyle dialled Quinn's mobile.

*

He arrived at the cemetery with Murphy in the passenger seat. He had the flashing blue light on the roof of the car. Quinn got up from where he was leaning on the wing of his own car. 'Stay here, would you, Keira?' he asked. 'When scene-of-crimes arrive, phone me. I don't want anyone in the cemetery until I've had a chance to look again properly.'

'OK,' she said.

'Tell them the scene is secure and cordons are in – the inner ones, anyway. Get someone over here to establish an outer cordon.'

Looking into his eyes, she nodded.

Quinn spoke as he and Doyle made their way to the grave. 'Tell me about the picture, Doyler,' he said.

Doyle walked with his hands in the pockets of his coat and his collar up. 'What's to say? It's a Polaroid: a patch of sand with a stone on it. It looks like it was taken on a beach somewhere, and it came in an envelope with your name on it.'

'Handwriting?'

'No, it was cut-out letters. Posted here in Dublin.'

Quinn stopped for a moment with his hand on the sergeant's

arm. 'The grave,' he said. 'There was a scuffle or something, I'm sure of it. You can see it in the footmarks; you can see it on the grave itself.' His eyes were suddenly hunted. 'She's been abducted, I know it.'

His face like stone, Doyle gazed beyond the patchwork of graves to the open ground and the trees, where the railway forked. 'Who in the world would abduct a copper's wife? Do you realise what you're saying, Moss? You're a Guard, for God's sake! Who's going to do that?'

'I don't know,' Quinn replied. 'But someone sent me a photo, and something went on at Danny's grave. Just now, whoever it was rang to tell me the clock is ticking.'

He considered the grave again. One arm across his chest, elbow cupped, and a finger to his lips, he studied the way the broken stems of carnations were scattered around the headstone. They were fresh flowers; they'd been put there less than twenty-four hours before, and the damage could not be put down to the rain. Going down on his haunches, he studied the layer of tiny white chippings he and Eva had spread so evenly. Here and there, they had been shunted into a ridge. He looked again at Doyle. 'Someone was lying on the grave.'

Frowning deeply now, Doyle bent beside him.

'See the way the flowers are flat and some of the stems are broken?' Quinn said, gesturing. 'Look at the pebbles, Doyler. Look at the prints: the heel of a woman's shoe and the sole of a man's. See how one is facing the other. See how close they are.' He could feel a pulse begin to thump at the side of his head. 'She came here to see Danny, and either he followed her or he was here already, waiting.'

Eyes pinched, he studied every stone, every green stem, every separate petal. He could see something sparkling about halfway up the grave. Taking a biro from his pocket, he picked up a piece of chain from among the stones. It was just a couple of links, but they were twisted, the metal stretched out of shape. He knew what they were; knew exactly where they'd come from. The necklace she'd been wearing yesterday: whoever had taken Eva had ripped it from her throat first.

Monday 1st September
9.30 am

She was in a hole somewhere; she didn't know where. She was covered with boards, and on top of that with carpet or linoleum, maybe. She was bound hand and foot. Like ice, the sweat clung to her clothes. In turn, her clothes clung to her, damp and chill, sucking the heat from her body. She was listening, trying to work out where she was. She thought she could hear water dripping. Water; water. She desperately wanted water. But no, it wasn't water, it was the faint sound of a clock. 'Tick-tock, tick-tock': as she lay there, it seemed to grow louder. And then she heard another sound: a footstep. She could feel it reverberate through the floor. Was somebody there?

Lying perfectly still, she listened, but the seconds became minutes and she heard nothing more. If someone was there, they were not moving now. Nevertheless, she had the feeling that something was watching her: a silent spider in the corner of the web, where she was trapped like a fly.

She lay on her side with her knees bent and her arms behind her back. Her hands and feet were so numb from lack of blood she could not feel them. Her right cheek was frozen; there was no sensation at all. Damp ground beneath her. She could smell water; she could hear trickles of water: water was all she could think of. But there was no water; she couldn't get to water. Her throat was so dry it felt as though it would crack. She had no idea where she was or how long she'd been there. Some kind of building; the shadows of walls; a partial roof. She'd watched him tear up floorboards before he'd covered her eyes.

He had carried her from her son's grave and laid her in the boot of his car. Darkness, confinement; she'd been restricted not just by the bonds but by her very surroundings. She had smelled petrol; she'd felt the weight shift, the whine of the engine, and all she could think about was Jess and Laura.

She could've screamed at the horror, the desperation, the fear. But black tape was stuck to her mouth and she could barely part her lips.

She could part them a little now, though, and she was trying to draw the tape into her mouth so that she could grip it between her teeth and bite a hole in it. She could breathe, but only just – through her nose. He hadn't left her to suffocate; he'd left her to dehydrate. Water: she swore she could hear it, and smell it in the earth against her face. Rainwater; rain falling, rain across the city. Daylight now; it had been dark when he brought her here, but now light edged the boards that covered her.

Jess and Laura; Laura and Jess. Why had she left them alone? What if he'd gone back for them?

For a few moments, the horror threatened to swamp her, but somehow she got a grip of her emotions and told herself that the girls would be all right: they'd wake and find her missing and then would phone their father.

She told herself she had to remain calm, she had to think, she had to try and get out of here. She bitterly regretted leaving the house and driving so far so that she could be with her son: but there had been too many people, so many people coming to pay their respects. All she had wanted was a moment where she could try and explain what had happened – and why it had happened – between her and his father.

She wanted to tell Danny how losing him had cut her in two and how she didn't know if she could ever be whole again.

She knew he would understand. She knew she should never have left his sisters by themselves.

She should never have pushed his father away; it was selfish, she knew that now. There were four of them; she wasn't alone in her grief. But she was a mother, and only a mother knows.

Danny would understand, she knew he would. Please God if she could only get the chance to explain, his sisters would understand too.

Monday 1st September
9.30 am

Back at Harcourt Square, Quinn was in his office with the door closed, poring over the Polaroid photograph they were about to send to the lab.

On the other side of the desk, Superintendent Frank Maguire sat with his arms folded, and Doyle hovered with a little box of snuff in his hand. The phone rang and Maguire picked it up. He cast a quick glance Quinn's way and then cleared his throat.

'Yes, sir,' he said, 'that's what we think: Inspector Quinn's wife from Glasnevin Cemetery.' Again he squinted at Quinn. 'Yes, sir, he's right here. I know, sir: unprecedented.' Covering the mouthpiece, he spoke to Quinn. 'Tom Calhoun,' he said, and passed him the phone.

'Hello, commissioner.'

'Moss, how are you? Look, this is outrageous, I mean absolutely outrageous. If your wife has been abducted, we will find her, I promise you that. Frank Maguire will have every detective in the country at his disposal.'

'Thank you, sir. I appreciate your concern.' Quinn glanced at Doyle. 'We know she was at home just before ten last night, but that was the last contact anyone had with her. We've checked the hospitals and the morgue, but then I got the phone call.' He paused then for a moment. 'Eva's not just my wife, of course, she's Sergeant Doyle's niece.'

Calhoun cleared his throat. 'Of course she is; I'd not forgotten that.'

'Would you like to speak to him, sir?'

'No, that's all right. Tell him he has our support; tell him what I told you.'

'I will.'

'There'll be no stone unturned, you have my word on that.'

'There's one other thing though, Commissioner.'

'What's that?'

'I know I'm not supposed to be anywhere near the case, but you know – of course – I will be.'

Calhoun was silent.

'There's no way I'm sitting at home.'

'What about your daughters?'

Quinn thought about that. 'They're at school, which right now is the best place for them. Don't tell me to back off, Commissioner. Not when we're talking about my wife.'

'Moss,' the commissioner said with a sigh, 'all that matters is finding Eva safe and well. But tread carefully: we need objectivity, not emotion. I'll let Frank Maguire be the judge of how to play it. I'll field any questions that he can't answer, and for what it's worth, if this was my wife, I'd be sitting right where you are.'

'Thank you, I appreciate that.' Passing the phone back to Maguire, Quinn smiled grimly. 'For the first time in your life, Doyler, you've got the commissioner's support.'

'Have I now?' Doyle muttered. 'After thirty-two years, lad. Don't be damning me now.'

Quinn returned his attention to the Polaroid. 'What does this mean?' he said. 'A beach, is it? Sand, maybe? A stone, a pebble, a hunk of rock?' Doyle didn't answer. 'And who sent it? Who abducted my wife a year to the day after my son was killed?' Balling a fist, he stepped away from the desk and gazed through the glass into what was now an incident room. More and more detectives were arriving there.

'Moss, notwithstanding what the commissioner just said, neither you nor Doyle can work this investigation.'

'The fuck we can't.'

Maguire lifted a placatory palm. 'You know I have to tell you that, the commissioner knows I have to tell you that. The fact that you'll be in the loop is neither here nor there, and what the pair of you do on your own is up to you. Just keep away from the cameras, all right? They're going to be camped all along Harcourt Street, not to mention outside your front door.'

Outside, Quinn lit a cigarette. His phone rang and he stared hard, still hearing the voice in his head. He answered now but it wasn't the caller, whoever he was; it was Paddy Maguire.

'Moss,' he said, a little breathlessly. 'Jeeze, man, I've been trying to get you. Have you found Eva?'

'No, Pat. She's been abducted.'

'She's what?'

Quinn stared the length of the drive to the gate, where the press were already beginning to gather. 'Someone took her: someone who knew it was the anniversary of Danny's death.'

'Who the hell would do that?'

'I don't know. But there are plenty both inside and out who'd like nothing better than to see me in the ground: maybe if they cannot get to me personally, this is another way.'

'But Moss,' Maguire said, 'we're talking about a guard's wife for Christ's sake. Who on earth would do it? None of the regulars, surely? Not Finucane or McGeady: they wouldn't be so stupid.'

'Of course they wouldn't, this is nothing to do with them.' Quinn drew hard on the cigarette. 'It's either some last anarchic faction of a war that finished years ago, or it's one psychotic individual who doesn't understand or doesn't care what he's getting himself into.'

'Have you any idea who?' Maguire asked him.

Quinn was thinking of the gold links he had found on the grave. He could see the man in his mind's eye: sitting there in the dock, with dark hair and darker eyes.

'Moss?'

'Only one person, but he isn't in Dublin.'

'Conor Maggs,' Maguire said. 'Of course, who else. Listen, Mossie, I should maybe have told you before, but Eva made me promise not to. He's been in touch. I know he's phoned your house as least twice since the trial.'

Quinn stiffened. 'He phoned Eva? What the hell did he want?'

'I think perhaps he was trying to see her.'

'But she didn't see him, did she?'

'Not as far as I know.'

'Jesus, he's never left her alone, not since they were kids. But he's supposed to be in London, Pat; I'm sure he's still in London.'

'So who else could it be, then?'

Quinn thought about that. 'There are a few maybe with the balls. You've probably visited most of them at one time or another.' He glanced up then as Doyle came out through the main doors. 'Look, I have to go. I'll be home with the kids tonight, though, and we should talk, Patrick. Maybe there's something Eva said to you that might mean something to me.'

'Call me whenever you want,' Maguire told him, 'and in the meantime for Christ's sake keep me posted.'

Upstairs again, Quinn considered the portrait of his wife that Maguire had asked him to bring in so they could release it to the press. It was the most recent picture he had: Eva every bit as beautiful as the day he first saw her.

He looked long and hard at the necklace, the gold pendant, and he had to remind himself that her wearing it had been nothing to do with anyone else; it was what it symbolised that mattered. It was an icon, a popular symbol; it wasn't that long ago you'd see the things made into broaches young mothers pinned to the hoods of their babies' prams.

He and Doyle were alone, Maguire having decamped to brief the gathering of detectives next door.

Quinn was staring at his wife's picture but all he could see was Mary Harrington with ligature marks on her throat. They were not what killed her, though: Mary had died of thirst.

The pathologist believed that, due to a combination of hypothermia and the fact that she had been tied up, after seventy-two hours she had probably developed postural asphyxia and gone into a coma. Dizzy at first, she would gradually have grown faint, the potassium levels in her body rising as the fluids started to go down. Then she started to cramp. She would have been crying without any tears; her skin, her lips cracking; her tongue swollen; sickness and dry-heaving as her stomach and intestines dried out. Quinn could see the plastic tarp and black tape that swaddled her; he could see dried blood on her upper lip where the mucous membranes in her nose had withered to the point of breakdown. He could see the skin of her face with no elasticity, wrinkled like a woman three times her age. After that, her blood pressure had dropped to the point where she slipped into the coma. Not long later, there was no blood pressure at all.

In Doyle's car, they headed for the river. Quinn was on the phone to 'Busy' Phillips, his best informant; Doyle was speaking to 'Jug' Uttley, an old water rat of a man who prowled the Bridewell area in his Hush Puppies and raincoat like some back-street solicitor. Doyle had him on a retainer and paid for his mobile phone. They found him waiting at a café across the cobbles from the viewing tower at Smithfield.

He had black hair, flaked with dandruff, heavy-lens glasses hooked over the mighty, hobbitlike ears that gave him his nickname. He was drinking a latte and chewing a Danish pastry. He considered Quinn with a little compassion in his booze-reddened eyes.

''Tis a bad business when they start in on the guards,' he said. 'It'll bring war to the street, so it will. You mark my words.'

'What is the word, Jug?' Doyle rested on his elbows, leaning across the small table and peering into his face.

Uttley loosed an audible breath. 'Shock, Mr Doyle. I suppose the word is shock.' He looked a little furtively at Quinn. 'Grace O'Malley, Lorne "The Thorn" McGeady, they're not saying it outright, but if it's help you're wanting, Inspector . . . ' He swept the room with his hand. 'All the old Dubs: they need something like this as much as they need another hole in their arse. Notwithstanding the personal hurt to yourself, Mr Quinn, this kind of situation is very bad for business.'

'So who's heard what?' Quinn demanded. 'Somebody must know what this is about.' Uttley sat back and looked reflectively at him. Arching his brows, he crossed one skinny leg over the other. 'It's a puzzler,' he said. 'Really it is. There's no word. I don't know if it's shock or that some people do know and they're not saying, but in all my years on the street I've not seen the city so silent.'

'Are you telling me nobody has heard a whisper?' Quinn asked him.

Uttley shrugged. 'I'm telling you the street is quiet.'

Quinn got to his feet. 'Well it better get unquiet, and it better do so quickly. Spread the word, Jug: let everyone know I'm calling in favours. Somebody has my wife. The last time anyone spoke to her was ten o'clock last night, and if we don't find her by Wednesday, she'll be in a coma she might not come out of.'

Monday 1st September
2.30 pm

Murphy was shuffling between her desk and Quinn's office, where Superintendent Maguire had set himself up. They had divers in both canals and at intervals along the Liffey. They had people going door to door in Glasnevin with questionnaires, and the incident room was in full swing.

Maguire had been over to Phoenix Park to brief the deputy commissioner for operations, and now he kept looking at Murphy as if there was something he wanted to bring up but wasn't sure how to do it. She didn't give him a chance. She was on the phone and on her computer; she was liaising with the detectives flocking in from all over Dublin, as well as those coming up from the country.

A young guard who'd been seconded to plainclothes came over to her desk. 'Murph,' he said, 'the photo is back from the lab. No prints, no marks, nothing.'

Maguire was hovering in the doorway of Quinn's office. 'There's nothing at all?' he asked.

'I'm afraid not, superintendent.'

'They don't sell Polaroid cameras any more,' Murphy told him.

'They went out when the world turned digital. But they do still sell the paper. The batches are all numbered, so we should be able to find out roughly where that print came from.'

'Good thinking,' Maguire told her.

'There's another thing,' she added. 'The action is mechanical; inside each camera there's a tiny set of wheels which rolls the picture out. If we can locate the camera, we can match the picture to it.'

'OK, we can work on that,' he said. 'Are there any other leads? Anything else come in while I was at Phoenix Park?'

'There's Blackrock, sir.'

He furrowed his brow. 'Blackrock?'

'The stone in the Polaroid is almost black,' she said, 'and it looks to me as though the picture was taken on a beach. I was thinking about Blackrock beach, sir.'

'That's a good point,' he said. 'Organise a search. While you're at it, organise searches of every beach within a thirty-mile radius of the city. Get people out to Dun Laoghaire and Shelley Banks and, as you say, Blackrock.'

'I'll get down there myself,' Murphy told him. 'We should appeal to the public as well, get them involved. The more people we have looking, the more chance we'll find her.'

Back at her desk, she organised a search team with dogs, then called the police in Dundalk and asked them to get officers over to Blackrock right away. While she was on the phone, Maguire went downstairs, where live-TV cameras were waiting.

Just before she left the office, Murphy phoned Quinn. 'Moss, it's me,' she said. 'How are you?'

Quinn was sitting outside his daughters' school waiting for them to come out. 'I'm all right,' he said.

'What's going on?'

She told him that the crime-scene technicians had come up with more links from the gold chain, including the one they thought might have been attached to the jump ring. There were also some decent shoe prints and a couple of fibres that had been taped and sent to the lab.

'They're still doing a fingertip search,' she said, 'but they did say the striation marks on the chain links were pretty distinctive, so that might give us something.' Then she told him about the search of the beaches and what she'd thought about Blackrock.

'That's a great idea,' Quinn said. 'You know, you might be on to something. Look, I'll come down and join you.'

'What about the girls?'

'I'll find someone to sit with them until I get back.'

'The super doesn't want you visible, remember.'

'Fuck what the super wants, Murph. I'm not going to worry about him.'

'Well, if you're coming, bring something of Eva's so the dogs can get her scent. Listen, Moss,' she added, 'this is hardly the time, but I get the feeling Maguire knows. It's like he can smell scandal, you know. Do you think he suspects we've been seeing each other?'

On the other end of the phone, Quinn was silent.

'Sorry,' she said. 'I shouldn't have brought it up. Hardly appropriate now, is it. God, what am I thinking?'

'Forget it,' he told her. 'We'll talk later. Look, you get down to Blackrock and I'll join you as soon as I can.'

An hour later, Quinn parked his car on the headland at Sandymount. He'd phoned Pat Maguire and asked him if he would come over to the house and stay with the girls. They knew him well, of course: he'd been a frequent visitor when he was counselling their mother. He was more than happy to help, and cancelled his appointments.

From where he stood now, Quinn could see the uniforms scouring the beach: volcanic sand broken by clusters of black rock. At low tide, the sea went out three miles, leaving sand and mudflats in its wake. Closer to the road, there were larger rocks split by crevices deep enough to hide a person Eva's size. They searched them all; the dogs with her scent now from the blouse she'd been wearing yesterday. But as the tide turned and the time slipped by, they didn't find a trace.

Quinn could hear the hiss of the smaller waves that were gradually chewing up sand. He studied the landscape: the Cooley Mountains behind them in the west. His mind was running with questions, ideas and possibilities. He kept asking himself: why send them a photo if there was no chance Eva would be found? He was a detective; his job was to sift possibilities. He tried to separate his fears and suspicions; he tried to think about it rationally. What did the picture hide? Where was the message? Was it the sand, the stone, the beach. Was it a beach at all, or just a patch of sand?

Blackrock was man-made. Back in the 1960s, people used to come here on holiday from Cavan and Monaghan. There were still a few guesthouses and a handful of old beach huts, but it was no longer any kind of resort. A few new-agers still came, however – in August, mostly, around the harvest time.

'Lughnasa,' Quinn told Murphy, who was standing alongside him. The sky was darkening now, and any hope they had of finding Eva was beginning to fade fast. 'It's a festival. Old Irish; the word means "hand-fasting".'

'What's hand-fasting?' she asked.

'It was a trial marriage. In pagan days, people would get together for a year and a day to see how it would work out. If it was no good, they'd part, but if they got along, they'd make it permanent. A marriage that lasted a year and a day: is there something in that, do you think? Yesterday was a year to the day that Danny died, so today is a year and a day. Jesus Christ, would you listen to me.'

Murphy could see him struggling; she wasn't sure what she could say. She thought about last night and how she'd known that sooner or later it was going to happen. They had worked so closely for so long, and Quinn's home life had been so chill and empty. Her own marriage, young as it was, was not all she'd hoped it would be. She knew she had feelings for him, deep feelings, but standing there with the tide coming in, she didn't know what she could say. The radio crackled, and word came that the team searching the southern end were packing up.

Murphy acknowledged the call, then slipped the handset into her bag. 'When I spoke to the crime-scene manager, he told me that Eva's necklace had been ripped from her throat,' she said. 'The way the links were scattered, the striation marks – it had to have been violent.'

Quinn nodded.

'It might've been just because of the struggle,' Murphy said.

He didn't say anything.

'Then again, it might not,' she continued.

Quinn watched as grey waves broke on a rock. 'The necklace was the one Maggs gave her,' he said.

She was silent for a moment, then said: 'Moss, if it was deliberate, the only person who'd rip it off is someone it meant something to.'

'That's what you'd think, isn't it?'

'There's only one person then, isn't there?' As she turned her back to the sea, the wind caught her hair and blew it around her face.

'Again, that's what you'd think, but Doyle's been keeping tabs on him, Murph: he isn't in the country.'

They walked back to his car, and Quinn considered the battered old beach huts they'd searched and searched again: they'd asked in every guest house, every shop; teams of volunteers had fanned out as far as the mountains. With the window rolled down, he smoked a cigarette; he picked up the phone and spoke to Paddy Maguire.

Murphy was sitting next to him, wanting to hold him, wanting to comfort him, but not knowing how.

'You and Pat go back a long way, don't you?' she said when he hung up.

Quinn nodded. 'We played rugby for Dublin seconds; he was a pretty good scrum-half, and at one time there was talk of him having trials with Leinster.' He looked sideways at her then. 'We were on a rugby tour in Kerry when I met Eva. Back in the days when Maggs was convinced she was his girlfriend. What she was was the only girl in Listowel who had any time for him: because she was a nice person, Murph – she had time for everyone.'

'But he took it that there was something more between them?'

He nodded. 'When they were kids, he persuaded his auntie to buy that necklace so he could give it to her at her First Communion. That's how far back they go.'

Murphy was still for a moment. 'I didn't work that case, but I remember seeing Maggs on the TV outside the Four Courts. That eulogy he gave: all that bullshit about forgiveness, Christ in his cell in Rathfarnham.'

'I suppose you can sort of see where it came from, what with his mother and all,' Quinn said.

'His aunt was the religious one. When he was a boy, she got him down to the church and I guess the old priest gave him the benefit of the doubt.' Dragging on the cigarette, he added: 'But when he was sixteen, his mother died after drinking drain cleaner, and Doyle believes it was no accident that she found it in a wine bottle.' He glanced sideways at her. 'He knew the history long before I'd ever been down there, and that was why, when Mary went missing, he was so adamant Maggs was our man. '

'But Eva was his friend?'

'She took some notice of him, Murph: I'm not sure she ever really liked him. Everyone liked her, though; she was that kind of girl. She was one of those people who could never see the harm in anyone, and as far as she was concerned, Maggs was the victim of a set of circumstances, so she treated him as she did everyone else.' He broke off then, realising that he was speaking in the past tense.

'Why did she push you away?' Murphy asked gently.

'You know why.'

'But it's so obvious that you still love her.'

'Does that bother you?'

'Of course not. Jesus, I feel guilty enough as it is.'

'Look,' he said, 'last night was last night, and for what it's worth I don't regret a minute of it. '

'Neither do I.'

'No one's being punished here, Keira: the two things aren't related.'

She nodded then and, taking his hand, she offered a smile of encouragement. 'We will find her,' she said.

Quinn peered through the windscreen. 'The necklace is significant,' he said.

'Unless it did just come off in the struggle,' Murphy said, lifting her shoulders. 'I mean, that's more than possible, isn't it?'

'Yes it is, of course it is. But I don't think that's what happened. It's significant, Keira, and if Maggs is in London, then there has to be someone else out there it means something to.'

Monday 1st September
5.30 pm

Leaving the square, Frank Maguire drove south on Camden Street, passing Jocky O'Connell's bar, where Quinn and Doyle used to wind up on a Thursday night. No doubt the Doyler still did, but Quinn had a career to take care of, and to that end he'd curtailed his drinking.

Doyle had never cared about a career: he said it as he saw it, and he knew that no matter what he did, after thirty-two years, no one in Phoenix Park would do anything about it. The judge had called for an inquiry after the Maggs debacle, but so far no one had seen any paperwork. The whole affair would die quietly, as it always did, and Doyle would go on being Doyle until he retired back to Kerry.

Maguire had been in the job almost thirty years himself, and he knew it was sergeants like Doyle who really ran things. In a way, Maguire envied him. For him, the career climb had been everything; he'd laid foundations for each rung religiously; from the golf and the lodge to the work he did for charity. Since childhood, he'd had a burning desire to advance as far as he could. That's partly why he'd married an investment banker; it's why they'd never had children;

and it's why they lived in Donnybrook when really they couldn't afford it. Donnybrook. It was funny to think that as recently as a hundred years ago, that had been the place you went if you wanted a fight on Saturday night; now it was about as affluent a Dublin suburb as you could get.

Maguire had managed to avoid the media scrum that was gathered in force now outside the Bureau. Not only was he fielding questions from TV and the newspapers, he also had the deputy commissioner on his back – who in turn had the commissioner on *his* back, who had the minister for justice breathing down his neck. Their combined weight was heavy, and on top of that Maguire had other things to think about.

On the south side of the canal, he made a left and trundled along under the gaze of the old Georgian houses until he found a space near Charlemont Lock. He was not far from where the statue of the poet Patrick Kavanagh sat on a bench seeking inspiration from the water. Thinking about him now, the words of a verse were in Maguire's mind suddenly:

Winter encloses me.
I am fenced,
The light, the laugh, the dance
Against.

A few lines, something Maguire remembered from his school days; words that right now captured everything he was feeling. In all his years as a police officer, he could not remember a day such as this.

Crossing the road, he entered a four-storey Georgian house that had long since been converted into apartments. The top one belonged to his little brother, who was at Quinn's place right now looking after his kids.

Inside, he picked up Patrick's mail and climbed the stairs to the flat. It wasn't much, but on Paddy's wages he couldn't afford much. It was more of a studio really, although the bedroom was separate. The flat overlooked the canal, however, and when the trees were in leaf you couldn't see the trolleys and plastic bottles and other bits of rubbish that littered the water. Right now, though, Maguire wasn't interested in the canal. Kavanagh's words haunted him; there on the mantelpiece was the photograph his brother insisted on keeping. Maguire peered at her; those sallow features; the way her hair lay lank and plaited, greasy across one shoulder.

*

His brother didn't have a name.

He was already three months old and they'd been back in the grubby tenement for weeks. Frank's mother told him that the midwife was on her way and he was in a panic about getting the place tidy.

She issued orders from where she sat, smoke lifting in a spiral from her cigarette. The skin seemed to hang from her face; there were greying sacks of it beneath her eyes; she never wore any make-up.

'Will you get the place cleaned up, Frank? Come on, you can get the dishes in the sink and wash down that surface.'

The kitchen formed part of the living room, and as he hunted under the sink for a cloth, she was still in the chair. It was how he always saw her. She didn't move from that seat, even when the baby cried.

He was crying now as Frank took a cloth to the spillages on the worktop: baked beans and HP sauce, egg ground into the draining board. He'd made his mother an egg the other day when she was too drunk to eat anything but had demanded it anyway. When he brought it to her, it was rock solid and she'd hurled it at him.

'Come on, Frank,' she cajoled. 'She'll be here in a minute, and if this place isn't as clean as a new pin you know what's going to happen. The school, Frankie: where the priests are in charge and you have to work till you fall over.' She leered at him, still cupping the glass she'd hide, as she always did, when somebody came to visit. At the last minute she'd wash it up, then rifle in her handbag for chewing gum, even though it did nothing to mask the sickly-sweet stench that clung to her breath.

Cloth in hand, Frank turned to her. 'Mam,' he said. 'She's going to ask about the baby.'

'What?'

'The midwife, she's going to ask about the baby.'

'What about the baby?' She sounded even more irritable. One last swallow, and she handed him the glass.

'Mam,' he said again. 'The midwife, she's going to want to know about the baby.'

'For Christ's sake, what about the bloody baby?' She turned on him now. 'He's clean, isn't he?'

'No, he's not. I can smell his nappy.'

'Then change him, for pity's sake. He's your brother, boy. It's your job to change him.'

He opened his mouth and she glared at him.

'Don't you dare talk back to me; one brat in the house is bad enough. Get him changed, will you? Go on, unless you want the midwife to take you both away.'

'But Mam,' he stammered, 'she's going to ask, isn't she?'

'Ask what, for heaven's sake?'

'What we called him. She'll want to know his name.'

She stared at him for a moment. Then she stared at the baby lying soiled still in the second-hand Moses basket they'd got at the charity shop.

'He needs a name,' Frank insisted.

'Well, why don't you think of something, then, instead of just yapping about it? And while you're about it, change his bloody nappy.'

Frank lifted his baby brother from the basket and took him into the bathroom, where water dripped and lime scale gathered around the plughole of the sink. He laid him on the mat, took off the rubber pants and grabbed an almost-dry nappy where it hung over the radiator. He was worried now after what his mother had said and, working too quickly, he pricked his thumb on the safety pin.

The midwife was a baby-catcher. That's the picture his mother painted, and if she remembered to tell him about a visit the day before, his dreams would be plagued by images of industrial schools where priests wandered never-ending corridors and far in the distance children were crying.

He cleaned his brother's mess, washed his arse and refastened a new nappy as best he could, then carried the boy through to the living room. His mother was back in the chair, her glass clean and put away, and she was chewing gum.

'I've thought of a name,' he told her. 'What about Patrick Pearse? We could call him Patrick, couldn't we? I mean, Patrick is the Saint of Ireland, and Pearse was . . . well I don't remember, but my teacher told me something about him, I know he did.'

'What're you prattling about?'

'Patrick, Mam: we could call my brother Patrick.'

She didn't look up; she was staring into space, hands buckled like claws across her lap.

'Mammy?'

'For Christ's sake,' she muttered. 'Call him what you like, boy, I couldn't give a shit.'

Monday 1st September
6 pm

Doyle parked outside Liberty Hall, which, at sixteen storeys – one for each of the martyrs shot during the Easter Rising – was the tallest building in Dublin. Few remembered this detail, and perhaps fewer still even cared, but Doyle was fifty years old and history, particularly Irish history, had been his subject ever since he'd been spellbound by James O'Donohue, his old schoolteacher back in County Kerry.

One of those who'd been executed was James Connolly, who stood truculent as a prizefighter, his feet apart and his chin high, as defiant cast in bronze as he had been in life. Ironically, the Brits had shot him sitting down because he was already wounded in the ankle after the siege at the old post office. The statue had been erected on the eightieth anniversary of his death, and Doyle had been one of those at its unveiling.

He was a dinosaur and he knew it, but there were a few still like him. He went his own way, always had, and though his family had been staunchly republican, it hadn't stopped him joining the police force. He'd had more enemies in the IRA than just about any other detective, yet towards the end of the Troubles there was rumour that his eldest brother, Cahal, had been on the Army Council. Those days were long gone now, though, and Cahal was in America.

Back in 1974, when Doyle was only two years into the job, he'd been walking the beat in Talbot Street when three bombs went off; one right in front of him. Thirty people were killed that day; the Ulster Volunteer Force from the north took responsibility, but the closer the Garda looked, the more the evidence pointed to British Intelligence.

Nodding deferentially to Connolly, Doyle left the car and walked to the quay. The rain had started again, worrying the surface of the Liffey. It had been a summer of nothing but rain. A burly-looking skinhead was on the deck of Finucane's boat. Doyle didn't know him, and the man clearly didn't know him either, because he looked down with a snarl on his face like a rabid pit-bull terrier.

'Get over yourself, would you?' Doyle said as he climbed aboard. 'Jesus, I'd eat two of you before my breakfast. Run along and tell Johnny the Doyler wants a word.'

The younger man's hands were fists now, and for a moment Doyle thought he might actually hit him.

He laughed in his throat but his expression was cold. 'I've little time, lad. Do as you're told before I toss you in for the trout. '

'Dessie!' Like a gunshot the word was fired from the stairs below the wheelhouse. Looking beyond the skinhead, Doyle saw Finucane watching them. 'Let him past, will you?'

Finucane was no more than five feet six in his socks. He was red-faced and rotund; his pate was completely bereft of hair, and the monk's crown that partially encircled it was shaved close to a bristle: at fifty-two or thereabouts, he'd been a gangster as long as Doyle had been a cop. The salon was both spacious and luxurious, with leather sofas and a massive high-definition TV. The picture was frozen on a rerun of last year's All-Ireland football semi-final; Doyle paused in front of the screen.

'Do you not know what happened, Johnny? Kerry beat you Dub bastards 1-15, then hammered Cork in the final.' Picking up the remote, he switched the TV off, and turning to where Finucane hovered at the bar, he nodded to the bottles on the shelves. 'I'll take a large Jimmy with a splash of port; you can hold back on the ice.'

Finucane poured the drink and handed it to him. Doyle raised the glass and swallowed, then looked the old northside gangster in the eye.

'How's your cousin, Johnny?'

Finucane gave a short, cold laugh and, moving to a leather recliner, sat down and tipped the seat back. 'The last time I clapped eyes on her was when she was on the TV with your man outside the Four Courts. Made a right fuckin' plank of yourself that day, didn't you? Letting a maggot off the hook. Always were too handy with the paws, though, even for an old bog-warrior'.

Doyle curled his lip. 'Are you starting, Johnny?'

'The fuck I am, Doyler. I've a game to watch, so what is it you're wanting?'

'I want to know who's been so stupid as to abduct a guard's wife.'

Finucane lifted his shoulders. 'Right now, I haven't the faintest.'

'Bad fuckin' business, and bad *for* business, if you know what I mean. Every car stopped, every van. Every business premises searched from Cork as far as the border.'

'Tell me about it. '

'So what's the word?'

'There *is* no word. This is no one that matters – not as far as we're concerned. Maybe it's the little gobshite you whacked coming back to haunt you. After all, she's your niece, isn't she?'

Doyle considered him coldly. 'I'd like to think it was, Johnny – so I could squash the fucker for good this time. But he's in London shacked up with your second cousin.'

'We might be related, but she's only my cousin's daughter, and I've said bugger-the-fuck-all to him in years, Doyler.'

'Well, somebody knows what's going on, and what you don't know you need to find out. When this is over, we'll not be particular about who we're cleaning up. That means you, Johnny; it means McGeady, Minty . . . '

Finucane looked sour. 'And the pirate queen?'

'Do us a favour, would you?' Doyle gave a half-smile. 'She's always had a thing for Moss Quinn, but it wouldn't stretch to doing away with his wife, now. Besides, she knows we like her pirating from Alexei Bris.'

'She's still selling the skag, man. What's the fuckin' difference?'

'She's not selling it in Ireland, clogger. *That's* the fuckin' difference.'

Finucane sat up straighter. 'That Russian scrote knows it's her – which means sooner or later there's going to be blood spilled, and there can only be one winner.' Getting up, he crossed to the bar.

'We can talk about the battle lines another time,' Doyle said. 'The clock is ticking, Johnny – and I mean literally. As you pointed out, this is my brother's babby we're talking about. Someone knows what's happened, and they know why. If she's not found, then me and Quinn are going to blame people like you, and God knows every copper in the country will be behind us.'

Finucane didn't say anything.

'I'll leave it to you then, will I? I'm taking it you're still the man when we're talking north of the river.'

Still Finucane didn't reply.

'I want my niece alive and well and the fucker's head on a platter. Am I making myself plain enough for you, Johnny?'

'You know, Doyler,' Finucane said quietly, 'you push it for an old feller. One of these days you'll be finished with the guards, and one dark night when you're done supping in some scabby bar in the back of beyond in bog land.'

Doyle patted the grips of the .38 he carried at his hip. 'Johnny,' he said, 'any time you think I'm old enough, you just come a-calling.'

Monday 1st September
6.30 pm

Laura Quinn watched Nickelodeon with her sister, though her mind was as far from the cartoon as it could be. Her dad was still out, and though the teachers had tried to keep it from them, she knew that her mother had been taken away by someone. Her Nan had been on the phone from Kerry. Grandad and Nana Quinn had been on the phone as well, and they told her to tell her dad they were coming home from their holiday early. She told them that her Uncle Paddy was looking after them while their dad went down to Blackrock; people said her mam might be at Blackrock beach. She hoped so.

She cast a short glance at Uncle Paddy, sitting at the table in the dining end of the living room. He had the evening newspaper spread out and was hunched on his elbows with his fists at his cheeks. Laura crossed to the bay window and stood with her head pressed to the glass staring at the empty space where her mother's car would normally be. Some of the kids at school had found out what had happened, and during the afternoon she and Jess had been asked loads of questions. People told her that her mam's car had been found in the cemetery where Danny was buried.

Looking round again, she saw Uncle Paddy watching her. He smiled. 'Are you OK, Laura?'

Laura shrugged.

Jess looked up, as uninterested in the cartoon as her sister.

'What would you like for your tea?'

'I'm not hungry,' Laura said.

'Me neither.' Jess drew her knees up to her chin.

Folding away the paper, Uncle Paddy came over. 'Look, girls,' he said, 'I know you're worried, but I know your mam, and she'll be all right.'

'But someone took her.' Laura sounded panicky. 'Someone abducted her.'

'That's what they call it,' Jess piped up. 'I heard it at school.'

Gently, Uncle Paddy stroked her hair. 'It is what they call it, yes; and there are some wicked people in the world; but your mam is strong, and every guard in the country is looking for her. Not just every guard, but every person, Jessie. They'll find her, and it'll be soon, I promise. She'll be back here in a jiffy and everything will be all right.'

Laura was contemplative, narrow lines appearing in the smooth skin of her forehead. She frowned at Uncle Paddy out of half-closed eyes. 'She's not been happy. She's not been happy ever since Danny was killed.'

'She blames Dad,' Jess said.

Laura looked angrily at her.

'It's true,' Jess repeated. 'She blames him because Danny was knocked down by a car, and Dad's a guard, and he couldn't catch whoever it was that was driving. I heard Mam on the phone to Nanny; she said that to Nanny: she said she thought it was deliberate and whoever did it must have had a grudge against our dad because he's a guard. Or something like that it was, anyway.'

'Listen.' Uncle Paddy took each of them by the hand now. 'I know your mam thinks that, she's said as much to me. You know that she and I have been talking. Your dad wanted us to talk; in fact, he asked me. I've known your mam as long as your dad has, and she's a good woman, a lovely woman, and she loved Danny very much. Yes, she is blaming your dad, and there's no reason for that, but she's a mammy and sometimes the love a mammy feels is so deep that things don't always seem as they actually are. What happened to Danny was an accident, and it's not your dad's fault, and deep down your mam knows that.' He smiled gently. 'You mustn't blame her for it. She'll get over it, and you'll be back together again as a proper family.'

Laura shot him a fierce look. 'She left us,' she stated. 'First she sent our dad away, then she left us on our own. Me and Jess: she left us by ourselves.'

'She's not herself, love,' Paddy said soothingly. 'Your mam is not herself.'

'And what if she doesn't come back?' Laura demanded. 'What if she dies, Uncle Paddy? What will we do then?'

Monday 1st September
6.30 pm

From three directions they converged on Harcourt Square: Quinn heading back from Blackrock beach with Murphy just behind him, Frank Maguire from Rathmines, and Doyle from the quays. Four cars sweeping past the massed ranks of reporters, the TV vans crowded along the street. The justice minister had expressly requested that the press keep away from Quinn's house in Glasnevin, and so far at least, that wish had been respected.

Quinn called home and spoke to his daughters: they wanted him with them, and he knew he ought to be there, but he couldn't just sit in the house while every copper in the country searched for his wife. Patrick told him he was happy to babysit for as long as he wanted, and his sister-in-law had been on the phone telling him that she might drive up from Kerry and take the girls to their nan's house. Hanging up, Quinn called 'Busy' Phillips. 'What's going on?' he asked him. 'I need information.'

'Inspector, I'm sorry, but I've not heard so much as a whisper.'

'Who's out there, for God's sake? Who is doing this to me?'

Busy was a runner for Trisha 'Grace' O'Malley, the mother of all gangsters. She had been nicknamed 'the Pirate Queen' after the six-teenth-century Grace O'Malley, who ruled the islands off the Mayo coast. She pretty much ran Limerick, and Quinn had a soft spot for her.

'I've no idea, Mr Quinn,' Busy was saying. 'Truly I don't. Right now there's not a lot being said, and I think that's because genuinely nobody seems to know anything. Believe me, if they did I'd know about it, and of course then so would you.'

Quinn believed him. 'All right,' he muttered. 'Keep me posted.'

'I will, Mr Quinn. I will. And I tell you what, everyone is up in arms about this. Miss O'Malley; your man down there at the Moorings; I've heard whispers from the southside that even Minty is offering to help.'

'That tattooed fuck! His days are numbered. You can tell him that however this turns out, he's leaving these shores, even if I have to commandeer *The Jeanie Johnston* and ship him out myself.'

Quinn paused for a moment, thinking. 'What about McGeady?'

'I've no idea about him, Mr Quinn. You'd need to be talking to someone else.'

Quinn made a mental note to go to Mountjoy and see 'the Crawthumper'. Hanging up again, he sat there gathering his thoughts. He was still holding his phone when it started ringing. 'Quinn,' he said. For a second there was nothing. His heart began to pump. 'This is Moss Quinn,' he stated.

Then he heard it, the same gravelled tones from his son's grave. *'Mary, Mary, quite contrary, or so the story goes. A maggot in her head, that's what they said, but only Mary knows.'*

The line went dead, and Quinn sat there, his skin crawling and sweat moving as if it were alive in his hair. He was upstairs in a flash, and he handed his phone to a young guard named McKinley. 'Get this checked,' he said. 'The last call. It's an unknown number, and I want to know where it came from.'

Maguire was in the inspector's office with Doyle and Murphy. Quinn strode across the room and opened the door. 'I've just had another call,' he stated, 'and he all but named Conor Maggs.' He told them what the caller had said, and then he turned to Doyle. 'Is Maggs in London? Do we know that for sure?'

'I'm pretty certain he is, yes.'

'Can you find out? Make a call or something? We need to know, Doyler. We need to know for sure.'

Doyle went over to Murphy's desk and picked up the phone. Quinn sat down heavily, the words working again through his head. *A maggot in her head, that's what they said, but only Mary knows.* He snapped a glance at Murphy. 'Get me Mary Harrington's file, would you?' She went to the filing cabinet at the far end of the incident room and, looking beyond her, Quinn spotted a young man with a ponytail and jeans, sitting in a chair against the wall.

'Who's that?'

Maguire lifted one eyebrow. 'A feller from Trinity, Geological Studies. I got him over to look at the picture.'

The academic's name was Townsend, and he taught geology, though he had a passion for Irish history. He told Quinn that the physical land was as much a part of the history of Ireland as the people who lived on it. They sat him down, closing the door against the hubbub of voices.

'What can you tell us, Dr Townsend?' Quinn asked. 'We're up against the clock here.'

Townsend nodded. 'Is the picture all you've had? I mean, is it in isolation?'

Quinn shook his head. 'No, it's not. I've received two phone calls.'

Lips pursed, Townsend looked very thoughtful. 'Is this person just taunting you, or do you think he really is giving you a clue to your wife's whereabouts?' Murphy came in with Mary's file. 'What difference does it make?' she asked.

'Well, it's probably not my place to say, but if he really does want you to have a chance of finding her, then what that Polaroid depicts might be as simple as what you see.'

'We thought it might be a beach,' Quinn told him. 'So far we've searched every stretch of sand within a thirty-mile radius of Dublin.'

'A pebble on a beach,' Townsend nodded. 'It could be. The stone is dark, so I imagine you already thought about Blackrock.'

'We've just got back from there,' Murphy told him.

'What else could it mean?' Quinn was sitting forward now.

Townsend gestured. 'It could be as simple as the two words indicated. Sand and stone: sandstone.'

'Go on.'

'There's not much sandstone quarried in Ireland, and most of it is the red colour you see in the mountains in the south-west, but there is grey sandstone in County Clare. It's referred to geologically as Liscannor, and of course there's a town over there of the same name.'

'County Clare?' Maguire looked doubtful. 'Eva was abducted in Dublin, Dr Townsend. Are you telling me she was taken all the way to Clare?'

'I don't know,' Townsend shrugged. 'Is it possible?'

Quinn was on his feet. 'Anything is possible.'

Townsend continued: 'Well, there is an old Liscannor quarry that's not been used in years. It was run by a family called Scanlon but closed in the 1970s. I've been there on field trips with my students. It's on the cliff and there's an ancient derrick for loading the stone straight onto ships. There are also a couple of ruined buildings.'

Picking up the phone, Maguire spoke to the crew of the police helicopter at Baldonnel. Doyle was waiting for a callback from London, so Murphy suggested she go with him.

'Tell them to pick us up from Phoenix Park,' Quinn instructed Maguire. 'They can land with no problem, and it's only five minutes with a blue light from here.'

'Keep me posted, Moss,' Doyle told him as they headed for the door. 'Eoin Slattery's your man down there. I'll talk to him and get a team out right away.' He turned to Townsend.

'Where is it, exactly, this place?'

'It's on the coast; I can give you the details.'

Doyle was scratching his jaw. 'Scanlon, you say. That rings a bell, I swear it does. But for the life of me I don't know why.'

Quinn grabbed the Harrington file and stuffed it into his bag.

'Are you taking that with you?' Maguire asked him.

'*Only Mary knows*, Frank: that's what he said.'

'Then what about the others? If Eva's abduction is linked to Mary's murder, what about the others?'

Quinn lifted his shoulders. 'The others were single mothers.'

'And Mary was pregnant.'

'Six weeks, the pathologist said. None of us believed she knew.' Maguire nodded.

'He referred to her on the phone, though, so we can't ignore it, can we?'

Monday 1st September
8.30 pm

The closer they got to the coast, the darker it seemed to become, and the engine noise, the whistling whine of the rotors, filled Quinn's head. Through their headphones, the pilot told them they were almost at the coordinates, and before they knew it, the land was gone and they were above the sea, with the tail of the helicopter swinging round in an arc. Now they were nose-in to the cliffs, buffeted by the wind, with thirty million candles worth of searchlight playing across slabs of stone that fell in steps to a sheer face and white-capped waves below.

Quinn could see a multitude of bobbing yellow lights, guards on the ground with torches, dogs barking in silence at the massive black bird hovering above them. The whole side of the cliff looked as though it had been quarried: on the southern stretch, the staggered walls were serrated. Directly below them, the hillside sloped in banks of gravel to where the rock was cut into the stripped plateaus. They could see the ancient rusting derrick Townsend had mentioned, its hook and cable high above the sea.

Quinn's gaze fixed on the shabby-looking machine shed that

dominated the open ground. Beneath them, where the sea broke, was a cave: a gaping black maw barely visible in the darkness. The sea itself was littered with rocks that broke the surface like teeth from some monstrous creature crawling below.

'Mother of God,' Murphy's voice came through Quinn's head-phones. 'It's a hell of a place, isn't it?'

'Think about the boats, Murph,' Quinn pointed down. 'Imagine trying to take on a load with rocks like those itching to scythe through your hull.' He spoke to the pilot then. 'Can you land?' he asked him.

The pilot peered through the windscreen, the searchlight picking up two rank-looking boats lying upturned by the machine shed. He shook his head. 'Not there, I can't. It'd be too unstable. I might be able to set you down on top of the hill maybe, let's see.'

They climbed above the cliff face and the derrick and the ruined building. Staring down at the gaping holes in the roof, Quinn could feel the ache in his gut and his pulse rushing with blood. Murphy was in radio contact with the guards below; turning to Quinn, she gave a short shake of her head. 'They've found nothing so far,' she told him.

On the ground, they procured torches and fluorescent jackets from two guards, who had guided the pilot to a safe spot. The guards repeated what Murphy had heard over the radio. Upending a three-cell torch, Quinn led the way down. It was awkward and slow, the land slippery and sloping sharply, littered with a million holes that were potentially ankle-breaking. Taking Murphy's hand, he guided her across some loose shale, and then stopped for a moment. Murphy knew what he was thinking; she knew what he was feeling, and she was feeling it too.

The wind had lifted, and the salt spray seemed to tighten the skin of his face. Quinn could see more lights where dozens of guards were working their way across the cliff with poles and sticks, one or two carrying shovels, just as they'd done at Blackrock.

'It's OK,' Murphy said. 'It'll be OK, Moss. It will.'

He didn't reply, but he let go of her hand now and continued down to where the boats lay in ruins next to the shed.

A guard in uniform came up to meet them: dogs were barking, voices echoing across the open cliff.

'I'm Sergeant Slattery,' he told them. 'You must be DI Quinn.'

Quinn peered into his face. 'Have you found anything?'

'No, inspector, not yet.'

'It was a long shot, a hunch: we knew that.' Quinn was talking as if trying to convince himself. 'We're clutching at straws, we know we are, but that's the way it is.'

Together, he and Murphy descended the last few paces. Then they were on the flat step with gravel underfoot and the rotten walls of the shed climbing in shadow before them.

Inside, it was one cavernous space, with some rickety iron steps leading up to two rundown offices, which were silent, dark and cold. Quinn climbed to a door where the padlock was hanging off. Forcing the door open, he could smell salt, and damp. There were a couple of desks, a battered filing cabinet and an old typewriter sitting on top of it. Everything was covered in dust, and cobwebs hung in tattered strings, shrouding the window. Quinn poked under the desks, but the office was tiny and there was nowhere to hide anyone. Outside again, on the gantry, he gripped the iron rail.

'Eva!' he called. 'Eva, can you hear me?'

The shout echoed across the empty space, the floor patched by bits of old machinery, a conveyor system, winches and pulleys, lengths of chain link chewed ochre by the salt. Nothing but his words came back to him; nothing but the howl of the wind, the sound of crashing waves. Standing there, he passed the beam of his torch across the concrete floor, where there was nowhere to hide anyone. There was nowhere for a tongue to swell or lips to crack;

there was nowhere for blood to weep from broken veins. He covered every inch of the floor, the walls; he even shone the light at the ceiling.

But there was nothing.

Eva wasn't there.

Monday 1st September
8.45 pm

In her hole in the ground, Eva managed to work herself onto her knees. It wasn't easy, with the weight of the boards across her; the weight of old linoleum; the weight, it seemed, of the sky.

She may have slept; she may have been delirious; she didn't know. She had no idea of time. But she dreamed of her children, of Jess and Laura; she dreamed of Danny. When she opened her eyes through the blindfold, she thought she could see them.

All she could think about was water.

She was desperate now, her tongue filling her mouth, so thick and dry she could barely breathe.

She'd bitten through the tape, a tiny hole. She'd managed to drag the sticky mess past her lips, suck it in, tease it with her teeth.

Now she was on her knees with her arms locked, she had no balance, her face against earth and a terrible ache in her neck. Using her forehead to support her, she was trying to suck up the trickle of rainwater where it had gathered beneath her.

A tiny dribble, no more than a taste. Her tongue ballooned in her mouth. Gagging, she coughed into tape. She couldn't breathe. She was sobbing, her eyes burning up with tears that were not there.

And the cold seeped into her bones. She asked herself if she would die of cold first or would the thirst get her?

Using all her strength, she tried to force the floorboards up, heave back the weight so she could work herself out of this grave. But she slipped and slithered, cocooned like a larval fly. She thought of Danny. When would she see Danny? Was he calling? Was that his voice she could hear? Was that her only son who'd been lost to a man who drove too fast, a man her husband couldn't catch?

Would catching him bring Danny back?

Would it bring back her husband?

She swore she could hear voices. And frantically, she tried to cry out, to let them know she was there. But her own voice was a murmur, a gurgle. A tiny sound barely audible, it was lost to the world and to her.

Listening hard, she was drifting. The voices seemed to drift. They were getting weaker and weaker now, and when they died finally, there was only the clock.

Suddenly thinking clearly, Eva realised what she had heard. There was no one out there calling. It was only the cry of a gull; solitary, mournful as the wind.

Monday 1st September
11.55 pm

The helicopter dropped them back at Phoenix Park, and Quinn felt weak now, empty, as if the life had been hollowed out of him and all that remained was a shell.

Lights burned in the incident room, and upstairs another shift of detectives was manning the telephones. To a person, they looked up grim-faced as Quinn and Murphy walked in. Maguire came out of the office with his jacket hung over his shoulder.

'Where's Doyle?' Quinn asked him.

Maguire shrugged. 'I've no idea. He went out not long after you two.'

'Did he hear back from anyone in London?'

'If he did, he didn't tell me. But then he only ever seems to tell me what he thinks I need to know.'

Quinn managed a smile. 'It's not personal, Frank. You should know by now: he's like that with everyone.'

Maguire yawned. 'I need a couple of hours' shut-eye,' he said. 'You better get some sleep as well. You look banjaxed, the pair of you. Moss, is my brother still up at your place?' Quinn nodded. 'I'll get home; let Pat get home himself. He's been a star, Frank, a real trooper. And not just today: he counselled Eva for weeks.'

Maguire looked beyond him. 'For all the good it did her.' He lifted a hand. 'I'm sorry, I didn't mean that. It sounds defeatist: that's not what I mean, and not how I feel at all.' Quinn offered another shallow smile. 'It's all right,' he said, 'we're knackered the lot of us. Go home and get some sleep. There's nothing more you can do tonight.'

Maguire indicated the file he had carried to the coast and back. 'I've been thinking about that,' he said. 'It's vital we don't overcomplicate things. There's no way Mary Harrington is connected with the other five, Moss. It's like you said: she probably didn't even know she was pregnant.'

Quinn nodded. 'I'm taking the file home anyway, and I'm going to go through it. Who knows, maybe I'll come up with something.'

He crossed the Liffey again on O'Connell Bridge, passing the statue where Daniel stood, together with his four angels, one of whom had taken an IRA bullet during the Troubles. He passed the old post office and the site where Nelson's Pillar had mirrored the column in Trafalgar Square until it was blown up. Ten minutes later, he pulled up outside the house. He saw that Laura's bedroom light was still on.

Patrick opened the door just as Quinn was fitting his key in the lock. 'There you are,' he said.

'Pat, I'm sorry. I . . . '

'For Christ's sake, forget it. It's the least I could do.'

Closing the door, Quinn went through to the lounge and, taking the decanter, poured a heavy slug of Jameson. 'Sweet lamb,' he muttered, 'I could do with tying one on.'

'You'd be hanging come the morning. It'd do you no good, Mossie, not with what's going on.'

Quinn gave a half-laugh. 'Are you lecturing me on my drinking,

Patrick Pearse Maguire? For the life of me, you're in no position to talk.'

He smiled then, glad that his buddy was there. 'Boy, but we were the pair, weren't we, back in the day? That turnover, the flying pass, and the drop goal to beat those deadbeats down in Kerry.'

Sitting down, he laid the file on the coffee table. 'That was when we met Eva, remember? That tour, Listowel and Ballybunion, Ballylongford.'

Maguire nodded. 'And you got in there before I had the chance, you horny old fucker. Paired me off with that Corin when I'd just told you how I felt about redheads.'

Quinn smiled. 'There was a queue, Patrick, and I was at the front of it.' He paused then. 'Are the girls all right? I saw Laura's light on just now.'

'She's asleep. She asked me to leave it on tonight; I don't think she wanted to be alone in the dark.'

'No, of course she didn't. What about Jess, is she all right?'

'They're both fine. But they're worried, Moss, of course they are. Both of them scared to death.'

'The poor lambs, their brother in the ground, their mammy gone.' Quinn took another glug of the whiskey.

'Eva's sister phoned again,' Maguire told him. 'She's definitely coming up very early tomorrow. She says she'll either stay here with the girls or take them back to their Nan's house. Both your brothers phoned as well, Moss, and your mam and dad. They're leaving you alone on your mobile, told me they don't want to clog up the line.'

'Thanks, Paddy. I appreciate you being here.'

'You look exhausted. You ought to try and close your eyes for a couple of minutes at least.'

Quinn worked a palm across the stubble that laced his chin. 'I'd not get a minute, would I? There's no time, Patrick. There's no time to sleep.'

Opening the file, he sucked a breath as if breathing was suddenly difficult and in some way he was taking a breath for his wife. It was only last night that he had been reading the abortive confession, and here he was with the same file again.

He could hear the voice still, like a rattle inside his head. He could see Conor Maggs in the dock, tears of pathos glistening as the judge was shown the hospital stills after Doyle had taken the hammer to him.

He considered the first few pages, determined to read the statements as if for the first time, and to fit the events together again to see if they told him anything he didn't already know. The first one had been taken from Jimmy Hanrahan, who lived with his dad in the old house directly across the water from the ruins where they'd found Mary's body. Jimmy the Poker; he claimed he'd seen Maggs that night talking to Mary, when Maggs claimed he'd never even set eyes on her.

It was suddenly fresh in Quinn's mind: so fresh he could hear music lifting from the various bars; he could see Doyle supping milk stout in Jett O'Carroll's; he could smell the fetid stench of Mary's body when they eventually found her.

'What have you got there?' Patrick asked, indicating the paperwork.

'The file from the Mary Harrington case – the *fleadh cheoil*,' Quinn told him. 'I had another call, Pat; another Dublin phone box. That's twice now. The first time he was talking about a clock ticking, the next he was talking about Mary.'

Maguire looked puzzled. 'Why would he call you at all? And why would he mention Mary?'

'I don't know.' Quinn shrugged. 'I've always thought Mary's death was a one-off. But whoever it was, he talked about Mary, and indirectly he talked about Maggs too. So I have to look, don't I?'

Sitting back, he lifted a foot to rest on the table. 'Listen,' he said, 'it's late, and you've been here forever. Don't feel as though you have to stay. I'm a big lad: I'll be all right. I'm just going to sit here and work through what happened, see if I missed anything.'

He could feel fatigue beginning to haunt his eyelids. Hunting in his jacket pocket, he found a cigarette.

'On the phone, you said he wasn't in Ireland, but do you think this is Maggs?' Maguire asked him.

Quinn narrowed his eyes. 'As far as we know, he's in London.'

'Who else then?'

'Whoever killed Mary Harrington; and for all I know, five other missing women maybe.' Quinn lit the cigarette. 'Though if it's one and the same man, why they should want to abduct my wife is beyond me. And as you say, why get in touch now after being silent for all these years?' He made a face. 'On the other hand, if you spoke to a forensic psychiatrist, he'd tell you that if you're on a killing spree and nobody knows you're doing it, then eventually you're going to ask yourself: where's the fun?' He sipped his whiskey. 'I've always been a street copper, followed my guts too much maybe, like Joe Doyle – though perhaps my interviewing technique is a little subtler.' He gestured with an open palm. 'I'm not sure about all the profiling stuff, you know? I suppose it has its place, but who've we had in this country that could be classed as a serial killer – apart from Shaw maybe, the Englishman back in the 1970s.' He pursed his lips. 'This isn't the States, is it? But talk to someone like Liam Ahern down there on the quays, and he'll tell you that there's a part of every psycho that wants to get caught. They *want* to stop killing maybe, I don't know; but they sure as hell want someone to know they did it. Recognition, Pat: it's human nature.'

Maguire lifted his eyebrows. 'Is that what you think this is, then: a serial killer who wants you to know he's out there? I thought you and Doyle discounted those other five abductions when you were investigating Mary.'

'We did.' Quinn worked the points of his fingers into his eyes. 'If you're asking me, then no, I don't actually think it is the same man. I still don't think Mary's murder had anything to do with those other five, but it looks like it's everything to do with what happened to Eva.'

Maguire got to his feet. 'Maybe now's not the time though, Moss, eh? You look deadbeat. You should shut your eyes for an hour or so and look at the file in the morning.'

'Yeah, you're probably right.' Quinn shot a concerned glance at the clock. He was acutely aware of the knot tightening in his belly once more. 'But we only have till Wednesday night; after that, it could be too late.'

'You don't know that for certain.'

'I don't,' Quinn said, holding up the file, 'but according to whoever called me, Mary does, doesn't she.'

Tuesday 2nd September
1 am

Maguire left him lying on the settee with his eyes closed. As if in testament to his mood, the half-empty whiskey bottle sat before him on the coffee table and the stubs of a couple of cigarettes lay crushed in a glass ashtray. He took a last look round the stripped-pine lounge, at the Victorian fireplace and pastel prints on the walls. He thought about the delicately inspired way Eva decorated. She was that kind of woman: gentle, subtle. There was a beauty about her that lingered even after she was gone. He thought about how they'd sat together so intimately in the kitchen; how she'd confided things to him she had never confided in anyone. With another quick glance at her husband, Maguire let himself out and, crossing the road to his VW, headed south to his flat.

The Portobello Hotel was silent: no music this late on a weeknight. They had bands playing at the weekends but his place was far enough down towards Charlemont Street not to be disturbed by this. An avenue of grass divided the Georgian homes and the canal: bordered by trees, it gave the area a suburban air that Patrick liked.

He thought about tomorrow morning and the visits he had

scheduled at Mountjoy before he headed for 'stab city' and the back of Shaws. He thought over this morning and Karl Crame from the Kilmahon estate, how he'd promised to go and speak to his girl-friend.

After the conversation just now with Quinn, he could not help but think about Conor Maggs – and that took him to Quinn's tout on the inside, the one who hung out with Christian Brothers incarcerated for abusing children.

The Crawthumper; so named because not only did he hang out with monks and priests, he defended the church like an old soapbox preacher. Quinn didn't know that Maguire knew about him, because Maguire kept what he did in the prison confidential, but he was in and out all the time and he picked up all kinds of information. There were a couple of hard cases he spoke to who were sure the Craw was informing. If he was, they left him alone, though, because he was a number-cruncher who had taken the fall for Lorne 'the Thorn' McGeady, and that bastard rivalled only the General in his cruelty. One of the old school –and long dead at the hands of the IRA – Martin Cahill, aka the General, had nailed one of his lads to a snooker table when he thought he'd been stealing from him.

Upstairs in his flat, Patrick saw that his mail was piled neatly on the table and knew his brother had been there.

A little suspicious now, he had a look round to see whether any of his stuff had been moved. He went into his bedroom and opened the drawer in the bedside table. He checked the shoebox he kept under the bed and he checked his cupboards. Nothing had been touched. He told himself there was nothing malicious, it was just that after all these years Frank still came and went as he pleased; as if he didn't quite trust his little brother, Patrick, to be able to take care of himself. He fussed over him, mothered him, as he always had.

In the living room, he noticed that the photograph had been

moved and then put back – but not quite in the spot it normally occupied. Frank hated that picture and he was always asking Patrick why he kept it. All the same, he could imagine him standing there with the frame in his hand, peering at their mother's face.

'Frankie,' he muttered. 'Frankie, Frankie. It's over, lad. Why don't you leave it alone?'

He stared into her eyes then, and the muscles tightened around his mouth. 'Did he come to see you, love? Did he? Somehow I doubt it.'

Tuesday 2nd September
5 am

Quinn had been awake for a couple of hours already and, with a cup of coffee at his elbow, he was poring over Mary's file.

The *Fleadh Cheoil na hÉireann*, the annual Irish music festival; two years ago, it had taken place in Eva's home town of Listowel.

That was where he'd met her, years before, when he and Paddy were in the south-west for the three-match rugby tour against a combined Kerry XV. They had won the first game by a single point, Quinn kicking the drop goal they'd talked about last night.

*

Ten of them gathered in Jett O'Carroll's, a pub in the centre of Listowel, afterwards, with a few pints already in their bellies and a few more settling on the bar. A TV fixed to the wall was showing highlights from the game between Munster and Leinster the day before, though one toothless old guy kept switching it over to the racing.

Quinn had been in the guards for about a year and was stationed in Rathfarnham with Joe Doyle. This was the Doyler's home-town local, and everyone knew the big man. His parents still lived in the area, as did his brother Cahal, who had affiliations with some people that Doyle didn't talk about.

He had a pint in one hand, and a Jameson with a drop of port in the other, and he was propping up the bar with a local copper called Martin McCafferty, as well as a couple of other lads who now and again would duck across the street to the bookies. Pat Maguire was regaling those who'd listen with how good the match had been and how game the Kerry side had been. He explained that it had only been his moment of brilliance at scrum-half that had allowed Quinn to kick the goal that won it.

Quinn rested an elbow on his shoulder, taking time out from the craic to consider two girls sitting with a young man at a table under the window. One of the girls was stunning: Quinn couldn't take his eyes off her. She was sitting almost demurely, sipping wine. Green eyes; her hair looked burnished in the sunlight. The lad with them looked out of place, though. Diminutive, with sloping shoulders; his hair a shaggy mop that covered his skull like an ill-fitting hat. Though they weren't being rude, it was obvious that the girls didn't want him around them. He felt Doyle's mighty mitt come to rest on his shoulder. 'What do you think you're looking at?' he said gruffly.

Quinn indicated the girl with the auburn hair. 'Mine's the one on the left, Doyler. You'll have to make do with the tug.'

Doyle's grip tightened a little. 'Mossie,' he said softly, 'the one on the left is my niece.'

'You're joking?'

'Eva, my brother's youngest, so keep your sweaty mitts to yourself.'

'Your brother Cahal's daughter?'

Doyle shook his head. 'No, Cahal has no children. Eva was Tom's babby: Tom who was killed in a car accident north of Ballybunion.'

'I'm sorry.'

'So was I, and so was she. She's been like my own ever since.' His eyes fixed on the lad with them.

'And talking of which, I cannot tell you how many times I've warned that little *ciaróg* to keep away from her.'

Quinn looked quizzical.

'It means maggot, lad,' Doyle explained, 'in the old language. The boy's name is Maggs, and he reminds me of one – which is close enough. Remember, when I joined An Garda Síochána you still had to be a native speaker.'

Quinn laughed. 'Doyler, when you joined, "Lugs" Brannigan was still taking his fists to anyone who'd lip off to him.'

At the window, Maggs was staring at them, conscious perhaps that they'd been talking about him.

'It doesn't look like your man's your biggest fan,' Quinn commented, 'and it seems to me he's taking precious little notice of you not wanting him around your niece.'

'He's trouble,' Doyle whispered. 'I'll tell you why some day. Eva's a sweetheart, Moss; she's the soul of Bernadette, she has. I want him away from her, but I can't go over there and shift him, not without embarrassing her.'

Quinn was smiling now. 'You want me to make my move then; is that what you're saying to me?'

'I'd appreciate it, only don't be making any more than the one move or you'll find out how Lugs got his reputation.'

Behind them, Patrick Maguire had finished his story, and he thrust another pint into Quinn's hand.

'Jesus, but she's the beauty, isn't she?' he muttered, indicating Eva.

'Joe Doyle's niece, Patrick.' Quinn motioned to where Doyle was back at the bar. 'The lad there with them . . . Doyle's not a fan, and he'd appreciate it if we found a way to move him on.'

'I can think of a way; I can think of lots of ways. I've always had a thing for redheads, and you know what Bruce Springsteen says about them.'

'No, Pat, what does he say?'

'That they always get the dirty job done.'

'Well get yourself in line, son. That dirty job is mine.'

Together they wandered over to the window and Eva looked up, wineglass to her lips, and smiled at Quinn. 'Hello, Eva,' he said. 'I don't know your friend's name.'

'Corin,' she told him.

'Hello, Corin, this here is Patrick Pearse Maguire, the most notable scrum-half to ever venture west from Dublin. He's a bit of a coward, though, and he asked me to ask you if you'd mind if we sat down.'

Corin laughed. Eva laughed. Maguire just wagged his head.

Maggs sat there looking awkward, angry even: they'd completely ignored him. Pulling out a stool, Quinn sat down. 'Joe Doyle told me you were his niece, Eva. I'm Moss Quinn, I work with him up in Dublin.'

'So you're Moss: he's talked about you.' Her eyes seemed to light up, and for an instant Quinn felt his heart quicken. Next to them, Maggs shifted in his seat and Eva gestured. 'This is Conor, by the way.'

Quinn offered his hand, working Maggs's knuckles with a little squeeze. 'Nice to meet you, Conor,' he said. 'Joe Doyle told me all about you.'

*

Quinn went through to the kitchen to refill his coffee cup. Outside in the garden he sucked on a cigarette, thinking back on that day and thinking again about what Doyle had told him later. In a way, he'd felt sorry for the lad, and knowing his wife as he did now, he could understand how she'd sort of befriended him. Eva was like that, she only had to look at a stray puppy to want to adopt it. The trouble was that this stray puppy followed her home; this stray puppy thought she was his mistress; and according to Doyle, this stray puppy had sharp teeth.

*

With Maggs sitting awkwardly on the periphery, they'd fallen into conversation, Quinn telling tales about Doyle that made Eva laugh out loud, and Maguire chipping in with the odd comment about how the old bog man had no real mates and that was why he'd tagged along with the rugby tour.

Eva assured him that her uncle had plenty of mates and that he'd tagged along because the tour was in Kerry and it gave him an excuse to do the stations in his home town rather than crawling the pubs in Temple Bar, or wherever he drank up in Dublin.

'He drinks everywhere in Dublin,' Quinn assured her. 'He's like a student, for Christ's sake: fourteen pints in fourteen pubs on a Thursday night, and that's before he settles down for a real drink.'

'You'd know all about it, wouldn't you?' Corin said with a laugh. 'From what I've seen, you two can down a pint yourselves.'

'I've been known to have a tipple,' Quinn said, trying his best to imitate his mentor. 'That and the odd pinch of snuff – though it's a habit that went out with my grandfather.'

Eva fell about, and Corin was laughing too. At that moment, Doyle placed a very large fist in the middle of the table.

'What's with all the racket?' he growled. 'Jesus, Mary and Joseph, can you not see there are people in this pub trying to have a quiet pint?' Then he looked at Maggs. 'And how are you, Conor lad? How's yer auntie? Keeping well, is she?'

If Maggs had felt uncomfortable before, he felt even more so now. Getting to his feet, he smiled briefly at Eva. 'I have to go,' he said. 'I'll see you later, will I?'

'I'm taking her out to dinner,' Quinn told him. 'Me and Eva, Patrick and Corin here; we're on a double date. Maybe she'll see you another time, but Eva's busy tonight.'

Maggs's face seemed to fill with blood. He looked at Eva as if waiting for her to refute the statement.

But she didn't.

Something seemed to die in his eyes then, as if a little of the life literally went out of him. He sucked his lip like a child and, muttering again about later, he pushed open the swing door. Eva looked after him, red all at once in the face. 'Shit,' she said, 'that wasn't right.'

Doyle twisted his mouth at the corner. 'Don't worry about it, Eva. Conor's a big boy.'

'Uncle Joe,' she said. 'I know what you think about Conor. You've told me a million times. I don't need you to look out for me, so why don't you fuck off back to those who want to listen to you?'

Doyle wagged his head sadly. 'Just like her mother: angelic to look at, yet a gob on her like a fishwife.' With a grin, he patted Quinn on the shoulder. 'I'll see you later, lad. Let me know if you need back-up.'

Tuesday 2nd September
8 am

Doyle had been on the street most of the night, only going home to his digs now to change his clothes. Mrs Mulroney, his landlady of twenty years, made him a bowl of porridge, which he shovelled down gratefully, eating it with one eye on his watch and the other on his mobile phone. All night he'd been kicking arse, shaking down as many people as owed him favours, and as many others who didn't. But for the first time in thirty years, nobody seemed to know anything. He'd been from Finglas to Tallaght and Poolbeg to Ronanstown, tapping up touts, tack-heads, bank robbers and brassers. He'd spoken to Grace O'Malley; he'd spoken to Lorne 'the Thorn' McGeady. He'd even roused the Monk, a player from the old days of Gilligan and Cahill.

"'Tis a terrible business, Joseph,' Mrs Mulroney said to him. 'Really it is.' She crossed herself. 'I've never known anything like it, not in all my days. Your niece an' all.' She was almost in tears.

'There now,' he said, placing the bowl on the kitchen surface and patting her a little awkwardly on the shoulder. 'Eva's tough, Mrs M. she might look delicate, and she's the sweetest-natured woman a man could lay eyes on, but she's her daddy's girl and my brother was no man's patsy, I can tell you.'

His phone started ringing. Squinting long-sightedly at the screen, he saw there was no number registering. 'Excuse me, Mrs M,' he said. Wandering through to the lounge, he answered the phone.

'This is Doyle.'

'Joseph, lad, how are you?'

Doyle recognised his elder brother. 'Cahal, how's things? How's the craic?'

'Things are fine, and the craic is ninety. I'm sitting here in a bar on the lower east side with a couple of lads from the old days.'

'Are you, now? Anyone I know, is it?'

'I'd imagine it might be, yes. But listen, I'm watching Fox News and they've just now broadcast from Harcourt Square. Fuck it, Joseph, is what I'm hearing right: some gobshite's made off with our Tommy's babby?'

'It is right, yes. We're pulling up trees looking for her.'

'Great God almighty. Is there anything I can do?'

'Not from there, there's not.'

'I know that; I mean from Dublin. I've plenty as still owes me. Do you want me to call in a couple of favours?'

'Call them in, by all means, Cahal; time is running out.'

Hanging up, Doyle went back to the kitchen. 'That was my brother, Mrs M – from America.' She looked at him then with the maternal expression she liked to keep especially for him.

'You must be hurting, Joseph: you've been like a father to that girl, I know you have.'

He blew out his cheeks. 'In my way, maybe – cack-handed though it probably is. I promised her mother I'd look out for her, but you know the poor woman never forgave me for introducing Eva to Moss Quinn.'

Mrs Mulroney looked a little shocked then. Almost sixty, she had been widowed for twenty years; she was short and round and she wore cat's-eye-style public health glasses.

'I'm joking, Mrs M,' Doyle grinned.

He was interrupted by the phone ringing again. This time it was Uttley. 'Jug,' he said. 'Not before time. For Christ's sake, tell me you have something for me.'

'Oh I do, Mr Doyle, I do. I'll meet you at the usual place in half an hour.'

'Talk to me on the phone, Jug, will you?'

'No, no, we'll make it the usual place. I never conduct business on the telephone, Mr Doyle, you know that.'

'Jug,' Doyle said with a sigh, 'it's eight o'clock in the morning; the usual place isn't open.'

The water rat seemed to think about that. 'No, you're right; of course. Best make it the church, then. St Peter's in half an hour.'

Doyle met Uttley in the church that dominated the fork between the Cabra and North Circular Roads. Normally they met in the bar of the Conan Doyle pub, just a stone's throw from the gates of Mountjoy Prison. The tout was sitting facing the altar with a bag between his feet and his hands in the pockets of his raincoat. From behind, his ears were very pronounced, and even more distinctive because of the thick, curling hairs that sprouted from them. Doyle crossed himself with a dab of holy water and sat down.

'Make it snappy, Jug,' he said. 'What've you got for me?'

Without looking behind him, Uttley lifted a sweaty palm and worked fingers and thumb together in a gesture that told Doyle he wanted money. Taking a short breath, the detective reached over the back of the pew, grabbed his fingers and squeezed so hard the old man yelped.

'You're on a fucking retainer, you mouldy-arsed gobshite. Now, what is it you want to tell me?'

Uttley prised his fingers free, then rubbed them with his other hand. 'Mr Doyle,' he said, 'the retainer doesn't cover this kind of information.'

Doyle looked wearily at him. 'You know what, if I had the time I'd extract it from you tooth by fuckin' tooth. For months now, you've told me nothing I don't already know. I swear you're as much use as an old nun's fanny.' He shook his head, cursed under his breath and peeled thirty euro from his wallet.

'Fifty, Mr Doyle, if ya don't mind; I'm wanting at least fifty.' Cursing softly, Doyle found another twenty and handed it to him. Uttley took the notes and slipped them into his pocket. 'Your man's in town,' he said gleefully. 'Him that's walking out with Johnny Clogs' cousin. He's staying with her, back of the Portobello.'

Tuesday 2nd September
8.30 am

Head bowed, Maggs stood in the shower. He and Jane were so loved-up they'd spent much of yesterday in bed, and when he'd woken this morning he could feel her pressing against him.

She was not attractive – she was too chubby and a little too pale – but she was a good sort, and one of the things he really liked about being with her was that she too had had a difficult time. The second cousin to the gangster Johnny Clogs, her story of life in the shadow of Dublin's underworld tallied with his own troubled childhood.

They kept quiet about the fact that they were living together, because some of the evangelicals didn't appreciate that, in this day and age, it wasn't actually living in sin. Jane had been unsure about a sexual relationship to begin with, but when he explained that all they were doing was celebrating the fact that God had brought them together, she was fine with it. The pastor at Harold's Cross was a stickler for a literal translation of the Bible, though, and didn't believe in sex before marriage. That was why Maggs had decided to be out when he popped round for a visit on Sunday night. Maggs was trying to establish himself as a speaker: an evangelist; the man who, while lying in a police cell, had been visited by Christ himself. That kind of conversion was very powerful, and people wanted to hear about it.

Jane was glued to the TV news. The television hadn't been on at all yesterday, and anyway, they'd not bothered with anything much, they'd been so into each other. But now she was watching a press conference coming from Garda HQ in Phoenix Park, and it looked manic. There were numerous TV crews – not just Irish channels but stations from all over the world – gathered outside the old building. The deputy commissioner for operations was speaking to the media, reiterating the fact that on Sunday evening, Eva, the wife of Detective Inspector Moss Quinn, had been abducted from Glasnevin Cemetery.

Mouth agape, Maggs stared at the screen.

It was 'unprecedented in the annals of crime in this country'; whoever had her might as well have abducted the president. The deputy commissioner made it clear that there would be no hiding place. The broadcast cut to the Dáil, where Ivan Chambers, the justice minister, echoed the deputy commissioner's sentiments.

Back at Phoenix Park, the deputy commissioner was fielding questions: no, the guards were not ruling anything out, but as he'd already stated, they weren't necessarily linking this abduction with the other cases of missing women either. He did point out that a brand new unit had been set up in Naas. It was operational as of yesterday morning; ironically, DI Quinn had been tasked to lead it. The fact was that they weren't necessarily linking the abduction with any other case at all – including, as one reporter repeatedly asked, the murder of Mary Harrington.

Maggs sat down heavily on the arm of the chair. 'Are you all right, pet?' Jane asked him.

He didn't reply. He was still staring at the screen: he recognised the plain-clothes officer standing next to the deputy commissioner.

'Frank Maguire,' he said softly. 'My God, that's Frank Maguire.' Dropping to one knee, Jane took his hand. 'Conor, what on earth is the matter?'

'That's Frank Maguire. He was the senior officer when Quinn and Doyle came after me.' He touched his ribs as if they were black again with the memory.

'Love, that's all over. The judge threw the case out: they can't hurt you now.'

Maggs stared at her. 'Jane,' he said, his voice edged with panic, 'did you not hear *when* they said she went missing: Sunday night. I wasn't here on Sunday night; I took a walk along the canal, remember? You had the pastor round and I was out for a walk. I had to go so the people at Harold's Cross wouldn't think we were living together. Don't you see? As soon as they find out I'm in the city, they'll be round here, and I won't have anyone to vouch for where I was.'

'Now calm down, Conor, come on. Ray Kinsella was gone by nine thirty,' Jane reminded him.

'It doesn't matter. I wasn't home by nine thirty, was I? You were in bed when I got back. Any moment now, we're going to have Sergeant Doyle hammering on the door. This is a guard's wife we're talking about – and not just any guard, it's Moss Quinn. You heard them just now: it's 'unprecedented'. The kicking they gave me the last time will be nothing compared to what they'll do now.'

'Conor,' she snapped, 'please would you calm down.'

He peered hopelessly at her.

'Doyle won't do anything,' she assured him. 'After what happened before, there's no way he'd even think about it.'

He laughed scornfully. 'You don't know Doyle. Don't you see? He's Eva's uncle. He hates me; he's always hated me; and he still swears I killed Mary Harrington. I've no alibi, Jane, and you know what happened the last time. My God, it'll look like a slap compared to this.'

'Doyle won't do anything,' she reiterated.

He was shaking. 'But he will. Of course he will. I wasn't here at ten: I came in after.'

For a long moment she just looked at him, with pity in her eyes; tenderness; love. 'No you didn't,' she said. 'At ten o'clock, you were tucked up in bed with me.'

He stared at her almost angrily. 'But I wasn't.'

'We'll tell them you were. You were back here by a quarter to ten, and we were together all night. Apart from an hour or so, that's absolutely true.' She smiled now and held his hand tightly. 'I'm not about to let it happen again. There's no way, Conor. I promise you, not after what happened the last time.'

Tuesday 2nd September
8.45 am

Doyle drove from St Peter's church to Quinn's house and found him on the steps waving his daughters goodbye. His sister-in-law had driven up from Kerry in the early hours and was taking them straight back to their grandmother's house so that Quinn could get on with trying to find their mother.

Doyle watched them go, then, rolling down the window, called to Quinn. 'Moss,' he said, 'I just met with Uttley. Maggs is back in Dublin.'

Quinn looked round sharply. For a moment, he peered across the roof to the empty space where Eva's car should have been – instead of at the lab with forensics experts taking it to pieces.

'Come inside a minute,' he said.

'Did you not hear me? The Maggot is in Rathmines. Get in the car, will you? Let's get ourselves down there.'

'And do what?'

Doyle stared at him. 'What do you mean: do what? Bring him in; interrogate him; find out what the little shite was doing on Sunday. Find Eva, for pity's sake.'

Quinn rested an elbow on the roof. 'What if it wasn't him?'

'What're you talking about? Of course it's him: we know it's him.'

'We *don't* know it's him. The mistake we made before was deciding it was him and not looking any further. You can't rely on instinct
alone, Doyler. The last time we did, we ended up with nothing.'

Climbing out of the car, Doyle looked Quinn in the eye.
'Instinct,' he said, 'is the one thing you can rely on. Instinct told me
he'd murdered Mary Harrington, and for all that happened in the
Four Courts, I've not changed my mind. Sometimes your gut feeling
is all there is, and it's served me pretty well these past three decades,
I can tell you. '

'But it wasn't enough, Doyler, was it?'

'He made a full confession: you know those words weren't mine.
I may've given him a little slap, but the words were his – every one
of them.'

'Doyler, you lathered the shit out of him.'

'But the detail, man; the detail!'

'He knew the fuckin' detail!' Quinn threw out a hand now. 'He
knew what she looked like when we found her, and he knew what we
thought he'd done to her. We'd told him a dozen times; all he had to
do was recite what we'd already told him.'

Doyle took a step back. 'Well bugger me,' he said. 'Bugger me
blind, why don't you: you really don't think it was him, do you?'

'Look, Eva is lying in a hole somewhere. That's all I know for
sure right now. Nothing matters except finding her.'

'Exactly, so let's drag the bastard in.'

Quinn looked witheringly at him. 'Why would he do it? What
would be his motive? In all the years he was living up here, he never
tried to contact her. You told me yourself he used to trail around
after her like the proverbial puppy.'

'He was no puppy, Moss. A wolf, maybe; a rabid dog.'

'You're going on what we thought we knew,' Quinn told him.

'Nobody ever proved he had anything to do with what happened to his mam, and you're the only person I've ever heard actually voice it. So he had a shitty childhood: what with who his mother was and every man Jack lipping off about it, it's hardly surprising. It doesn't necessarily make him evil, though, and it doesn't mean he put drain cleaner in a wine bottle. I tell you, I'm not playing that game again. We have to get this right. We've little time, and we can't afford to waste a second of it.'

'Listen, Moss,' Doyle told him, 'she may be your wife, but Eva is still my niece, and I made a promise over her dad's coffin that I would take care of her. Would you stop for a minute and think about it: who else would take the necklace?'

'I *have* thought about it, but as Murphy pointed out, it might've just come off in the struggle.'

'So where's the pendant, then?'

'What?'

'The Sacred Heart. If it was lost in the struggle, why didn't Scene of Crimes find it along with the broken chain?'

Quinn couldn't answer him. Instead, he turned and went inside. Doyle followed, cursing under his breath. 'And if you're talking motive, it's simple,' he said. 'Revenge, Moss: revenge on you for taking her away in the first place; revenge on both us for dragging him into court; and revenge on me for kicking his skinny arse to Connacht and back again.'

Quinn held his eye. 'Doyler, he's hardly the type to think of sending us a picture. And what about the phone calls? Why would he do that?'

'Jesus, would you listen to yourself? You told us the caller all but named him.'

'I've not forgotten that, and I've not forgotten what the profilers tell us either. People want recognition, Joseph. Did it not occur to you that if we got it wrong, whoever did kill Mary might've taken offence?'

In the living room, Doyle helped himself to a slug from the whiskey bottle. 'Do you want one of these?' he growled.

Quinn shook his head. 'I had enough last night.'

'Is that why you're coming up with such a fuck-crazy notion? You're hanging this morning, is that it?'

'Fuck off with you and sit down.' Quinn had Mary's file in his hand. 'The fleadh cheoil,' he said. 'I want to go through it again. And if we come up with nothing but maggots, believe me, Doyler, I'll be the first down to Rathmines to stomp on the toe-rag's head.'

*

August two years before, and the Maguire brothers were staying at the holiday home Frank and his wife had bought in Ballybunion. Frank was playing golf, and Patrick had arranged to meet Eva in Listowel. Quinn and Doyle would join them later – either that night or in the morning, depending on how quickly they finished an investigation they were carrying out in Cork.

A balmy night, and the little Kerry town felt as alive with visitors as it did during the racing festival.

Eva looked beautiful, and Maguire was thinking that Quinn really was a lucky man. She wore a gypsy-style top and a pair of jeans that flared over tan-coloured cowboy boots. The children were in Dublin with Quinn's parents, and Eva told Pat she was looking forward to a weekend with her husband, her old mates and the craic. That was, if Quinn and Doyle ever made it.

'I tell you what,' Maguire told her. 'If Moss doesn't show in time, I'll make sure you don't miss him.'

Eva laughed. 'I'll bet you would too, Patrick Pearse – mad thing that you are.'

'I tell you something else,' he went on. 'I've told Moss hundreds of times, so it's no secret: if he'd not had the good sense to pursue you when he did, I'd have been the veritable bloodhound, believe me.'

'Is that why you never got married? Because you thought all the best girls were taken?'

'No, love. I never got married because *you* were taken.'

They parked in a side road and Eva took his arm as they walked towards the town centre, where already music was drifting from various doorways. 'I love this,' she said. 'It's such a fantastic atmosphere. There's nothing like it, Patrick. I mean really, is there?'

In the first bar, there was a solitary singer, but after a couple of numbers he was replaced by a guitar-and-fiddle duo that was really good. Eva was drinking wine, Patrick pints of Smithwicks, with the odd whiskey to chase them down. He was people-watching. He was a social worker and prison visitor: people were his business. He'd come here straight from the jail in Limerick.

A group of young women came in. They were dressed to the nines, and one of them was more than a little drunk already; she was not unlike Eva to look at, although she was much younger. She caught Maguire's eye and he flashed the cheeky little smile that had worked so well when he had the muscles of a scrum-half to go with it.

He fetched another round; when he got back to the table, he was amazed to see Conor Maggs in his seat. 'Conor,' he said, placing Eva's drink before her, 'what a surprise seeing you again after all these years.' He couldn't help it, not after what had happened before, and with a wicked grin he nodded to Maggs's nether regions. 'Got yourself all tucked away, I see. Good lad.'

Maggs went scarlet. Then his eyes dulled and he gave Maguire as cold a stare as he'd witnessed. 'You've a mouth on you for a Dublin boy a long way from home.'

Maguire was amazed at the aggression. 'Well, well,' he muttered. 'Got yerself an attitude finally, did you?'

'Fuck you.' Maggs shot a stiff glance at Eva. 'Sorry, Eva, I have to go. Nothing to do with you, love; just the company you're keeping.'

When he had gone, Eva's gaze was cold. 'That was out of order. He wasn't doing any harm, Pat. You should leave the man alone.'

'I suppose it was a little uncalled for,' Maguire admitted. 'But give us a break, would you? The last time I clapped eyes on him, he was watching you from the bushes with his pants around his ankles.'

*

Quinn looked up from the handwritten sheet of paper. 'Patrick's statement from the night Mary was abducted. You remember, Doyler?'

'Course I do,' Doyle said. 'She was my niece, Mossie, and he was talking about the night you were with her down by the river.'

*

Patrick and Eva moved from pub to pub before making their way down to the square, where a large marquee had been erected. Eva hooked up with Corin and some old school friends, so Maguire went to watch a couple of bands by himself. There was a lad from Dublin he'd seen playing on Abbey Street. He was good: a throaty-sounding voice that seemed to fit someone older. The marquee was packed; people standing shoulder to shoulder, whooping and clapping every time he finished a song. There were other acts waiting in the wings but the kid was so good he was encored again and again.

Having heard enough, Maguire headed for Jett O'Carroll's. He caught sight of Maggs watching him from further up the road.

'Yup,' Maguire muttered to himself. 'An attitude, all right. He's braver than he used to be, that's for sure.'

Maggs was wearing Levis, Chelsea boots and a Paisley waistcoat; he had leather bands round his wrists. It occurred to Maguire that this was the guy who'd grown up with no friends and had had to deal with everyone looking at the Polaroid Jimmy Hanrahan had taken.

A kid like that could turn out any which way.

Jett O'Carroll's was heaving, and it took him ten minutes to get served. Finally he did get a pint, though, and standing at the door to avoid the scrum, he noticed the same girl he'd seen before – the one who reminded him of Eva. She was on her own, stumbling up the street and bumping into a few people along the way. Maguire saw Maggs cross from John B. Keane's and wondered if he'd been back to try and see Eva. He wasn't looking where he was going, though, and neither was the girl: they clattered into each other right there on the corner.

*

'Mary Harrington did look like Eva when she was younger,' Doyle observed. 'And that sighting was backed up by Jimmy the Poker. We did our jobs, Moss. We didn't just go after Maggs with no good reason.'

Quinn was quiet for a moment. 'You and me were still in Cork then, weren't we?'

'We were.' Doyle looked suddenly wistful. 'I remember missing the music; I remember missing the craic; and above all I remember missing the kind of porter only Eamon O'Carroll can pour.' Sitting forward now, he placed his empty glass on the coffee table. 'We're wasting time here. I'm making the call. I'll get a-hold of Murphy and we'll pick up the Finucane girl too; see what she has to say for herself.'

Ignoring him, Quinn was studying the topmost statement.

'Paddy's word backed up by Jimmy Hanrahan,' he murmured. 'Whose mother drowned and whose dad sees the dead in his kitchen.'

*

Jimmy hated the guards: he freely admitted it to anyone who asked him. He hated Joe Doyle the most because he'd given Jimmy quite the slap after he whacked the old woman with her poker.

He hated the festival – the music, at least. The only thing it did was bring a bit of cash into the place; a few cars he could've broken into if he was still in the business. But the only illegal activity he was engaged in these days was a bit of poaching when his dole money ran short. His old feller liked a bit of fresh meat, and it was nothing for Jimmy to bag a deer out of season. Where they lived, the coppers left them alone, and nobody liked to come to the house anyway – not with some half-crazed old man spouting about the souls of the dead and sprinkling holy water.

Jimmy was on the corner of the square when the Maggot showed up. 'Hey, Jimmy.' Maggs walked over to him and, with a look of contempt, Jimmy dragged on his cigarette before dropping the stub to the pavement and letting it burn.

'Maggot,' he muttered, 'what brought you out of your hole.'

'I live in Dublin now,' Maggs told him. 'I'm here with my girl-friend.'

'Are you?' Jimmy looked up and down the street. 'So where is she, the old tug? Is it the one I saw you with her just now – about as pretty as your ma's hairy arse?'

Maggs stared coldly at him. 'You're a piece of shite, aren't you, Jimmy? How's your old man? Seen your mammy yet, has he?'

'Careful,' Jimmy warned, 'don't be starting. I gave you a piece before, maggot; I can always do it again.'

'Can you, Jimmy? Can you still?' Maggs held his eye. The malice there was almost unnerving. 'I'll see you around,' he said.

'Not if I see you first.'

Jimmy did see him; he'd gone into John B.'s and was out the back having a smoke when Maggs wheeled his drunken girlfriend outside and sat her down with a pint of iced Magners.

'See, maggot,' Jimmy hissed from a darkened corner, 'told you she was a witch. Just like your mam, only this one has more teeth.'

Leaving the bar, he crossed the street to the battered old Land Rover that he had parked near the corner shop. When he tried to start it, the damn thing flooded, though, so he sat there and smoked another cigarette. Five minutes later, he saw a girl with long hair totter up from the square on a pair of ridiculously high heels. At the same moment, Maggs crossed the road. The girl bumped into him, then lurched back and sat down on the windowsill.

Tuesday 2nd September
10.25 am

No matter what Jane told him, Maggs could not shake his sense of trepidation. He hovered around the balcony outside just waiting for the guards to show up.

And show up they did.

The sound of a car turning in from Richmond Street made him jump. He watched it trundle up the service alley and come to a halt below. Jane came out of the flat and peeked over the rail. Searching for her hand, Maggs squeezed tightly.

'It'll be OK, love,' she told him. 'I'm right here with you. Nobody's going to hurt you. Nobody's going to do anything, I promise.'

Below them, a young woman got out of the passenger side. Then the driver's door was thrown open and a bulky figure in a grey suit emerged. Square-shouldered, he stood with his back to the balcony rail, his jacket open so that the leather holster was visible at his hip.

Then he turned and looked up.

The colour was gone from Maggs's face. He was hanging on to Jane's hand. Then, stumbling backwards, he raced inside the flat.

With the door closed, he pressed himself to the living room wall, and for one terrifying moment he was back in the police cell with the door ajar and the sound of footsteps in the corridor.

*

Knees to his chest, he hunched on the narrow bunk. He'd been the only prisoner since late afternoon, and now he knew why. Molly had betrayed him: the guards had leant on her, and she must've told them she'd been too drunk to know if he'd been with her or not. That's what had happened: she'd taken away his alibi, and now they wanted a confession.

He could hear heavy footsteps echoing on a stone floor. Outside his cell, the footsteps stopped, and there was silence; a silence so dense it deafened him. He saw a gloved hand push the door open. Sergeant Doyle, who'd haunted him since childhood. Heavy-set, he dwarfed Maggs. In one hand he held a pad of paper and a ballpoint pen, and in the other a copy of the Dublin phone book.

Maggs stared at him. He could smell the excitement, the adrenalin almost, pumping like a drug.

He tried to look away, he tried to ignore him, but Doyle stood like a boxer now, imperceptibly shifting his weight.

'I can hurt you, Conor,' he whispered. 'God knows I should. I know what you did to your poor mother, and I know you put Mary in your car when she was five sheets to the wind and Molly was spark out in John B.'s bar. You were pissed off because after all these years you still thought my Eva held a candle for you. Only she never has, you sick puppy, has she?'

Maggs wouldn't look at him. He sat with tears in his eyes, shaking his head from side to side.

'Paddy Maguire put you in your place, remember?' Doyle bent closer to him. 'He told you how it was that night; reminded you of exactly what kind of a little pervert you are. And Eva didn't say a word to defend you, did she? That's because she doesn't give two fucks about, you lad; she never did.'

Still Maggs shook his head.

'Mary reminded you of her, didn't she? Mary looked just like Eva used to, with that long hair and those big dark eyes. And she was so drunk she was reeling; she'd not say no to getting in your car.'

Maggs couldn't speak. He opened his mouth, but his throat was dry and he couldn't get any words out.

'You see, Molly told us the truth finally.' Doyle sat down next to him now and he scuttled for the corner like a spider.

'Molly, who was stupid enough to listen to the lies you fed her. She'd been smoking a little weed and she was pretty drunk herself, but she wasn't so out of it that she couldn't remember how it was when she came to.'

'I was in the bar,' Maggs pleaded. 'I was in the bar all the time she was outside. You can ask anyone.'

'I did, lad, I did.' Doyle worked the fingers of his right hand deeper into the fingers of the glove. 'I spoke to Jimmy Hanrahan, and he told me he saw you outside the Spar. He told me you were talking to Mary.'

'What does he know? His old man is mental, and Jimmy's the kind of scumbag who batters old women.'

'Jesus, is he?' Doyle said softly. 'The kind of scumbag that batters old women. You're some can of piss, maggot, aren't you: the feller who let his own mother neck a glug of drain cleaner.' He was silent for a moment. 'You took Mary because she looked like Eva, and Eva had really upset you that night. You took her away in that car you're so proud of. You put your hands around her throat and strangled her till you thought she was dead. Then you left her buried under the floor in the abandoned place across from Jimmy's house.'

*

He could hear the same hollow footfall now as Doyle walked the length of the concrete landing.

'We should've stayed in London,' he whimpered. 'I can't do this. I can't take it, Janey. Not again; not any more.'

'It's all right.' Smoothing his hair, Jane turned to the door, where a shadow filled the reinforced glass.

Doyle's knock was surprisingly light, and his smile looked almost genuine as she opened the door and looked defiantly into his face.

'Hello, Jane. I saw your cousin the other day,' he said. 'The Clogger sends his regards, he does. Hopes you're all right.'

'What do you want, sergeant?' she asked him.

Doyle didn't reply. He was looking over her shoulder into the living room, where he could see Maggs standing against the wall with his hands behind his back, just as he'd been in that council house the day his aunt called the guards.

*

It was Friday evening, and Doyle was down from Dublin for a weekend's fishing with Martin McCafferty. They were into a couple of pints in Jett's pub when Eamon took a call and passed the phone across the bar. When McCafferty put it down, he sank his stout and wiped his mouth with the back of his hand.

'Cora Maggs,' he said to Doyle. 'She just found her sister lying dead in the kitchen.'

Doyle accompanied him the short distance to the council estate, where an ambulance was already parked out the front. Getting out of the car, the two men crossed themselves, then walked up the path, where another, uniformed guard stood by the open front door. Cora was sitting on the stairs, her shoulders shaken with sobs.

Gently, Doyle asked her what had happened.

'I kept the drain cleaner under the sink,' she said. ''Twas in a tin, I swear it was. Mother of God, Mr Doyle, if she put it in that bottle, whatever was she thinking?'

Doyle narrowed his eyes. 'Tell me that again, Cora,' he said.

'The drain cleaner; the caustic soda, or whatever it is. We've had awful problems with the drains here, and I got the most powerful stuff I could find. From the ironmongers in Listowel. It was industrial strength, they said. 'Twas under the sink in a tin, I swear it was, or maybe . . . ' – she shook her head – 'maybe I'm losing my marbles. I don't know, but sweet Jesus, she's been known to drink the meths when she's been bad, but this . . . '

Leaving her, Doyle went into the other room, where he saw Maggs's mother lying on the floor with her legs crossed at the ankle and one arm thrown out. Beside her was an overturned wine bottle, empty now; the spilled contents had burned right through the linoleum. Martin McCafferty was looking down where her eyes were open, her tongue burned so it stuck to her teeth, burns across her cheek and lips; the expression on her face, one of absolute horror. The ambulance crew were attending her, and the paramedic, a young woman, shook her head in disbelief.

'Jesus,' she said, 'I've seen some sights in my time but . . . ' – she indicated the bottle – 'she must've tipped it down her throat without thinking. One good glug, and it wouldn't stop burning until it had gone all the way through her.' As if to underline her point, she covered the dead woman with a blanket.

It was only then that Doyle noticed Conor in the corner pressed against the wall. For a moment, he regarded him. 'Conor, do you know what happened here?' he asked. 'Did you see it?' The boy shook his head.

'Were you here?'

Again he shook her head.

'How did the stuff get in the wine bottle? Your auntie says it was in a tin.'

Still Conor did not look at him.

'Conor?'

'Mam did it,' the boy said quietly. 'The tin me auntie bought went rusty. She thought it was going to leak, so she poured it into that bottle.'

'How do you know?' Doyle asked him. 'How do you know she did that?'

Again he was silent.

'Conor, how do you know she did that?'

He shrugged. Eyes downcast, he wouldn't look at Doyle, and he wouldn't look at his mother lying prostrate under the blanket. 'I don't know,' he muttered. 'She must've told me, I suppose. I don't know. I don't remember.'

Tuesday 2nd September
10.35 am

Frank Maguire drove quickly back to the Square, Dublin's roads choked with traffic, as they always were. He had the blue light going on the roof, and now and then he'd flick on the siren. Doyle had phoned to tell him that Maggs was back in Ireland and that he was on his way to the Tom Kelly flats to pick him up. It was a breakthrough, there was no doubt about that, but Doyle had a history, and that was why Maguire was scuttling back from his briefing with the commissioner.

As he crossed the river, his phone rang. Clipping the Bluetooth earpiece in place, he answered.

'Superintendent Maguire.'

'Hello, Frank, it's Paddy.'

'Patrick, what's going on?'

'I'm on my way to Limerick,' his brother told him. 'I was with Moss last night, but I've not seen him today. Is there any news?'

His brother sighed. 'I'm afraid not – not as far as where she might be, anyway.'

'God, I was hoping you'd turn something up by now. How is

Moss this morning? He was getting through the Jameson when I saw him.'

'He's all right. He's re-looking at the Mary Harrington case.'

'Yeah, I know. He had the file with him when he got back last night. I suppose it makes sense, given the phone call.'

'He told you about that?'

'We're buddies, Frank. And I was counselling Eva, wasn't I.'

'There is a snippet of a lead,' his brother told him. 'Conor Maggs is in Dublin.'

Patrick gave a hollow laugh. 'Of course he is; I knew he would be. I'm with Doyle on this, Frankie. I saw Maggs the night Mary was abducted, remember, and he wasn't the Maggs from before. Did Moss tell you he's been on the phone to Eva since the trial? She told me he called a couple of times trying to meet up with her, but she wouldn't see him.' He was quiet for a moment and then said: 'Listen, big brother, there is something I want to ask you.'

'What's that?'

'Were you checking up on me again yesterday?'

Frank didn't reply, but he caught a glimpse of his sudden embarrassment in the rearview mirror.

'I'm thirty-eight years old, Frank. You don't need to worry about me.'

'Not on the phone, Pat, eh.'

His brother laughed. 'You don't change, do you?'

'What do you mean?'

'I mean, you're so terribly concerned about what people think: about you; about us. You and me, Frankie: where we came from; who we really are.'

'Pat, please, I just said not on the phone.'

'Nobody's listening, you idiot. Since when did Phoenix Park start bugging your mobile phone?'

'That's not the point, you know it's not. What people think

matters, Paddy. How do you suppose I've got this far without worrying about what people think?'

'You're a politician, Frank, and a consummate one at that. That's how you've got as far as you have. But listen now, would you. I'm a grown man. We're through the difficult years: you don't need to keep going into my flat.'

His brother was silent.

'You were there yesterday. You picked up my post and left it on the table. You were looking at the photo you're always telling me you despise. I know you were, Frankie. You being a copper and all, it's taught me to pick up the details.'

'Paddy, I'm not checking up on you. The truth is I had every reporter in Ireland wanting a piece of me. I needed five minutes to think, and your place was close by. Look, if you want your key back, you can have it. I only kept one for security reasons anyway.'

'OK, I understand. You've a lot on your plate just now, which is why you don't need to be worrying yourself about me. I'm just fine, Frankie. I go my own way, and I can look after myself.'

'I know you can.'

'Good, just so long as we understand each other. Everything will be fine, Frank. Everything will be fine.'

Tuesday 2nd September
10.35 am

Exhausted from forcing herself onto her knees, Eva had slithered over, and she lay in a kind of claustrophobic delirium where now and again screams of panic leapt to her throat, only to be lost in a mouth too dry to utter a sound.

She was slipping in and out of dreams; her mind wandering; thoughts; words; the *tick-tock* of that clock.

Macabre images plagued her. The blindfold had slipped, and when her eyes were open she could see cracks of light; when her eyes were closed, the darkness melted into the past. That first night with Moss in Listowel, the curry house on the corner: hot food and jugs of iced water.

*

Although Patrick was sitting opposite Corin, it was obvious he wasn't interested in her. He only had eyes for Eva, just as Moss only had eyes for Eva. Afterwards, Corin told her it didn't matter; that after all these years she was used to it. But it was embarrassing nonetheless. Eva spotted Conor through the window. He walked past with his head down, as if he didn't know they were there. Half on her feet, she watched as he crossed the square and took up a position like some kind of unwanted sentinel outside McMahon's solicitors.

'That your man again, is it?' Moss asked her. 'He seems to have it very bad for you.'

'He's all right. My Uncle Joe gets on his case all the time, but he's not that bad.'

'He's sort of got that look about him. You know, when a person thinks they've a call on somebody else.'

'I was friendly to him when we were kids, that's all.'

'Soft bitch, so she is,' Corin muttered.

Eva looked sideways at her. 'He's not a bad person, Corin. He has his moments, but he's not like people say. He's had a hard time, that's all.'

'That's not what your Uncle Joe says,' Quinn told her.

'Yeah, well my Uncle Joe thinks he's my dad these days, though he's never been married and wouldn't know the sick end of a babby from the shitty one.'

*

Awake again, the whole of her left side was numb. From the cold, from the stone or the damp soil – whatever she was lying on under the broken boards. The horror of her plight hit her suddenly: she was buried under a floor, just as poor Mary Harrington had been. Only he'd been back to look at her. She knew he had. She had seen nothing and she'd heard little save the sound of that clock, but every now and again she'd swear he was standing above her.

*

There had been quite a crowd gathered for the last match of the tour, Eva on the sidelines with her pals, cheering on the locals, although she only really had eyes for the Dublin number ten. He kicked every penalty and every conversion, and he scored an individual try when he ran it into the corner.

Man of the match, they gave him a bottle of champagne. Instead of opening it, he shoved it in his coat. Later, when everyone was deciding where they would eat, he took Eva to one side and they got in her mother's car.

Patrick watched them go. There was something in his eyes maybe – a hint of envy – and across the car park Conor watched them too. He hated rugby, hated all sports, and Eva knew he was only there because she was, and she was wondering now whether he took a masochistic pleasure in seeing her with another man.

She *was* with another man, though the reality was that she'd never been with Conor in the first place. She was with Moss Quinn from Dublin, and that first night he'd walked her home and they'd talked about his job, his flat; the opportunities for a girl up in the capital. Eva was not yet nineteen, and she was just working locally. She'd talked about college, she'd talked about redoing one of the A levels she'd flunked and perhaps going on to university. She'd known the moment he kissed her that it wasn't going to be just a fling.

They drove to the river. It was a warm night and hadn't rained in a week now – which was unheard of for this part of the country. Her mother kept a rug in the boot of the car; they spread it on the grass and Moss cracked open the champagne.

They had no glasses so they swigged straight from the bottle.

Eva could smell the water; she could smell the rushes that gathered along the bank where terns nested, and she could smell the hint of Moss's aftershave. He kissed her. He kissed her again and again, sending shivers across her skin.

He kissed the tops of her breasts through her blouse, and she could feel the flight of a single butterfly inside her chest. She let her hand slip from his shoulder to the flat of his stomach. Her blouse was off, her bra, sending a thrill through her as the breeze began to pick up. It was cooler now. No cloud tonight; the hint of a moon, perhaps.

Moments later, she was completely naked and he was kneeling, his hands, his lips, his tongue probing, caressing.

Gasping suddenly, Eva locked fingers deep in his hair.

Opening her eyes, she caught a glimpse of Conor half-hidden among shadows on the bank. She couldn't tell whether he knew she could see him, but she could: he was spying on them. She didn't say anything to Moss. She didn't call out or try to scare him off: she just lay back while Moss pressed his tongue against her.

She was toying with him and she knew it; she was punishing Conor for following them, for taking things too far. She was punishing him for his foolishness, his loneliness; for believing things that could never be. The moonlight danced on the black water; tugging off Moss's shirt, she kissed the ridge of muscles across his stomach. Then, with a glance once more to the bushes, she began to unbuckle his jeans.

*

She opened her eyes, and vividly she remembered not just Conor but Patrick. She hadn't seen him, but suddenly she'd heard him yelling out. It had all kicked off: Moss pulling on his jeans, and Eva covering up; Patrick accusing Conor, and Conor denying everything.

That had been the last time she'd seen him for ages: a few weeks later, she moved to Dublin, and though she and Moss had been married in Listowel, there had been no sign of Conor anywhere.

She was muddled now, her mind wandering, and she wasn't sure if the whole thing had been a dream or not: she and Moss, Conor and Patrick, the four of them on the banks of the river so many years ago.

She was slipping away, her eyes closing. She had no strength, and no sooner did she decipher a thought than it was lost again.

Tuesday 2nd September
10.45 am

Sitting at Quinn's desk, Frank Maguire mulled over the conversation he had had with his brother.

They had Jane Finucane waiting downstairs, and Doyle, God bless his cotton socks, had taken Maggs to the same Rathfarnham garda station where he had coaxed a confession from him.

Taking a moment to think, Maguire worked a hand across his scalp. He was trying to figure out whether to make this public – at least the fact that somebody was being questioned. If he didn't, and Maggs asked for a solicitor – which he undoubtedly would – it might look bad if that was how the news came out. As it was, he had the world's press camped across the street: they'd taken rooms in the Harcourt and other hotels.

'Superintendent?'

He looked up to see a young detective from the country at the door. A fresh-faced lad, he hardly looked old enough to have done the training.

'Detective McMichael,' the man said by way of explanation, 'from Wicklow.'

Then Maguire saw the envelope he held edgewise between two fingers.

Grabbing a couple of Kleenex, he spread them out and McMichael laid the envelope down. Behind him the doorway was full of guards. Murphy pushed her way through and was about to speak when she saw Quinn's name in bold, hand-printed capitals.

Maguire took a pair of surgical rubber gloves from a package in the top drawer, then turned to McMichael. 'Who's had contact with this, besides yourself?'

'Only the post room, sir, but they were instructed not to handle anything that was addressed to Inspector Quinn.'

Maguire peered at Murphy. 'Where is Quinn? I thought he was coming here.'

Murphy coloured slightly at the fact that he was addressing the question to her, but she looked him in the eye and told him that Quinn had gone to Rathfarnham to meet Doyle.

'Has he, by God?' Maguire muttered. 'That's all I need. Get him on the phone, would you?'

He slit the top of the envelope and withdrew a piece of lined A4 paper that was folded in half. Looking up, he saw that Murphy was still there.

'Now, Keira, please.'

Picking up the phone, she punched in the number, all the while watching the superintendent. She saw him unfold the paper and touch his lips with his tongue, a line of perspiration creeping across his brow. Quinn answered, and Murphy passed Maguire the phone.

'Moss?' Maguire said. 'This is Frank.'

'Hello, Frank. What's happening?'

'Have you spoken to Maggs yet?'

'No, but I plan to.'

'I ought to tell you to back off and have somebody else do it.'

'Frank, I'm here to keep a muzzle on Joe Doyle.'

'Listen, there's something you need to know before you go in. We've just received a note: hand-printed capitals, and addressed to you again.'

'What kind of note?'

'*Two, two, the lilywhite boys, clothe them all in green, ho, ho.*'

On the end of the phone, Quinn seemed to force a breath. 'What the hell does that mean?'

'I don't know. But a Polaroid, Moss, two phone calls and now this little message. Quite the cryptic, isn't he?'

'He's playing with us,' Quinn told him. 'Dangling me on a bit of string. The bastard: he's no intention of us ever finding Eva.'

Tuesday 2nd September
10.55am

Doyle sipped weak machine coffee from a plastic cup, watching his partner, who was on his mobile phone further along the corridor.

Waiting in the interview room, Maggs seemed to have recovered his composure. He wasn't quite the gibbering wreck he had been when he saw Doyle at the door; in fact, he'd been calm and measured all the way here in the car, and as of this moment he hadn't asked for a solicitor.

Doyle was tapping his foot and chewing on the lip of the plastic cup. 'Come on, Mossie, would you? Get off the fuckin' phone.'

As if he heard him, Quinn pocketed his mobile and walked back down the corridor. He told Doyle about the note.

'Lilywhite boys,' Doyle said. 'What the hell is all that about?'

'It's not about anything,' Quinn stated grimly. 'It's all bullshit, designed to give you and me the run-around.' At the door, he paused. 'Did he change his mind about the lawyer?'

Doyle shook his head.

'Are you happy about how we're going to play this?'

'I'd be happier bouncing him off the wall. '

'Course you would, but that's not going to get us anywhere.' With a shake of his head, Quinn pushed open the door.

Maggs was sitting at the table looking pensive. He glanced at the tape recorder and the video camera, and then at the two police officers.

He smiled nervously at Doyle. 'Don't take this the wrong way, sergeant,' he said, 'but could we make sure we film this interview, please? You told me I'm not under arrest and I don't need anyone with me, but there are two of you and one of me, and we have a bit of a history, don't we.'

'It's being taped, Conor, don't worry.' Quinn sat down opposite him. 'And you're right: you're not under arrest; not at the moment. Jane told us you were with her on Sunday night.'

Maggs sat up straighter now. 'And you believe her? You're not going to try and persuade her she's lying, like you did the last time?'

Pursing his lips, Quinn cast a look at the digital clock on the tape recorder. 'The sergeant thinks she's lying,' he said. 'She's Johnny Clogs' cousin, and that – in Doyle's black book – makes her a liar by nature.'

'It's in the genes,' Doyle added.

'He also believes you murdered Mary Harrington,' Quinn went on, 'and the fact that you claim he beat the confession out of you has no bearing on the truth of anything.'

Maggs raised his eyebrows. 'That sounds like Sergeant Doyle. No doubt he still believes I killed my mother too. And while we're at it, I'm sure he thinks I was giving myself a hand-job when I saw you and Eva down by the river.' He seemed to grow in confidence. 'But that wasn't me, Moss. That was Patrick Maguire.'

Quinn stared at him and, with a slow nod, Maggs added: 'Have you never asked yourself what he was doing there? Have you never thought it just a mite coincidental that Patrick should turn up like he did and start lipping off?' He looked bitter suddenly. 'I saw them together the night of the *fleadh cheoil*, remember: long before the pair of you made it down. I could see how he was then, all loved-up sitting next to Eva; wishing it was him that had married her instead of you. The truth of it is I could see how it was that very first night in the pub when he had to make do with Corin.' With a shake of his head, he added: 'Moss, Patrick's had a thing for your wife for almost as long as I have.'

Now he turned to Doyle. 'I admit it: I did have a thing for her, and when I was a kid perhaps I was guilty of misreading the signs. But she was good to me, and as God is my witness, I've never done anything but cherish the girl. I'd never do anything to harm her.'

He placed the flat of his hand on the table. 'Years ago, I gave her a necklace.'

'I know you did.' Quinn was looking closely at him now.

'My auntie paid for it because I was only ten. I told her that of all the people in the whole school, the only one who ever had a kind word for me was Eva.' Tears glistened as he spoke. 'You know how it was with my mam. Jimmy the Poker lost his virginity to her. He paid her for sex so she could buy booze, then took a picture that he showed around the playground.'

'Conor,' Quinn interrupted him. 'We need to talk about Eva. I know you gave her the necklace: it was taken from her this past Sunday.'

Maggs stared at him now, his mouth open, and a hint of spittle dragging his lip. 'Taken?'

Quinn nodded. 'It was torn off; we found links from the chain on my son's grave. Sunday was the first anniversary of his death, and I think Eva was there because she had to have some time alone with him.

'I want you to help us,' Quinn told him. 'I want you to help me. I know you think I stole her from you, but that's not how it was.'

Maggs nodded slowly. 'I know that, Moss. I understand. It's why

I was quite happy to come and talk to you now; it's why I don't need a solicitor. I'm not a kid any more, and I don't dwell on the past.'

He threw a short glance at Doyle, who was watching every move, every expression, every jerk of his head.

'I'm not lying, sergeant.'

'Conor,' Quinn said, 'we've received a photograph, a Polaroid: a picture of a stone lying on a patch of sand.'

'Jimmy Hanrahan,' Maggs curled his lip. 'He was the one with the camera.'

He bowed his head, working a palm across his face, then looked once more at Quinn. 'I didn't kill Mary Harrington. You hit me with what had happened to her so many times: you told me all the gory stuff about how she was, and how she'd jerk like a chicken when she was unconscious. You told me all that, and I wrote it down like you made me.' He gestured to Doyle. 'I didn't kill her, Sergeant. No matter what Molly tells you, the fact is, she was so shit-faced she didn't know if I was there or not.'

'That's not what she said.'

'It's what she said before you started threatening her.'

'Nobody threatened her, and she only said what she did because you told her to.'

'No.' Maggs shook his head. 'That isn't how it was. The fact is, Molly only changed her story after I stopped seeing her. She was hurt, upset; she was pissed off enough to want to get even with me.

'Mr Doyle,' he stated, 'I did not kill Mary. I barely spoke to Mary. The only people you had to tell you otherwise were Jimmy Hanrahan, who took pictures of my alcoholic mother when she was naked, and Paddy Maguire, who made claims about me to cover up what he was doing himself. He didn't happen upon me that night, I happened upon him.'

He turned to Quinn now. 'That's all you ever had, isn't it? My barrister told me there wasn't a trace of physical evidence linking me to

Mary Harrington. All you had was a girlfriend I dumped, and two fellers who hated my guts. The reason you went after me was personal. You should admit it. You wanted it to be me; you both did.' He sat back in the chair. 'But that's all right. Maybe you'll believe me now. Maybe, finally, I have the chance to set the record straight, and just maybe I can clear my name.' Again he looked at Doyle. 'My name's been sullied, Mr Doyle. The judge threw the case out, but he didn't exonerate me. I'm a man of God, I'm a pastor soon to have my own flock, and the people who follow me need to know that my character is beyond reproach. That's why I'm here now; that's why I'll help you. I want to clear my name.'

Quinn looked sideways at Doyle. He looked at the clock and then peered across the table.

'Where's my wife, Conor? Where's Eva?'

Maggs's eyebrows shot up.

'Where is she?' Quinn asked him. 'The clock is ticking, you told me yourself, remember. *Tick-tock. Tick-tick-tock.*' Brow furrowed, he was staring hard at him.

'I'm sorry,' Maggs said, looking helpless. 'I have no idea what you're talking about.'

'And then of course there was Mary.'

'I just told you, I didn't kill Mary.'

'*Mary, Mary, quite contrary, or so the story goes. A maggot in her head, that's what they said, but only Mary knows.*' Quinn cocked his head to one side. 'Was that you trying to tell me that somebody else killed Mary? Was that you trying to tell me that if I find that somebody, I'll find my wife?'

Maggs looked bewildered. 'Now you've lost me completely.'

'If it was you, then you know where she is, don't you? Where is she? You love her, I know you do. You wouldn't want to hurt her.'

Quinn's gaze shifted once more to the clock. 'Time is running out,' he said. 'There are only a few hours left. Mary died of thirst:

you know that. She may have been partially strangled, but she died because she had nothing to drink. Seventy-two hours, and that's pretty much it. A person can starve for days, weeks even, and still survive, but much more than seventy-two hours without water and there's no coming back. Eva is tied up somewhere and she's thirsty, Conor, thirsty. Before long, she'll look just as Mary did when we finally found her.' He leant across the table.' Eva, Conor; little Eva from catechism; the girl you gave the necklace to.' He cocked his head to one side then and looked quizzically at him. 'Why did you take it back? You gave it to her; it was a gift. It wasn't yours to take back.'

'I didn't take it back,' Maggs said quietly. 'I wasn't there, Moss. I had nothing to do with any of it.'

'You phoned her, didn't you?' Quinn pressed him hard now. 'After the trial collapsed, you called her on the phone. What did you want? What did you say to her? She was wearing the necklace at your trial. Did you think it was a sign: a secret symbol, a code to tell you that it was you she wanted all along, and not me? I bet you just loved it when you found out she and I were separated. Did you call her because you knew I wasn't there? She flipped you off, didn't she? You finally found out that even when I'm not around, it isn't you she wants.'

Maggs was silent. Arms across his chest, he regarded Quinn evenly. 'I'm sorry,' he said. 'I'm really sorry this has happened. But it's nothing to do with me; I was with Jane on Sunday night.'

'That's what she says,' Quinn told him. 'But then that was what Molly said too, until you thought it was safe to dump her.'

'Exactly.' Maggs leered at him suddenly. 'I dumped her, and she was that pissed off she set me up with the guards. Come on, Moss, you've heard the old saying about hell having no fury. Of course you have: it happened to you when you couldn't find who killed your son.'

For a moment, Quinn was taken aback. He sat there stiffly in the chair.

Still Maggs held his eye. 'Women are like that: they'll find a way of making everything your fault. You should know that; you, of all people, should know it better than anyone.'

For a few moments, Quinn regarded him. And then he got to his feet. 'OK, Conor,' he said, 'that's all for now. Thanks for coming in.'

Maggs stared incredulously at him. 'You mean I can go?'

Quinn jerked a thumb at his partner. 'Would you rather I tuck you up in a nice quiet cell and send your man along?'

Tuesday 2nd September
11.25 am

From the window, Doyle watched Maggs saunter out the front door, where hordes of news people were waiting. Needless to say, he seemed happy to pause and speak to them.

'I can't believe you let the bastard go,' he muttered.

Quinn was standing next to him. 'Phone Martin McCafferty in Kerry,' he instructed. 'Have him bring a team to Jimmy Hanrahan's house and see what they can find.'

'Jimmy the Poker? What for?'

'I told you, we're walking through it again. There was one thing Maggs said in there that might've made some sense.'

'You mean about Jimmy being the one with the camera?'

Doyle nodded.

'OK,' he said, 'I'll phone Martin. But I tell you, boy: this has nothing to do with Jimmy.'

Quinn drove back to Harcourt Square. As he pulled up at the barrier, the car was swamped by reporters. Parked underground, he smoked half a cigarette and thought about Maggs, sitting across the table looking as calm and confident as he'd ever seen him.

Pinching the end of the cigarette, he shoved it back in the box, then went up to the incident room. In his office, he closed the door, and on the far side of the desk Frank Maguire steepled his fingers. 'So what do you know?' he said.

Quinn shook his head. 'I let him go. No sense in holding him. There was nothing to charge him with, and of course he denied he had anything to do with it.'

'What do you think?'

'I don't know.' Quinn glanced up as Doyle strode in, snuffbox in his hand and some of the red dust shading his lapel.

'He'll tell you it's Maggs,' Quinn went on, 'but then of course he's the nose for it.'

'That's right, I do,' Doyle told him. 'He's our man, Moss. There's no doubt about it.'

'Did you speak to McCafferty?' Quinn asked him.

They told the superintendent what Maggs had said about Jimmy Hanrahan and Patrick.

''Tis funny,' Doyle observed, 'but I don't remember any of this being relevant when we were investigating Mary's death.'

'My brother, you mean?' Maguire looked quizzical. 'Maggs's version of events?'

'Not just your brother, Frank, but Jimmy the Poker.' With a glance at Quinn, he added: 'Clearly none of us thought it very important.'

Quinn ignored him. 'It's just maggot-speak. Even if he didn't do it, he's never seen the world as normal people do.'

'So what now?' Doyle said. 'We wait for the Kerry guards to give the Hanrahan place a spin and come up with sweet fuck all? She's my niece, Moss: you should let me take a piece of him, then we'd know for sure.'

Quinn rolled his eyes to the ceiling. 'What if he's not lying? Has that ever occurred to you? What if he doesn't know? What if he didn't do it?'

'He is. He does and he did.' Doyle turned for the door. 'Remember,' he said, 'all the time we're sitting around with a thumb shoved up our collective arse, Eva is slipping away.'

When he was gone, Quinn shook his head wearily. 'I love him to death, really I do. But sometimes, Jesus, I swear he's only half a door.' He worked the heel of a palm against his eyes.

'What if he's wrong and I'm right? What if Maggs didn't take Eva, and what if he didn't kill Mary?'

'That's a lot of what-ifs, Moss,' Maguire suggested. 'And it doesn't get us any nearer finding her.'

On his feet again, Quinn paced the floor. 'What if it was pure prejudice that put him in the frame?'

'Are you telling me you think it was?'

'My wife thought it was. And as he himself just pointed out, we didn't have a shred of physical evidence.'

'He lied about talking to Mary.'

'I know he did. Paddy saw him, and Paddy I believe. Jimmy Hanrahan I don't know: he's a scrote, and he and Maggs have never seen eye to eye. But Maggs was scared, Frank: he knew what people thought about him, and a long time ago Doyle let him know he believed his mother's death was no accident.' He spread his palms. 'What would you do if you were him and your girl had had such a skin-full she'd repeat anything you told her. Think about it from his point of view: to admit to even talking to Mary was to invite the devil in.'

Maguire showed him the note from the post room. 'What do you make of this?'

'It's just more cryptic bullshit. Like I said on the phone, whoever this is, he's playing with us.'

The door opened then, and Murphy put her head round. 'Inspector,' she said, 'Jane Finucane is still downstairs. I've interviewed her, and she's sticking to her story. Do you want me to see if I can find Molly Parkinson?'

'Molly?' Quinn arched one eyebrow. 'What for?'

'I thought she might be able to help. I mean, we do think Jane is lying, don't we?'

'I don't know. I haven't spoken to her.'

'Sergeant Doyle thinks she's lying.'

'Of course he does: Doyle thinks everyone's lying.'

'It was just a thought,' Murphy said, 'but Molly lied to begin with. Then she came to court and testified. She would have seen Jane then, wouldn't she? Maybe she can enlighten her, I don't know. But if Jane is covering for him and we can prove it . . . '

'It's a good idea,' Maguire told her. 'See if you can locate her.'

When Murphy had gone, Quinn shot half a smile at his boss. 'At the risk of sounding like Doyle,' he said, 'wouldn't it be better to drop Jane off at the moorings? Half an hour with her cousin, Frank; we'd soon know if she was lying.'

Tuesday 2nd September
12.15 pm

Jimmy Hanrahan was in the shed cleaning his guns. He had a second-hand Winchester rifle he used for deer, together with a twelve-bore under-and-over shotgun.

The old man was in the house hollering his head off. Last night had been bad: he'd come down and there was the devil cutting cards with a woman he swore was Jimmy's mother. He was pleading, begging for her soul, and he was so loud that Jimmy had to get up, and the only way he could calm his father down was to tell him that he could see her too, and it wasn't his mother.

All morning, the old lunatic had been muttering about it, and he was still muttering when Jimmy went back to the house. He was in the lounge sitting in his chair, what little hair he had sticking to the powdery white scalp. He wore his pyjama bottoms and an old jumper, a pair of woollen socks.

'Sprinkle the water, son,' he muttered. 'Your mother, God rest her. I know what you said, but I swear 'twas her. Sprinkle the water, and maybe she'll have some peace.' He shifted uneasily in his seat, making the sign of the cross again and again and again.

His son looked wearily at him. 'Do you want a cup of tea, Dad?' he asked him.

Again his father crossed himself. ''Twas your fault.' He jabbed a finger without turning his head from the TV screen that was blathering away in the corner. 'Without what you done, she'd be here, so she would, and I'd not have Beelzebub at my kitchen table.'

'For fuck's sake, would you listen to yourself?' Jimmy yelled suddenly. 'There's nothing there. There's never been anything there.' He tapped the side of his head. 'It's the drink, Dad: the gin. You're bally; mad; loco.'

'The shame it was,' the old man went on. 'Her own boy, her only boy taking a poker to that poor old woman. She blamed me, I know she did, but it was your fault they found her floating out there with her eyes gone to the fish.'

With a bitter shake of his head, Jimmy turned away, telling himself that if it wasn't for the money, he'd have taken the old fool out to meet his mother years ago.

The sound of a car made him look up; through the kitchen window, he saw three marked police vehicles pulling up. Then half a dozen uniforms were on the path, and Jimmy opened the door.

'Well, well,' he said, 'I've the old feller shooting his mouth off, and now the shades are on my doorstep. Come on in, why don't you? Sit yourselves down and play a few hands of cards with the devil.'

Standing aside, he ushered them in. His father turned round from his chair in the living room.

'Mother of God,' he muttered, 'what have you gone and done this time?'

'Shut your noise, will you?' Stepping across the kitchen, Jimmy slammed the door. Then he turned to the uniformed inspector, a tall man with sandy hair and kindly eyes. 'So, Mr McCafferty, is it me you're wanting, or have you come for the old feller?'

Tuesday 2nd September
12.30 pm

Murphy headed across the river to Mountjoy Square. The houses here were four-storey terraces; she rang the bell at an attic flat she'd been to a couple of times before. She waited, gazing across to the tree-lined square. The buzzer sounded, and she asked if Molly was in.

'Who wants her?' the voice came back.

'Is that you, Molly?'

'Who's that?'

'Detective Keira Murphy. Can I come in?'

For a moment there was silence, then: 'What do you want?'

'I need to speak to you. I need to speak to you about Conor Maggs.'

She climbed the stairs to the top-floor flat, where Molly let her in. The place was a mess; four girls sharing a handful of rooms; there were clothes dumped in piles all over the place. One of Molly's flat-mates stood at an ironing board in front of the TV; she looked up with a nervous smile. Murphy considered her for a moment, then suggested they go somewhere a little quieter.

Reluctantly, Molly led the way into a bedroom, where twin beds lay unmade and makeup was scattered on the dressing table.

'How's business, Molly?' Murphy asked her. She touched the ends of her hair. 'I might ask you to do mine one of these days; I've not got anyone regular.'

Molly had a mobile hairdressing business, driving from client to client. 'Business is all right,' she stated, a little irritably.

'Look,' Murphy told her, 'we'd not bother you again after what happened, but . . . '

'A guard's wife has been abducted, and you're looking at my ex-boyfriend.' Molly shook her head bemusedly. 'I've never seen anything like it; I swear there are more coppers on the street than there are people. I was listening to the news yesterday, and they were even talking about it in the Dáil.'

'It's about as serious as it gets,' Murphy told her.

'And you've Conor for it, have you?'

'We spoke to him, but there's nothing we can charge him with. At least not yet.'

'So what do you want with me?'

Murphy perched on the bed beside her. 'Do you remember Jane Finucane?'

'The girl at the trial? Of course.'

'She claims he was with her on Sunday night around the time we think Eva Quinn was abducted.'

'And you don't believe her?'

Murphy made a face. 'We didn't believe *you*.'

'No, well, I wasn't very convincing, was I? But then I'd drunk half of Kerry by the time it all kicked off.'

'Conor claims you only changed your story through spite.'

Molly laughed. 'Because he dumped me: that's a laugh. I was about to dump him, guard: that's the truth of it. Anyway, the judge threw it out, so me changing my story did no good at all, did it?'

'You told the truth, that's what mattered.'

'Right, I told the truth. So what do you want from me now?' Molly asked her.

'I want you to talk to his girlfriend. Tell her what happened. Tell her how he made sure you gave him his alibi. If he's done the same with her, I want her to ask herself why. I want her to understand that another woman's life is at stake, only this time we might be able to save her.'

She patted Molly on the knee. 'Do you think you can do that?'

Sitting in the passenger seat of Murphy's car, Molly could see the flashing blue light reflected in shop windows. She'd met Maggs here in Dublin back when she was working in a regular salon close to St Mary's Cathedral. He had come in with his shaggy black mop and dark eyes. He was a quiet soul, but well spoken. He was about thirty-five – a lot older than her – and she'd just split from a much younger lad who worked in the power station at Poolbeg.

There was something about him; he was cultured compared to most of the men she'd dated. She didn't see him for a while, then six weeks later he came back for another haircut and he had two tickets for the All-Ireland football semi and asked her to go with him.

*

Back at his flat afterwards, they drank a bottle of wine sitting together on the sofa. They made small talk, and whereas before he'd been fairly chatty, now he seemed almost nervous.

Finally he kissed her.

He was trembling: a thirty-five-year-old-man, and he was trembling. There was something engaging about that: he had a boyishness, a sense of caution about him; a sense of uncertainty. They had a few more drinks, then she slipped his hand inside her shirt and pressed his palm to her breast. She could feel the tension in his touch: she could see the erection beginning to strain at his zipper. She took him out, and he came right there in her hand.

Face scarlet, he was on his feet and muttering a panicked apology.

'Hey,' she said, 'it's all right. Really, don't worry about it: it's OK, Conor. I'm sure it happens to lots of men.'

His vulnerability attracted her; there was something about the way he looked – his physical frame, perhaps –that made her want to mother him – and Molly had never wanted to mother anyone.

'I've got something,' she told him. 'Something that'll chill you out. And later we can do it again.' She had a little grass she'd scored a few nights before, and she fetched it now and rolled a modest joint.

'It's all right,' she reassured him, 'I don't mind. We'll just chill out and you can relax and then we can try again.'

A few weeks later, he took her to the music festival in his home town in Kerry. He'd rented a caravan above the cliffs at Ballybunion.

Before they went into town, Molly sat in the evening sunshine smoking dope and drinking wine. By the time they got into the car, she'd drunk a whole bottle and was pretty merry. Conor was silent, and she was beginning to think the quietness she'd been attracted to at first might actually be a little irritating.

In fact, she'd been debating whether to come at all: as the weekend grew closer, he seemed to have more and more on his mind, as if he was expecting something and wasn't sure how to handle it.

'So will she be there, then?' she asked him, as they headed towards town.

In the driver's seat of the old Granada, he stiffened. She'd hit a nerve: there *was* someone; that was what had been bothering him. 'Just lately, you've been even more subdued than you normally are. You ought to learn to chill out, Conor. All that pent-up anxiety in a man your age: it'll be the death of you.'

He turned his head and stared at her. 'And all that shit you smoke,' he said. 'That'll be the death of you.' In that moment, she realised that she may not have known him at all. But she'd had a few to drink, and the dope had dulled her senses enough that she just kept going.

'Who is she, then? An old flame you don't want to see?'

He smiled coldly. 'You've got it wrong. There's no one, Molly; I mean, no one that matters. I know lots of people, of course I do: I lived here for the first twenty years of my life.'

'There's someone, I can tell. Someone you either want to see or don't want to see, I can't decide which.' They were pulling into town and already plenty of people were on the street. Conor nodded at a scrawny-looking man getting out of a battered Land Rover.

'There's someone I don't want to see,' he stated. 'Jimmy the fucking Poker.'

They moved from bar to bar and tent to tent listening to different kinds of music. In John B. Keane's bar, Molly went out the back for a cigarette and downed a couple of pints of cider. Conor was inside, where she'd left him sitting at a table by the window. She'd noticed that wherever they went, he always wanted to be near the door or the window. He kept glancing up and down the street. He was anxious; excited, maybe, about seeing someone – and it sure as hell wasn't Jimmy the Poker.

And then she felt his presence. When she looked up, he was behind her; she'd not even seen him coming.

'Are you all right?' he asked her. 'Can I get you another drink?' She had a pint of Magners still in front of her, and she was already bleary-eyed.

'I've a full glass,' she told him.

'Are you coming in?'

'I'm staying here.' She was slurring her words. 'I need the air, and I can still hear the music.'

She'd passed out. Closing her eyes to stop her head swimming, she'd woken up God knows how long later. She was hunched in a corner against the wall. Getting to her feet, she left the still-brimming glass and stumbled into the bar. It was packed; everyone singing; the music pounding in her head. She looked for Conor but, not able to find him, she picked her way awkwardly out to the street.

There was no sign, though, so she went back to the bar. Outside, she smoked cigarettes. Some time later – she couldn't remember how long – she looked up as he tapped her on the shoulder.

Tuesday 2nd September
12.45 pm

The Kerry police were searching Jimmy's house. His father was moulded into his chair, his arms tight around his chest, and he was shouting at anyone who walked across the room. Jimmy was in the kitchen smoking roll-ups.

The place was filthy; a chipped table and metal chairs; dog bowls that hadn't been washed in weeks. There were dishes piled in the sink, and the smell of grease permeated the whole house.

'Your father seems to be getting worse, Jimmy,' McCafferty observed quietly. 'Maybe you ought to think about getting him some proper care.'

'Ah, you'd like that, wouldn't you? Get the nutter to the nuthouse and give the neighbourhood a bit of peace. Would you look around you, guard?' Jimmy gestured through the window to the open fields, the estuary and the ruins of Carrigafoyle. 'There *is* no fuckin' neighbourhood.'

'Calm down, lad. I was only suggesting.'

'Yeah, well, don't. He's my dad, and I've been taking care of him since you dragged my mam from the water.'

At that moment, a younger officer came padding down the stairs carrying an old shoebox, which he placed on the table.

'Found this lot in your man's room.' He jerked a thumb at Jimmy.

McCafferty considered the contents: a whole stack of Polaroids, together with the camera that had been used to take them. 'What's all this, Jim?' he said.

Jimmy rolled his eyes to the ceiling. 'What does it look like?'

'That's a lot of photos.'

'So? Is there some law against that then now, is there?'

Stepping outside, McCafferty gazed across the water. Taking his mobile, he phoned Dublin.

'Joseph,' he said when Doyle answered, 'Martin McCafferty here. I thought you'd like to know we've found a Polaroid camera.'

Tuesday 2nd September
12.50 pm

Quinn was at the door to his office when Doyle came in to tell him the Kerry police were on their way up with Jimmy Hanrahan and a Polaroid camera.

A breakthrough, finally. Quinn's heart began to beat that little bit faster: *A maggot in her head, that's what they said, but only Mary knows.*

Was Jimmy Hanrahan capable of coming up with a line like that? Jimmy, who'd dished out thirty-two stitches to an old woman before his mother drowned and his father disappeared into the hellish prison of his own drink-sodden conscience. Jimmy, who'd wasted no time in blabbing to them how he'd seen Maggs with Mary Harrington and who lived within spitting distance of where they found her body.

He moved to the window. Hands in his pockets and shoulders stretched, he spoke without looking round. 'Did it ever bother you that we had no physical evidence, Doyler?' he asked.

'No fibres or anything from that old Granada?'

'No, it didn't.' Doyle exhaled audibly. 'We had what we had, and we did our jobs accordingly.'

Crossing to his desk, Quinn opened Mary's file and began to flick through the pages.

'Jesus, you're obsessed with that now, aren't you?' Doyle commented.

'The way you are with the Maggot, you mean?'

'I know a guilty man when I see one.'

'So you keep telling me, and I suppose if we can prove it this time, it'll vindicate you being in that cell.'

'Moss,' Doyle said, 'I'm not looking for vindication, and both you and Frank knew fine what was going on that night.' He looked at his watch. 'Eva's been gone almost two days. It's the Maggot, for Christ's sake. Let's pick him up again, and this time let *me* ask him.'

Quinn didn't reply, and for a few minutes there was silence, with Doyle restless at the window and him restless at his desk.

'Do you really think it might be Jimmy then?' Doyle shook his head. 'I can't see it; for the life of me, I cannot see it at all.'

'He gave us Maggs, didn't he?' Quinn stated. 'And he was quite capable of beating an old woman over the head for a few quid. He'd have known we'd be looking at him, so he made damn sure we knew Maggs had spoken to her. Everyone in Listowel knew how it was with us, and Maggs and Jimmy the Poker was no exception. Let's face it, we didn't let them down, did we? We went after him with everything we had. All we needed was the right word, and we got it both from Jimmy and from Patrick Maguire.'

'And we got *him*, Moss: we found out the Maggot lied through his teeth.'

'He could've lied just because he was frightened.' Quinn looked hard at him then. 'Do you not think – standing back now, I mean – that the pair of us might not have been just a little bit prejudiced?'

Doyle sat down. 'I don't know,' he said. 'I suppose it's possible. But Jimmy the Poker? He lives in Kerry. Was he even up here on Sunday night? And if he was, what the hell's he ever had against Eva?'

'I don't know, but when he gets here we can ask him.'

Quinn looked at his watch. He could feel the tension eating away at him. 'You know, Eva and I argued about Maggs,' he said.

He could see her in front of the Victorian fireplace telling him pointedly that he was wrong. And for all the man's failings, his misconceptions, there was no way Conor could kill anyone. He had no history of violence, no matter what her uncle claimed. 'She told me straight it wasn't him: she said that you and I were going after him for personal reasons, and she'd lost respect for the both of us because of it.'

Doyle considered the hive of frenetic activity outside in the incident room. 'So if it isn't Maggs,' he said, 'if this is someone else, what's with all the cryptic bollocks, then?'

Quinn lifted his palms. 'Maybe he's pissed off, Doyler: a little indignant or something. Maybe he's telling us that we have to look again; maybe he's telling us we got it wrong with Mary and if we find who really killed her, we'll find Eva.'

Doyle lifted one eyebrow. 'So the lilywhite boys then; they're from the poem, aren't they: 'Green Grow the Rushes O'. *Two, two, the lilywhite boys, clothe them all in green, ho ho.*'

'I thought about that,' Quinn stated. 'The "clothe in green" part, at least. I don't know, but it could be something to do with being buried, maybe; some connection with what happened to Mary.'

'Mary wasn't clothed in green though, was she? There was no turf on her, Moss: she was hidden under the floor.' Doyle considered for a moment. 'Kildare, maybe,' he muttered. 'A lilywhite is what they call someone who comes from Kildare.'

Logging on to the internet, Quinn called up a search engine, then typed the words 'Green Grow the Rushes O' and hit 'Enter'.

Doyle leant on the desk next to him.

Going to the Wikipedia entry, Quinn read from the introduction: '"The song is referred to as 'The twelve prophets or the carol of the twelve numbers'. *I'll sing you one, ho, green grow the rushes, o. What is your one, ho? One is one and all alone and ever more shall be so.*'' He read to himself for a moment, then all at once he glanced up. 'Look at this,' he stated: "The phrase '*Green grow the rushes, o*' sounds sufficiently out of place that one is inclined to ascribe it to the same origin as '*Fine flowers in the valley*', which is a similar type of line and can be found in one version of the ballad "The Cruel Mother".'

'Click on it,' Doyle said.

'What?'

' "The Cruel Mother": click on it.'

Quinn did as he suggested, and another page popped up.

'A woman gives birth to one or two illegitimate children (usually sons). She kills them and buries them. Going home, she sees children playing, and says that if they were hers, she would dress them in fine garments and otherwise take care of them. The children tell her that when they were hers, she did not dress them so but murdered them. They tell her she will be damned for it.'

Doyle flared his nostrils. 'Maggs was an illegitimate son,' he said, 'whose mother made his life a misery.'

'She did,' Quinn agreed. 'The piece talks about one or *two* illegitimate sons though, doesn't it?' He thought about that for a moment. Then, going back to the previous page, he read the original poem again. Another line caught his eye and it bothered him; it bothered him a great deal.

Seven for the seven stars in the sky; or seven for the seven who went to heaven.

He glanced through the open doorway to the incident room, where, on Murphy's desk, the files they were supposed to be taking to Naas were piled one on top of the other.

'Seven for the seven who went to heaven,' he murmured. 'Six women are dead, Doyle, and one more is missing.'

Tuesday 2nd September
1.15 pm

The interview room was small and cramped, and Jane Finucane was sitting with her hands clasped as Murphy showed Molly in. For a moment, the two women regarded each other carefully, the atmosphere a little awkward.

'I'm not sure that you were ever introduced,' Murphy said. 'Jane Finucane, this is Molly Parkinson.'

'I saw you at Conor's trial,' Jane said. 'You testified against him.'

'That's right, I did.'

'What're you doing here?'

Molly didn't reply. She looked at Murphy for encouragement.

'I thought you girls might like to have a chat,' Murphy explained. 'After all, you've quite a bit in common.'

Taking a seat, Molly looked a bit nervous. 'I think the guard is talking about Conor, Jane. I know you were with him at the trial: I saw you on the steps when he was giving that press conference. Are you still seeing him now?'

Jane nodded. 'We got together when he was on remand. He sent an open letter telling everyone what had happened to him and how it led to such a dramatic conversion. I belong to a church group, you see, and his letter touched not just me but all of us.'

'So you wrote back to him?'

'Yes, then I visited him in Mountjoy.'

'And that's when you fell for him?'

'It was pretty instant.'

'I suppose it can be like that,' Molly agreed. 'I remember I wanted to mother him, and that isn't like me at all. But he was always a little vulnerable. I remember when he came to the salon, I saw it even then. I'm a hairdresser, you see, and Conor came in one day. He didn't say much, but there was something about him that really seemed to get to me.'

'He's genuine,' Jane told her. 'That's a rare quality these days. There's no second-guessing with Conor: what he says is what he means.'

'He appears genuine,' Molly told her. 'But the night Mary Harrington was murdered, he told me what to say.'

'You mean he had to remind you. I heard your testimony, Molly, and Conor and I talked about it. We have no secrets. He told me he had to tell you what happened because you'd had such a load to drink you couldn't remember anything.'

'I'd had a few, it's true.'

'You passed out completely.'

'And when I woke up, he wasn't there.'

'That's what you say.'

'It's how it was, Jane. I've nothing to gain by lying to you, he's already walked from the Four Courts. The fact is, when I woke up, Conor wasn't there.'

Jane sat for a few minutes digesting what she had heard, then she spoke to Murphy.

'Look, guard,' she said, 'I appreciate how serious this is, but I also know how you coppers work. I've a second cousin who's right up there on your wish-list, and I've been spoken to by the guards more times than I care to remember. When someone goes missing, you're under pressure for a quick fix. It really doesn't matter who you get, so long as you get someone.'

Molly looked across the table at her then. 'I suppose if you think like that, it makes it easier to give a man his alibi,' she said. 'I suppose it's OK to lie if you think you're in love. As far as you're concerned, the police set him up once, which means they must be trying to do it again.'

She glanced at Murphy briefly. 'The thing is, I never had any of that. When I was going out with him, I'd no experience of how sneaky coppers can be, and I didn't think I was in love. I was just so shit-faced I'd no earthly idea what was going on. Conor told me there wasn't a minute we weren't together, save when he went to get me some fags. But the guards told me he'd been spotted by two different people talking to Mary Harrington, and after a bit the reality that a girl had been murdered came home to me. It was serious; very serious. Not just because of the killing, but because if I got it wrong, I might implicate a man who had nothing to do with it. I thought long and hard, believe me: I made myself work it through again and again, until I thought I'd got it right. I went back over it after me and Conor broke up, and what I told the guards was that I couldn't account for where I was myself that night, let alone anyone else. It was the truth, Jane. You heard me testify, and I'd have thought that to someone like you, there isn't much that's more important than the truth.'

Pushing back her chair, she got up. 'That's all I've got to say: a woman is missing, just as Mary was – only this time, she could still be found alive. Because I couldn't remember to begin with, I thought it best to go along with what Conor told me, and that's why I gave him his alibi. I wasn't lying, I just didn't remember.' She broke off then and looked Jane in the eye.

'You, on the other hand, weren't drunk on Sunday night, so if he wasn't with you, you're lying – and given all that's happened, maybe you should ask yourself why.'

Tuesday 2nd September
2 pm

In the visitors' reception at Limerick Prison, Patrick Maguire was signing in. He knew the desk sergeant well: an old friend of his brother, he'd come down to the house they owned in Ballybunion when the racing festival was on.

'Is there any word on Quinn's wife?' the sergeant asked him. 'I've been listening to the news, but it seems the media doesn't know a whole lot.'

'My brother is running the show,' Maguire told him, 'and I imagine he's keeping things pretty close to his chest. He's not a believer in investigation by television, John. He's no time for the pundits who follow a thing blow by blow, broadcasting what the guards are doing almost before they do it.'

'No, and I don't blame him either.'

'Having said that,' Maguire went on, 'I think that what you're getting on the TV is just about all there is at the moment.'

'Have they no idea where she is?'

'They know she's not in the canals or the Liffey, at least, which is something.'

'Well, when you see Moss Quinn, tell him I send my best.'

'I'll do that, John. Bless you.'

Maguire was visiting Willie Moore, a twenty-three-year-old who was doing seven years for dealing heroin on the streets of Limerick. He had angular features, both his ears were pierced, and he had a tattoo of the three-legged Isle of Man triskelion on his right arm. Maguire had first spoken to him a couple of years ago when he was on remand. He was not only very intelligent, but also ice cold and calculating in his opinions. Despite his young age, he was old beyond his years: he'd formed a particular view of how the world worked, and rightly or wrongly, he was living by it.

He was from a middle-class family and had been well educated, but had dropped out of university to take up a life of crime. During their first few meetings, he'd explained to Patrick that he had looked at various careers and thought about how much money he could make from them, then compared it with what he could make as a heroin dealer.

A warder brought him into the interview room. The first thing Moore did was glance at the clock, then check the time with the warder's wristwatch.

'Just making sure I get my full hour, Mr McShane,' he said.

'You'll get your hour, Willie, don't worry about that.' The warder nodded to Maguire. 'Patrick, good to see you, as always.'

'How are you, Willie?' Maguire asked, when the warder was gone. 'How're things?'

Moore waggled his hand from side to side. 'Things are OK, Patrick. I look forward to talking to you because it's pretty much the only decent conversation I get. There's no doubt that one of the downsides of being in here is the level of intellect, but that's something I just have to deal with.'

'Are you still thinking of the time as an occupational hazard, then?' Maguire asked him.

'Of course. I told you that when we first started speaking: this was a decision I made having studied all the evidence.'

'Becoming a drug dealer was a calculated step, you mean?'

'A heroin dealer, if we're being exact. It's just a market, like any other: there's a product, a customer base and a price.'

'It's costing you seven years, Willie. Is it really worth it?'

'Of course it is. I'd not be here if it wasn't. When I started, I worked out what I was likely to get in terms of a sentence if I was caught, and then I worked out how much I needed to stash in order to be able to afford the time.'

Maguire looked puzzled. 'Afford it?'

'It's all part of the equation. Even with seven years – of which I'll only do about three, by the way – I'm still way ahead financially. I've money aside, and plenty of it: when I get out, I'll restructure, regroup, and off I go again.'

'Just like that, with no compunction? Even though this country's got a drug problem like never before?'

Moore offered a sardonic smile. 'Come on, Patrick, what do any of us care about a drug problem? This is the Celtic Tiger, one of the fastest-growing economies in Europe; we've more millionaires per square mile than just about anywhere. So we've a drug problem? So what? We've always had an alcohol problem, and we've still got a tobacco problem. The only difference is the taxes. When you get right down to it, I'm no different to the brewers or the cigarette manufacturers, other than the taxes. I'm supplying a demand at a rate people can afford. The prison time has to be accounted for in terms of the balance sheet, but the numbers still add up.'

'Jesus, Willie,' Maguire said, 'I ought to know it by now, but you really are a cool one, aren't you?'

'You don't get anything for nothing,' Moore stated. 'If you can't do the time, don't do the crime: it's a cliché, but it's still a fact.'

'But seven years, Willie, come on. You're a young man, and surely life's not just about making money. What about your mam and dad, your family? What about girlfriends, a wife maybe, children? How are you going to balance that side of life if all you intend to do is carry on dealing?'

Moore made a face. 'My family know what I'm like, and we all know how girlfriends come and go.'

For a long moment, Maguire studied him. 'You never told the police about her, did you?'

Moore looked scornful. 'Of course not: that was information, and information costs. I was waiting to go to trial, remember, and as far as I was concerned, I needed all the bargaining chips I could get. They asked me, of course, but when I tried to broker a deal, they were having none of it.' He smiled then, mercilessly. 'With what's going on right now, though, that little snippet might be worth something.'

Tuesday 2nd September
2.35 pm

Murphy drove Molly Parkinson north of the river. When she got back to Harcourt Square, the incident room was buzzing with talk of Jimmy Hanrahan. Quinn was at the computer and Doyle was on the phone. There was no sign of Frank Maguire. Murphy took a moment to see Quinn on her own.

'How are you, Moss?' she asked him. 'How're you coping?'

Sitting back with a sigh, he tried to raise a smile. 'To tell you the truth, I don't know. All the time I thought this was Maggs, there was hope that Eva was OK, that perhaps she wasn't crammed into some godforsaken hole somewhere, because once upon a time, at least, he loved her. If it was Maggs, she might be able to reason with him.'

'Are you saying that you don't think this is him? Is that why there's all this fuss over Jimmy the Poker?'

Quinn glanced beyond her to the detectives, who were hunched over their desks in the outer office. He thought about the thousands of uniforms still searching. He thought about sandstone cliffs and a gravelly voice in his head.

'Jimmy has a history with Maggs,' he said. 'We've always known that. And the Kerry lads found a Polaroid camera in his house.'

Murphy sat down. 'Was his house not searched when you found Mary's body?'

'Why would it be? Maggs was well and truly in the frame by then, wasn't he?' He thought for a moment. 'I've had to re-evaluate. I've had to rethink what might've happened with Mary. I was so convinced it *was* Maggs, perhaps I was blinded to other possibilities. Jesus, it shouldn't happen, but in this job sometimes it just does.' He paused for a moment, reflecting.

'You know Jimmy's mother went for the rope, don't you?'

She nodded. 'So?'

'I just think it's interesting, I mean in the context. At first glance, Jimmy doesn't strike you as the poetic type. But he likes to take pictures and he likes to take them with a Polaroid camera.' He indicated the computer screen, where he'd called up the information he and Doyle had looked at before. 'The lilywhite boys, Murph. It meant nothing at all at first, but when you begin to look deeper . . . '

'"The ballad of the cruel mother."' Murphy peered at the screen. '"A woman who gives birth to one or two illegitimate sons." Moss, are you telling me there are two of them?'

'Of course not. Look at the seventh line, though: "*seven stars in the sky; or the seven who went to heaven*". Six women are dead already and now a seventh is missing.'

Brows arched, she stared at him. 'Are we talking about a link between them all, then?'

'To tell you the truth, I'm not exactly sure what we're talking about. All this crap we're getting, though, all this cryptic bollocks: it's the stuff of movies, for Christ's sake. This doesn't happen in real life.'

Murphy was thinking hard. 'Moss, they can't all be linked, because five of them were single mothers and the sixth probably didn't even know she was pregnant. The seventh . . . '

'Has lost a son and pushed her husband away.' Quinn gestured with an open palm. 'With me leaving home, you could argue that Eva became a single mother. I'm covering all the bases, Murph, or at least I'm trying to. But whoever is behind this knew that when we got the note about lilywhite boys, we were bound to look it up. That means they knew what we were going to find.'

For a moment, he broke off. 'I've said it before: serial killers don't just like the killing, there has to come a point when it's no fun if nobody knows you're doing it. I'm not saying this is how it is, but nobody is going to tell me now that Eva's abduction is not linked to Mary Harrington. Liam Ahern talks about how when a person is born, they have all the hardware they need to be a human being. But they don't have any of the software. The actual business of being a person is programmed into them, and it's generally done by their mother. If for some reason it doesn't get done, then potentially you're left with someone who has no idea of how to behave, and sometimes you wind up with a psychopath.' He pointed to the screen. 'Whichever way you look at it, this whole thing is in part at least about motherhood: five victims were single mothers, Mary Harrington was pregnant, and my wife left our daughters on their own.'

Maguire walked into the incident room and Quinn got to his feet. 'Keira, listen,' he said, 'when the Kerry guards get here, I want you to take the camera to the lab yourself. They need to look at it under polarised light. They know that, of course they do; but they're looking for a mechanical pattern we can match to the print. Have you got that?'

'Yes,' she said with a smile. 'I was the one who told the super, remember?'

'Course you were. I'm sorry.'

He turned then as Maguire came in. 'Frank,' he said, 'let me talk to Jimmy Hanrahan, will you? I took his statement at the *fleadh cheoil*, and Doyle was there when his mother's body washed up.'

Maguire nodded. 'Is there anything else happening?'

Quinn showed him what they'd got from the computer. 'Doyle reminded me that a lilywhite is someone who comes from Kildare,' he said. 'That's the only Irish connection I can find. But we looked at the poem, and the poem led us to the seven stars, as well as this "cruel mother" reference.'

For a moment Maguire was still, and when he spoke it was almost a whisper. '*O mother dear, when I was thine, Fine flowers in the valley, You did na prove to me sae kind, And the green leaves they grow rarely*. That's Robbie Burns, Moss. I can quote Kavanagh, you know, but that was Robbie Burns.'

Sitting down, he looked suddenly weary, the bags heavy under his eyes, his skin waxen and sallow.

'Kildare, you say?'

'A lilywhite, yes: that's the only Irish connection.'

'But hold on a minute: single mothers, I thought that was the link we'd established, a link that rules out Mary Harrington and certainly Eva.'

'Not necessarily.' Quinn told him what he'd discussed with Murphy.

'That's stretching it, to say the least,' Maguire stated. 'And you're forgetting that nobody knew Mary was pregnant, not even her girl-friends.'

'You're right,' Quinn agreed, 'that's the bit that doesn't make any sense. But maybe we've missed something; perhaps there *is* someone who did know: the child's father, maybe.'

'We spoke to him: the boyfriend. It's in the file.'

'We did, yes. He was on remand in the 'back of Shaws' and he didn't deny or confirm anything: he just said that whatever information he may or may not have, had a price tag. He told me he knew the value of information and he'd talk only if we negotiated a price.

I was in no mood to play that kind of game, and back then it didn't matter anyway. We were looking at Maggs, weren't we? Me and Doyle, we were all over him like a bad haircut.'

Maguire looked askance at him now. 'Are you saying there *was* prejudice then, Moss?'

Quinn's expression darkened. 'We both had reason to hate the Maggot, and at the end of the day I can admit to my failings. Sometimes you find yourself dealing with someone who is just asking to go down. You know how it can be, Frank: you've been a copper long enough.'

He thought for a moment, then said: 'Maybe Willie Moore did know something. Maybe he still does.'

Tuesday 2nd September
3.35 pm

Maggs was in the living room when Jane got back. He heard the taxi pull in from the main road and he sat there working his fingernails into the arm of the chair. He heard the key turn in the front door and the door close, and then he heard Jane.

'Conor?' she called. 'Love, are you there?'

'In here, pet,' he replied.

The living-room door opened and there she was, looking a little red in the face.

'What happened?' she dropped to one knee beside his chair and took his hand in both of hers. 'What happened, love? When I heard Doyle say he was taking you to Rathfarnham, I was . . . '

'Where did she take you?' he interrupted. 'That female guard, where did she take you after you left Rathfarnham?'

'To Harcourt Street. You know, the building with all the satellite stuff on the roof.'

'What did they say to you?'

She stroked the hair from where it had fallen in his eyes.

He pushed her hand away. 'What did they ask you, Janey?'

Rocking back on her haunches, she looked troubled. 'They didn't say anything very much; they sat me down in an interview room and just made me wait.'

'Did you ask for a lawyer?'

She shook her head. 'I'm Johnny Clogs' cousin: I can deal with the guards.'

'Are you sure? You know what they're like; they're clever, very clever, and very, very sneaky. They manipulate what you say: they twist it around so it means something other than what came out of your mouth. I know: they did it to me, remember? They made me write it down.'

Again, Jane took his hand. 'It's all right,' she said, soothingly. 'That's all in the past. They used the past: twisted things so they looked different, then used it against you.'

He was nodding now like a child. 'That's right,' he said, 'that's what they did. That's what happened.'

Then he was himself again and, sitting up straight, he held her hand and looked her in the eye.

'So what did they say to you, Janey? What did you say to them?'

'They brought in that girl, the one from the court, the one who testified against you.'

His eyes were orbs suddenly. 'Molly Parkinson?'

'That's right, they brought her in and she told me how she lied when she said you were with her that night in Kerry.'

'But she didn't lie,' he stammered. 'I was with her. I never left her side except to buy her a package of smokes. Two minutes, that's all it was.'

'Exactly,' she said, smoothing the skin of his face. 'No time to do any of what they made you say you did.'

'Of course not. So what happened?'

'Nothing. I'm not stupid: I know what they were trying to do, a bit of emotional blackmail from a girl who can't hold her drink.' She smiled then. 'It didn't stand up in the Four Courts, and it doesn't stand up with me now.'

Tuesday 2nd September
2.45 pm

Frank Maguire went outside to get a breath of air; one hand in his trouser pocket, he fingered the rosary beads he carried, wandering around the back of the main building to get away from the press.

His head was full of memories: recollections of a past he'd managed to brush under the carpet. But like the odour of something that's festered, the memories were seeping back.

He could remember his brother's dad, though he couldn't recall his own. He showed up one day after a Russian ship docked in Dublin, only for the entire crew to defect. That had been back in the days of the iron curtain: lots of men jumped ship. Good-looking enough to charm a single mother who drank too much, he was looking for a place to hide out, and he found it. He stayed for nine months: just about long enough to know his son was born, and then he was off. From the day she left hospital, his mother blamed the boy.

*

It was a day like any other: when Frank came home from school, his mother was asleep in the chair. Climbing concrete steps to the grim little flat, he found Patrick sitting on the floor beside the chair, where she was slumped, as usual, in alcoholic oblivion.

'Hey, Paddy lad, how are you?' With the smile he reserved just for his brother, Frank picked him up in his arms and hugged him.

'Frankie, our ma's asleep; she's still asleep. She's been that way for ages.'

'She's always asleep. But what about you, are you all right, wee feller? Have you had anything to eat?'

Paddy shook his head.

Frank looked at him, then, with a stab of pain in his chest, he looked at his mother with an intense hatred, he wondered if it wasn't time he told someone. He'd hidden this for as long as he could remember, because for as long as he could remember he'd lived in fear of being taken into care and being separated from his brother.

Sitting Patrick down at the tiny table, he took the empty glass from between his mother's fingers: he tipped out the ashtray and cleaned it, and still she didn't stir. Her head lolled to one side, her hair thick with grease.

He hated her: he'd not known what hatred was until his brother was born. Before then, there had only been the two of them, and Frank could deal with that. She didn't drink so much then, or perhaps she did, only he was younger and didn't understand.

'Are you hungry, Paddy?' he asked.

'Yeah, I am.' His brother patted his stomach and Frank could hear it gurgling. He knew he would've had nothing since the cereal he'd given him at breakfast. Sometimes, if there was bread, he'd make him a jam sandwich and leave it hidden so he could munch on it until Frank got home.

But there was no bread today and very little else, and when Frank looked in the fridge he thought they'd have to go hungry.

Then he spied his mother's handbag on the worktop. She had a couple of quid in her purse: enough maybe to get a saveloy and chips from down the street. It would have to do: if she found out, she found out. They couldn't just starve: with all she drank, she never seemed to need any food, but the boys had to eat.

An hour later, having shared a couple of battered sausages and a portion of chips, Frank took his brother home. Quietly he unlocked the door, then, finger to his lips, he led Patrick to the bedroom they shared.

Before they knew it, the door swung open and their mother stood there like some kind of witch, with her hair hanging over one shoulder. She peered at them in turn, her eyes wide, head bobbing, then, with incredible dexterity, she flicked out a hand and caught Frank across the face.

'You little shit,' she hissed. 'You sneaky little shit. Thieving from your mammy, Frank; thieving from your mammy.'

'Mam!' Patrick yelled at her. There was such venom in his five-year-old eyes that his mother took a step back.

But she recovered herself. 'What do you think you're doing, boy, screaming at me like that?'

'Let Frankie be!' he shouted.

She lashed out again, with her fist this time, and knocked Patrick right across the bed. He came up with blood on his lip and the same murderous expression in his eyes.

Again his mother stepped back. 'Mother of God, would you look! I swear you've the devil in you.'

Tuesday 2nd September
4.05pm

How long had she been gone?

How long had she been lying here under the eye of the clock? She could see now, having finally worked the blindfold from her eyes. She was out of the grave. Thirst had driven her; the water in her hole all gone, she'd summoned every ounce of strength to break the weight of the floorboards and inch her way – a painstaking wriggle – across the floor to where a puddle had formed from the rain. Lying on her side, she managed to tilt her head and bury her taped mouth in the water, then suck what she could through the hole. It was not enough; it would never be enough; but even a little moisture might keep her from slipping deeper into delirium.

She could hear the clock but she couldn't see it: *tick-tock, tick-tock* from somewhere high above her.

She knew the clock mattered: she knew all about time. She knew what had happened to Mary Harrington and she knew she was dying of thirst. Her senses, her stomach; her lips were dying of thirst; her tongue, her throat; her limbs; her guts were shriveling, intestines loose like rubber bands that had been stretched once too often.

Face pressed to the floor, she tried to listen for the voices she thought she had heard before, and she felt sure Danny had been calling. He was beckoning, calling out for her to join him; he was so close now she could almost touch him.

It was tempting: her little boy, who'd got on his bike and cycled so far away. All she had to do was close her eyes and drift off to sleep, and then she would be with him.

Jess and Laura: their faces were etched suddenly in her mind. Opening her eyes once more, she could see the roof above her head; she could see gaps in the tiles and clouds; clouds massed in the sky.

Life.

A single word, distinct and separate in her head.

I am alive: my name is Eva. I'm Eva-Marie Quinn and I have two little girls. I know I have two little girls.

My husband is Moss and he is looking for me. My husband's name is Moss; he is a policeman and he is looking for me.

Then she heard the footsteps. Slow, they seemed, like a distant kind of echo: footsteps coming from outside.

And she lay there helpless, an escapee from the grave.

Closer they came, and closer; an even, deliberate step; she knew he was coming back. After a moment's silence, the door began to open. He stood with gloved hands hanging loose at his sides. His image was blurred, his features swimming in the haze of her confusion. But she saw his fingers flex and then that same gravelled rasp carried to her.

'Eva, darling, what're you doing out of bed?'

Desperately she tried to call out, but all she had was the tiny hole in the tape and she could not show him that. Crossing the floor, he took the blindfold and worked it back into place. Then he lifted her, and in a few paces she was carried the short distance it had taken an eternity to crawl.

Tuesday 2nd September
4.15 pm

O'Connell Bridge was alive with traffic, the first of the evening's commuters scurrying for the tranquillity of the seaside or the country, maybe. In the taxi heading for the flat, Maggs tapped a fingernail against his teeth, thinking about the prayer meeting he'd called tonight in Harold's Cross.

For two days, Dublin had been a sea of police officers – the usual clamour with the scream of sirens and the blur of flashing lights. A couple of Fords went rattling by now, blue lights flashing. They roared around the cab on the wrong side of the road, and for the second time since he'd flagged him down, Maggs could feel the taxi driver scrutinising him.

'Don't I know you from the telly or something?' the man asked him.

Maggs studied the back of his head: white-haired, a man in his sixties, a rattle in his voice from too many cigarettes.

'You might,' he replied matter-of-factly.

'So who are you, then?'

Maggs chuckled softly. 'I suppose that depends on who you talk to. If you ask my girlfriend, she'll tell you I'm a man of God; if you ask the police, on the other hand, they'll tell you I'm a murderer.'

The cabbie squinted at him. Then recognition flared. 'Jesus, now I know you: you're the feller they beat seven kinds of shite out of, aren't you? That trial back in the spring.'

Maggs didn't reply.

'The Four Courts; the lass whose body they found in Mayo?'

'Kerry.'

'Right, right, Kerry. You're him, aren't you?' He grinned then, a little awkwardly. 'So what really happened, eh? Did you do it, did you?'

'Of course I did,' Maggs told him.

The driver peered at him in the mirror. Then his whiskered lips parted in a grin. 'Suppose I asked for that, didn't I?'

'I suppose you did, yes.' They were at the southern end of Lower Camden Street now, and Maggs handed him a ten-euro note. 'Here's just fine,' he said.

He didn't go straight back to the flat; instead, he took a stroll past the Portobello and along the canal towards the bronze of Patrick Kavanagh, as he'd done the other night. This was where Patrick Maguire lived. Maggs knew his flat: the last of the older homes before the squared sixties-built blocks that overlooked the lock. Patrick Maguire, whom he'd met in Kerry all those years ago; Patrick Maguire, who came to Mountjoy as a visitor; Patrick Maguire, who had testified against him.

Maggs was feeling liberated after his meeting with Quinn, although the old resentments still lingered, as far as Doyle was concerned. It made him angry, but bad blood was bad blood, and he supposed that was just how it was. He had had another moment on the TV, though, and he'd enjoyed that: his first interview since back in April. Lost in thought, it was only when he looked up as a car came by too close that he saw the water rat sitting on a towpath bench.

He recognised him immediately: Jug Uttley, the man with the big mouth he'd first come across in prison. He looked like he was taking a breather on his way to the next watering hole, and of course the canal was where drunks like him hung out in the daytime. Then it dawned on him: now he knew how Doyle had found his way to Jane's door.

Unaware of his approach, Uttley got up from his bench. Above him, Maggs leant over the wall.

'Jug,' he called, 'you ulcerated boil. Been lipping off to the guards again, have you?'

For a moment, Uttley gawped at him. He looked left and right, but the towpath was empty save for a couple of tramps further on, squatting with bottles of cider.

In one athletic spring, Maggs was over the wall and sliding down the bank. Then he was face to face with the informant and pressing him down on the bench.

'Tell me, Jug, what were you doing bringing Sergeant Doyle to my door?'

Uttley shook his head, fear in his eyes behind the black-rimmed glasses. 'I wasn't bringing him. Jesus, I didn't even know you were here.'

Maggs had him by the lapels, grime-laden and stinking. So disgusted was he that he almost let go. He could smell the old man's rancid tongue, his breath reeking of whiskey.

'I swear: the last I heard, you were in London,' Uttley spluttered. 'Saved, they said: saved by the blood of Jesus, and doing his good works.'

'I'll give you the blood of Jesus, you misshapen gargoyle. Spill your guts, or I swear I'll spill them for you.'

'I said nothing,' Uttley wailed. 'I told no one anything. I never knew you were here.'

Maggs gripped him tighter. 'I'm a man of God, Jug, not a man of violence, but so help me – with you I could make an exception.

'Jesus, will you please . . . '

'Tell me.'

'All right, all right: I heard a whisper, and so I spoke to Mr Doyle. Mother of God, I needed a couple a quid, and what harm could it do? After what he did, and everyone knowing it – I knew he'd not touch you again.'

'How much did he pay you?'

'Thirty euro.'

'I said, how much?' Maggs shook him then, viciously. 'How much, Jug? How many pieces of silver?'

'All right, fifty.'

'Give it up.'

'That was yesterday. I spent it.'

'Give it up, or you're going in the canal.'

'OK, OK, but you're a whore's melt, so you are.' Shaking free, Uttley fumbled in his pocket and brought out a bundle of notes. Before he could peel off a fifty, Maggs had taken the lot.

'Jesus, man, will you give a feller a break? That's all I got, Conor: you've taken all my money.'

'So phone your pal Doyle and tell him you were mugged.' Maggs stuffed the cash in his pocket. 'This is payment for betraying me. Now go on and get yerself lost. You're lucky I'm in a good mood, otherwise you'd be picking up bits of yourself all along the towpath.'

Tuesday 2nd September
4.25 pm

Stoked now by memories, Frank Maguire stepped over the pile of letters inside his brother's front door. Recalling their last conversation, he left them where they were. And he was reminded again of childhood: the stone steps he'd had to climb above a rubbish-strewn quadrangle in a battered council block. There had been a handful of children's swings, though they were useless with the seats torn from the chains. The older boys used the dangling links to tie up the smaller kids, and he recalled coming home one day to find three of them tying up his brother. He sent the ringleader home with a fat lip and carried Pat upstairs.

He'd kept it secret, the past: as far as the job was concerned – as far as *anyone* was concerned, in fact – he and his brother were a couple of local lads whose parents lived abroad. There had been nothing in it other than the desire to cover the embarrassment of a childhood that should've been banished to the dark days when the Irish were burning everything British but their coal.

Inside Patrick Pearse's flat, he climbed the three stairs that led to the living room. All was quiet apart from the traffic on Charlemont

Bridge. All was quiet apart from the ticking of the clock. Frank considered the hands against those of his wristwatch: a little fast. He went to adjust them but then changed his mind.

Next to the clock was the photograph, featureless save for the wasted look in her eyes. He studied her plaited hair; he studied the broken line of smoke lifting from her cigarette. He considered her throat and the hint of gold, the Sacred Heart pendant he'd last seen as he and Patrick had looked down on her open coffin.

As a kid, Paddy had been fascinated by it, and in his mind's eye Frank could see him with their mother passed out from drink and her unrecognised son climbing into her lap. He would sit there and fiddle with that necklace as if she were holding him, as if she were mothering him – when she never did.

A maggot in her head, that's what they said, but only Mary knows.

The words echoed in Frank's skull and, sitting down at the table, he looked out over the trees and the parked cars to the canal. He could hear the clock: *tick-tock, tick-tock, the mouse and the clock, the clock's going to stop.*

Eyes closed, he could hear his brother crying.

*

Crossing the quadrangle, he heard the shrieking sobs. He'd spent his life listening out for his brother, and he recognised the voice immediately. Almost eighteen, Frank was desperate to join the police, and he'd been trying to think of a way of telling his mother. Paddy was eleven, and Frank going to Templemore would mean him being left alone with her. He'd talked about it with him; tried to explain that Pat was older now and it would be all right; but the boy had fallen to pieces.

Breaking into a run, Frank was across the grass and into the stinking concrete stairwell that climbed to the floors above. On the landing, he ran to the door – which was locked, as usual. With one hand he was thumping, and with the other he was fitting the key.

He burst into the tiny hall and, throwing open the living room door, he saw Paddy squatting on his heels looking up at their mother, who was slumped in the chair with her arms rigid and her head thrown back.

*

A massive stroke, or so the doctor told them: brought on by years of depression and years of the drink. Even if he'd been at home, there was nothing Frank could have done. She was dead, and with her gone there was nothing to stop him joining the guards. God forgive him: six weeks later, Patrick was at Islandbridge and he was training at Templemore.

Tuesday 2nd September
4.45 pm

Quinn phoned the Kerry guards and asked them to take Jimmy the Poker to the station in Terenure in the south of the city. It was an old-fashioned four-storey brick building with a slate roof. The local DI was a friend, and he said he'd make sure that Jimmy was nice and comfortable.

The guards came on up to the square afterwards, and Murphy took charge of the camera. Quinn and Doyle took the box of Polaroids and sat down to flick through them.

They were mostly pictures taken when Jimmy had been out hunting: deer he'd shot, and birds; lots of rabbits. There were others, though: a few of his poor old dad asleep in the chair, and a couple of him shuffling around the ratty kitchen, sprinkling holy water. There was another when he was scampering up the stairs with his pyjamas all but falling off him. 'Sick fucker, isn't he?' Doyle commented.

Quinn came to the picture they had been looking for. 'Take a peek, Doyler,' he said. Doyle studied the now rather grainy image: an older woman lying on her back with her legs open. 'The infamous memento,' he muttered. 'Let's have a word with the cockroach, shall we?'

Taking the photo, they drove to Terenure, and a guard brought Jimmy to an interview room, where Doyle was seated at the table and Quinn was leaning against the wall. There was no tape, no video recorder, and no duty solicitor.

The clock ticked towards five o'clock.

Jimmy was wearing jeans and a pair of work boots, an open-necked shirt and a body warmer. His thin face and narrow eyes gave him the look of a cornered animal. Lips twisted, he folded his arms.

'A long fuckin' ways for a chat,' he muttered.

'You're used to it, lad,' Doyle told him. 'After all, you were only up here on Sunday.'

'Was I fuck: I was in Kerry, where I always am.'

'Rubbish, you were at Glasnevin Cemetery watching Eva. '

Jimmy gawped. 'Jesus,' he said, 'so that's what this is about: you think it was me that took your wife? I was in Kerry, for God's sake: what would I be doing up here?'

Doyle had the photo, and placing it on the table now he rotated it so that it faced Jimmy. 'Quite the snapper, aren't you?' he said. 'Did your mam see that, Jimmy, or was it just what you did to poor Mrs Bolton that made her throw herself in the river?'

Jimmy's eyes clouded.

'You like taking pictures, don't you?' Quinn asked from where he leant against the wall. 'I mean, you've a whole stack of them.'

'So what? Is there some kind of law I don't know about as regards a bloody camera?'

Doyle tapped the Polaroid. 'How old were you? Thirteen, fourteen maybe?'

Jimmy didn't reply.

'How much did she charge the poor soul?'

'I don't know.' Jimmy smiled cruelly. 'I know I got my money back, mind: that picture made us quite a few quid, I can tell you.'

'Did Conor see it?'

Jimmy shrugged.

'Course he did. He started on you because of it, didn't he?'

'If he did, he never finished.'

Doyle looked at the picture himself now. 'Imagine that was your mam,' he said. 'How would you have felt? Did you ever think about that? No, of course you didn't. But then you always were a scumbag, weren't you? As far as you were concerned, she was just an old tart: some old bag who liked them any which way; old or young, it didn't matter. That's what you thought, wasn't it?' He leant towards him then. 'How many of you were there? A whole bunch, I heard: regular little gang-bang, eh?' His face was set, the muscles stiff at his jaw. 'Conor found out, didn't he? And he dumped you on your arse before your mates beat him up.'

'Just like you beat him up, eh, Mr Doyle?' Jimmy curled his lip. 'What's the matter with you? I was just a kid; it was twenty years ago. What's it got to do with anything?'

'The camera, Jimmy. The camera you used to take this picture, and the one you used the other day. On the beach, was it? Down there where you live? That little stretch over by the castle?'

Jimmy looked genuinely puzzled. 'What're you talking about? I haven't used the bloody thing in ages.'

'Yes you have. You took a picture of a bit of stone on the sand, a pebble on the beach. What was that about, son? Sand and stone, stone and sand; sandstone maybe, was it?'

Quinn spoke then from where he stood behind him. 'What did you do with Eva, Jimmy?'

Jimmy looked back at him. 'I don't know what you're talking about.'

'Eva,' Doyle said, pressing him. 'The girl all you horny little gobshites were having wet dreams over when you were growing up.'

'I have no idea what you're on about.' Shaking his head, Jimmy spoke as if to himself. 'Can you believe this? I mean, Jesus, there I am, a law-abiding feller with a sick old man to take care of, and they send Martin McCafferty to my door. Then I'm dragged halfway across the country. Have you nothing better to do with your time lads, is that it?'

'Time, is it?' Gripping him harshly at the shoulder, Quinn twisted him round so he was looking straight at the clock. 'A few more hours and she'll be dead. Is that what you want?'

Jimmy looked suddenly cautious. 'You really think I took your wife, Mr Quinn? What kind of a moron are you? I live in Kerry, for Christ's sake. When did she go missing? Sunday, was it? I just told you, I was home with my dad; you can ask him.'

'We did ask him, and he told us you weren't there.' Quinn eyeballed him. 'So where were you?'

'Listen,' Jimmy said. 'The old man wouldn't know one day from the next. He's not right in the head. I was home on Sunday, I swear.'

'So what about the photo?' Doyle demanded.

'What photo? I told you, I don't know anything about any photo.'

'You've a history with the camera. You took advantage of a poor old drunk, remember?'

'I shagged a poor old drunk, is what I did, and got a dose of something for my trouble too: itching like a flea-bitten dog for weeks after.'

'Then there was Mrs Bolton, the old lady whose house you broke into before taking the poker and giving her thirty stitches.'

'That was years ago, for Christ's sake. Honestly, I've not the slightest idea what you're going on about. I was home Sunday, looking after my dad.'

Pulling out another chair, Quinn sat down and peered into his pinched features. 'Tell us about Mary,' he said. 'The girl we found under the floor in the cottage across from your house.'

'I've told you all I know about that. I told you back when it happened. I saw her talking to Conor Maggs: that's all I know.'

'You didn't talk to her?'

'No.'

Doyle laughed softly. 'So what would you say if we were to tell you a little bird said you did?'

'I'd say you were trying to fit me up like you did the Maggot.'

'Fitted him up, is that how it was? You were the one who fingered him, Jimmy. You were the one who was only too happy to come in and tell us how you'd seen the two of them talking by the corner shop.'

'That's because I did.'

'Since when did you start grassing on people?'

'I didn't grass. You asked me a question and I gave you an answer. That's all there was to it.'

Sitting back, Doyle stretched his fingers across his belly, his jacket falling open, the gun holstered on his hip. 'You do a lot of travelling when you're after the deer, don't you? You and that old shortbed of yours. From Kerry to the midlands and right up here to Dublin: there's plenty to be poached when the season's over, and you don't want to be shitting on your own doorstep.'

'Is that what you were doing on Sunday?' He looked coldly at him now. 'Your father told us you weren't there. And he did know it was Sunday, because the priest came round to give him Holy Communion. So where were you, eh? Looking for deer? A doe ripe for the taking?'

'Listen,' Jimmy told him. 'I've told you, priest or no priest, my old man wouldn't know Sunday from Saturday, or any other day for that matter.'

'What is it about you and the women,' Quinn said. 'When did you start hating them? Did it begin with Maggs's mother letting a fourteen-year-old ride her for the price of a bottle? Or was it the fact that your own mother despised you so much she preferred purgatory and the bottom of the Shannon?'

Suddenly Jimmy lashed out; swinging his fist, he almost caught Quinn across the nose. The next thing he knew, Doyle had him in a wrist-lock and was twisting his arm so hard he yelped. On his feet now, Doyle shoved him to the floor.

'What does it mean?' Quinn demanded. '*A maggot in the head, that's what they said, but only Mary knows.*'

'You can tell us, son,' Doyle told him. 'Come on, get it off your chest. After all you've been through with your mam and the old man, God knows we understand. Losing her like that in the water with the fishes chewing on her: it'd be enough to turn any lad's head.'

Jimmy was squealing, screeching like a child. 'You're breaking my arm, for fuck's sake! You're breaking my fuckin' arm!'

Doyle held him a little longer, then Quinn nodded and he hoisted Jimmy to his feet. Quinn told him to sit down. 'Now I'm going to ignore that you just tried to whack me,' he said. 'You might not believe it, but I know how the frustration can get you: all these years looking after for your dad, what with him and your mam and everything.' He glanced briefly at Doyle. 'You know, from what Martin McCafferty tells us, people down in Kerry actually think you've done a good job keeping him out of the nuthouse.'

Looking a little bewildered now, Jimmy was rubbing his wrist.

'Tell us about Eva,' Quinn went on softly. 'Come on now, there's no time. I'll forget you tried to assault me. Just tell me where she is.'

Jimmy shook his head. 'I swear to you, Mr Quinn. I swear to you on my mother's grave: I know nothing about what happened to her.'

Tuesday 2nd September
5.15 pm

Outside in the car park, Quinn leant with his back to the car door and his hands in his pockets.

'What do you think?' he said.

Doyle made a face. 'I don't know. It's hard to tell with a lad like that: all his life he's been a toe-rag, but is he capable of the kind of planning and pre-meditation we're looking at? I don't know.' He let go a breath. 'We'll find out when the results come in from the lab though, won't we?'

When they got back to the incident room, the superintendent was behind Quinn's desk with the files on the five missing women spread out in front of him.

'Anything happen, Frank?' Quinn asked. 'Any new leads?'

Maguire shook his head. 'What about Hanrahan?'

'He's not telling us anything.'

Closing the door, he perched on the edge of the desk. He indicated the files. 'Have I convinced you then, with all my errant rambling?'

Maguire managed a half-smile. 'I want to find Eva, Moss. What you said made some sense, and of course we'd be fools to ignore it.'

'So, the lilywhite boys: who do we know from Kildare?'

Maguire didn't reply. Resting on his elbows, he leafed through the pages. 'Five single mothers,' he said. 'Six, if you include Mary.'

'And seven if you include my wife.'

Maguire looked unimpressed. 'Moss, even if we do include Mary — which we haven't until now — I have to draw the line with Eva: that just does not stack up.'

'Maybe not to you, Frank. Maybe not to me or Doyle or any other copper. But to this fucked-up scumbag . . . ' Quinn gestured. 'We know he's punishing women for some reason — and not just women, but mothers. Which brings us to Maggs's mother, who drank drain cleaner, and Jimmy Hanrahan's, who drowned herself. I tell you what: if you put those two lads in front of a forensic psychiatrist, he'd tell you they might have issues.'

'You're right,' Maguire nodded. 'He would. And that brings us back to Mary Harrington. Moss, there is no way that either Maggs or Hanrahan could ever have known she was pregnant.'

'No, there's not,' Quinn said. 'But we have to consider every option.' Opening the door, he called across the incident room. 'Doyler, do us a favour, would you? Get on the blower to the back of Shaws and tell them we're coming down to talk to Willie Moore.'

Tuesday 2nd September
6 pm

The Baldonnel helicopter landed in a park in the centre of Limerick, where a guard in a marked car picked up Doyle and Quinn. Hitting the lights and sirens, he took them to the prison close to where the old Shaws department store used to be – which was how the place had got its nickname.

Quinn made a phone call to the pirate queen. 'Grace,' he said, when she answered. 'Moss Quinn, how are you?'

'I'm taking Russian lessons, Mossie. What about you?'

He laughed. She was a gangster – as ruthless a woman as there was – but she had a sense of history as well as a sense of humour, and he liked that.

'My wife is missing, Grace. It's been almost two days now, and time is running out.'

'I know, I've been following it on the television, and it's not good, it's not good at all. We have our differences, of course we do, we're playing for different sides, but to do this to a guard's wife is taking things too far.'

'Listen, Grace, there's a kid doing a seven-stretch in the back of

Shaws. He's in for dealing smack he bought from Alexei Bris. I need someone to lean on him and I need them to do it now.'

'The back of Shaws, you say?'

'That's right. Doyle and me are on our way right now. His name is Willie Moore.'

She didn't say anything further, but then Grace would never openly offer help to the police: she didn't know who might be listening.

'She's all right, you know,' Doyle commented when Quinn had hung up. 'As far as the criminal fraternity goes, I mean. She's about as good as can be expected.'

'She's careful too,' Quinn told him. 'We've never been able to lay a finger on her, have we?'

'No, and right now if she's doing battle with Mintov, then she's doing us a favour. It makes me think, though,' he added. 'I ought to get down to the moorings again maybe, have another word with your man about his cousin's attitude.'

'Jane Finucane?' Quinn looked sideways at him. 'You think she's lying, don't you?'

'Course she is.' Doyle tapped a thick finger against the side of his nose. 'Thirty-two years, Moss: I can smell it as plain as I smelled the Brits the day I was blown through a plate-glass window.'

The guard dropped them outside the prison, and a few minutes later they were in reception, where they were told that Moore had been held up due to a disturbance on his landing. Quinn and Doyle exchanged a glance; while they waited, they grabbed a cup of coffee.

'Good old Grace,' Quinn observed quietly. 'You never spoke to this guy, did you, Doyler? He's a calculating fucker.'

Willie Moore had a slight swelling under his left eye; a little reddening of the cheek. He sat with his hands in his lap; he had an expression of disgust on his lip.

'Willie,' Quinn said, 'I'm Moss Quinn. I . . . '

'I know who you are,' Moore told him. 'I never forget a face and rarely – if ever – a name.'

'Then you know why I'm here.'

Moore touched his cheek with the tip of his index finger. 'To offer me parole?' he said. 'Have me out on licence maybe?'

'You're a scumbag drug dealer,' Doyle reminded him. 'Licence is for political prisoners.'

'Political my arse: they were the biggest fucking gangsters in Irish history.'

'We're not here to talk about that,' Quinn said. 'The last time I spoke to you, I asked you a specific question.'

'I remember.' Moore leant towards him now, his forearms cross-wise on the table.

'I'm going to ask you that same question again,' Quinn said, holding his eye. 'I've no time to dance with you, Willie, so just give me an answer.'

'An answer, is it?' Moore dabbed his cheek a second time. 'What's it worth, inspector? Just how much is an answer worth to you?'

'You little shit.' Reaching across the table, Doyle grabbed him by the collar.

Moore laughed in his face. 'Sergeant,' he said, 'this is the back of Shaws. The odd screw might get away with giving out a kicking now and again, but not a copper – even one with a reputation for it.' He turned to Quinn. 'You want an answer; I say "how much?"' Once more he touched his face. 'And by the way, there's a premium on it now.'

'Listen, Willie,' Quinn said. 'My wife is lying in a hole somewhere, and in another twenty-four hours she'll be beyond help.'

'It's a shame.' Moore sat back in his chair. 'I'm not in the people-hurting business, but I *am* in business.'

'Shall I tell you about the people-hurting business?' Doyle jutted his chin in Moore's direction. 'All we have to do is let a few folk in here know how cooperative you were' – he indicated the swelling on Moore's cheek – 'and that little gnat bite will be the least of your worries. By the time they get done, you'll wish you'd been rogered by the crew of a Liberian fishing trawler.'

'Then the price goes up,' Moore told him, 'and it keeps going up. Sergeant, you might as well shut your fat gob, because there's no way you're going to intimidate me.'

Quinn shook his head. 'I tell you something, Willie,' he said, 'I'm going to remember you.'

'Course you are, Mr Quinn: I'll be in business a long time.'

Quinn regarded him coldly, then said: 'Mary Harrington was six weeks pregnant when she died.'

Moore looked nonplussed.

'I asked you before if you knew that. We know she came to see you: it's in the prison records.'

'I might've known, inspector. Then again, I might not.'

At that, Doyle got to his feet. Walking round the table, he took hold of Moore by the collar and yanked him to his feet. Squeezing stiff fingers into the drug dealer's throat, he pressed his lips to his ear. 'Now you listen to me, shithead. You're going to answer the inspector's question, and you're going to do it now, because if you don't, I'm going to bounce your head off that wall.' With that, he marched Moore backwards across the room.

Moore tried to laugh, but his face was the colour of ripe beetroot and there were tears in his eyes.

Doyle kept squeezing, and when finally Moore spoke, his voice was a shrill squeak. 'Let me go, will you? Jesus,' he cried. 'OK, all right. I knew.'

Doyle released him and, working a palm against his throat, Moore took a couple of steps backwards. 'You're a psycho, Doyle, you know that. What they say about you isn't the half of it.'

'Sit down, Willie,' Quinn growled. 'Or I'll let him off the leash.'

Moore sat, and Doyle stood right behind him. 'Tell us,' Doyle said. 'Tell us now or I'll tear your voice box out and you'll have to write it down.'

'What did you know?' Quinn asked him.

'That she was six weeks up the duff. She came in here and told me I was the brat's father and that she wanted to keep it. She knew I had money and she wanted as much as she could get.'

Looking over his shoulder, Moore glared at Doyle. 'Did you hear that, you fucking ape? I'm worth a few quid: more than enough to pay someone to whack you.'

Quinn grabbed his arm. 'Concentrate, for God's sake. We've not got all day.'

'Six weeks, the stupid bitch.' Moore looked as though he could spit. 'Like I told Paddy, she'd forgotten, hadn't she: we'd only been going out a month.'

'Paddy?' Quinn was peering into his face. 'What do you mean you told Paddy? Who's Paddy?'

Moore lifted his shoulders. 'Paddy Maguire, the prison visitor.'

Tuesday 2nd September
7 pm

All the way back to Dublin, Quinn was thinking about Willie Moore. They'd checked at reception and it was confirmed that Patrick Maguire had indeed been his prison visitor. Quinn wasn't sure what it meant, except that Patrick had known that Mary Harrington had been pregnant and he hadn't thought to mention it.

'I tell you what,' Doyle said, his voice crackling through the headphones, 'at least we can stop worrying about any kind of a link now. Mary was random, Moss, she was spur-of-the-moment, and the other five are nothing to do with it.' He looked at his watch. 'Patrick should've told us, though. God knows why he didn't. Some kind of visitor-inmate confidence or some such bollocks, probably.' He looked sideways as they came in to land. 'We're running out of time. I'm away down to the moorings as soon as I get hold of a car.'

The chopper dropped them at Phoenix Park, where Murphy was waiting. Climbing into the passenger seat, Quinn asked her to take them back to the square. She was looking pensive.

'What's up?' Quinn asked her.

'The lab, Moss. The camera: the mechanism doesn't match the pattern on the picture.'

From the back seat, Doyle snorted. 'There you go,' he muttered.

'I called the station at Terenure,' Murphy went on, 'and asked them to give Jimmy the bus fare back to Kerry.'

Quinn could feel the minutes slipping away now, and for the first time he began to doubt that they would find her. The possibility made his blood run cold. All he could think about was the look on his daughters' faces when he had to tell them.

In the car park at Harcourt Square, he took another cigarette from the now-nearly-empty pack. His hands shook slightly as he lit it.

'Did you get anything from the back of Shaws?' Murphy asked him.

He told her what Moore had told them — and to keep it to herself for the time being. When she was gone, he dialled Patrick's mobile.

'Paddy, it's Moss,' he said.

'Moss, how are you? Is there any news?'

'We thought we had a lead with Jimmy Hanrahan but that went to rat-shit.'

'There's nothing else?'

'Only that I thought there might be a connection with Mary Harrington. I told you that. I was thinking that if anyone knew Mary was pregnant, then there might've been a link with the other women too.'

Maguire was quiet.

'Me and the Doyler flew down to the back of Shaws just now and spoke to her old boyfriend. You know him: Willie Moore. Mary told him the baby was his, but it couldn't have been because she was six weeks gone and they'd only been going out for a month.'

'And Willie told you that he told me,' Maguire finished for him.

'Why didn't *you* tell me?' Quinn demanded.

He heard his friend sigh heavily. 'I thought about it, Moss. I thought long and hard. But when I started talking to these lads, I made a commitment that the conversations would remain confidential.'

'Regardless of what they told you?'

'They have to know they can confide in me without worrying about whether I'm a tout. Otherwise, what's the point?'

'You're fucking mollycoddling them. Jesus, Pat, they're villains, for fuck's sake, and you're worrying about their trust? They're lucky they have anyone to talk to at all: most people don't, you know.'

'Oh come on, Moss, you know how it works. Without trust there's . . . '

'No, *you* come on, Patrick. I was investigating a murder, for God's sake, and you had information that could've been pertinent.'

'I made a commitment, a promise.'

'It's not the confessional, it's a prison visit for pity's sake.' He broke off then, drawing hard on the cigarette.

'Look Moss, I'm sorry, but what else could I have done?'

'You could've told me, Patrick. That's what you could've done.'

Doyle drove to the Liffey and Johnny Clogs' boat. The same bodyguard was on deck, and he gave Doyle the same hard stare he'd given him the last time he'd been there.

'Where's the boss?' Doyle said as he climbed the steps.

'He's not in.'

'Where is he?'

'I don't know: the dogs, mostly likely.'

Doyle nodded slowly. 'Get a-hold of him, Dessie. Get a-hold of your man and tell him to stop taking the piss and phone me, all right? Tell him to do it right away or I'll come back with a can of petrol and a box of fucking matches. '

'Jesus, you're something, aren't you?'

'Believe it,' Doyle said, and jumped down onto the quay.

Walking back to the car, he heard a voice call from the shadows.

Looking over his shoulder, he saw Jug Uttley, a little the worse for drink, leaning against the railings between Finucane's boat and *The Jeanie Johnston*.

'Jug, what do you know?'

'Mr Doyle, all right?' The water rat was slurring.

'What is it, lad? I'm busy: if you've a word, give it to me.'

'The Maggot, Mr Doyle: he only fuckin' mugged me.'

'He did what?' Doyle squinted at him.

"'Tis true; down by the canal. I'm walking along minding my own business when up pops the bastard and strips me of my cash.'

'I'd take the gobshite for a lot of things, but a mugger? Are you sure that's how it was, Jug?'

'Course I am, Mr Doyle.'

'Then report it: the biggest police station in Dublin's just over on Amiens Street.'

'You don't understand.'

'Understand what? If there's something I need to know, then spit it out, would you?'

'Can you spare me a couple a quid maybe? The fucker cleaned me out.'

Reaching for his wallet, Doyle peeled off a couple of notes and handed them to the old tout.

'Ah, bless you, Mr Doyle, bless you.'

'Tell me what you know,' Doyle said.

'Well, after the scumbag took my money, it set me thinking. I made a couple of calls, and while I was talking to one lad, he told me something I thought you ought to know.'

'What was that?'

'Patrick Maguire, Mr Doyle, the superintendent's brother: he visited two men in Mountjoy whose wives were two of the ones that went missing.'

Doyle opened the car door. 'Janice Long and Karen Brady: I

know. It's in the prison records, Jug. It's no secret.' He shook his head. 'Jesus, and I gave you money too. Do us a favour, would you? In future, don't come looking for me when you've had a couple over the eight.'

'That's not all though, is it? There's something else, Mr Doyle.'

'What else?'

'It wasn't just that pair of hardchaws he was talking to: Patrick spoke to the Maggot as well, didn't he.'

Doyle stared at him now.

'That was the point of what I was coming to. It was a bit of a joke: the super's brother visiting Conor Maggs on remand. I mean, it made no sense, did it? Maggs knew Patrick was going to testify against him.'

'Who told you this?'

'The Crawthumper, Mr Doyle. Your man what cooked the books for Lorne McGeady'.

Tuesday 2nd September
7.15 pm

The church in Harold's Cross was little more than a bible-study group, but Jane had been one of the founder members, along with the self-styled pastor Ray Kinsella. When Maggs had written his open letter from Mountjoy, Jane had read it to the group. It was then that, collectively, they had decided to take up his cause.

Kinsella had contacts in London. Believing that both Maggs and Jane had stories that would inspire others to join their church, he arranged for them to spend some time with another group who met in Muswell Hill. The few months they spent over there had allowed the dust to settle after the trial, but it had always been the intention to bring them back to Dublin.

Kinsella was younger than Maggs: around Jane's age, no more than thirty. He was a small man with thinning hair and designer glasses; he wore flared jeans and pointed shoes; and he had the sleeves of his shirt rolled back on the inside at the cuff.

They were all gathered: a fledgling community, but a vibrant one, and when they met there was plenty of singing, hand-clapping and dancing.

They were due to begin the prayer meeting, but before they did, Maggs asked to say a few words.

'You have to understand,' he explained, 'that in the circumstances of it being Inspector Quinn's wife who was abducted, I was bound to be questioned.' He regarded the group carefully. They were meeting in a school hall close to the Franciscan hospice. 'You saw me on television – of course the clip is being repeated endlessly – and you know what happened at the Four Courts.' He smiled then warmly. 'But as I said that day, I bear no grudge towards the police, and if it hadn't been for what happened with Doyle, I'd never have witnessed what I did at Rathmines.'

'Amen to that,' one of the younger girls said.

Maggs glanced at her. 'Unfortunately, the guards still believe I was responsible for what happened to Mary Harrington. They can't seem to understand that the eloquence, as they put it, of my so-called confession was down to the fact that Joseph Doyle composed it.'

'It's a sad indictment of our society that the police can never admit when they're wrong, or indeed offer any kind of meaningful apology.

'I'm telling you now so we're all clear about what happened. When they interviewed me, I had no representation and I was not under caution. I told them I had no objection to talking to them; on the contrary, it gave me an opportunity to clear my name. '

He took Jane's hand now, and with a warm smile he went on. 'I want you all to know how this lady has stood by me: she will tell you that I was pretty shocked when I saw the news. I knew they'd be coming as soon as they found out I was in Ireland, and I was scared, I don't mind admitting it. I've known Quinn and Doyle a long time, and Quinn could never deal with the fact that even though he'd usurped me in her affections, Eva and I remained very close. When we were kids, she wore a necklace I'd given her.' For a second or two, he broke off, his eyes narrowing slightly. 'She wore it during my trial,' he said more quietly. 'She may have been Quinn's wife, but she never thought me capable of abducting Mary Harrington.' He was smiling again. 'Anyway, I just wanted to share that with you so that perhaps you can appreciate the bigger picture. I've been accused of a lot of things in my life – and none of them very pleasant.'

He was quiet for a while then; they all were; each of them contemplating what he had said. Then he sat forward. 'You've all been very kind. I mean, you've been kinder than kind; kinder than any kindness I've known, in fact. I don't want to sound self-pitying, but my life has been spent largely without family and with precious few friends.'

'Well, you have both now, Conor,' Kinsella stated.

'Thank you,' he said. 'Thank you very much. I want you to know how much I appreciate it, and also how much I appreciate being able to call this meeting. Her husband and uncle might not have a lot of time for me, but Eva certainly used to.' His voice wavered suddenly, and he took a moment to gather himself. 'She's one of the sweetest souls God ever placed on the earth, and I believe that with the power of our prayers, he will protect her.'

Tuesday 2nd September
7.15 pm

Jimmy the Poker was sitting in the bus stop with the wind blowing litter up the street. He was beyond the bowling green at the junction of Terenure Road where it joined Harold's Cross. One of the guards had suggested he take a coach to Kerry from the station on Amiens Street, on the north side of the Liffey. He was angry: he had been dragged all the way up here from the west coast, then chucked a couple of euro and told to clear off. They hadn't given him back his camera – or the box of photographs. Every picture he'd ever taken was in that box.

He was sucking so hard on his cigarette that his cheeks all but met in the middle. He was thinking about his stuff, and he was thinking about his dad telling the guards he'd not been home on Sunday.

He'd have to put the bastard straight when he got back. The people from social services didn't like him being on his own, but that's how he would've been since this afternoon.

Fuck him, Jimmy thought. *Serves him right.* There was no gathering of souls. He didn't see dead people in the kitchen, he saw only what his mangled liver showed him: hallucinations – the kind that came when a conscience as troubled as his was mixed with bottles of neat gin. Jimmy knew what he told everyone: how he'd not been near a drop of alcohol since his wife passed. But that was all rubbish; he was the same old drunk he'd always been.

He supposed that the Social might send someone round to make sure he was all right: no doubt McCafferty had phoned to say the guards had picked his son up and that the old fool would be by himself. They might have asked the Slovak woman who was supposed to keep the place clean to go over and cook him a bit of food. Jimmy could hear him muttering as he sat there; he could see him in his chair with his red face and bulbous nose, the skin marked with thread veins that grew ever more prominent with each drop he supped.

There was no sign of the bus. Looking at his watch, he threw away his cigarette. What was he doing sitting here anyway, just because the shades told him he had to? The bastards had brought him up here; *they* should be taking him back.

He had a couple of euro in his pocket, and there had to be a pub nearby. He'd overheard one of them mention that there was a meeting at the Harold's Cross dog-track tonight. As he knew a little about greyhounds, Jimmy decided he might try and win a few quid. It would serve the old man right. He could lie there in his own sweat listening to the voices inside his head. After what he'd said on Sunday, he could put up with the devil by himself tonight.

Tuesday 2nd September
7.40 pm

Quinn drove to his house in Glasnevin to pick up a fresh shirt; he had none left at the Garda Club and hadn't changed when he woke up this morning. After two days, the collar was rubbing his neck raw.

The house was silent and empty, yet it smelled clean and fresh, as it always did: it smelled to him of his wife. Standing in the hall, the extent of his loss suddenly hit him, and it was all he could do not to slump on the stairs and cry.

The light on the telephone answer machine was blinking; he thought his daughters might've phoned while he was out. The timer indicated that the call had come in just after seven. He pressed the button and listened.

'Three little mice, they couldn't find their way: for three little mice, the clock stopped that day.'

Murphy met him on the stairs at Harcourt Square. 'I don't know what the hell is going on,' he said. 'But Jesus, we're going around in circles. Someone has to know something. I'm going to talk to Maggs again, Keira. Do me a favour, will you: get hold of Doyle and ask him to meet me at Jane Finucane's.'

Downstairs he walked outside, and taking the 9mm Glock from his shoulder holster, he slipped out the magazine. Carefully he checked the rounds and slid the magazine back again. Replacing the gun in its holster, he got in his car and drove the short distance to the service road that branched off Richmond Street.

His eyes were cold, his jaw set; parking the car beneath the concrete balcony, he trailed the fingers of his left hand along the spiked railings.

Almost eight o'clock: forty-eight hours since Eva had been abducted. Trembling slightly, he could see her with her auburn hair cropped short. After Danny was killed, she'd cut it off as if in some kind of penance; since then, nothing had been the same.

Climbing stone steps, he rapped on the door. But the hall was dark through the reinforced glass and there was no light in the kitchen window. Instead, he hammered on the neighbour's door; a moment later, it was opened by a pudgy-faced man wearing a pair of running shorts.

'Garda,' Quinn told him. 'Sorry to bother you, but next door, do you have any idea where they are?'

A glimmer of recognition passed across the man's face. 'You're the copper whose wife is missing,' he said. 'It's been all over the TV.'

Quinn thought for a moment. 'What's your name?' he asked.

'Harry Long.'

'I'm Moss Quinn. Were you in on Sunday night, Harry?'

The man nodded.

'Did you hear any coming and going from in there?' Quinn jerked a thumb at the house next door.

Long made a face. 'She had a visitor, I think. Came early, went about nine maybe.'

'Was she in on her own?'

'I don't know. He came back with her though, didn't he? They'd been in England or somewhere – or that's what I heard.'

'He?'

'The other feller, the one from before.'

'Conor Maggs, you mean?'

'Is that his name? I don't know: black-haired lad, anyway.'

'Did you hear anything else?'

Long shook his head. 'If you want them now, I reckon they might be over in Harold's Cross. She goes to this leaping-and-wailing church. You know – the happy-clappy brigade.'

'Does she now?'

'Aye, she does.' Long gave a thin smile. 'She keeps trying to get me along there with her. No chance of that, mind. Anyway, I think they meet in a school not far from Mount Jerome.'

'Thanks, Harry,' Quinn said. 'I'm obliged.'

'You're welcome, inspector. I hope you find your wife.'

Quinn was about to get back in the car when Doyle pulled up next to him. Walking over, Quinn leant on the roof.

'The bastard called me again, Doyler: the answer phone at home.'

'What did he say?'

Quinn told him. Quinn glanced up at the balcony. 'Given how Jimmy the Poker is in the clear, I came looking for Maggs again, but there's no one here. The neighbour reckons they might be over in your neck of the woods.'

The school abutted the hospice, which in turn bordered Mount Jerome Cemetery. It was a modern building with a red-tiled roof; a handful of cars were parked outside. Although there were lights on in the hall, the main door was locked. They pressed the buzzer and waited.

Quinn could see that Doyle had something on his mind. 'Did you see Johnny Clogs, then?' he asked him.

'No, but I put a flea in his lad's ear and he told me Johnny might be across the road there betting on the dogs.' He nodded in the direction of the track.

'Who did you see then?' Quinn asked. 'You've a face on you like a bulldog chewing a wasp.'

At that moment the door at the far end of the hall opened, and a young blonde woman walked the length of the corridor.

Taking his ID from his pocket, Quinn held it up to the glass. 'Are you from the church group?' he called.

Unlocking the door, she nodded. 'We're holding a prayer meeting. Why, is there a problem?'

'Is Conor Maggs with you?'

She looked into his face then, recognition flaring. 'You're Inspector Quinn, aren't you? Inspector, the prayer meeting is for your wife.'

For a moment, Quinn just stared at her.

'It's true, we arranged it specially. Actually, it was Conor who called us together.'

A man, sandy-haired and not very tall, appeared in the corridor and made his way towards them.

'That's Ray Kinsella, our pastor,' the girl said. Then, turning towards him, she said: 'Ray, it's the police. This is Inspector Quinn.'

Kinsella hovered momentarily as if he did not know what to say. Then Maggs appeared.

'Been on the phone again, have you?' Quinn stared at him coldly, one hand in his jacket pocket, the other loose by his side.

Maggs looked wearily at him. 'We're praying for Eva, Moss.'

'I tell you what,' Quinn said, 'instead of praying for her, why don't you give her up?'

Kinsella moved in front of him. 'Inspector Quinn, please.'

Quinn looked down at him. 'Has he been here all the time?'

'Of course; we all have.'

'What time did you get here?'

The pastor shrugged. 'Around seven, maybe.'

Maggs stepped forward now. 'What is it, Moss? What do you want?'

Quinn flared his nostrils, every muscle tense as he stared into Maggs's eyes. 'Sergeant,' he said to Doyle, 'escort Conor to the car, will you? I'll join you in a minute.'

'Is he being arrested?' Kinsella asked.

Quinn turned back to Maggs. 'I don't know. Are you being arrested or are you coming of your own accord?'

With a shake of his head, Maggs stepped past him.

'Sergeant Doyle,' Kinsella said, 'I am a witness to this, and if there's a single mark on him, you will answer for it.'

Doyle spoke without looking round: 'I'll bear that in mind, Father.'

Quinn went into the hall, where he spotted Jane Finucane sitting on a high-backed chair with another girl alongside her. Jane was red around the eyes and had a handkerchief in her hand. Crossing the room, Quinn waved the other girl away, then, resting his palms on his thighs, he bent towards Jane and looked her in the eyes.

'My wife is missing,' he told her. 'She's lying somewhere with her lips cracked and her tongue swollen. When she cries, there are no tears because after forty-eight hours her tear ducts have dried up. She can last until tomorrow night and then she'll be in a coma. Once that happens, her organs start shutting down, and even if we find her there's no guarantee we can get her back.' Pausing for a moment, he added: 'Do you understand that?'

Jane nodded.

'I'm going to ask this only once: on Sunday night, was Conor with you or not?'

Jane held his gaze. 'Yes,' she said, 'he was.'

'If you're lying and Eva dies, you're going to the women's prison as an accessory to murder.' He straightened up now. 'Just so you know, Jane; just so you understand.'

Doyle had Maggs in the back seat of his car, and Quinn got in beside him. He thought about taking him to his rooms at the Garda

Club or Glasnevin even, but given what Kinsella had said, he decided against it. 'Take us to Crumlin Road, Joe,' he commanded.

They drove in silence, Maggs with his hands in his lap and Quinn
staring ahead. They made their way to Parnell Road, then, for a short
distance, skirted the Grand Canal. At the junction with Crumlin
Road, they swung south-west until they came to the police station.
Dragging Maggs out of the car, they marched him in through the
back door, where a uniformed sergeant greeted them. Doyle
explained that they needed an interview room. Another younger
guard took Maggs down the corridor and then came back to find
them again.

'Inspector,' he said, 'do you want me to set up the tapes?'

Quinn shook his head.

The guard seemed a little unsure, and Doyle laid a firm hand on
his shoulder. 'He's not been arrested, lad: he's here of his own
accord.'

Quinn turned in the direction of the interview room but Doyle
checked him. 'Moss,' he said, 'you asked me who I spoke to down by
the river.'

'Yeah, I did. Something's on your mind, Doyler; what is it?'

Doyle told him what Uttley had said. 'He told me the source was
Lorne McGeady's accountant.'

'The Crawthumper?'

Doyle nodded. 'He and the Maggot were tight as a drum, apparently. He told Jug that Maggs was visited by Pat Maguire – which for
the life of me I just don't get.' He paused. 'I'm the last person to be
making connections, but he also visited both Janice Long's former
husband and Karen Brady's.'

Quinn nodded slowly. 'I thought about that as soon as Willie told
us.'

'So,' Doyle continued, squinting towards the interview room, 'the
question is: do you still want to talk to your man, or do we go and
see Paddy?'

Maggs looked nervous, drumming his fingers on the table.

Doyle sat; Quinn took his jacket off and removed the Glock from its holster. He racked a round into the chamber then walked behind Maggs and, taking him by the hair, jerked his head back.

He pressed the barrel of the gun under his ear. 'Where is she, Conor? Where is Eva?' Maggs stared wildly, the whites of his eyes fully visible.

'What have you done with Eva?'

'Nothing . . . I haven't done anything with her.' He was stammering. 'I told you, I know nothing about it. For God's sake, what do I have to do?'

'Tell us the truth: that's what you have to do.'

'I am. I swear. I am telling the truth.'

'Tell us where she is.'

'I don't know.'

'What about the others?' Doyle fired the question from across the table. 'What about the five we never found? Did you do the same to them, maggot? Strangle them until they danced, before you buried them?'

'I don't know what you're talking about, honest to God I don't.'

Quinn slammed him face down onto the table. 'I told you to tell us the truth.'

'I am, I am. For God's sake, I am.' Maggs was spitting, his face red, saliva drooling from his lips.

Quinn let him up and Maggs took a moment to gather himself. He touched his lips and inspected his fingers, then wiped them on his jeans. 'There you go again,' he muttered. 'How utterly predictable.' He looked up savagely. 'There'll be marks, Moss, just like before – only this time I'll sue the shit out of both of you.'

Quinn grabbed his hair. 'Do you think I care about marks? You little fuck, when I'm finished they'll not be able to see you for them.'

Holstering his gun, he stood back. 'Three little mice,' he said.

'*Three little mice couldn't find their way; for three little mice the clock stopped that day.*'

'Poetry, you toe-rag,' Doyle said. 'Another little rhyme to get us going.'

'Not from me,' Maggs said.

'Of course it was from you. You're having a laugh, playing a game with a couple of guards you've been fucking with forever.'

Maggs touched his forehead where it was marked red and a lump was already beginning to swell. 'I think I need a lawyer,' he said sarcastically. 'You know, before things get out of hand.'

Quinn snorted. 'You have no idea.'

'I'm entitled to a lawyer.'

'You're entitled to fuck all.' Again Quinn was alongside him. He clamped his hand over the back of Maggs's. 'What's Eva entitled to, eh?'

'Prayer,' Maggs said. 'She's entitled to prayer.'

'Jesus, but you're a sick fucker.' Doyle shook his head.

Maggs rounded on him now. 'What's sick about praying for a friend? What's sick about the fact that I forgave you, Doyle, for the kicking you gave me? How sick is that, compared to the feller who dished it out?'

'You confessed, you gobshite.'

'Rubbish.' Maggs glowered at Quinn once more. 'Go ahead, Moss. Get your gloves and your phone books and your armlocks. Get the thumbscrews and the rack while you're at it. Do what you like, because I can't tell you where she is, no matter what you do to me.'

For a few moments nobody spoke, then Quinn sat down heavily. He studied his watch. 'It's eight-thirty, Conor.'

Maggs spread his palms. 'I don't know where she is.'

'Why did you ask to see Patrick Maguire when you were locked up in Mountjoy?'

'I didn't ask to see him.'

'That's not what we heard.'

'I don't care what you heard, Moss. *He* asked to see *me*.'

Now they both stared at him.

'How do you know about it anyway?' Maggs asked.

'Maggot,' Doyle said, 'do you not know we know everything about you? We know you spoke to Patrick, and we know what happened on the canal with the old water rat.' He jerked his thumb over his shoulder. 'Mugging the poor bastard. How much did you take, eh? And how does it square with your friends back there?'

'I've another question for you,' Quinn interrupted. 'Who do you know from Kildare?'

Maggs looked bewildered.

'The lilywhite boys: *two, two, the lilywhite boys*. You know the poem, don't you?'

'Of course I do.'

'Lilywhites are people from Kildare. So who do you know from Kildare?'

All at once, Maggs started laughing.

'What's funny?' Quinn demanded.

Maggs shook his head.

'What the hell are you laughing about?'

'Maguire, Moss: Patrick Maguire.'

'What about him?'

'He's from County Kildare.'

Quinn stared at him. 'No he's not: he's from Dublin.'

'No.' Maggs leant towards him now, eyes dark, hair hanging to his brows. 'He's from Clane in County Kildare.'

'How do you know that?' Doyle asked.

Maggs spread his palms again. 'Because he told me.'

Tuesday 2nd September
7.45 pm

They left him alone then. Outside in the corridor, Quinn looked bemusedly at Doyle.

'What do you reckon?' he said.

Doyle hunched his shoulders. 'I'm buggered if I know. The whole thing: it beats the shit out of me.'

'Is he telling the truth?'

For the first time, Doyle hesitated.

'Did we fuck up, Doyler?' Quinn asked. 'Did we allow the past to cloud our judgement? Did we let personal feelings get in the way?'

Doyle made a face. 'All this time I would've sworn my instinct was right. I thought he was our man for sure . . . '

'And now?'

'I don't know. If I'm to be honest with you, Moss, I don't know. She's my brother's girl. I promised I'd look out for her. And now I just don't know.'

When they went back inside, Maggs was sitting exactly where they had left him. Doyle had organised some tea; a few minutes later, the young guard from before set three cups on the table.

'Do you want sugar?' Quinn asked Maggs.

Maggs glanced furtively at him.

'What's the matter?' Doyle said. 'Do you not know if you want sugar?'

Maggs laughed nervously. 'It's not that, it's you two: one moment you've a gun in my ear, and the next you're asking me if I want sugar in my tea.'

'How would you play it if you were us?' Quinn asked him. 'Just supposing it was you who'd married her, and I was sitting where you are, and she was missing. With time running out, how would you play it, Conor?'

Maggs sipped tea, both hands hooking the cup like a child. 'Why were the two of you separated?' he said. 'I thought you were always so tight.'

Quinn thought about this before answering. 'You knew about my son?'

Maggs nodded. 'A hit-and-run, north of the river. I heard about it, of course.'

'It came between us. Sometimes these things do.'

'Grief is a terrible thing,' Maggs said, glancing at Doyle again. 'Everyone handles it in their own way. When my mother died, I didn't know what to do with myself. I know what people thought of her, but she was my mother. She was an alcoholic; addicted. It was a sickness; it wasn't her fault. I hated what she did, but she had no choice: she'd never have been that way in any other circumstances.'

His gaze seemed to fasten on the floor. 'I had nothing to do with Eva's disappearance. Moss, you have to know I would never hurt her. When I was a kid, she was my only friend. You never understood that, but when you came down to Kerry, it was my only friend you were taking. That's what she was. I may have loved her; I may have wished our relationship could've been more than that; but whatever anyone thought, Eva was my friend.'

Taking a shallow breath, he gestured. 'Everyone decided that because I asked my auntie to buy her a necklace, I somehow thought I had some kind of claim on her. But it was never like that: I didn't follow her around like the lost puppy everyone said I was.' He squinted darkly, tilting his head so he could look at Doyle. 'You were suspicious because of how my mam died. I know you were; I heard the rumours. But Jimmy paraded that picture around the school, and even though he had twenty-odd backing him, I went for him. I took them all on, didn't I? I'm not going to defend my mam like that, then put drain cleaner in a wine bottle knowing that when she's drunk she's likely to guzzle it.'

Quinn was scouring his face now, seeking the hint of a lie. 'Did you kill Mary Harrington?'

Maggs shook his head. 'No,' he said, 'I didn't.'

'Do you know where Eva is?'

Again he shook his head.

'Why did you ask to see Patrick?'

'I told you, that's not how it was. It was him that asked to see me.'

Quinn and Doyle glanced at each other.

'I couldn't work it out either,' Maggs said, gesturing. 'I mean, he'd told you he saw me with Mary Harrington, and I knew he was going to testify, so what the hell did he want to see me about? He knew I was never with Mary Harrington – not in the way he told you, anyway. She might have been at the corner when I nipped over to buy Molly a package of fags, but I never spoke to her, short of asking if she was all right.'

'He told us you had your heads together,' Doyle said. 'That you spoke to her for at least a couple of minutes.'

Maggs snorted. 'So did Jimmy Hanrahan.'

'They got it wrong then, did they?'

'Sergeant, I told you how it was when you first interviewed me: I didn't speak to Mary other than ask her if she was all right. I mean, she was drunk, wasn't she?'

'Talking of drunk,' Quinn said, 'why did you get Molly to say what she did when you both knew she was in no state to remember?'

Maggs gave a short, scornful laugh. 'You know why. Sergeant Doyle was convinced I killed my mother, and you thought I'd been spying on you down by the river. I'm not stupid: it wasn't going to take much for the pair of you to come after me.'

'What did you and Patrick talk about?' Quinn asked him.

'What do you think we talked about? Mary Harrington, of course. I was sure he was looking for something.'

'What d'you mean: "looking for something"?'

'I mean something other than the confession you got; something that wasn't forced; something that would make him sleep a little easier.'

'What do you mean: "sleep a little easier"?'

'You're the detective; you work it out.'

'Are you saying that Patrick had something to do with Mary's death?'

'I'm not saying anything: whenever I open my mouth, I get my teeth kicked in. '

'What else did you talk about?'

Maggs shook his head.

'Come on, I'm asking you: what else did you talk about?'

'That night down by the river.'

'You mean, when he found you in the bushes with your trousers round your ankles?'

'So he says.'

'What were you doing there, then?'

Maggs didn't reply.

'Conor, I'm asking you a question.'

'And you wouldn't believe the answer. You were on a rugby tour with your best mate and I was the little gobshite who wouldn't let

Eva alone.' He shook his head dejectedly. 'Ah, come on, I'm done with this. I've told you all I know.'

'No you haven't. And I'm asking,' Quinn said. 'How come you were down by the river?'

Maggs peered at the floor. 'If you must know, I was there because it was obvious how Patrick had been looking at Eva. I saw him that first night in the pub, remember, and I saw him when the two of you took off. He followed *you*, Moss; all I was doing was following *him*.' He looked closely at Quinn. 'I didn't like the way he was looking at Eva. And why do you think he made such a hullabaloo lipping off like he did? I mean, if it had been you coming upon me like that, what would you have done, yelled your head off? I don't think so. More likely you'd be dragging me off somewhere to give me a quiet kicking.'

Tuesday 2nd September
8.30 pm

The canal looked very peaceful: the shadows of trees in the street lights; a few people wandering the towpath on the other side. With the flat in darkness, Patrick Maguire stood at his window and watched as he liked to do: with no light to distract him, he was able to pick up the subtleties, the nuances of the night. He thought of Eva. He thought of Willie Moore and his calculations. He thought of Quinn on the phone earlier.

He poured another slug of Bushmills. Adding a splash of water from the kitchen tap, he drank it down and set the glass on the draining board. He felt a little nervous: he moved about the flat with a sudden sense of trepidation, the kind of feeling he'd not had in a long time. Sitting in a chair, he lifted a foot to rest against the hearth, and, as always, his gaze was drawn to her picture.

Frank was right: he should have ditched it long ago.

He thought about pouring another shot of whiskey but he'd had two big glugs already: anymore and he'd get a headache. He couldn't remain in the flat, though: it seemed very cramped indeed.

He made his way across the road and onto the towpath. Here he hesitated, thinking he'd make a right and head towards Lansdowne Road. Instead, he walked the other way towards Richmond Bridge, planning to stroll down past the barracks.

But he didn't.

Crossing the bridge, he paused to wrinkle his nose at the smokers gathered outside the Portobello. Wandering a little further on, he stopped at Jocky O'Connell's pub. He bought a pint of lager and sat at the bar shooting the breeze with Marie, the barmaid. He knew her well – they all did – and Marie told him to tell Moss that everyone was praying for the safe return of his wife.

Tuesday 2nd September
9 pm

Eva had no idea of time, though it was dark again and the clock was ticking. She knew that her life was slowly ebbing away.

She could see Danny, though his face was dim. She could see Jess and Laura, though theirs were dimmer still.

She could see her mother and her sisters; she could see her Uncle Joe.

She could see Moss when he was nineteen. She could see Patrick Maguire.

Words; sentences; half-phrases; things people had said; pictures; images from the past swimming before her eyes. This must be how it was then: this was how it was before you died.

Then she heard the footsteps.

No matter how weak she was, she could always hear the footsteps.

And she would begin to tremble: her bowels would weaken; she could feel urine that wasn't there.

She could hear the clock and she could hear his footsteps.

She heard the door swing open and he was in the room and she waited for his voice. She wept tearlessly: knowing he was standing right above her; knowing there was nothing she could do.

She wanted to cry out but her limbs were so weak, her mind so confused. Even if she had no gag, there was nothing she could say. But she could hear him, she could feel him and she could almost smell him now as he stood above her looking down on the grave.

That's what this was now, a resting place where there would be no rest. Sooner or later, her periods of unconsciousness would lengthen and lengthen until she never woke again. When she thought of it like that, she was almost calm: she would be with Danny, and Moss would look after Jess and Laura. They would be all right. They wanted their daddy, and they were so young that they had never understood why she'd sent him away in the first place.

And then she heard his voice again. It assaulted her, life something physical. That hoarse whisper. 'If they're clever enough, they will find you. Do you hear me, Eva? If they're clever enough, they will.'

They won't, she thought. *It's too late.*

And in her mind's eye, she could see his face and knew at last who he was.

Tuesday 2nd September
9.20 pm

Quinn and Doyle collected the other car from the school. Back at Harcourt Square, they met up on the stairs, and Quinn took his partner by the arm. 'Keep what we know to ourselves, Doyler,' he instructed. 'For now at least; until we've figured it out.'

Doyle gave him a laboured smile. 'So what is it you think we know then? I'm only a sergeant, and I tell you I'm confused.'

Frank Maguire met them as they came into the incident room. 'Moss,' he said, 'if you're going after Maggs, I need to know about it beforehand. The man is a delicate issue, and the press just love the fact that we're speaking to him again. If he wants to have a go at us, they'll be falling over themselves to give him the platform he needs. If he's been arrested, then someone who is officially tasked will need to interview him, not you.'

Quinn looked him in the eye. 'He's not been arrested, Frank.'

Maguire furrowed his brow.

'Not yet, anyway,' Doyle added. 'We spoke to him again just now, but it was all very amicable.'

Maguire took Quinn's arm and took him to one side. 'What's he going on about? Nothing between him and Maggs has ever been even vaguely amicable.'

'It's all right, Frank,' Quinn told him. 'We spoke to him and then we let him go.'

Murphy was at her desk. 'Where are the files, Murph?' Quinn asked her. 'The five missing women; what did we do with the files?'

'They're still in your office.'

Maguire followed him to his desk. 'Moss,' he said, 'I really think we should discount the other files. What's important is finding Eva; they're just complicating the issue.'

'Are they?' Quinn sat down at his desk.

'Three little mice,' Doyle stated. 'Mice and clocks: another nursery rhyme, for God's sake. Hickory dickory dock or something, is it now?'

'Who knows?' Maguire said helplessly. 'It's all cryptic nonsense, and none of it ties together.'

'Like the lilywhite boys,' Quinn said without looking up.

'Yes, like the lilywhite boys. And maggots in her head, and a photo of a stone on a patch of sand.'

Quinn checked the clock on the wall against his watch and the clock on his computer screen. Then he opened the file on Janice Long, the first woman to go missing, almost six years previously.

Half an hour later, he was outside in the car park with Doyle. 'Joseph,' he said, 'whatever Frank says, we've five missing women, all of them single mothers, and two with husbands doing time at the Joy. On top of that, we've Mary Harrington, who was pregnant, and we have Eva . . . '

'And the super's brother with access to them all,' Doyle said, finishing his sentence.

Quinn thought for a moment. 'We need to talk to him, but first I want to see what the Craw has to say. Let's get ourselves up to the North Circular and drag the tout out of bed.'

Without speaking to Frank, they crossed the river, Doyle driving and Quinn on the phone instructing the duty officer at the prison to have his informant waiting to speak to him. The man started to argue because of the time, of course, but Quinn told him that it was in direct relation to his missing wife. By the time they got beyond the grey Victorian walls, Lorne McGeady's accountant was waiting in an interview room.

Quinn had a carton of cigarettes for him: he'd make more money selling those than if he was given straight cash, and it would keep his reputation intact. The Craw was in his forties, with greying hair. He was slightly built, gaunt even; he looked as though he'd never eaten enough. He had one of the sharpest minds in Mountjoy, however, and nothing ever escaped him.

'Hello, Craw,' Quinn said, sitting down in the white-walled room with a single table and three chairs.

'Do you know Sergeant Doyle?'

'Who doesn't know Sergeant Doyle, at least by reputation?'

'Craw, you know my wife is missing.'

'Of course I do; everyone does; and I can tell you it is causing great consternation not just on the streets but behind these hallowed walls. It doesn't do to cross the lines of demarcation; even sociopaths like the Ukrainian understand that. '

'Listen,' Quinn said, 'I need help to find her, and whoever offers that help will be remembered.' He passed him the box of cigarettes.

'Inspector,' Craw said, 'I can tell you that even as we speak, the fraternity of Mountjoy Brothers is kneeling in supplication.'

'I need more than fucking prayers, Craw, I need information.' Quinn drew a sharp breath through his nose. 'Why, when he was going to testify against him, did Paddy Maguire want to visit Conor Maggs?'

Craw sat back. 'Now, who spoke to me about that just recently,' he mused. 'Ah, I remember.' He spread his palms. 'I can only tell you what Maggs told me, but if you speak to Patrick, I imagine he'll tell you it was Conor that asked to see him, and not the other way round.'

Quinn considered the comment for a moment.

'Well, he would, wouldn't he?' the Craw responded. 'That's the way of it in here: never me, sir, always the other fellow. Unless of course there's some advantage in it.'

'But Maggs told you Patrick asked to see him?'

'That's what he said.'

'What did they talk about?'

'Maggots,' the Crawthumper said.

*

Maggs was sitting at the table when Paddy Maguire came in. Arms folded, he looked up as the door was closed, and the prison visitor placed his soft leather briefcase on the table.

'Well, well, Brother,' Maggs said. 'A visit from you, this is a surprise.'

Maguire looked him in the eye. 'I'm not your brother.'

'No, of course you're not. I know you're not. It's just a figure of speech.'

'Yeah, well don't use it with me. Do you understand?'

Maggs nodded. 'So tell me – I'm curious, given how you're going to testify against me – what did you want to see me about?'

'Conor, *you* wanted to see *me.*'

With a nod of acknowledgement, Maggs indicated the leather briefcase. 'I get it,' he said. 'You've a tape recorder in there, and you're hoping maybe I'll give you another confession.'

He laughed then without humour. 'What is it, Paddy? Quinn and Doyle send you, did they? Hoping to get something they can say wasn't forced?' He blew the air from his cheeks. 'Well they can think again, brother. You'll not have me putting my name to any more of their lies.'

'I've told you,' Maguire said, 'I'm not your brother, and there's no tape in my bag.'

'So what do you want then? Have you come here to counsel me? Is that it? Is it the power you like, maybe?'

Maguire didn't answer him.

All at once, realisation seemed to dawn, and Maggs sat back in his chair. 'You've come to gloat, haven't you? Of course you have; that's what you do. Of all people, I should know. You get your man in a spot and then you like to gloat. It's what you did in Kerry, remember, when we were down by the river.'

Leaning forward once more, he brought the flat of his hand down on the table. 'The crack you made in front of Eva in the pub on the night of the *fleadh cheoil*. I understand. Of course I do. No wonder you told them I was speaking to Mary.'

'What're you talking about?' Maguire asked him.

'I'm talking about how I saw you watching Eva that night all those years ago, when all the time you've been claiming it was the other way round. Is that what you're doing now, Patrick, making sure I take the fall?'

Patrick was trembling slightly.

'You're here to ensure I go down.' Maggs's gaze was dull suddenly. 'Well you won't get away with it. I'm going to get off, and when I do, where will you be then?'

He was silent for a moment, then he added: '*Aithininn ciaróg, Paddy. Aithininn ciaróg ciaróg eile.*'

Tuesday 2nd September
9.22 pm

For a few moments, the two detectives just sat there with the Craw opposite them, his expression grave and his hands clasped in his lap.

'*Aithininn ciaróg,*' Doyle muttered, '*aithininn ciaróg ciaróg eile.*' Turning to Quinn, he translated: 'One maggot recognises another.'

Quinn was considering the informant. 'What was all that talk about a brother?' he asked.

'It was a joke, Mr Quinn; a little dig, I'm thinking.'

'What do you mean?'

'Patrick, he almost joined the Society.'

'What're you talking about?'

'The Society of Christian Brothers: we've one or two in here at the moment.'

'Them and the priests,' Doyle muttered. 'Jesus, there must be more Mass said in Irish prisons than Irish churches these days.'

'Craw, what do you mean Patrick almost joined the Brothers?' Quinn asked.

The tout looked across the table at him. 'Inspector, you played rugby with the lad, did you not?'

'For years, yes.'

'And you'd no idea?'

'No.'

'From the age of eleven, he was brought up at Islandbridge.'

Quinn stared at him.

'He was a full-time boarder at St Boniface. One of the monks that taught him is right here in the Joy: they say he buggered some other lad, but I don't believe it. He's a man of God and I'm sure he's innocent. If not, God will forgive him.'

'Paddy was brought up at Islandbridge?' Quinn cocked one eyebrow. 'But his mam and dad, Craw, they're ex-pats; they live in Dubai or somewhere.'

The tout shook his head. 'No they don't. When they were kids, Frank and Patrick lived in a council block in County Kildare and neither of them ever knew their dad. Their mam was dead from the drink by the time Patrick was eleven.'

Both Quinn and Doyle were silent, sitting with their arms folded, gazing across the table.

'Frank went straight to Templemore,' the Craw went on. 'He'd always wanted to be a copper, and he'd always wanted to be accepted. It was him who let folk believe all that stuff about their parents: he didn't want anyone to know the truth; what he wanted was respectability. Patrick was only eleven and he had nowhere to go, so Frank asked the Brothers if they would take him, and from eleven to eighteen he lived at St Boniface. He was all set to become a monk himself, apparently, then all of a sudden he left, claiming he's an atheist.'

'What happened?' Doyle asked him.

'I have no idea, but these days "Brother Patrick", as Conor used to refer to him, has no time for religion or the Church; all he believes in is survival of the fittest.'

Outside, the wind was up. The clouds were heavy and rain was spotting the roof of the car. Quinn stood in the darkness with his jacket buttoned.

Doyle faced him from the driver's side. 'So Maggs was telling the truth,' he said. 'In part at least, anyway.'

'What part?'

'The part about Paddy being from Kildare,' Doyle said, opening the door. 'Do you not think it's time we went and spoke to him?'

Quinn got in the car. 'I think it's time we spoke to Frank, Doyler: let's get back to the Square.'

They bumped into Murphy in the car park, and Quinn asked her to find out where the call to his home phone had come from.

'Already on it,' she said. 'I'm getting the Eircom team to look into it, but they won't be there till tomorrow.'

'That'll have to do, then.' They carried on to the stairs, then something else occurred to Quinn, and he called to Murphy again. 'Listen, Keira, when you send Jimmy Hanrahan's pictures back, take out the photo of Maggs's mother, would you?'

'What do you want me to do with it?'

'Put a match to it; tear it up; just get rid of it – I don't care how.'

Doyle's phone was ringing. Unhooking it from his belt, he peered at it long-sightedly. 'Your man from the moorings,' he muttered. Then, turning away, he spoke into the phone: 'Johnny Clogs, how are you?'

Finucane's voice was surly in his ear. 'What do you want, Doyler? My boy Dessie tells me you've been down to my boat again, only this time you were threatening to burn it.'

'Did he say that? He must've misheard.'

'Listen, you gobshite, I've told you before: one of these days you'll be retired and you won't have the uniform to protect you.'

'No, but I'll have my guns, Johnny. I'll always have me guns.'

'For fuck's sake, what do you want, Doyler? It's bad for business, the guards all over my boat.'

'We've had words with Maggs again, and your cousin is still say-ing he was with her at the time Quinn's wife went missing.'

'So what're you telling me for?'

'I want to know for sure.'

'And if I find out for sure, will you leave us the fuck alone?'

'Course I will. You're a gangster, Clogger: I only speak to you if I have to.'

Hanging up, Doyle followed Quinn up to the incident room, where Frank Maguire was briefing a group of detectives. Murphy grabbed him at the door. 'Sarge,' she said, 'I've been thinking about that last call: the one to Moss's home number.'

'What about it?'

'What if *three mice who couldn't find their way* weren't so much lost as blind?'

Doyle squinted at her now. 'Three blind mice. Now that's a thought, Murph. Look into it, why don't you? And let me know what you find.'

Finished with the briefing, Maguire stepped into Quinn's office. With black bags crawling under his eyes, Quinn had the look of a man who needed a good night's sleep.

'What gives?' Maguire asked. 'Moss, I've seen that expression before, remember. Speak to me, will you? Tell me what's on your mind.'

Quinn glanced briefly at Doyle. 'It might just be that we're all of us exhausted, Frank, but a couple of things have cropped up that we need to talk about. '

'I'm all ears,' Maguire said, throwing out a hand. 'Heavens above, am I. I mean, there's nothing else. We've a photo but no camera; we've a bunch of cryptic clues that don't . . . '

'Like the cruel mother, you mean,' Quinn said softly. 'And a cou-ple of lilywhite boys from Kildare: Clane to be exact, Frank. Clane in County Kildare.'

The colour drained from Maguire's face. 'What do you know about Clane?'

'I know about a council flat. I know about a couple of lads with a drunk for a mother, and neither of whom knew their father.'

'Who've you been talking to?'

'It doesn't matter. The question is: is it true? Is it true that you and your kid brother are a couple of lilywhite boys from Kildare?'

Maguire looked coldly at him now. 'Are you accusing me of something, inspector?'

'I'm asking you if it's true.'

Maguire regarded Doyle for a moment, then slowly nodded.

'So why the bullshit? Why pretend you've a mam and dad living out in Dubai?'

Maguire didn't say anything.

'Do you really think people give a shit?'

'When I was eighteen I did.'

Quinn sat down heavily. 'Tell me,' he said. 'Tell me about Paddy. I know he ended up at Islandbridge, but before then, Frank? What happened before?'

Maguire seemed to slump in the chair. For almost a minute, he sat there without answering. 'I looked after him,' he said finally. 'I brought him up, even though I was only a kid myself. You see, his mother – *our* mother – never gave him the time of day. If you asked Liam Ahern, he'd probably tell you that Paddy wasn't programmed properly.'

Tuesday 2nd September
9.30 pm

The sudden stillness was punctured only by the ticking of the clock. Both Quinn and Doyle were staring at their boss now, and he was staring at the carpet on the floor.

'Programmed, Frank?' Quinn asked softly.

'Isn't that how the good doctor refers to it, when someone doesn't get that initial injection of love, of care, of understanding? That's the profile you've been working on, Moss. You and Murphy – that's what you've been thinking when you look at those other files.'

'Is that what you're thinking?' Doyle asked him.

Maguire didn't answer. Instead, he got to his feet and paced to the window, where he stood with his back to them.

'Paddy visited Janice Long's husband in Mountjoy,' Quinn said. 'It's always been in the file – her and Karen Brady – but we never thought anything of it, not until we spoke to Willie Moore.'

'What about Willie Moore?' Maguire said, turning suddenly to Quinn. 'Moss, I'm supposed to be leading this investigation. What about Willie Moore?'

'There was someone who knew Mary was pregnant,' Quinn said

coldly. 'Patrick knew, Frank: Willie Moore told him.'

Maguire's mouth was hanging open.

'I've asked him about it, and he says he didn't tell me because the conversations are supposed to be confidential. I suppose I can just about deal with that, but it's not all: according to Lorne McGeady's accountant, he also spoke to Maggs when Maggs was on remand. That's not in any file, Frank, and it's not on any prison record.'

Maguire was ᵂ : te now. 'What're you saying to me?'

Quinn lift᷅ . nis hands. 'I don't know. Perhaps I'm asking why I don't know my old buddy as well as I thought I did. Perhaps I'm asking you what happened to him. Perhaps I'm asking why, when he was due to join the Society of Christian Brothers, he suddenly upped and left.'

Maguire sat down behind the other desk now. He looked exhausted, ill, haunted. 'Patrick told us he saw Maggs with Mary Harrington,' he said. 'So did Jimmy Hanrahan – the two of them saying the same thing independently of each other. It means that Maggs *did* speak to her and that he *did* lie to us.'

'Yes,' Quinn agreed. 'But it doesn't mean he killed her.'

The superintendent clasped his hands together. 'Spit it out then, Moss, will you? Are you accusing my brother of murder? Are you accusing him of abducting Eva?'

'I don't know, Frank, are you?'

Outside in the car park, Quinn felt for a cigarette but the pack was empty. 'Let's get a beer,' Doyle suggested. 'Fuck, could I do with a couple.'

Crossing the street, they bellied up to the bar in the Harcourt Hotel. Billy stuck glasses under the Guinness taps and poured them each a shot of Jameson.

'Put a drop of port in mine, would you?' Doyle asked him. He looked sideways at Quinn, then took the box of snuff from his pocket and worked some into his nose.

'Jesus, I need a smoke,' Quinn said. 'Billy, have you got any fags?'

The barman tossed him a pack of Embassy; taking their whiskeys, they stepped outside. Quinn stared at the darkened brick building across the street, the lights on the fifth floor.

'It isn't the first time it's occurred to him,' Doyle stated.

'What?'

'Frank Maguire; the implication of what we were saying: it's not the first time it's occurred to him. I could see it in his eyes, Moss: he's thought about this before.'

Wednesday 3rd September
8 am

Waking up on the sofa, Quinn had never known such silence: his son dead, his wife missing and his daughters with their grandmother in Kerry. He could've wept; his face ached with fatigue and the circles under his eyes seemed not to be part of his skin. The doorbell rang; crossing the hall, he could see Doyle's bulky frame in the glass.

'Did you sleep?' Doyle asked him.

'Some, maybe. Did you?'

'Mrs Mulroney had a bottle of Bushmills in the house. I think I managed a couple of hours.'

He followed Quinn to the kitchen and spooned coffee grounds into a filter. Filling the jug, he added water and stood back as the percolator began to gurgle.

'So listen,' he said, 'there's something I've been meaning to ask you.'

'What's that? '

'How long have you've been sleeping with Garda Murphy?'

Quinn was bent to the fridge, poking around for something he could stuff into his mouth. He spoke without looking up. 'How did you find out?'

'I'm not stupid. I've seen you around her, boy: I know how it is.'

'It's only been the once. '

'The night Eva was taken.'

Quinn closed his eyes.

'Makes you feel guilty, does it?'

'Yes, it makes me feel guilty, what with the kids not being able to get hold of me. Yes, Joseph, it makes me feel very guilty. Does that make you happy?'

Doyle inhaled sharply. ''Tis none of my business what you do, Moss – unless of course it affects me. And given that Eva's my niece, I think it does affect me. But I'm not judging you, and I'm not really making a comment, I just thought I'd let you know that I know, in case you wanted to get anything off yer chest.'

Quinn looked sourly at him. 'You sarcastic bastard; you're telling me to get even. You're telling me because I've been on at you about your gut feelings and how you battered the Maggot.' He paused.

'Does Murphy know you know?'

'I haven't told her.'

'Well don't. It was a one-off, Doyler, all right?'

Doyle brought the coffee through to the lounge. 'I was just letting you know I know, that's all,' he repeated. 'You don't have to explain. I saw what was going on: Eva blaming the both of us for not being able to do anything about Danny. Juxtapose that with Maggs being charged with murder and throw in her Uncle Joe and his loose hands and what've you got? A woman on the edge: a woman who's thrashing around and hitting out at those she loves.'

'And those who love her,' Quinn added. 'I've never stopped loving her, and I never blamed her for pushing me away.' There were tears in his eyes suddenly. 'When a child dies, you don't get over it. You never get over it. You never make it back, Doyler, you just have to learn how to cope.'

Doyle sat down on the sofa and considered the younger man now with kindness in his eyes.

'We'll find her,' he said. 'We will, lad, I know it.'

They ate breakfast in a café they frequented on the Cabra Road. Notwithstanding the tension, the anxiety, Quinn realised he'd hardly had a mouthful since Sunday and he was ravenous.

'Do you want to go and see if Paddy's home?' Doyle suggested. 'Do you want to call him up?'

Quinn shook his head. 'No, I think we should leave him to Frank. Frank's a good copper; he'll do what he thinks he has to.' He swallowed a mouthful of coffee. 'What I want to do is go to Islandbridge and speak to the Brothers.'

St Boniface was situated on the south bank of the Liffey close to the war memorial. To the north, the river widened to encompass a series of leafy green islands, the mini lagoon punctuated by the tumble of a weir.

Parking the car, the two detectives got out, and for a moment Quinn just stood there and reflected: he could see rowing boats on the south shore; he could see the whitened height of the buildings on the road beyond; he could see the bridges and pathways that linked the islands.

'Not so bad a place to grow up,' Doyle commented. 'Beats the bejaysus out of some crappy estate in Clane.'

Brother Peter Farrell met them at the main door. He was wearing a long black cassock and full white collar that denoted him as a monk and not a priest. He was in his late fifties, with weathered features, and white hair cut short like a US Marine. Brother Peter led them down to the banks of the river with his hands in his pockets.

Quinn could hear the sound of the weir, and he imagined his wife hidden somewhere with nothing to drink. By ten o'clock tonight, she could be in a coma.

'What is it you wanted to speak to me about, inspector?' Farrell asked him.

'Patrick Pearse Maguire.'

Farrell's expression darkened. From his pocket, he brought out a rosary, considered it for a few moments, then worked a couple of the beads between his fingers before hiding it away again.

'He was with you twenty years ago,' Quinn went on. 'From the age of eleven to eighteen. He was going to join the Society, but something changed his mind.'

'Is this official, inspector?'

Quinn half-closed his eyes. 'I'm trying to find my wife, Brother Peter.'

The wind lifted, and the Liffey was flecked with whitecaps all at once. 'You remember him, then?' Doyle asked.

Farrell nodded. 'Of course I do. He's Superintendent Frank Maguire's brother. Frank is a good man, a good Catholic. To this day, he supports us with fund-raising, letters of referral, that kind of thing. You realise I'll have to tell him you're asking.'

'Of course you will,' Quinn said. 'That's your prerogative. But in the meantime, you can tell us.'

'Tell you what, exactly?'

'How Patrick Pearse came to be here, and why he left when he did.'

Wednesday 3rd September
9 am

When Patrick came out of the front door, his brother was leaning against his silver Opel with his arms folded.

'Frank?' Patrick exclaimed. 'What're you doing here?'

Frank didn't answer immediately; pushing himself away from the car, he crossed the road.

'I was waiting for you, Pat. Let's go inside.'

Patrick looked puzzled. 'I can't, Frankie, I've an appointment at the prison. '

'It can wait.'

'What are you on about?'

'It can wait, Patrick,' his brother insisted. 'Let's go upstairs.'

At the window, Frank gazed over the canal. 'This is a nice place,' he said. 'You know, living right here in the city . . . you could do a lot worse.'

'I know I could. I've seen a lot worse, believe me.' Patrick was standing beside the fireplace.

'What's up, Frank? What's all this about?'

His brother didn't answer.

'Frank, what is it? Is it Eva? Is she all right? Have you found her? Is everything all right?'

Frank looked round at him now. 'I don't know, Paddy? Is everything all right?'

Patrick furrowed his brow. 'What're you talking about?'

'Eva: do you know where she is?'

'Of course I don't. How could I?'

'Moss thinks you might.'

'What?' Patrick was aghast, shock standing out in his eyes. 'What're you talking about?'

'He told me you were Willie Moore's visitor.'

Patrick's shoulders slumped then, and with a heavy sigh he sat down. 'Of course he did,' he muttered.

'Why didn't you tell him, Paddy? Why didn't you tell *me*?'

Patrick peered at now with a bemused shake of his head. 'My God,' he said, 'I'm not sure I believe this. A woman is missing – and not just any woman, but a friend I've known for twenty years – and you're telling me I'm a suspect?'

'I didn't say that.'

'That's the implication.'

'Why did you go and see Maggs when he was on remand?' Frank asked him. 'And why didn't you tell anyone?'

'I didn't go to see him. I'm a visitor, Frank; I was in Mountjoy, and he asked to see me. Jesus, I was with him for all of five minutes.'

'It's not in any record.'

'Why should it be? It was impromptu: I was already there seeing other inmates.'

'You didn't think it was a conflict of interest then, given that we were relying on your testimony?'

'The case was thrown out, Frank, long before I got anywhere near the witness box.'

Frank peered at him. 'What did he say to you? Did he accuse you of killing Mary Harrington?'

'Something like that, I suppose. I don't really remember.'

'And you didn't think that was very important?'

'It was Maggs, Frankie. He was just mouthing off.'

'And did you?'

'Did I what?'

'Kill Mary Harrington.'

'Jesus, Frankie.'

His brother looked at his watch. 'Eva is still alive, Paddy. If our reckoning is correct, there's still time to save her. If you know anything about this — anything at all — you have to tell me.'

Patrick was on his feet. 'Jesus H. Christ,' he said, 'I really do not believe we're having this conversation.'

'Do not blaspheme. Do you hear me?' Frank was shouting now. 'There's enough godforsaken language I have to listen to without you adding to it.'

'Frank!' Patrick's gaze was fierce suddenly. 'Have you heard yourself? I mean, have you? You're my brother, not my dad. For all you did for me, you're not my mam. You just can't help yourself, can you? All my life, on and on and on. Coming in here with your key, snooping around and telling me what to do and when to do it, wondering where I am. You're the one who dumped me at St Boniface while you went off to play at being important. Where do you get off telling me anything at all? Where do you get off asking me these questions? I know nothing about what happened to Eva and nothing about Mary.'

'I can ask because of Willie Moore and Karen Brady, because of Janice Long. I can ask because of how it was when we were kids.'

'Do I fit the profile, Frank, is that it?' Patrick bent close to him. 'I'd never have made any secret of the past if you hadn't gone on about it so much. You're the one who invented all that crap about us being Dubs with parents in Dubai; an old feller who didn't exist, working in the oil business.' He turned to the photo of their mother. 'Respectability; acceptance, or whatever it was. Fuck it, Frank: I was the one she couldn't stand looking at, and I was the one who didn't give a shit.'

'You knew Mary Harrington was pregnant,' Frank reminded him. 'You spoke to Maggs and you visited the husbands of Karen Brady and Janice Long.'

'So what?'

'So it doesn't look good, Paddy.' Frank regarded the photograph. 'And you hated her. I mean, you truly despised her every bit as much as she despised you. She said you had the devil in you.'

Patrick laughed out loud. 'Oh for heaven's sake, don't go getting all religious on me, on top of everything else. There's no such thing as the devil, Frank. There's no God, no virgin birth, no m—'

Frank interrupted him. 'No perfect mother, Patrick, is that what you're telling me?' For a moment he stared at him. 'Is that why you did it before you left St Boniface? Desecration, Patrick: the Holy Mother of God.'

Wednesday 3rd September
9.30 am

Quinn and Doyle sat across the desk from Dr Liam Ahern in his office overlooking O'Connell Bridge.

The forensic psychiatrist, who was in his forties, with longish hair and blue eyes, was as good as any in his field. He worked in the UK and America; he advised courts and police officers in Australia, New Zealand, South Africa and many European countries. He retained a residency with the FBI at Quantico but he had been born in Dublin and chose to work from this office overlooking the streets of what had once been the second city of the British Empire.

The garda didn't need to use him very often, though he had been asked to assess some people who had been victims of child abuse at the hands of Catholic priests.

Quinn knew him through discussions they had had about the five missing women; Dr Ahern had created a 'suspect profile' for him.

Dr Ahern wore an open-necked shirt under a designer jacket and reclined in a handmade leather chair. 'Are we talking about your wife, Moss?' he asked.

Quinn held his gaze. 'Is it possible that someone with the kind of profile we discussed before could consider Eva in the same fashion as the others?'

'It's possible, yes. Given that you and she were estranged – and from what you say it was at her instigation – if someone was aware of it, they could stretch it, maybe, if they were of that mindset.'

'In two of the other cases,' Quinn went on, 'the fathers were doing time in Mountjoy. They were in the process of getting divorced, Liam, remember? By getting rid of their husbands, both Janice Long and Karen Brady became single mothers. With me and Eva, it's not that dissimilar, is it?'

'Moss,' Ahern looked closely at him, 'I've just said: if we're talking about that kind of mindset, it's possible. Now, I've been as worried about your wife as the rest of Ireland. What've you found out that I don't know about?'

Quinn sat forward. 'A woman gives birth to two illegitimate sons. She kills them and buries them. Then on the way home, she sees two boys playing and tells them that if they were hers, she would dress them in good clothes and take care of them. The boys tell her that when they *were* hers, she didn't take care of them; she murdered them. They tell her she will be damned for it.'

For a few short seconds, there was silence. Considering Quinn for a moment, Ahern gazed out of the window. 'The Ballad of the Cruel Mother', he said:

> *'She sat down below a thorn,*
> *Fine flowers in the valley,*
> *And there she has her sweet babe born*
> *And the green leaves they grow rarely.'*

> *'She has taken out her penknife,*
> *Fine flowers in the valley,*
> *And robbed the sweet babe of its life*
> *And the green leaves they grow rarely.'*

He turned again, and Quinn sat forward in his chair. 'There was once a boy who in his mother's eyes barely even existed. She never fed or changed him; she didn't even give him a name. She never bothered to load any of the software you talk about. That, along with everything else, was left up to his elder brother. But his brother was only seven when this second lad was born. When he was eighteen, their mother died and the younger brother was placed with the Society of Christian Brothers. Big brother went off to join the police force, and everything seemed to be all right – that was, until his little brother reached eighteen. Then he went into the chapel and pissed on a statue of the Virgin.'

Wednesday 3rd September
10 am

Murphy was at her desk when the superintendent walked in. He looked drawn and pale, the fatigue of the past couple of days seeming to hang like weights from his shoulders. He didn't speak to anyone, just went into Quinn's office and draped his jacket over the back of the chair.

Grabbing the notes she'd made, Murphy knocked on the door.

'What is it?' Maguire said.

'The call, superintendent: the one to Inspector's Quinn's house. The Eircom team just told me it came from a phone box in Harold's Cross.'

Maguire sat back then, looking thoughtful. 'Where was Maggs when Quinn and Doyle picked him up?'

'He was attending a prayer meeting at the school next door to the hospice and Mount Jerome Cemetery.'

'And they interviewed him at Crumlin Road?'

She nodded.

'OK, thank you.'

'Jimmy Hanrahan was interviewed at Terenure, superintendent,'

Murphy added. 'When the results came in, he was given the bus fare home and told to get across the river to Amiens Street.'

Again, Maguire looked up at her. 'A route that took him through Harold's Cross.'

'That's right.' She glanced briefly at the papers she was holding. 'There's one more thing, superintendent, something I mentioned to Sergeant Doyle.'

Perching on the chair opposite, she told him about the idea she'd had about the lost mice being blind. 'I did some investigating into the origins of the "Three Blind Mice" nursery rhyme,' she said. 'And most commentators think it's quite modern – a couple of hundred years old, maybe. But there is one theory that claims it's much older.'

'What's that?'

'There's a school of thought that believes it refers to Bloody Mary, Mary I of England: Henry VIII's daughter by Catherine of Aragon. She came to the English throne in 1553 when her half-brother died of TB.'

'So?'

'So she was a Catholic like her mother, and she began to repeal the changes her father had made when he split from Rome. In 1555, she blinded and then burnt three men at the stake: Hugh Latimer, Nicholas Ridley and Thomas Cranmer, the Archbishop of Canterbury.'

Maguire considered her. 'A bit of English history, eh? It doesn't tell us a whole lot, does it?'

'Not on the face of it, I suppose, no, but it's all I managed to come up with. I don't know, I just thought I'd mention it.'

'Well thank you, guard.' Maguire took a moment to think. 'Tell me more about the phone box.'

'There's nothing to tell, really. I organised forensics; they might get a latent print.'

'Get hold of Moss, Keira, and tell him it was Harold's Cross.'

*

Quinn and Doyle left Ahern's office and walked back to their car. As Quinn opened the driver's door, his mobile rang. 'Keira,' he said. 'How's Frank this morning? Is he looking for us?'

'He asked me to phone you,' she said. Then she told him about the call box.

'Harold's Cross?' Quinn was squinting at Doyle.

'Just before seven o'clock. I've got a forensics team on its way, and I'm heading down there myself.'

'Maggs was in Harold's Cross,' Quinn stated.

'So was Jimmy Hanrahan: that's why the super wanted me to tell you. He asked that I call you specifically.'

'OK, we'll get down to Tom Kelly and see if Maggs is in. Stop off on your way, Murph. Meet us at the flats.'

There was no one home when they pulled up behind Richmond Street. Staring at the darkened front door, Doyle blew out his cheeks.

'What the fuck is going on here, Moss? First the Maggot, then Jimmy the Poker and Paddy bloody Maguire, now Maggs again. Jesus, Mary and Joseph, are we dancing to our own tune or is somebody pulling our strings?'

Quinn shook his head. 'I'm buggered if I know. Every time I think we might be getting somewhere, something else crops up.'

Doyle thought for a moment. 'So now we're in this neck of the woods, shall we nip along the canal and see if your man is home?'

'Let's wait for Murphy: she can give us the lowdown on Frank. He'll have spoken to Paddy by now; he's bound to have done the business by now.' He was leaning on the rail looking down at the spiked railings two storeys below. 'You know what?' he muttered. 'We're not going to find her in time. For all our efforts, Doyler, we're not going to find her in time.'

Doyle didn't say anything. Earlier he'd been encouraging, but now he wasn't so sure. Quinn looked round at him. 'We've no time left, and we're no nearer finding out where she is. For God's sake, what am I going to say to the kids?'

They sat in the car with the window rolled down and Quinn trailing cigarette smoke. He glanced at his watch. 'Twelve hours,' he said. 'That's all we've got left.'

Doyle didn't say anything. In the door mirror, he saw Murphy pull off Richmond Street behind the wheel of a Ford.

They all three got out, and they asked her if Frank had said anything about Paddy.

'Not to me,' she replied, 'but then he's not saying very much to anyone right now.'

Lips pursed, Quinn cast a glance at Doyle.

Murphy looked puzzled. 'Is there something I don't know?'

'I need to call the kids,' Quinn said. Taking out his mobile phone, he wandered towards the main road.

Murphy turned to Doyle. 'Sarge, what's going on?'

Doyle drew breath through his nose. 'You look knackered, Keira. Have you managed to get any sleep?'

'No, but then who has?' Still she peered quizzically at him. 'Are you going to tell me what's going on?'

'Did you turn anything up with that theory you told me about?'

'I had a look, but there wasn't much to be found. A bit of English history: how Bloody Mary blinded three Protestant martyrs. Put their eyes out, then burned them at Oxford University. I told Maguire but he didn't think there was anything to it.'

'No, I don't suppose there . . . ' Doyle seemed to freeze where he stood. 'Jesus Christ,' he murmured.

'Sarge?'

Whirling around, he called to Quinn. 'Moss, get off the phone.' Yanking the car door open, he was behind the wheel in an instant.

'Murphy,' he said, 'get the helicopter scrambled. Tell them to land at the sports ground on Crumlin Road.' He craned round in the seat. 'Moss!' he yelled again. 'For the love of God, man, will you get in the bloody car?'

With the passenger door open, he slewed the car around and screeched to a halt beside Quinn.

'What is it?' Quinn demanded, sliding in beside him. 'What the hell's going on?'

Doyle slapped the magnetic light on the roof. 'I know where she is, man. I know where Eva is.'

Wednesday 3rd September
10.25 am

With the siren screaming, Doyle pulled onto Richmond Street heading for the bridge. Across the canal, they were racing west following the water towards the Crumlin Road.

'Doyler, for God's sake!' Quinn demanded.

'It's Carrigafoyle, Moss. Eva is lying right where he dumped Mary Harrington.'

In his mind's eye, Quinn could see the ruins of the cottage across the estuary from the old castle.

'Three mice who couldn't find their way,' Doyle gesticulated. 'Murphy was right: they couldn't find their way because they were blind.' He overtook a lorry on the wrong side of the road. 'Three blind mice: she looked it up and found three Protestant martyrs blinded and burned by Mary I of England.'

He glanced sideways now. 'One of them was Cranmer, Henry VIII's archbishop.'

'So?'

'So Lislaughtin Abbey: 1580, Sir William Pelham, Elizabeth I's man – Elizabeth who was Mary's half-sister, and Henry's daughter by

Anne Boleyn. First he battered the O'Connor keep at Carrigafoyle, then he burned the abbey and hanged all the monks, including three old fellers in their seventies. They were blind, Moss, they were blind.'

Quinn sat there taking it in. Then he felt a shiver of hope rush through him. 'Jesus, Doyler,' he said.

'But Carrigafoyle, why would he go back there?'

'Why *not* go back there? Would we think to look there when Eva was abducted in Dublin? The photo, the picture: it's not sandstone, and it's not a stone on the sand. It's a stone *in* the sand. It's in an indentation, a hole: a rock in a hole. *The* rock in *the* hole, Moss. In Irish, that's Carrigafoyle.'

'*Only Mary knows*,' Quinn muttered. '*Only Mary knows* because Eva is lying right where Mary lay.' He slapped the dashboard. 'Christ, man, you're right.' Grabbing his phone, he dialled Harcourt Square.

'Frank, it's Moss. Is Murphy back there?'

'No, but she's been on the phone. The chopper is on its way, Moss. What the hell's going on?'

'She's in Kerry, Frank. Eva's at the dumpsite where we found Mary Harrington.'

Wednesday 3rd September
11 am

Old John Hanrahan heard the commotion from his living room, sirens howling from the Ballylongford Road. He had a mug of tea at his elbow and had been watching children's cartoons on the satellite TV system that Jimmy had got hold of. John loved cartoons; it was the simplicity, the way everything worked out, that made him happy.

Sirens meant trouble for someone, though, and he could hear them getting closer. He hated the sound; twice now he'd heard it along this stretch of water, and twice the guards had spoken to him. The first time had been to tell him his wife had been dragged from the Shannon; the second was a couple of years back, after he saw the girl in his kitchen.

They found her across the way in the old turf-cutter's cottage that nobody had lived in since before he could remember. He knew it was her as soon as the guards showed up, and he'd harnessed the horse to the cart in case they needed help to bring her out. He told them he'd seen her sitting at his kitchen table waiting on the devil, but of course they didn't believe him. Listening to the sirens, he could see her again; he could see her as if it was yesterday.

*

Whispers, that's what he heard: whispers and the sound of foot-steps. He saw a flash of light and bit his tongue so hard he thought he'd draw blood. Then the whispers died away and he heard a scrap-ing sound coming from the kitchen. The old fear gripped him; the fear and the anticipation. The gathering of souls in his kitchen. He might see his wife, he might see Elizabeth; he'd been waiting for her for so long; he knew he had to go down.

Lying in the dark with sweat prickling his brow like the legs of a hunting spider, the terror was all-consuming. He could feel the sheets sticking to him; the darkness of the bedroom was total.

But he knew he would have to get up.

Reaching for the bottle of water the priest had blessed, he swung his legs over the edge of the bed.

The house was suddenly silent; if Jimmy was home, he was in bed and not stirring: Jimmy never stirred for the dead.

The chill worked from his shoulders into his neck; it worked into his hair, fingers of fear plucking senses strung tight as strings on a violin.

He faltered, the door still closed, wishing he didn't have to do this. After so many years, he had never got used to it, and his nerves were frayed to the point where the slightest sound made him jump. The doctor, the priest: they told him he should leave this house and move into a care home, where the demons could no longer haunt him.

But he couldn't do that: this was his task, his duty, his penance for the years of neglect.

On the landing, he hesitated. The only light was now that spreading from the bulb outside the front door. It bathed the hall in a kind of distant gold. He could hear no sound but his footfall. One step at a time: his legs were not what they were. He gripped the ban-ister tightly.

In the hall, he paused again.

He moved into the kitchen. His heart was high in his chest; he could hear every hollow beat; he could feel the moisture on his palms; the knot that twisted his stomach so badly sometimes he pissed blood.

She was sitting at the table: long, dark hair; her head was bowed and he couldn't make out her face.

*

He could not make out her face, but he remembered that night as vividly as he remembered anything: he'd sprinkled water all around the room, but still she sat there waiting. He'd gone back to bed. Like a child, he lay down and pulled the covers up to his chin. A few minutes later, he heard a door creak and then the pad of someone on the stairs. The footsteps halted on the landing, and then Jimmy's door opened. He breathed a sigh of relief. At least he wasn't alone. He must've fallen asleep, because he heard no more; later, when they dragged the poor girl from across the way, he knew it was her he had seen. He told them: the guards. Not only had she been murdered, she'd had to cut the cards for her soul.

Shuffling to the window, he gazed across the water. It was a cold morning, rain brushing the coast from the Atlantic. He could see police cars driving past the castle. They didn't stop: they rounded the point and pulled up at the five-bar gate just as they had before.

Wednesday 3rd September
Midday

From the air, they could see the ruins of the ancient O'Connor stronghold. The windscreen was smeared with rain; the grey clouds were low and oppressive, as they had been all the way from Dublin. Quinn hunched in his seat as the pilot brought them into a hover. Below them, the grass, and the water that edged it, rippled as one in the downdraft. He could see where the British had breached the castle walls; he could see the old abbey and the graveyard where the monks had been hanged or put to the sword.

As they landed, Quinn's gaze was fixed on the almost-roofless cottage. It looked as though it had half-sunk in the sea of boggy grass. This was where they had found Mary. Looking down now, he could see guards in uniform wearing wellington boots; he could see spotters with dogs; he could see search specialists gathered in paper suits.

They hadn't been able to get anybody on the radio; either the helicopter system was playing up, or it was atmospherics, but right now he and Doyle were blind. They had no idea what the locals had found, but he could see from their body language that any urgency in the search was gone.

There was an air of defeat, of resignation. As the chopper descended, a chill seemed to surround him.

Doyle felt it too: the big man was almost rigid in his seat, grey stubble grazing his jowls, his iron-coloured hair sticking up at the back of his head.

'I'm not going to set her down,' the pilot told them. 'The ground's too wet: I'll be sinking in mud before I know it. I'll drop as low as I can, and you two will have to jump out.'

With a nod, Quinn opened the door. He could see the faces of his colleagues; the dogs held on shortened leashes snapping and barking soundlessly as the noise from the chopper drowned everything out. The rotors seemed to splutter and the aircraft dipped a little, then the pilot gave them the signal. Unclipping their safety belts, they dropped into the grass.

Quinn stared at the pockmarked walls of the broken-down cottage. He could see Mary Harrington covered in white maggots; he could smell the noxious, stomach-churning odour; he could hear the horrible squelch as her body, still wrapped in a plastic tarp, was lifted from the shallow grave.

He looked from face to face, and some of the uniformed officers avoided his eye. His sense of trepidation deepened.

His children were just half an hour from here, with their grandmother in Listowel, the small town where Eva had grown up, where she'd been loved by all who'd known her. What if he had to tell them now that she was dead? He was trembling so much that it was all he could do to remember how to put one foot in front of the other and hobble across the grass.

Martin McCafferty appeared in the doorway of the ruin.

'What've you found?' Quinn asked him.

'You better come and look.'

Quinn's heart was racing. He could feel the blood rushing in his head. He could smell rotten wood and wasted mortar; he could smell the estuary and the cow shit; he thought he could smell the dead. With Doyle behind him, Quinn approached McCafferty – who moved aside as they drew near. Inside, the cottage was chill; water clung to the walls, where the ancient horsehair plaster was falling away in chunks. The boards were up in the second room, just as they had been before.

But the hole in the floor was empty. There was no body; there were no clothes, no old tarp and no layer of hungry maggots. He looked round at McCafferty, and then he looked again: in the damp earth where the boards had been was a clear plastic envelope; inside, a single sheet of paper.

One is one and all alone and ever more shall be so.

Wednesday 3rd September
12.05 pm

Back at Harcourt Square, the incident room was buzzing with activity: everyone waiting for word to come through from Kerry. But the comms were out between the ground and the helicopter, and no one could tell them anything.

Maguire paced like a condemned man who, from his cell, can hear the nails being hammered into his scaffold.

'Sergeant Doyle picked up on it right away,' Murphy was telling him. 'Three blinded martyrs and three blind monks.'

Maguire nodded. 'The old bog-man knows his history; he always did.' He looked at the clock on the wall, back at Murphy and then at his watch. 'Is that Jimmy Hanrahan's stuff?' he asked, indicating the box on her desk.

She nodded. Then, recalling what Quinn had said, she sat down and began sifting through the photos.

The phone rang, and she grabbed it. But it wasn't Quinn and it wasn't Doyle or any of the Kerry guards: it was someone from downstairs wanting to know if they had a Detective Stevens up there.

Not as far as Murphy was aware; hanging up in frustration, she returned to her hunt for the photo. One of the other pictures caught her eye: a young woman sitting in the shadows at the kitchen table. There was something odd about the way she was almost hunched there; the way her hair fell in her eyes.

Finally, she found the one Quinn had told her about. It was obscene, degrading, in full colour and full close-up. The poor woman had passed out, and a fourteen year-old boy had been there to capture the moment. Murphy was about to tear it into pieces when, all at once, a shiver prickled her scalp. Laying the photo down, she picked up the other one. A girl in Jimmy's kitchen: it resonated with something she'd heard, something she'd read, maybe.

Something that didn't add up.

Glancing through the open door, she saw that the superintendent had the Harrington file on his desk still, along with the five others. He handed it to her when she asked for it. 'Is there still no word from Quinn?' he asked.

Murphy shook her head.

Back at her desk, she flicked through the pages, not really knowing what she was looking for. A note Doyle had scribbled the day they'd recovered the body; a remark from the old man about how he'd seen Mary's ghost sitting at his kitchen table. They'd dismissed it. Of course they had: John Hanrahan saw everyone's ghost at his table.

Murphy stared at the photo: no features visible but the hair. The shape of her hair; the way it fell across her shoulders. She laid it side by side with the photo that Mary's family had provided, and the touch of a chill finger skittered the length of her spine.

She placed the file under Maguire's nose.

With a click of his tongue, he looked up, agitation lining his already lined face. 'What is it, detective? I'm trying to write this report.'

'Have a look, superintendent,' she said.

With a weary sigh, Maguire did as he was asked. 'So?' he said. 'What am I looking for?'

'That's Jimmy Hanrahan's kitchen.'

'And?'

'Where his father sees dead people; where he saw the ghost of Mary Harrington. Doyle made a file note: the old man told him he'd seen her in his kitchen. It was the day they dug her up, sir: he was out there at the dumpsite with his horse and cart.'

'What are you saying, Murphy? What's your point?'

Murphy tapped the photograph. 'He did see her, sir: that is Mary Harrington.'

Wednesday 3rd September
12.10 pm

Quinn stumbled out of the broken-down cottage into the rain.

The rain fell against his face; it seemed to chill his bones. Beside the road, he could see John Hanrahan with his old horse harnessed between the shafts of the rank-looking cart. His cap was askew, he wore a weary-looking suit, and he had a scarf tied round his neck. Leading the horse, he paused at the gate and just stood there watching them, as he had when they'd brought Mary's body out.

Quinn felt Doyle move alongside him. His eyes were broken; the big man was trembling.

'The bastard,' Quinn muttered. 'The evil fuckin' bastard.' He sucked in his breath, watching Hanrahan watching him. 'We'll never find her now, Doyler – or if we do, it'll be too late.'

There was nothing Doyle could say: when he'd listened to what Murphy had discovered, the dawning had been so complete that he was positive they would find her. Which is exactly what her abductor had intended: so he could tell them they never would.

One is one and all alone and ever more shall be so.

Despair swamped him like waves washing over the grassy banks. He watched Quinn wander away, muttering about needing to see his children, about going over to his mother-in-law's house.

With their hopes dashed, he needed to be with his family.

Doyle needed a shot of whiskey and a pint or two of the black stuff. He needed a moment of solitude with his brother Tom, at whose graveside he'd made a promise to look out for his family.

His mobile phone started ringing: the office at Harcourt Square.

'Doyle, this is Frank Maguire.'

'Super?'

'Finally, we get a signal. Mother of God, what's going on?'

'She's not here,' Doyle told him. 'I thought she was, and in a way I was right: we were meant to think she was.'

'What? What do you mean?'

'He's leading us a merry dance, so he is.' Doyle told him about the note.

Maguire was silent and for a second Doyle thought they'd been cut off. 'Are you still there, Frank?'

'I'm here, I am. Listen, Joseph, there's been a development at this end.'

Quinn paused at the gate, where John Hanrahan stood with his horse and cart. The old man's eyes were rheumy; he looked tearful as he gazed the hundred yards or so to the cottage where the uniformed guards were putting in a cordon. He held the withered old nag at the bridle. 'I brought the horse over in case you might need her,' he said.

Quinn recalled how when they'd found Mary, he had offered to transport her body across the grass.

'Thank you, John,' he said, 'but she's not there.'

'Is she not?' Hanrahan looked puzzled. 'I thought she would be.'

'That was before, John. That was the last time, remember?'

'The last time?' He looked even more puzzled then. 'Right, yes. With you, guard: the last time.' Now he nodded. 'I saw her, you know. She was in my kitchen playing cards with the devil. I was looking for Elizabeth but she never comes.'

'I know, John, I know.' Quinn laid a hand gently on his shoulder.

'I saw her, though.' He nodded towards the cottage. 'Did I ever tell you that?'

'You did, John, you told us back when it happened.'

'I get confused, I know I do, but I remember seeing that one.' He snorted phlegm and spat. 'So you don't need the horse, then?'

Quinn shook his head.

Doyle came over, and together they watched the old man lead his horse and the flat-bed cart back across the road.

A short-wheelbase Land Rover swung round the bend and pulled into the overgrown yard.

Doyle looked on as Jimmy jumped down, gawping at the police activity.

'What was old John saying?' he asked.

'He was telling me how he saw Mary in his kitchen that time playing cards with the devil.'

Doyle hadn't taken his eyes off Jimmy. Opening the five-bar gate, he flipped the leather catch from the hammer of his .38.

The rain came down at an acute angle, lines of grey breaking like twigs against him. In the driveway of the house, Jimmy was rolling a cigarette.

'Don't give up, Moss,' Doyle said. 'It's not twelve thirty yet, and this isn't over.'

With that, he stalked across the road, and as he did so he took a set of handcuffs from his pocket.

In the driveway, Jimmy watched him, the cigarette pinched between his fingers.

'Stay where you are, lad,' Doyle growled.

Jimmy looked left and right. He looked towards where his father was turning the horse. He gave the impression of a man who was about to take off. Doyle pulled out the pistol. 'You misbegotten arse-wipe, don't give me an excuse to shoot you.'

Wednesday 3rd September
2.30 pm

Dublin was cold and grey, the rain following them like some bestial fog all the way back from Kerry.

Jimmy Hanrahan, sitting handcuffed between them, had been stony-faced and silent throughout the journey. He was the same way now, sitting with a duty solicitor at the police station on Amiens Street. The three of them were there this time: Quinn and Doyle across the table, with Maguire riding shotgun.

Quinn had the box of photos in front of him. He had the camera and was holding it under Jimmy's nose.

'Where's the other one?'

'What other one? There is no other one.'

'Sure there is: the one you used to take the picture you sent to us. What have you done with it, Jimmy? What've you done with my wife?'

Jimmy shook his head. 'I've told you, I've *told* you till I'm blue in the face, I don't know anything about your wife, and I don't know anything about Mary Harrington.'

'Last night,' Quinn told him. 'You were supposed to be on the bus to Kerry but you never went. Where did you go? What were you doing in Dublin?'

Jimmy wagged his head. 'No one told me I had to go anywhere, and the last time I checked this wasn't East Berlin. Jesus Christ, you drag my carcass up here all over again and ask the same stupid questions. If you want to know, I've had a gut-full of looking after the old man. I spent the night, check it out: I stayed in a B&B round the corner from the dog track.'

Quinn's eyes blazed suddenly. Throwing back his chair, he reached across the table and gripped Jimmy by the lapels. 'You piece of shite. Where's my wife? What've you done with my wife?'

'For fuck's sake!' Jerking himself free, Jimmy looked to his solicitor for help. 'Jesus, man, would you do something?'

'Inspector!' the solicitor snapped. He looked then at Maguire. 'Superintendent, do something about your man, will you? I'll not sit here and have my client intimidated.'

Lips tight, Quinn sat back in silence while Doyle took over. The big man tapped the photo of Mary sitting unconscious after partial asphyxiation, her body supported by the table.

'Taking a risk, weren't you, lad?' he said to Jimmy. 'This being in the box all the time. You must have laughed your socks off thinking how we missed it.'

'Mr Doyle,' Jimmy was looking earnestly at him, 'I swear I never took that photo.'

'So who did: Beelzebub?'

'Look, I've told you already,' Jimmy said almost desperately, spreading the fingers of his right hand out. 'I told you the last time. I told you in Kerry. I'm telling you now: I have no idea where Eva is. I swear to God. I don't know anything about her and . . . ' He looked again at the picture. 'I never took that. I never even knew it was there.'

Leaning forward suddenly, Quinn snatched up the photo of

Maggs's mother. 'You took this, though, didn't you?'

Falling silent again, Quinn glanced at Doyle, then at the solicitor, and finally at the skinny man with the pinched face hunched across the table from him. 'Take a moment, Jimmy,' he said, 'and think about it. You're so screwed right now, we could hang a picture from you. We've got you for Mary's murder. You throttled her till she was unconscious, and then you thought what a laugh it would be to sit her up at the table, knowing the old man would be down with his holy water.' He let out a breath. 'Jesus, when I spell it out, you really are a bucket of shite, aren't you?'

'Listen,' Jimmy thrust a finger at him, 'I would not do that. I love my old man. I'm the sad fuck who's spent twenty years looking after him.'

'You do it so's you get your dole money, Jimmy,' Doyle reminded him, 'so's you can keep the carer's allowance, which means you can clean your guns all day and go poaching at night. That is, when you're not taking pictures of women you've just strangled.'

Jimmy's face was bright red, his eyes whitened saucers in his head. 'Do you think I'd do that to my dad when the only reason he sees what he does is because he's looking for my dead mother?'

'And why is he looking for her?' Quinn asked. 'Because of you, Jimmy.'

'Oh come on, I was just a kid when I broke in that old biddy's house. I didn't know what I was doing. I was a kid when I shagged Maggs's mammy. Come on now, for God's sake, ask yourselves: have I been in trouble since my mam drowned? Have I been arrested? Have I touched a single hair on another person's head?'

'You strangled Mary Harrington and left her to die across the way where you thought no one would think to look for her.'

'No I didn't. Christ, for the first time in my life I even spoke to the guards. I tipped you off, didn't I? I told you what I'd seen.'

'Course you did, Jimmy.' Doyle pressed his face close. ''Twas the perfect way of keeping attention away from yourself.'

'Oh for heaven's sake.' Jimmy sat back then with his arms hooked across his chest. He looked sideways at his solicitor. 'If I'd taken that picture, would I really put it in a box with all the others? Would I leave it there for anyone to come along and find it? Would I have let the guards put me on a bus back to Kerry when they still had the bastard thing?' He rolled his eyes to the ceiling. 'Course I wouldn't, I'm not a fuckin' idiot.' He looked beyond Quinn and Doyle to Maguire. 'And what would I be doing with *two* bloody cameras? You can't buy them. It's hard enough just getting the film.' He leered at Quinn. 'I haven't got two cameras, and I didn't take that picture. Don't you get it: the Maggot took the picture.'

Doyle laughed out loud. 'Now I've heard the lot. How the hell do you figure that?'

'You great bag of piss.' Jimmy slapped the photo of Maggs's mother. 'Because I took *that* one.'

Outside in the corridor, Quinn pressed a palm to the wall. Doyle looked at his watch. 'He's lying,' Maguire stated, before Quinn could say anything. 'We know he's lying. He was in Harold's Cross: he's admitted that. He made the call, Moss. It was him that phoned your house.'

Quinn thought long and hard. Time was running away from them, but he forced himself to stay calm and try to think clearly.

'So why won't he give her up?' he asked. 'I mean, he knows we've got him. He knows he's going down. Why doesn't he try to make a deal?'

Maguire threw out a hand. 'Why should he? Why should he make it easy for us? As you just said, no matter what we promise, he knows he's going down.'

Quinn looked unsure. 'There was no sign of the necklace,' he said.

'What?'

'When we searched his house just now, when Martin McCafferty searched it before, there was no sign of the necklace. If he had the photo of Mary lying around, why not the necklace?'

'Because it didn't mean anything to him,' Doyle stated quietly.

'Then why bother to take it?' Quinn was shaking his head. 'I can see him killing Mary: no problem with that at all. He tried it on, and she blew him out, or they went for a drive or whatever. I can see him doing that to his dad too, what with the picture and everything. But that necklace meant nothing to him, so if he abducted Eva, why bother with it?' He lifted his palms. 'It doesn't stack up. And, as he says, neither does the notion of him having two Polaroid cameras.'

He walked away a few paces. 'We can't afford to waste time. Charge him for Mary's murder, that's fine. But the only person the necklace meant anything to was Conor Maggs.'

'Moss,' Maguire's tone was laboured.

Quinn looked back at him.

'You're wrong.'

'What do you mean?'

'He's not the only person.' Maguire shook his head; eyes downcast, he stared at a patch of floor where the linoleum was worn. 'We need to talk to my brother,' he said. 'We need to talk to Pat.'

Frank made the call, and when they got back to Harcourt Square Patrick was waiting in Quinn's office.

Quinn shoved the door open and for a moment the two men just stared at each other, the silence between them brittle.

'I hear you want to talk to me.' Patrick's tone was terse, the look on his face almost angry.

His brother opened his mouth to speak, but Patrick waved him down.

'I don't need any help,' he asserted. 'There's nothing here I can't deal with.' He turned again to Quinn. 'Just because I had a shitty upbringing, and you think I fit the psychological profile, doesn't mean anything.' Pausing for a moment, he glanced briefly at his brother. 'Now, do you want to talk in here with all those detectives watching, or shall we go somewhere where it won't embarrass Frank?'

They went down the hall to a meeting room, Frank's face the colour of slate. Patrick was defiant as he turned once more to Quinn. 'So tell me, Moss, what is it you think you know, exactly?'

Quinn considered him carefully. 'I know you cared about Eva,' he said. 'I know you wanted her and I know you put all that aside to counsel her.'

Patrick lifted one eyebrow.

'If you have any idea where she is, then please, for the sake of all that, just tell me.'

'I have no idea where she is. Of course I don't. Why should I?'

Quinn stepped a little closer to him. 'Because she's a single mother like Janice and Karen, and just as you counselled Eva, you counselled their husbands.'

'So?'

'You counselled Willie Moore, the drug dealer who calculates every equation, be it financial or emotional, down to the last penny. Tell me, why didn't you let anyone know he'd told you Mary was pregnant?'

'Moss,' Frank butted in, 'we've got Jimmy Hanrahan for that.'

'Shut up, Frank.' Quinn bristled suddenly. 'Your brother said he'd talk to me, so let him talk, will you?'

'Mossie,' Doyle said, laying a gentle palm on his shoulder. 'Easy boy, that's the super you're talking to.'

Quinn threw off his hand. 'Right now, I couldn't give a fuck if it was the commissioner.' He turned back to Patrick. 'Answer the question, Paddy.'

'It was confidential. I told you, client confidence.'

'You're not a doctor, you're not a lawyer, and you're not a fucking priest. You're not even a monk, are you? You blew any chance of that when you took a piss on the Virgin.'

Patrick held his gaze. 'I was eighteen and I was drunk.'

'Drunk, were you? Is that how it was: so shit-faced you didn't know what you were doing? Maybe you were, Paddy; maybe you were. On the other hand, maybe you did it because you imagined you were pissing on your own dead mother, who'd never given a shit about you.'

Patrick sucked breath. 'Now I told you I'd talk to you, but you've the charm of a peat bog, so you do. You're out of order, Moss. She may not have got along with me but she was my mother, and no matter what any of you says, I got along with her.'

'Bullshit. You hated her, you despised the drunken bitch.'

Patrick levelled a finger at him. 'You keep on and I'm going to knock you flat on your arse.'

Frank stepped forward, but again Patrick waved him away. 'Stay out of it, Frank,' he snapped. 'I told you, I can fight my own battles.'

He looked darkly at Quinn. 'Now, I know you're under pressure, Moss, and I know time is running out. But I came here of my own accord, so if you want to talk, keep it civil. If not, you can charge me with something or you can shove it. It makes no odds to me.'

'This is getting us nowhere,' Frank butted in. 'Moss, you get a hold of yourself, or you can get out of here. Shouting the odds is not the answer to anything.'

Quinn was in his face then, spittle flying from his lips. 'I want a warrant to search his flat,' he demanded, 'If you won't get it, I'll go down to the Bridewell and put a case to the judge myself.'

Fumbling in his pocket, Patrick brought out his house key. 'You don't need a warrant, inspector. Be my fucking guest.'

Doyle took Quinn outside while Frank spoke to his brother. Lighting a cigarette, Quinn squatted against the wall and drew smoke into his lungs. 'Sorry about that, Doyler,' he muttered. 'I lost it there for a moment.'

'Course you did, lad. Who wouldn't?'

'I'm thrashing around, I know I am. I suspect everyone. Call myself a policeman? Jesus, am I fuck!'

'You're personally involved, that's all. It's hard to be objective – no, it's nigh-on *impossible* to be objective – when the clock's almost to zero and you're personally involved.'

'Jimmy Hanrahan,' Quinn stated, staring across the car park to where a large black cat sauntered from bonnet to bonnet. 'I can see him for Mary, no problem: I can see him stuffing her in his car and taking her home. I can see him taking that photo.'

'But you can't see him abducting Eva, and you can't see him being responsible for the others.'

'No, and whichever way we look at it, Patrick's the only person who knew Mary was pregnant.'

'But would he smuggle her into the old man's house and take a snapshot of her?'

'He might if he was trying to frame Jimmy. He knew the history. He knew about the old man and his ghosts: everyone did. Doyler, if he wanted someone to take the fall, Jimmy the Poker was perfect. Short of that, there was the Maggot, only he crawled away.' Getting to his feet, he stamped on the butt of the cigarette. 'I don't know. I don't know. Jesus, fuck this.' He stared at the cat, which was sitting on the roof of one of the cars now, looking back at him. 'Talking of maggots, Doyler, has Johnny Clogs been in touch?'

Doyle shook his head.

'The bastard. When all this is over, I'm going to remember how helpful he was.'

Doyle paced the yard with his hands in his pockets, ignoring the rain, which was falling more heavily now. 'It wasn't just Willie Moore or Janice and Karen, was it?' he said. 'Whoever said what and whoever asked to see who, there's no getting away from the fact that when Maggs was in Mountjoy, he and Patrick were face to face.'

Quinn was looking bitter. 'He's been my friend for twenty years. But the dog that bites you, Doyler, is the one you least expect.'

Murphy came outside then. Looking up and down the drive, she spotted them, threw a raincoat around her shoulders and walked over.

'Moss,' she said, 'we're going to search Patrick's flat, and the super wants to know if you're coming with us.'

Wednesday 3rd September
3.30 pm

A handful of cars made their way along the canal, with Quinn and Doyle following Murphy and Maguire.

The two detectives were silent. Soon, Eva would have been missing for seventy-two hours.

Quinn had confirmed the reality of her situation with Doctor Ahern before they left his office that morning. It was as he feared: much longer, and his wife would go into a coma which she would be unlikely to come out of.

In Kerry, he'd spoken to Laura and Jess and to Eva's mother and sisters; the whole town was keeping a vigil for her safe return. It wasn't just them: her plight had captured the hearts of the nation, and it seemed as though everyone was looking for her.

Quinn felt nauseous with worry; the weariness lined his face and dulled his senses; he could no longer think clearly. As they pulled into a parking space, he turned to Doyle in the driving seat alongside him.

'What're we doing?' he spoke, as if he was asking the question of himself. 'This is Paddy we're talking about: my mate, for pity's sake. So his brother kept their past to himself. If I was the super, so would I, probably.'

Inside the flat, the atmosphere was electric, static bouncing almost visibly between Quinn and Patrick as they faced each other across the tiny living room.

'Here we all are then,' Patrick said. 'It's not very big, so it shouldn't take long.' He indicated the photo on the mantelpiece. 'There she is, Moss, the drunken bitch. Just like Maggs's mammy, only ours didn't open her legs but for a couple of fellers, eh Frank?'

'Shut up, Patrick,' Frank told him. He went through to the bedroom.

Patrick called after him: 'Don't worry about what anybody thinks, you already made superintendent, and you were never going to make commissioner.' He turned again to Quinn. 'The truth will out, eh Moss? The truth will always out.' He looked bitter suddenly. 'By the way, while we're here, what else did the Maggot tell you – apart from accusing me of murder? Did he say it was me giving myself a hand shandy while you and Eva were at it?' He winked then at Doyle. 'Good-looking girl, your niece; worth a shuffle she is, for sure.'

Frank called from the bedroom. 'Patrick, shut your foul mouth or I'll kick you down the stairs myself.'

Patrick slumped into a chair. 'By the way, Moss,' he said, 'who've you been talking to over at Islandbridge? Peter Farrell, is it? When he was younger, he had the hots for me: used to walk around with no underpants under his cassock because the material rubbing his cock gave him a hard-on. Did you hear that, Frankie? Our mam only threatened to send us to the men in black dresses, but you had the beating of her.'

Again his brother appeared in the doorway. His face was hard as stone now; he had one hand thrust in his pocket and the other fisted at his side. For a long, chill minute, he stared at Patrick where he sat in the chair. 'You're letting yourself down, Pat. You're letting yourself down.'

Patrick made a face. 'Well bugger me, there's the shame of it.'

Still Frank held his eye.

Patrick was about to make another crack but he caught himself. He stared at his brother now, and his face gradually lost its colour. Lifting his closed fist, Frank uncurled fingers to show what he held in his palm. 'In the shoebox under your bed.'

Patrick stared, Quinn stared; Doyle took a couple of paces towards Frank, then stopped.

'What the hell are you doing with it?' Frank demanded. 'Why was it under your bed?'

The silence that followed seemed to echo from the walls.

The Sacred Heart in tarnished gold; there was no chain.

Quinn's mouth was dry. In his mind's eye, he could see Eva lying on Danny's grave.

Patrick didn't say anything. His mouth was open but he uttered no words; he just sat there, his face white and both hands pressed between his legs.

Trembling, Quinn turned to him. 'If she's dead when we get to her, I'm going to kill you,' he said. 'Do you understand? I'm going to put my gun in your mouth and blow the back of your head off.'

Patrick was on his feet suddenly, crossing the room, but his brother was in the way. Grabbing him by the wrist, he bent it back and forced him onto his knees.

'It's not hers,' Patrick cried. 'It was our mother's, for God's sake.'

'Our mother's went into the ground with her.' Frank spat out the words so violently that a string of saliva flew with them.

'No it didn't: I took it.'

'I was there, you bastard. I was fucking there.' Frank was shaking; still holding Patrick, he pressed him closer to the floor.

Patrick wailed in pain.

Eyes closed, Frank drew a shortened breath. 'Patrick Pearse Maguire,' he stated, 'I'm arresting you on suspicion of abducting Eva-Marie Quinn. You do not have to say anything, but anything you do say . . . '

'Frankie,' Patrick interrupted. 'For Christ's sake, it's me. It's Patrick, Frank. You've got the wrong man.'

Wednesday 3rd September
7.30 pm

The mood in the incident room was somber, to say the least; the time ticking away and the tension tinged with shock now that Superintendent Maguire's brother was in custody. The pendant had gone to the lab, so that the linking ring could be compared with the chain links that had been recovered from Danny's grave.

Frank was personally involved now, and he wanted to draft in another senior officer to interview his brother. The deputy in charge of operations was on his way from Phoenix Park to discuss exactly how they were going to move forward.

'There's no time to bring in anyone else,' Quinn was saying. The three of them were in his office with the door closed and the blinds pulled down. He indicated the clock. 'Every second is precious, Frank. We can't waste time briefing somebody else now.'

'You can't go near him if that's what you're thinking,' Frank told him. 'I've bent the rules enough as it is.'

Doyle sat on the edge of the desk. 'Moss is right, Frank,' he said. 'There's no time, and the best person to do any talking to Patrick is you.'

Frank didn't look very encouraged. 'Do you think so?'

'Of course. The lad looked up to you. When he was a kid, you were his rock; you were all he had.'

'That's right, I was,' Frank said, nodding. 'Up until he was eleven, at least.' His eyes reddened suddenly. 'Then it all went to pot.'

'Frank,' Doyle said, 'you can't blame yourself. Even if you'd not been intent on joining the police, there's no way the social services would have let you bring up your brother. He'd have been in some home or other, regardless. Better it was Islandbridge, where at least you knew the monks. And for all his taunting just now, they've no history of anything even vaguely dodgy at Islandbridge.'

Frank took his head in his hands and for a moment he looked as though he was going to weep. But he gathered himself and cleared his throat, then turned to Quinn.

'That necklace . . . Our mother was wearing one just like it when she was dressed for her funeral. Paddy and I went to see her in the chapel of rest.' He worked the points of his fingers into his eyes.

'Did you speak to Liam Ahern about any of this?'

'We did,' Doyle answered, 'though we didn't mention your brother by name. He fits the profile, Frank: you don't need us to tell you.'

Pushing back his chair, Frank got to his feet. 'You're right,' he said, 'the only person who can talk to him is me. When the deputy commissioner gets here, let him know what's going on.'

Grabbing his jacket, he left them, and they watched him cross the incident room with his shoulders square and every eye upon him.

Murphy tapped on the open door. 'Moss,' she said, 'I thought I'd mention it: we just had word from Scene of Crimes. The phone box in Harold's Cross; there are prints all over it, but nothing we can match. '

'Thanks, Keira. It was worth a try.'

'Now that Patrick's been arrested, what happens to Jimmy Hanrahan?'

Quinn exchanged a glance with Doyle. 'That's a good question. He's not out of the picture – not until we know what we've got. Leave him where he is, Murph: it won't do him any harm.'

He walked to the window. The images were blurred in his brain: Patrick's venom; old man Hanrahan with his horse and cart; Eva slipping away. He turned to the clock. The hands seemed to *tick* and *tick* as if they were mocking him.

He thought of the note, the final communication. His wife was alone, and if Patrick didn't tell them where to find her . . . she *ever more would be so.*

Wednesday 3rd September
9.30 pm

Frank Maguire sat down with his brother in the same interview room where they'd spoken to Jimmy Hanrahan.

Patrick was across the table, his anger gone. He looked forlorn, lost, confused – like the frightened child Frank had spent eleven years bringing up.

'Paddy,' he said softly, 'do you not want a solicitor?'

Patrick looked up at him. 'Do I need one?'

'You've been arrested.'

'I know – and by my own brother.'

'Do you want a solicitor?'

Patrick shook his head. 'No,' he said, 'I don't. I haven't done anything, and I'm sitting here trying to get my head around quite how I got here. But I had a right pop at you just now, and at Moss too, and I'm sorry for that. Jesus, but it got my goat though, what you were doing. And Moss . . . ' He paused for a moment. 'I suppose he's just worried to death, isn't he? Of course he is; who wouldn't be in his position?'

Frank studied him: his kid brother, his comrade in arms when they were growing up.

'Where is she, Pat? You have to tell us. You don't want her to die, I know you don't. Not Eva.'

Patrick didn't say anything.

'Did she remind you of our mam? Is that what this is about? Did they all remind you of her?'

Patrick peered across the table. 'Do you really believe I did this, Frankie? Do you really believe I could?'

'You had no love, Patrick; you had no mother. She never loved you, and it's bothered you all your life. Do you remember how you'd fiddle with her necklace? When she was so drunk she'd pass out, and you'd clamber up in her lap and sit there for hours just playing with it? Was it the way it sparkled, the gold maybe? Or was it just that when you were up there, you were close to her?'

Tears had worked their way into Patrick's eyes now. 'She hated me,' he mumbled. 'Didn't she, Frankie? She hated me so much it was you who gave me my name. You looked after me; you made sure I had something to eat. You were all I had. But then you put me with the Brothers and . . . '

Reaching across the table, Frank took his hand. 'I know, I know. And I'm sorry, I'm so sorry, but what else could I do?'

'I hated it there,' Patrick said. 'She told us that the boys who went there were never seen or heard from again. Frankie, for the first year almost, I slept on the floor under my bed.'

He gazed into space. 'Moss is right: I *was* always in love with Eva. That first time we met her she was over by the window, but Moss was in there before I could get a chance. She looked at me, though; she looked at me in a certain way. I reckon in any other circumstances, it could've been me instead of him.

'She turned to me when Danny was killed. She couldn't deal with Moss: she was so angry; so very, very angry. It wasn't rational of course, she knew that: it wasn't his fault that Danny got run over. But she watched how Maggs had been accused of murder, then confessed to Doyle, quick and simple, the kind of police work she didn't see when it came to Danny. I suppose it was a combination of those things – Maggs and Danny – that got her so confused that she pushed her husband away.'

He looked into his brother's face. 'That was when she started wearing the necklace.'

'Did it remind you of our mam?' Frank asked him.

Patrick pushed out his lips. 'In a way, I suppose it did. I'd never seen her wear it before, but there it was one day around her neck. She told me how she got it and that she'd not worn it in years. She had to wear it now though, because it was the heart of Jesus, and with Danny gone the religion was all she had to cling to.'

'You didn't tell her it was rubbish then,' his brother said. 'About Jesus, I mean. That the world and all of us – everything – was just some accident of the universe?'

Patrick shook his head. 'That would've been cruel, wouldn't it?'

'Where is she?' Frank asked him.

'I don't know.'

'You have to tell us.'

'I can't if I don't know.'

'There's no time, Paddy. If we don't get to her soon, she's going to die.'

'I know.'

'Then you have to tell us; you have to tell me.'

'I can't tell you if I don't know.' Patrick leant across the table and looked him right in the eye. 'Do you really think this is how it is, Frank? I mean, deep down in your heart of hearts, do you believe I could abduct my best friend's wife? Do you think I've buried her someplace, left her to die without water just like Mary Harrington?'

Frank studied him, the tension working across his shoulders a physical pain now. 'What about the others?' he said. 'What about the five missing women we've never found any trace of? Eva was a single mother, Pat, like you say. She'd pushed Moss away and she was all alone with those two girls. That made her just the same as the others. You knew two of them, didn't you?'

Patrick looked almost sadly at him. 'Do you think I killed them, I mean really? Patrick Pearse Maguire, a serial killer, the most brutal murderer this country has ever known?'

'Are you?'

Patrick closed his eyes. 'Just because I fit the profile doesn't mean I did it. And just because I had no love as a kiddie doesn't mean I did it. Did it never occur to you, Frankie, that because of you I turned out all right?' He shrugged his shoulders. 'So I took a leak on a statue at St Boniface. Big deal. It was a statue, Frank, that's all it was, and I was shit-faced drunk. '

'But why did you do that of all things, when you knew how it would look, you knew you'd have to leave.'

'I can't remember doing it. And I doubt I would've cared how it looked. I was eighteen and I wanted to leave: it was only ever the monks who said I should join the Society. I'd had enough of religion. I didn't believe any of it any more, and whatever anyone reads into it I'd had such a skin-full that night that I have no recollection of even being in the bloody chapel.'

He sat forward again, his shoulders hunched and his gaze fixed. 'I haven't done this. It isn't me. I no more abducted Eva than I abducted Mary Harrington. This isn't me, Frankie. You've got it wrong; you've all got it wrong. The necklace was our mother's, not Eva's.'

Frank shook his head. 'Our mother's was buried with her.'

'No it wasn't.'

'Paddy, come on, I was there.'

'Yes, you were: you and me in the chapel of rest. But I went back, remember? You were talking to the undertaker; you were being all grown up and dealing with everything as usual, and I told you I was going for a pee.' Reaching across the table, he took his brother by the arm. 'I went back, Frankie. I went back and I took it. I lost the chain years ago, but I always kept the heart. It reminded me of our mam; of being in her lap. And that was the only good memory I ever had of her.'

'Listen,' he said, 'I can see how this has come about. I've spent my life in prisons seeing how things get twisted, how they get misconstrued. But you're the one who hid our past, not me. If you hadn't, then Moss wouldn't even have begun to be suspicious. Don't you see? Half the reason things look like they do is because you were so worried about what other people might think. But you have to forget all that now and you have to trust me. You have to look me in the eye and you have to believe what I'm saying. I'm not your man. This isn't me. I didn't do any of it.'

Wednesday 3rd September
9.50 pm

In the living room at Jane's flat, Maggs was watching the garda commissioner making a statement to the press. He couldn't quite believe what he was hearing. Jane was sitting on the arm of his chair; she was holding his hand, and her eyes were bright with excitement.

'We have two people in custody,' the commissioner was saying. 'They're both currently assisting us in the search for Eva. That's all I have to say right now. I'm sure you have a multitude of questions, but you'll have to forgive me: I cannot answer any at the moment.'

With that, he walked up the drive.

Suddenly Jane was in Maggs's lap, her arms around his neck. She was smothering him with kisses. 'Oh, Conor,' she said, 'did you hear that? You're vindicated: your name is cleared finally.'

Maggs was still staring at the screen. Only he was no longer seeing it: he was in the dock at the Four Courts, and there in the public gallery Eva was twisting the necklace he'd given her around her little finger.

All at once his shoulders sagged, the relief suddenly visible. Jane had his cheeks cupped in her hands and she was kissing him again and again. 'Oh love, it's marvellous; it's fantastic. Praise the lord, Conor, praise the lord.'

Maggs didn't say anything. Getting up, he stood there for a few moments, gazing through the hall to the front door without really seeing anything.

'Conor,' Jane said, 'are you OK?'

'I'm fine. It's just that after all this time, I'm not sure I can get my head around it.' His eyes were wide suddenly. 'They no longer think it was me, Jane. Doyle and Quinn, after all they did: they no longer think it was me.'

Tears brimmed in his eyes now; he was trembling slightly. 'You believed in me,' he said. 'When nobody else was there, you always believed in me.'

'And I always will. I'll always be there for you. I love you, Conor. You know I do. I'm in this for the long haul.'

He slipped his arms round her neck. 'I love you too. And you know what? We should celebrate. This is a moment in history; a watershed, perhaps, in our relationship. We've won a great victory and we should celebrate. Let's buy champagne, Janey; let's buy champagne and go to bed. Let's celebrate in bed.' He smiled now and he kissed her. 'Get undressed,' he told her. 'Take off all your clothes and get into bed. I'll fetch the champagne.'

Grabbing his jacket, he picked up his wallet and stepped outside. Jane remained in the hall for a couple of minutes, basking in the glow. She knew how much she loved him; she knew how much he loved her; and she was thinking then that there wasn't much else in the world that really mattered right now.

She wondered if he might ask her to marry him. She was singing as she went into the bathroom to run the bath. While it was filling, she went through to the tiny bedroom and laid out her sexiest night-dress, then set about making the bed. She heard footsteps coming along the landing outside. 'Conor, if that's you back already, the door's open.'

There was no reply, and she wondered then if they had champagne in the corner shop or if he'd nipped up to the hotel. She heard the front door open behind her and, with a smile, she turned.

'That was quick . . . ' She took a step backwards.

Two heavily built men stepped into the hall. They were big men, hard men: one wearing a leather coat, and the other a donkey jacket. Both were skinheads; one had home-made tattoos scrawled on the backs of his hands.

'Who are you?' she demanded. 'What're you doing in my flat?'

The first one just stared at her. The other went into the bathroom and turned off the shower.

'Your cousin wants a word,' he told her. 'You have to come with us.'

Before Jane could say or do anything, he took her by the elbow and lifted her coat from the peg. 'It won't take but a minute, love. You have to come with us.'

Wednesday 3rd September
10.03 pm

Seventy-two hours. Quinn was staring at the clock. Doyle was on the phone; Murphy was on the phone. There was no sign of Maguire: as far as Quinn was aware, he was still across the river at Amiens Street.

He felt helpless, lost; more alone even than when he'd woken this morning. The noise from the incident room was incessant: the conversation, the hubbub of phones ringing and messages coming in. But it was seventy-two hours now, and he'd been to Blackrock, he'd been to Clare and he'd been to Carrigafoyle, where Doyle had told him not to give up. But all hope seemed to be lost now. Pat Maguire was in custody; Jimmy Hanrahan was in custody; and still nobody could tell him what had happened to Eva.

He just sat there. The frustration was so great that it was as if his muscles had seized and all he could do, as the clock ticked beyond the point of no return, was watch helplessly as people worked feverishly around him.

His phone rang. Shovelling a rough hand into his jacket pocket, he dug it out. For a moment he looked at the screen, not recognising the number, then realised that it was the lab calling from across the city.

'Quinn,' he said.

'Moss, this is John May.' May was a ballistics expert he'd worked with many times in the past.

'What do you know, John?'

'Is there any news on Eva?'

Quinn bit his lip. 'No,' he said, 'no news. We've two men in custody and fuck-all good it's doing us.'

'Jeez, I'm sorry. Look, Mossie, I wanted to talk to you as soon as I had anything on that pendant. The chain that Scene of Crimes picked up showed links with distinctive striation marks.'

'That's right.'

'Well, I'm sitting here now with the pendant under the electron microscope we use for bullets.

You've seen it: it magnifies two million times.'

'What's it telling you?'

'The striation marks don't match, Moss. I'm still checking, of course, and I've a couple of assistants checking it too, but as far as I can see the pendant you gave me was never attached to the chain.'

Wednesday 3rd September
10.03 pm

Jane had never been to her cousin's boat, and in the back of the car with the tattooed skinhead seated alongside her the nerves almost got the better of her. Johnny Clogs was actually her dad's cousin, and the two of them didn't get on at all. Whereas Johnny was a multi-millionaire developer and allegedly a gangster, her father had never amounted to anything more than a council worker in south Finglas.

'What does Johnny want to see me about?' she asked the man sitting next to her. He was looking ahead as they drove towards the quays and O'Connell Bridge. 'I haven't seen him in years. What does he want with me all of a sudden?'

The thug filling most of the back seat didn't answer. He didn't look at her; he sat stony-faced as the driver negotiated the midweek traffic. At the bridge, they swung along the quay past the service alley that opened onto Abbey Street. Jane could see the massive cabin cruiser tied up at the moorings. When they were on deck, they pushed her down the steps into the salon below.

White leather sofas, a flat-screen plasma TV and a well-stocked bar, where her cousin was standing in a silk robe and a pair of leather slippers. He had his back to her; he was shapeless and squat, the pink slab of skin at the back of his head glistening as if he'd just stepped out of the shower.

She heard the chink of ice in a glass and, looking back, she saw the man who'd been sitting next to her standing at the top of the steps with his tattooed hands clasped in front of him. Jane was trembling slightly: she could feel perspiration gather under her armpits and at the tops of her thighs. She thought of Conor coming back to the flat and finding no trace of her.

'John,' she said. Still he didn't turn around. 'Johnny, you wanted to see me?'

As if he didn't even know she was there, Finucane busied himself with making a drink. When he had poured it, he remained with his back to her while he sipped it. She saw him reach for a cigarette from the open packet and take his lighter. She could smell the smoke; it clogged her throat in the confined atmosphere. Then he turned and considered her: piggish-eyes buried in fleshy holes in the pudgy moon of his face.

'Jane Finucane,' he said softly. 'Tell me, how is your dad?'

Jane looked puzzled. 'He's fine, John – or at least he was the last time I spoke to him.'

'Still with the council, is he? I've a couple of projects going on up there in Finglas. Ah, but he works the roads though, doesn't he – nothing to do with the building.'

He motioned for her to sit down and then, taking a tub of fish food, he crossed the thick pile carpet to a large tank, where a number of brightly coloured exotic fish were swimming back and forth.

'I hear you're keeping the company of a maggot,' he said softly.

Jane coloured. 'I don't follow you, Johnny.'

'Conor Maggs, the lad the guards lathered before his case was thrown out.' He smiled to himself, dribbling a little fish food onto the surface of the water. 'That's what they call him, you know: the type of creepy-crawly thing I'd normally feed to the fish.'

'He's just been exonerated, Johnny, he's . . . '

'He's full of shite is what he is.' Setting the tub down, her cousin looked coldly at her. 'And he's caused me a lot of trouble just lately.'

'I don't understand. How could he be trouble to you?'

'The guards, Jane. One Joseph Doyle, an old bog-trotter from County Kerry.' He pursed his lips. 'Not a lad to cross is Doyle, and neither is Moss Quinn. You see, they're not the kind of coppers who understand the modern world. They live in the past: an Ireland that no longer exists. They don't understand that a citizen has certain rights and they're not to be intimidated.'

'But what's any of this got to do with me?'

'Sunday night, pet. Sunday last, around ten o'clock: where were you?'

'On Sunday I was home, Johnny. I was home at the flat.'

'And the Maggot? Was he with you?'

She faltered.

His eyes flashed darkly. 'Don't lie to me now. Fine for the coppers, if that's what you want, but do not lie to me.'

She opened her mouth, then closed it again, and her cousin nodded slowly. 'I always know when a person is lying, Jane.' He tapped the side of his head. 'I've this built in shit-detector, you see, had it all my life. And the one thing that really sticks in old Johnny's craw is a cheap fuckin' lie. We're family, Jane, you and me. But if I thought you were lying, I'd weigh anchor and off we'd trot up the Liffey and into the Irish Sea. Then I'd tie a set of chains around your ankles and lower you over the side.' He snapped his fingers. 'No more Jane Finucane, and no more little lies.'

Jane almost wet herself, sitting there on her cousin's leather sofa with his eyes boring holes in her. At the top of the stairs the skinhead was watching, with a wolfish grin on his face. Johnny sat down next to her. 'Now,' he said, 'I'm going to ask the same question again, and now you know how it works you can answer. I'll tell you, though, it's like a TV quiz: I can only accept your first answer. If you have to change your mind, then it's the boat trip, and before you go I'll let Dessie there have his way with you.' He looked over to the stairs. 'And Dessie likes it rough, Jane. He likes to hurt his women. '

She was shaking; it was all she could do to stop herself from urinating all over his furniture.

'So tell me,' he said softly. 'I'm asking you now, and I'm doing it once: was the Maggot there with you, or did you lie to the cops?'

Wednesday 3rd September
10.10 pm

Maggs bought a bottle of *cava* from the mini-supermarket on Lower Camden Street; he had had to walk all the way down there because there was nothing at the Spar. His pocket wouldn't stretch to a bottle of Moet but Jane wasn't proud, and this stuff tasted just as good anyway. Shoving the bottle inside his coat, he wandered back towards the canal. There was no rain now, though there was a wind blowing across the city.

Two men in custody; that brought a smile to his face. Quite the turn-up after all this time. But justice was justice, no matter how long it took.

Ten minutes later, he turned into the service alley and looked up at the sixties-built flats: the grey stone balconies, the cheap tiles and the large square windows. He was free, clear; finally they had somebody else, and that meant he could spread his wings if he chose to. He'd need to do something about earning some money, though: he had no job as yet, and sooner or later the generosity of groups like the one at Harold's Cross was bound to run out.

The stone stairwell was smelly; he'd not really noticed before, but perhaps with this newfound sense of freedom there was a freeing up of his other senses also. He could smell where some little scrote had taken a leak right where people had to walk. They'd move on perhaps, him and Janey: they could do better than a place like this. Taking his key, he let himself into the flat. 'I'm back, love,' he called, 'but we'll have to settle for *cava*.'

There was no answer.

'I'm back,' he called again. 'I couldn't get proper bubbly, so I picked up a bottle of the Spanish stuff, and I had to go all the way down to Camden Street just to get that.'

Still there was no answer. Pushing open the bedroom door, he saw a nightdress laid out, but there was no sign of his girlfriend.

'Jane?' he called. 'Janey, where are you?'

She wasn't in the kitchen or the living room, but the shower looked as though it had been running, because the inside of the bath was wet. Then he noticed that her coat was gone – though her phone was still on the kitchen worktop, together with her handbag. He scratched his head: what would she be doing going out without either her phone or her money?' Outside on the balcony, he leant on the rail looking up and down the service alley, but there was no sign of her anywhere.

It didn't make any sense.

And then he was cold suddenly, and his heart began to pump. He worked a palm across his jaw. He was thinking, and thinking hard.

Wednesday 3rd September
10.15 pm

Maguire walked into the incident room just as Quinn put the phone down to the lab.

Doyle looked over from his desk, where he had just finished a call. He was still holding the handset, but when he saw the superintendent he put it down. Ignoring the detectives who tried to speak to him, Maguire strode into the office, opened the bottom drawer of Quinn's desk and took out the half-bottle of Jameson he had stashed there. There were two glasses; taking one, he poured a hefty measure and knocked it back. Then he poured another and waggled the empty glass at Quinn.

Quinn shook his head.

Stepping past him, Doyle took the glass and poured three fingers. 'What did he say, Frank?'

'He says he doesn't know where she is, and he says he didn't do it.' Maguire sank the second whiskey. 'I know what you're going to tell me: of course he says he didn't do it; none of us has ever met a guilty man, have we?'

Quinn drew his top lip in with his teeth. 'Your mother's necklace,' he said. 'The one in the photo in Paddy's flat.'

'I last saw it just before we buried her, but Patrick claims he took it when I was talking to the undertaker. '

'I just had the lab on the phone,' Quinn added quietly. 'The striation marks don't match.'

Maguire stopped dead. He'd taken the bottle from Doyle and was about to pour a third slug of whiskey, but instead he turned to Quinn. 'What did you say?'

'The striation marks created when the pendant was pulled off: they differ from the marks on the chain.'

Maguire looked stunned. 'You mean the pendant isn't Eva's?' He took Quinn by the arm. 'Is that what you're saying, Moss?'

'That's what I'm saying.'

Doyle was working the bottom of the glass against the palm of his hand. 'Shall I tell the pair of you something else?' he said.

They both turned to him now.

'Jane Finucane was lying. Maggs wasn't with her at ten on Sunday night. He wasn't home till gone midnight.'

Wednesday 3rd September
10.25 pm

Quinn and Doyle went ahead. Maguire told them he'd follow, and they left Harcourt Square, swinging right and left onto Camden Street. From there, it was barely a two-minute drive; Doyle pulled over before they came to the service alley.

'Let's not advertise the fact we're coming,' he suggested.

Quinn was on the pavement buttoning his jacket. They walked side by side up the street before turning left in the darkness. The squared block lifted in shadows cast by the lights from the rear of the Portobello, and Quinn was aware of the sound of his footsteps as they crossed the short expanse of concrete to the stairwell. Two flights and they were on the landing. Doyle walked ahead, where light spilled from the door to Jane's flat.

Suddenly the door was open, and Maggs stepped out with his back to them. He was carrying a canvas grip bag; the collar of his jacket was turned under his ears. One hand still on the latch, he looked round and saw them.

'Going somewhere nice, Conor, are you?' Doyle asked.

Throwing open the door again, Maggs leapt inside and tried to close it. Quinn was too quick and, shoulder to the wood, he smashed the door open and sent Maggs sprawling across the hall.

Maggs scrambled to his feet. 'For God's sake, what're you doing? I'm going to meet Janey. I'm going to meet my girl.'

'The hell you are.' Quinn had him by the arm now and, swinging him round like a hammer thrower, he slammed him into the wall.

Maggs crumpled, but almost before he hit the floor, Quinn had one hand knotted in his hair and was dragging him into the living room. 'Where is she?' he demanded. 'Where is Eva? What have you done with my wife?'

'Nothing, Jesus! I've done nothing. You know I've done nothing.' Maggs was crying; his eyes wide, his face twisted. 'I've told you; I don't know how many times I've told you. I don't know where she is. I don't know anything about it. I don't know where she is, Moss. I don't know where she is.'

'You spoke to her. In the Four Courts, you thought she was offering some kind of sign because she was wearing that fucking necklace.' Quinn hauled him upright. He could smell his breath. He could see the hunted look in his eyes. 'Where is she?'

'I don't know.' Maggs was wailing. 'I don't know. For God's sake, let me go.' His hands were buckled around Quinn's, his fingers tight, desperately trying to break Quinn's grip.

'I'll kill you, you sack of shit. I'll rip your fucking head off.' Quinn released him suddenly and, throwing him bodily into a chair, he stood over him with his fists balled. 'The Polaroid: the rock in the hole. Where is she?'

Maggs was staring goggle-eyed, saliva whitening his lips.

'The phone messages, the notes, all those bastard rhymes.' Quinn had Maggs's bag now and was rifling through it, tossing out shoes, clothes, a washing kit. 'What've you done with it? What've you done with her necklace?'

'I don't know what you're talking about,' Maggs was begging

him. 'Please, Moss, I don't know what you mean.'

Quinn hurled the bag and it hit Maggs in the face, splitting the skin at his eye. He yelped like a dog, one hand to his eye socket and the other thrust palm-out as if to fend Quinn away. Quinn dragged him to his feet. 'Just like you knew nothing about Mary, even though you strangled her till she blacked out, then carried her into John Hanrahan's kitchen. Revenge, Maggot, finally.'

'Moss, please.'

'*Only Mary knows*. Only you could think of that, because only you knew that Mary would lead us to Jimmy. With that picture, he goes down for the murder you committed. And Paddy, you sick fucker, you marked his card the day he caught you in the bushes, and when he told us he saw you with Mary, you marked his card again. The photos you took of yourself: the Crawthumper; the Society of Christian Brothers.'

Maggs broke away from him and, scrambling across the floor, he hunched in a corner like a frightened child. He squatted there shaking, blood smeared across his face, his limbs almost in spasm. He was coughing, convulsing; holding his sides with both hands, he spat on the floor.

Then all at once he was still. When he looked up, his eyes carried the emptiness of his soul. With a snarl, he flew at Quinn.

Doyle, who'd been blocking the door, weighed in with a fist but Maggs was too quick and, ducking sharply, he made it around the big man. Then he was at the door. Quinn was after him. As Maggs reached the balcony, he had him around the waist. Together they lurched across the concrete, before slamming into the hip-high wall with the worn metal rail running the length of it. Maggs was scrabbling for Quinn's eyes with his fingers, trying to gouge, tear. He was spitting like a cobra. 'Fuck you, Quinn, fuck all you bastards.'

Quinn hit him in the stomach.

Maggs doubled up.

But then he came up swinging and caught Quinn across the face. He swung again. He missed badly, and the momentum almost carried him off his feet. Quinn hit him again and again, and then, with his head low and leading with his shoulder, he sent him crashing into the wall. The rail caught Maggs in the small of his back. He was off his feet and for a moment his eyes were huge, his mouth open.

Then he was gone, toppling from the balcony with a short scream in his throat.

Quinn had slumped onto his hands and knees. Doyle hauled him upright, and together they looked over the wall. They saw Maggs at ground level, though he wasn't quite on the ground. It took a moment to work out. Then they realised he was impaled, the black spike of a railing thrust right through his chest. Like an insect pinned to a board, he was all arms and legs, the disbelief of what had happened, the horror of it, visible in his eyes.

Police cars pulled in from the main road. Quinn grabbed Doyle's arm and they raced to the stairs.

Moments later, Quinn was bending where Maggs was skewered, his feet, and the tips of his fingers, trailing the ground. His eyes were open, and he was blinking as if he couldn't focus. There was blood in his mouth, great gobs smothering his tongue; a burbling sound lifted in his throat.

On one knee, Quinn forced him to look up. 'Where is she?' he said.

Head tipped back, Maggs held his gaze, his brow rippled in a bloodied frown.

'You don't want her to die, Conor, you know you don't. Tell me where she is.'

Maggs opened his mouth; he blew bubbles of blood; his eyes were closing. He puckered his lips, and Quinn lowered his head so he could hear. But Maggs did not speak. He lolled on the spike, and with a hideous squelching sound his weight thrust it deeper still.

'Where is she, Conor?' Quinn demanded. 'What've you done with Eva?'

Maggs's eyes were closed now, his face an unrecognisable mask. A lung had burst and he was spewing blood; his mouth gaping, lips loose; his tongue quivering as if someone had cut it free.

Then all at once he was still.

Quinn let out a cry of pain, of grief; of sheer desperation.

On his knees, he hung his head, then, hopelessly, he got to his feet. He looked down at the prostrate form beside him.

Then Maggs opened his eyes.

He parted his lips and he stared. His gaze was hollow, as if he could no longer see anything. 'Moss,' he whispered, 'Moss.'

Again Quinn dropped to his knees. 'Tell me, Conor. For God's sake, tell me while there's still time.'

'She left you,' the words lifted in the same rasping whisper Quinn had heard on the phone. 'She left you and she left Laura; she left Jessie on her own.'

'Where is she, for Christ's sake?' Quinn was screaming. He was shaking him, punching the useless body where it hung on the spike. 'Tell me where she is.'

His lips twisted, Maggs bent bloody fingers to grip Quinn by the arm. 'She's with me now,' he whispered. And wearily his eyes closed, never to open again. 'She's with me.'

Wednesday 3rd September
10.35 pm

Stumbling away from the railings, Quinn stared without seeing anything. His mind was numb, his senses so stunned that nothing registered at all.

Behind him, sirens were wailing and more police cars were turning in from Richmond Street. Maguire arrived with Murphy, who was on the phone immediately organising an ambulance and the fire brigade. Quinn gawped. Maggs impaled with his arms splayed and his head back, mouth agape; his eyes closed for all time. Quinn felt Doyle's hand on his arm. 'Moss, let's search the flat.'

He looked round at him.

Then it registered. The flat, of course; there might be a clue. Yes, Doyle was right: they had to search the flat.

Murphy stepped towards them. She was about to speak but they were already headed for the stairs. On the landing, Harry Long, the neighbour whom Quinn had spoken to on his previous visit, was peering over the rail.

They took the flat apart: drawers, cupboards. Jane Finucane's computer was on standby, and Quinn got on the phone to ask Harcourt Square for someone who knew what they were looking for to come down right away. He could imagine Maggs trawling the Internet, looking up the very information they had found: the three Protestant martyrs, the lilywhite boys. How he must've felt that God was on his side when he'd found not only two boys from Kildare, but the ballad of their cruel mother.

He shivered at the evil.

He shivered when he thought of old John Hanrahan stumbling down the stairs to find what he thought was the ghost of Mary Harrington in his kitchen. He'd dealt with a few victims in attempted murder cases who had been strangled to the point where they'd blacked out, only to come round an hour or so later with no recollection of what had happened.

'He planned it in minute detail, Doyler.' He was rifling through drawers in the kitchen. 'Yet all the time I thought it was him, I believed she had a chance. I hoped that because of how he felt about her, he wouldn't want to harm her. But when she left me, she became a target. Maybe he didn't want to hurt her, but he had to take her: two birds with one stone; another mother who, in his eyes, didn't care enough about her children and, in the same moment, revenge.'

Doyle was in the bathroom with the door open, searching through dirty clothes in the laundry basket.

'He looked up everything exactly as we looked it up,' Quinn said. 'He led us by the nose, right down to the last note, the final bloody detail.'

Doyle paused then, his face expressionless, his eyes swimming in pools of fatigue.

'The nursery rhymes,' Quinn gesticulated, 'the Polaroid. For twenty-five years, he hated Jimmy the Poker. He hated me for taking Eva away and dragging his sorry carcass through the Four Courts. He hated you because you knew what he'd done to his mother.' He looked at his partner now. 'He did kill her, Joe. He did put drain cleaner in the wine bottle knowing full well she'd drink it. He killed Janice Long and Karen Brady, he killed the other three and he killed

Mary Harrington: *seven stars in the sky, the seven who went to heaven.* He knew we'd find that line, and either Paddy Maguire or Jimmy Hanrahan would take the fall for it. Imagine his delight when he found out we had them both in custody.'

'It means Eva is still alive,' Doyle said.

Quinn stared at him.

'The seven who went to heaven, Moss: it's his mother that makes seven, not Eva. She's still alive; there's still a chance we'll find her.'

Quinn stood there with his eyes wide and his mouth open. 'You're right,' he whispered. 'Jesus, Doyler, you're right.'

Coming through from the bathroom, Doyle took him by the arm. 'You just now said that you thought at least if it *was* him, there was hope. Well, you were right. There was, and there still is. There's still a way we can find her. Think about it: up until now, he never contacted us. Not a whisper. Then he takes Eva.' He paused for a moment, thinking. 'The day the trial collapsed, there she was in the Four Courts wearing his necklace. We believed he might've thought it was some kind of sign, some kind of come-on, but it wasn't: as far as the Maggot was concerned, she was no longer fit to wear it.'

Quinn could feel the blood draining from his face.

'But once upon a time, he loved her. He had to take her because of what she'd become, but unlike the others, he'd loved her, and because of that, he couldn't be responsible for killing her. That's why he made contact. He had to have his revenge, but he didn't need Eva on his conscience to take it.'

'You mean, to appease one half of his sick psyche, he had to give us a chance?' Quinn was nodding now. 'And if we found her in time, it wouldn't matter because we'd already have Hanrahan or Patrick.'

'Exactly; he'd walk away. And that means we still have a chance.'

'But Doyler.' Quinn could feel the panic rising again. '*One is one and all alone and ever more shall be so.*'

'I know, I know. I've thought of that: but only if we don't find her.'

For a few moments, Quinn stood there, considering Doyle's words. When he spoke, it was as if to himself. 'His mother had no idea who his father was. As far as Maggs was concerned, she didn't care; she didn't care about him. That's what started all this: the fact that even after she brought him into the world, she went right on opening her legs for whoever had the price of a bottle. And what turned him from just a pissed-off kid into a psychopath was Jimmy the Poker's Polaroid.'

There was movement at the front door now. Looking round, they saw Murphy standing there. 'Mary was different,' Doyle went on. 'All this time we didn't link her to the other five women because no one could've known she was pregnant. And the irony is, Maggs didn't know it either. But the night of the *fleadh cheoil*, Molly Parkinson was drunk and Paddy had been taking the piss out of Maggs, just like everyone used to. Eva was sitting right there, and yet she didn't defend him.'

Quinn nodded slowly. 'And Mary reminded him of her. She looked like Eva when she was younger: long hair the same colour, the same colour eyes. They went for a drive and he must've realised how he could get Jimmy. But for all of that, he once loved Eva. You're right, Joseph: it means we've still got a chance.'

Doyle moved into the living room. He stared at the TV, the book-case, the CD cabinet.

'Carrigafoyle; we're missing something. There has to be some-thing else.'

'We've no time,' Quinn stated. 'It's been seventy-two hours, if she's tied up and in the cold . . . '

'She can hold on,' Doyle said sharply. He looked beyond Quinn to where Murphy was watching from the hall. 'She's strong: she has two daughters to live for. She was taken from her son's grave when she had two little ones at home. Think how she must've felt. Think how determined that would make her. We know her, Moss; we know what she's like. She won't give up. She'll fight and fight; that's how she's built. She's a Doyle, for Christ's sake.'

Quinn snaked his tongue over his lips. 'Sunday, Doyler. He must've been in the cemetery; he must've seen Eva and realised what she was feeling. He knew her; he knew she wouldn't be able to leave it.'

'So he waited,' Doyle said, nodding, 'and when the time was right, he took her. In the morning, he told you the clock was ticking.'

'Then he gave us the cryptic message about Mary.'

'And the lilywhite boys from Kildare.'

'Three little mice who couldn't find their way.' Doyle glanced at Murphy again. 'Latimer, Ridley and Cranmer: it led us to the three blind monks of Carrigafoyle.'

'Don't forget the Polaroid,' Murphy reminded him. 'That brought Jimmy into the game, and not just him but the quarry.' She arched her brows. 'Did he want us chasing all the way to Scanlon's quarry? He'd love that, wouldn't he? Dashing here and there, and all the time the sand slipping through the narrows of an hourglass.'

Doyle stared into space. 'Scanlon,' he said. 'I know that name. I swear it means something to me.'

'Think what he did in the Joy.' Quinn's hands were fisted at his sides. 'Watching Paddy come and go, and seeking out men like the Craw so he could dig the dirt; find out what anyone knew.'

They slipped into silence; the only sounds now those that came from below. Doyle pursed his lips.

'Mother of God, but the name Scanlon means something to me. Come on, Doyler, think, you big lug. What've you got? Latimer, you've got Latimer, Ridley and Cranmer: three men blinded and burned for their faith. They led us to Carrigafoyle and three blind monks who were hanged because of theirs.' He stood there with his hands shoved in the pockets of his coat. He glanced at Quinn; he glanced at Murphy. He looked beyond them both to where Harry Long had appeared with a bottle of Jameson in his hand. Doyle peered at him; he peered at the bottle, the label; the name written on it.

The cold seemed to rush through him. 'Jesus and Mary,' he whispered.

'What?' Quinn had a hand on his arm. 'What is it, Doyler? What?'

'My God, Moss. It's not *where* at all; it's *who*.'

Quinn was staring at him. 'What're you talking about? I don't understand. What do you mean – who?'

Doyle wasn't listening; he was fumbling in his pocket for his mobile phone. 'What's Norma's number?'

'Norma?'

'Your mother-in-law, for Christ's sake. What's her phone number?'

Quinn told him, and Doyle dialed it. 'The little shit, the little fuckin' gobshite. He knew about Latimer; he knew about Ridley and Cranmer. He knew we'd find them, and he knew I'd know enough history to put the rest of it together and come up with Carrigafoyle. But it's not the place that's important – the scheming bastard – it's *who*.'

Quinn grabbed him by the arm. 'Doyle, for pity's sake, you're making no sense. What the hell do you mean?'

'The monks, Moss: the three blind monks. We need to know their names, lad; we need to know who they were.'

Murphy moved alongside them as Doyle spoke to Quinn's mother-in-law in Listowel.

'Norma,' he said, 'it's Joseph. I need James O'Donohue's number. 'Tis very important. My old history teacher from when I was at school. James O'Donohue; he still lives in the town. Look it up in the book now, and be quick, would you?'

Two minutes later, he had the number and was dialling again. 'It's not *where* at all,' he repeated. 'Of course it's not. It couldn't be, because she wasn't there. Christ, Doyle, call yourself a detective? You should've seen it earlier.' He glanced again at Quinn. 'We need to know who those old men were; I'd put money on one of them being called Scanlon. When we find the other two, we'll find her. I swear that's how he's set this up.'

'Jesus, Doyle,' Quinn said, arching his brows. 'But your history teacher, will he even remember? I mean, how old is he going to be?'

'In his eighties, ninety maybe. But he's all there, Moss, and if I know him, he'll not be in bed, he'll be having a small one in front of the History Channel.'

He waited; the phone was to his ear while Quinn hovered next to him. 'He's not there,' Quinn told him. 'Either that, or he's in bed.'

Doyle shook his head. 'He'll pick it up. He will.'

Then all at once, he smiled. 'Mr O'Donohue, is that you? It's Joseph Doyle, the guard. How are you?

'Good, good,' he said, nodding. 'Listen, I'm glad to talk to you after all these years. I was in your history class; it must be forty years ago. You remember? Mother of God, that's amazing. Listen, now,' he said, 'I'm sorry to phone so late, but I need to know something, and it's very important. It's a strange question at this time of night, but do you happen to remember the names of the three blind monks from Lislaughtin Abbey, the ones Pelham hanged back in 1580?'

He fell silent then and, listening, his eyes narrowed slightly. 'Ah, you've a wonderful head for the facts, Mr O'Donohue. Thank you, you've been a great help. The next time you're passing Jett O'Carroll's, tell your man Eamon you've a pint or two put by.'

Switching off the phone, he turned to Quinn. 'I was right,' he said. 'It's not Carrigafoyle that's important, Moss; it's the three blind monks. Their names were Scanlon, Hanrahan and Shea.'

Wednesday 3rd September
10.46 pm

Doyle looked beyond Quinn to where Harry Long was still hovering at the front door. 'Well come in lad, if you're offering,' he said. 'But don't touch anything.' Taking the bottle from him, Doyle grabbed some glasses, then poured a glug of whiskey into each of them.

'Scanlon, Hanrahan and Shea.' Quinn was thinking hard now, his pulse like a weight in his skull. He took a glass from Doyle and knocked it back. 'Jesus, but he planned this even more carefully than any of us could've imagined.'

'You're not kidding,' Murphy said. 'Telling us to re-look at Mary's file, and all the while that Polaroid was in the box.'

Quinn exhaled heavily. 'It had been there since Mary's death. If we'd found it then, as we were supposed to, Jimmy would've been locked up.'

'I'll lose no sleep over that little toe-rag,' Doyle muttered. 'He never did half the time he should've for battering Mrs Bolton.'

'But Shea?' Quinn asked. 'What do we know about Shea?'

'What *don't* we know?' Murphy replied. 'I mean, how many Sheas are there in the Dublin phone book?'

Neither of them answered her.

It was hopeless: they'd run out of time. With a name like that, perhaps Maggs was having his longest laugh last.

Resting a shoulder in the doorway, Harry Long shifted his weight. 'It's nothing to do with me,' he said, 'but what about the old ironworks?'

'What's that?' Doyle looked over at him.

'The old ironworks up there on Shelley Banks. It's been shut down for years, but my granddad used to work there when he was a boy. I'm sure that was Shea's: the old place up near the water.'

'Ironworks?' Pulse quickening, Quinn was staring at him.

'Yeah, it was called Shea's. Or maybe it was O'Shea's, I don't know. It was famous, though, back in the day. My granddad used to tell me about it. In Nelson's time, the British would have their fleet moored in the bay: he reckoned that the officers set the watch by the chimes of Shea's clock.'

The car was where they had left it, parked on double yellow lines with the magnetic light squatting on the dashboard. Doyle had the keys. In an instant he was behind the wheel, with Quinn slapping the light on the roof.

Gunning the engine, they pulled away from the kerb. They swung left just after the bridge. Doyle fairly punched through the gears, and they raced alongside the line of parked cars all the way down Canal Road. Beyond the lock, the road widened and he stamped his foot to the floor. With the siren wailing, they passed Lansdowne Road, then headed north towards the canal docks. There Doyle hauled on the wheel, and they barrelled across the bridge and around the greyhound stadium at Shelbourne Park.

Heading for Irishtown, Quinn hunched in the passenger seat with his knee to his chest and a fist against his teeth. He could see his daughters' faces when they waved him goodbye. He could see Danny fishing the Tolka the day before he was killed.

He could see Eva the first time he'd set eyes on her – when the man who might've murdered her was perched on the bench alongside.

They raced through Irishtown towards Poolbeg and the nature reserve at Shelley Banks. With the sea made choppy by the wind, they drove the length of the coast road, passing industrial buildings old and new, until they could see the shadows of what was left of the abandoned plant that Harry Long described as Shea's ironworks. There was little there now – just a handful of weathered buildings behind a broken-down wire fence.

Across the road was the beach – a great expanse of sand where, on Monday, search teams had been swarming like newly hatched flies. At the gate, Doyle slammed the brakes on so hard he almost put Quinn through the windscreen. Then Quinn was out, forcing his way through the fence and running across the puddle-pocked yard towards the shattered buildings. Above his head was an old clock with a square face. The hands were moving beyond eleven o'clock.

He was shouting; he was calling to his wife. 'Eva!' he yelled. 'Eva! Eva!'

Under the boards, under the carpet and strips of old linoleum, her face was swollen, her hands like wax from lack of blood. She could no longer feel any part of her body; she was no longer thirsty. She was slipping away; she knew she was, and there was a beauty in it. A long time ago, she'd stopped thinking about her children. A long time ago, she'd stopped thinking about her husband or her mother or sisters. She'd stopped thinking about the man who'd put her here.

There was no single thought in her head now. Her mind was a mish-mash of images: what had been and what yet might be.

She wondered where she was going. She knew she was on the very brink of the abyss, and she wondered if all was darkness, or whether there were colours, as some people said there were.

She wanted to know; she wanted to go; she wanted to find out for herself. Danny had gone ahead, and she was sure he'd been calling for her to join him. If that were so, then there must be light; there had to be some colour.

Someone was calling her now. She could hear a voice: Eva, Eva-Marie. She was Eva-Marie, and someone was calling her name. So there was more than the darkness; there had to be.

Was it Danny she could hear?

No, it couldn't be. Danny wouldn't call her by her name: he'd call her mammy or mam, maybe; he wouldn't call her name.

Opening her eyes, she looked up.

And the darkness was broken: her grave of carpet and linoleum, the boards of rotten wood.

She could not move, but whatever it was that covered her mouth was eased aside, and then she could feel strong arms raising her from the dead.

Still she couldn't see anything, but she could feel him and she could smell him and she knew that she was alive.

Danny would wait; of course he would. There was Laura to think about; Laura and Jess.

She felt lips brush her cheek, and for a moment she was lying beside the river again all those years ago.

She could hear his voice, and his voice was gentle. 'I've got you,' he told her. 'You're going to be all right. I've got you, Eva. I've come to take you home.'

She could feel dry tears in her eyes. *That's my husband*, she thought. *That's Moss. I know it is. That's Moss. He's found me.*